OBLIVION'S WAKE

JONATHAN SEAN LYSTER

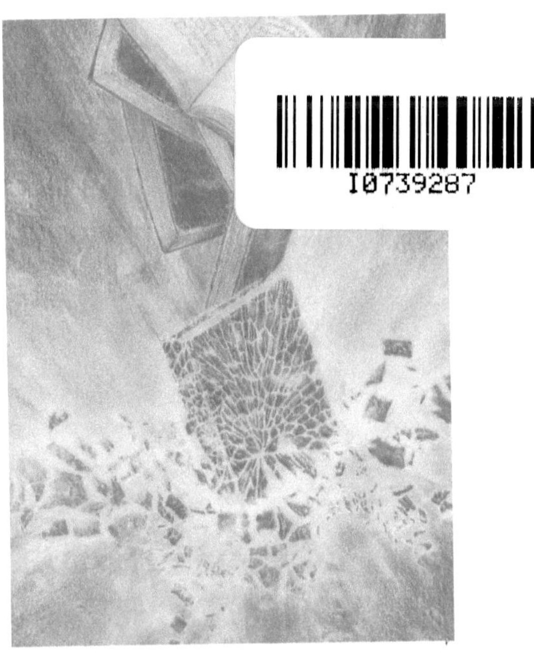

Heuronic Books

Published by Heuronic Books
An imprint of Heuronic Systems Inc.

Cover concept by Jonathan Sean Lyster

Cover images used with permission from Shutterstock, Can Stock Photo, and Heuronic Systems.

Title page artwork by Rick Sazon; see more of Rick's work at: http://s1128.photobucket.com/user/rick_sazon/profile/

Also available in ebook format through your favourite online retailer.

ISBN 978-0-9937570-1-3

Table of Contents

To Audrey, my mother

You told me about our ancestor who had his head chopped off
for writing scurrilous verse about the aristocracy.

I'm doing my best to live up to family traditions.

Autumn 2051

"Memory is a story the mind tells to itself."

1

DAVID IMAGINED THE DRUG AS an insect beneath his skin, climbing from the crook of his arm to his shoulder and neck, then catching the stream of the carotid artery that would carry it into his brain. It clung to that arterial wall, fought the flow, drew the journey out from hours to days to never.

Two weeks since the syringe bit his skin and still no flood of images, no spark of recollection.

David shut his eyes. Opened them upon the stones at his feet.

MELANIE REED   STUART REED
LOVING AUNT   LOVING UNCLE
1976 – 2028   1974 – 2028

He had hoped this would be his first visit to the graves where he could actually recall his family. Instead, a familiar hollowness remained in his mind. He knelt and brushed dirt from the base of the twin stones. Then, sighing, he looked up across the grass to where Ariel stood before the headstone of her grandmother.

Her hands made fists in her jacket pockets, knuckles pressing tiny indentations against the fabric. Seeming to sense his gaze, she turned, forced a smile, and came toward him. With her black hair tied into a bun, she looked like a schoolteacher too long in the jaws of public education. Her coat was identical to his: magenta, with more pockets than one could possibly need, and zipped to her chin against November's chill.

Ariel slipped her gloved hand into his.

"Thank you." David leaned down and kissed her. Her lips tasted of mint.

Her brow arched. "For what?"

"Being here. Being you."

"If that's all it takes to keep you amused, I can manage."

"Going to ask whether anything has come back yet?"

"I'm tired of asking." Ariel snorted and squeezed his arm. "I'm starting to think they shipped you a vial of Baltimore tap water."

The car crossed from Vancouver into Burnaby beneath a sky threatening rain, made its way to Watling Street, and eased itself into the driveway. David climbed from the passenger side. Ariel joined him, pressing herself against him as they strode across the lawn – a mess of maple leaves blown and scattered by storm winds. The car dutifully waited for the garage door to slide up, then rolled itself inside.

The huge house with its oversized living room and brooding black couches was strangely free of racket. The kids were away for the weekend – thanks to a few words from Ariel to their friends' parents. He had become used to family noises competing for his attention. There were times when he had longed for peace and quiet. Now it left him unsettled.

"Love?" Ariel said, stepping inside.

"Yes?"

Ariel cocked her left eyebrow. "That was a question. Was that your answer?"

"Always." David grinned back, enjoying the old game.

Ariel ran her coat's zipper from throat to waist and tugged it open with a flourish. Now David understood why she had put it on in the bedroom: to keep him from seeing her choice of garb. Ariel had opted for her burgundy vest with snaps up the front. Over the years she had grown somewhat thicker around her middle – a change only she and he were likely to notice – and the vest was a size too small now. But vanity or denial hadn't prompted her to wear it. She had clearly chosen it for the spectacular things it did to her breasts.

Ariel licked her lips. "Don't you know it's rude to stare?" She slipped her arms beneath his, breathing spearmint against his cheek. "I love you."

"Love you too."

"I love you more."

"Do not."

"Do – "

He shut her up with his tongue.

*****

> The lapses are here. Damn it damn it damn it. My mind wanders away from what I'm doing now. Got to get this down. Remember the time Auntie and Uncle took me to the fair in '26? They had those big fighting bots, the kind that can smash each other into pieces, but all the bits snap back together so the next player can do it again. Auntie kept saying, "Oh, that's so mean, Davie." I was beating up this other kid's bot.

David studied the page of his journal, neat black strokes in his younger self's handwriting. The wooden chair at the dining table chilled his naked behind.

The fair would have been in midsummer – weather for shorts and a T-shirt. He was thirteen. The place likely smelled of fast food.

> The other kid's name was Fredrick. I remember that 'cause he called himself Rick. It was his mom who called him Freddie. God, picture getting stuck with a name like that. "Davie" is bad enough.

The couch creaked as Ariel picked herself up.

"Been thinking," David said.

"Uh-oh." Ariel strutted to the table, hips swaying in a comically exaggerated stride, breasts bouncing. The surgical scar between them stood out in pink relief against her skin.

"Trying to distract me? The teenager I used to be thanks you from the depths of his libido."

"Are you sure? What if it turns out I'm not his type?"

"Him: hetero teenage boy. You: warm, female, sans clothing. Definitely his type. But not the point." David tapped the books in front of him. "I have an idea. I described Auntie and Uncle in these books. I can imagine how they looked, how the house must have smelled, even Uncle Stu's blustery voice. Maybe the memories are so close to what I've imagined that I just haven't noticed they've started coming back."

Ariel's gaze skipped away from his. "That's an interesting thought."

"You only say 'that's interesting' when you mean 'that's crap.'"

"Name one case of a patient who got a beta ephemerase dose and didn't have some kind of disorientation. It takes time for the stuff to kick in. Sometimes a month, or even more."

"Majority start getting their lives back in less than a week."

"And one in three start the week after, and one in seven the week after that. So you're special but not very. Live with it."

David slapped the notebook shut. "So, consensus: that was a stupid idea."

"Put it in context. Your magnificently bizarre mind cooked it up while you were rolling me around on the couch. The blood normally feeding your brain cells had better places to be." Ariel eased her arms around his neck. Warmth pressed against his back. "Let's go to bed."

"It's four thirty. Tired already?"

"Don't be silly."

*****

David woke to a stench of rotten meat. His stomach clenched and squeezed until he couldn't breathe. He tumbled out of bed and half staggered, half ran to the bathroom. His palm caught the light switch. The glare from the light strip above the mirror stabbed agony through his eyes. His belly heaved. He sank to his knees before the toilet and retched. Nothing came up but bile burning in his throat.

Ariel's voice roared in his head. "Jesus. What's wrong?"

"That smell. Something die under the bed?"

Ariel stood wide-eyed in the doorway. "No smell, David."

David rose and leaned against the sink. He twisted the knob for cold water, bent down over the basin to drink directly from the flow. Mouth full of water, he sucked air in through his nostrils. No odor of rotting flesh. David emptied his mouth and drew a long breath.

"Must have dreamed it."

"It certainly wasn't coming from me."

"Smelled like old meat. Roadkill. Strong and thick. As though it were all around me." David reached for his toothbrush for the second time this night.

A smile dimpled Ariel's cheeks. "So I guess we're getting our money's worth."

"What?"

"It's started."

David worked the brush along his teeth and tongue, killing the acid taste. He spit froth into the basin. "Maybe. Didn't write anything about old meat in my books."

"You had five months to write down fifteen years of your life. Odds are good you left out a few details. Remember anything specific?"

"Maybe."

"Coherent sentences, Mr. Glass."

The images in his thoughts broke apart, but one remained, like a still-frame photograph. "Ridiculous."

"What is?"

"You and Auntie Mel. Her with her hands on your neck. Choking you."

Ariel's brow shot up. "Not what I expected, considering."

David nodded. Not only was it creepy as hell, it was impossible. The fire had burned his aunt and uncle to ashes four years before he found this woman standing frightened and alone before her grandmother's grave.

2

DREAMS DROVE A KNIFE EDGE through David's sleep. The smell of rotten flesh clogged his nostrils and mind. Ariel, Aunt Melanie, and Uncle Stu all stood over him, Auntie Mel's face contorted in a rictus leer. David huddled at their feet, his body small and frail. Their bellows clashed in a din like a dozen trains rattling on parallel tracks. Then the scene in his mind shifted to a stench of plastic and tar and rubber: the house devouring itself with fire. The kids danced around the blaze.

David woke to see a face too close to his. He bolted back. His scalp struck the wrought iron at the head of the bed.

"Ari," he breathed, rubbing the back of his head.

Her fingers touched his face. "Just another dream, love."

"I know. Crazy."

"What do you remember?"

"Elizabeth and Warren around the fire."

"That isn't an old memory. That was two years ago, down in Washington."

"Dancing around the house fire. With Auntie and Uncle inside."

"That's – "

" – no memory at all. A dream. I know."

"What else? Your aunt throttling your lovely and brilliant wife again?"

David sat up and leaned against the cool black iron. "Random pictures. Sounds. Voices."

"Saying what?"

"Nothing I can make out." The bedroom window glowed with afternoon sun. "We better get the kids."

"I called Joleen's and Hoshi's houses. I'll collect Elizabeth and Warren in an hour. Stay put and let your brain stew." Ariel eased herself out of bed and reached for her robe. Her black hair hung free and straight now. David let his gaze take in the shape of her nose and jaw. Lines had sprouted in the corners of her eyes; he had watched them grow in her smooth skin over the years. They reminded him of feathers.

Why, he wondered, have we lasted so long? We never had much in common.

Then he thought of the cemetery, of standing over auntie's and uncle's graves while Ariel knelt where her grandmother lay. We have that in common, he thought. Loss.

At least Ariel had known her grandmother. David had only known a void that could not be filled by the words in his journals. But when the disease disconnected him from his childhood, it granted him a compensatory gift. He could remember everything Ariel had said when they first met. Like a film in his mind, he could play a montage of her swelling as Elizabeth grew in her belly, and then of standing next to her hospital bed as she declared her undying hatred of him when that doctor who looked like he could be fourteen ordered, "Push!"

Later: weeping and holding tiny Elizabeth to her breast, the baby's body still damp from the womb. Gracing Ariel's face was the most radiant smile David had ever known.

David frowned and turned his thoughts back to his dreams. Memories – his old deleted ones – should be like records in a computer or pad: distinct packages with dates and times and types. Beta ephemerase should have given him the code – the language – of those memories. Shouldn't he be able to flip through them, like the pages in his journals?

A scene from his dream blossomed into sensibility. The house in flames dissolved into the campfire two years ago, down in Washington. The family had crossed over to Port Angeles on the Vancouver Island ferry and driven into the foothills of Olympic National Park. Warren had announced at the beginning that he would be bored silly without his netpad or his games. Then he vanished among the cedars and firs behind the campsite and spent hours terrorizing Elizabeth, darting out at her until they wrestled like small animals covered in pieces of forest.

At dusk beside the fire, Elizabeth insisted that David re-create the chess game they had begun days before at home. He laid his small travel chess set on a stone between them and set the pieces into place. They cast dancing shadows across the board, shaped by firelight.

Fire moved also at the edge of what might be an older memory. David pursued it, slipping off the bed and making his way down to the basement. He turned left and strode past the rec room with its wall screen and oak chess table and worn brown paisley couch to the library. Cool air lifted the hairs on his arms. He slowed his pace as he moved along the wall, his gaze skimming the shelves. Ariel's grandmother had left behind a vast collection of fantasy novels. David ignored these. His own collection filled most of the shelves of one bookcase: Bennie Shimmerman's seven books on the nature of memory (one of them, *No Inner Voice*, was missing), and ninety-two other books on the subject of memory and ERIN – beginning with the first book on the topic, J. J. Sebastien's dreadful *Mindslayer*: three hundred pages of poorly researched sewage that painted the disease as a scourge that would bring humanity to its knees when billions succumbed to "amnesia on steroids," leaving a handful to care for the mindless.

David chuckled at the thought. How many at last count, worldwide? Eight hundred seventy thousand over the whole period of the outbreak.

The house computer had the same collection, along with thousands of articles from *Scientific American*, *Psychology*, and a long list of other publications. David preferred the hard-copy collection; paper had tactile appeal that digital print couldn't match. In with *Mindslayer* and the rest were his journals. He tugged at the first of the thick black notebooks, the only one that dealt with the fire. His younger self had written little about it. He let the book fall open in his hand and skimmed page after page until he found the part he wanted.

The fire just ate the house like a monster in a
B movie. This fireman (called John or Jim?) sat
with me while his friends hosed the flames. He
stayed on the bench waiting for the ambulance
and cops to show up. He was a nice guy, kept
saying, "We'll get them out, we'll get them out."
But I knew it wasn't going to happen. The fire
was too hot. There was too much smoke. I felt
like crying but I couldn't.

David slammed the book shut with a gunshot sound. "I remember that. I think." He strode back upstairs to the bedroom, thumping the book against his thigh.

*****

Ariel heard David moving around the house as she mixed pancakes in the kitchen, blending flour and honey and baking powder in a bowl.

"Keep it real," Gran used to say. "None of that processed crap."

The chai maker hissed and burped, filling the air with a spicy smell. Soon the machine quieted down; its hum became the only sound in the house.

The pancakes could wait. Ariel carried two earthenware cups warming against her fingers to the bedroom. Movement from the window at her right caught her attention. The little Husqvarna lawn mower had emerged from its doghouse-like shed behind the garage and now rolled back and forth in the backyard, negotiating its way around the perpetually green cedar tree and the two stark, skeletal maples whose leaves lay scattered across thick grass.

Ariel turned her gaze to David. He lay on his stomach, face toward her, sheets covering his legs. One of his journals lay open beside him. Surrogate memory, Ariel thought. Out of those records had risen a love for his aunt and uncle, a keen and painful loss over the house fire that had taken them when he was fifteen, a quiet, simmering rage at the drunk driver who had killed his parents on an Oregon highway. Ariel was sure – had always felt sure – that on some level David did remember it all. Never mind what Bennie Shimmerman had written: there was more to memory than those strands of protein woven into the nerve cells of the brain. His uncle and aunt had ingrained themselves in his spirit. They had shaped him into the man he had become.

Of course, Ariel thought as her gaze travelled up David's legs to his ass, his guardians probably had nothing to do with his tendency to wear nothing at all when the kids weren't home. She had never known anyone else so truly comfortable in bare skin. No, not comfortable: natural. Unselfconscious.

Deep in sleep, his forehead furrowed and his eyes danced beneath his lids. Ariel remembered waking beside him for the first time, seeing his eyes move as though he were watching a high-speed tennis match projected against the inner flesh of his eyelids. At times his eyes would pop open, stare at the wall, fix on hers, then close again.

I married a being from another world, she thought.

After twenty years, David continued to surprise and unnerve her. At times she felt as though he were in her head, walking through her thoughts, turning them over, examining them. The tinfoil-hat crowd thought ERIN survivors like David had some mysterious psychic power, some talent for reading minds. The reality was far simpler, far more subtle. David saw what was actually in front of him. His vision was not obscured by heaps of emotional baggage stretching back into his childhood. He saw without the blinders of assumption and expectation.

Thump. The lawn mower had run itself into one of the maple trees. It backed off and pounded against it again, the sound muffled by the windows.

Ariel grimaced. Stupid machine.

David's voice broke into her thoughts. "You're hovering." He turned onto his back and grinned up at her. "Put the cups down, woman. Gonna drag you into this bed."

"Yes, my master, my liege, my king, my something-or-other." Ariel set the mugs down and bowed. She glanced again at the machine in the backyard, rolling back and forth against the tree. Then she knelt on the edge of the bed and leaned over David. Her bathrobe slid down her arms, revealing her breasts. Her fingers ran along David's inner thigh. His penis twitched in response.

Ariel's voice grew husky and urgent. "Love, close your eyes. Imagine what you'd like to be doing to me right now." She lowered her left breast until her nipple touched his cheek.

David arched his neck back, nuzzling her breast, then shut his eyes. "Oh yes," he breathed. "Got it."

"Good." Ariel flung herself up. "The lawn mower is trying the same thing with a tree in the backyard."

3

While boarding the Airbus at Baltimore/Washington International, Jackie Olver palmed two Vaxodin tablets from the bottle stolen from the narcotics locker at the university hospital. One came apart in her mouth, leaving its raw-eggs-and-sand flavour on her tongue. She dropped herself into her seat and shifted the V-pad she carried under her arm to her lap. Four rapid blinks switched her contact lenses from Clear to Display. David Glass's children hovered before her.

What will David do when he remembers? Jackie pictured him, a boy barely older than his daughter today, his face contorted with madness, fingers tearing at her shirt, launching buttons free. Later, when she tried to shower his touch away, she found the claw-like imprint of his grip on her left breast.

The pills kicked the inside of her skull and a jolt of blue ecstasy arced across her brain. Jackie leaned her head against the seat and let the sensation pulse through her. Without the drug, sleep had eluded her these past two months – ever since a certain email appeared in her inbox. *David Glass, patient designation VBC-1105, registered for beta ephemerase September 6.* Jackie couldn't remember exactly when she had set up the alert in the medical database. Three years ago, maybe longer – back when beta ephemerase, BE, was barely a gleam in Mo's eye.

Why couldn't Mo have been wrong, just once?

The effects of Shimmerman's Disease were irreversible. It shattered the proteins of memory, boiling them into free-floating amino acids. Saint Bennie's victims could not get their souls back. That had been conventional wisdom until Mohammad Seraf said otherwise. Mo endured ridicule for his "handedness" theory of memory formation, and for pronouncing a connection between Shimmerman's Disease and influenza. His career nearly imploded when an elderly and famous neurophysiologist called him a joke in the New York *Times*.

These days Mo kept his gold Nobel medallion in a temperglass display cabinet in his office at Johns Hopkins. And these days, few called the illness Shimmerman's Disease. Most referred to it by the acronym Mo had coined:

ERIN.

Jackie woke in a haze, the kids still staring at her from her contact-lens display. Her brain refused to translate the rumble of speech from overhead speakers into words. Moments later the aircraft shook as its wheels bit a runway. She switched the lenses to Clear and joined her fellow passengers struggling with luggage from the overhead bins.

Sky Harbour in central Phoenix looked and smelled like a hundred other airports she had wandered through in her life. Jackie passed a yellow sign proclaiming, "BigBurger just fifty yards ahead." Next to it was the entrance to the restroom. Inside, she ran cold water and cupped it with her hands onto her cheeks, then gazed at herself in the mirror. Her eyes had begun to sink in recent days. She loosened her graying ponytail and ran her fingers through it. In her carry-on's front pocket she found her bottle of saline spray and shot a dose up each nostril, hoping to stave off cracked skin and nosebleed. Arizona was worse than the aircraft since the atmosphere started out desert dry even before the air conditioners and filters worked it over.

Her connecting flight was more than an hour from takeoff. In a seat near a row of screens showing arrivals and departures, she awakened her V-pad and blinked her lenses to Display. Her itinerary scrolled across her vision. Four days in Vancouver attending the Seventeenth Annual Convention on Neurological Disorders.

Jackie tapped the pad and opened a blue file folder in the air before her. David Glass had been a diligent former patient – dutiful to excess. Every six months for the past twenty-two years he had filled out the questionnaires the university emailed him. Jackie swiped her finger across the pad, turning pages past the intelligence profile, psychiatric analysis, and spatial acuity tests, until she found David's own words.

March 21, 2030
Simon showed me chess. I like it. It makes
music.

David was seventeen then. He had been her patient two years before, living out the final months of his old life in the North Vancouver Shimmerman Clinic. He must have written those words when Shimmerman's Disease was still widely believed to cause brain damage.

December 6, 2030
I am learning about computers. I found two in
the closet downstairs. I am going to fix them.

August 24, 2031
I like to read.
    Simon says I need to have friends. Simon
says I need people outside the house. Simon
says I need to relate.

Jackie remembered Simon Markson: a thin, grizzled man with an unfortunate penchant for Hawaiian shirts and khaki shorts. He trusted her to manage the Incoming Patients floor in the clinic, leaving him free to deal with those in Recovery. He and Mo Seraf were of a kind: brilliantly practical. Simon was one of the first to realize the illness didn't ruin its victims. It stripped away memory, certainly. It tore apart the soul until even the subconscious dissolved, leaving only kinesthetics and basic language.

The brain was undamaged, but empty – a *tabula rasa*.

Jackie spent the next hour wandering back and forth before the departure gate, drinking vending machine coffee and struggling to keep the effects of the sleep drug at bay until the announcement came, fed into her contacts in green text: *Flight 688 to Vancouver now boarding at Gate 24.* She shoved her pad into the pocket of her carry-on. Avoiding the gazes of her fellow passengers, she slipped into line behind a middle-aged couple and a young man in military pants and olive T-shirt. The couple were engaged in a hushed conversation which threatened to become a fight when they found somewhere more secluded. The military man wore fingertip gloves and motioned in the air before him, his gaze flickering over a view only he could see. Solitaire, she guessed.

The crowd flowed along the walkway into the aircraft. Jackie found her seat, settled into it, and shoved her carry-on under the seat ahead of her. She leaned back and prayed the drug would kick in once more.

It didn't. An hour later, the steel bird humming around her, she returned to the files in her pad. David Glass's kids peered at her again. Elizabeth was fourteen, hair cut short, laced with streaks of blonde. Warren, twelve, had a round face and his father's dark green eyes.

Jackie skimmed the paragraphs and bullet points. David Glass had turned thirty-eight in September. She could walk past him on a street in Vancouver without his giving her a second glance. It would have been easy to leave things that way, to let him be, if not for those two children and his wife.

Jackie found David's notes again and read:

February 30, 2032
I like playing chess at the library. They think I'm stupid until I beat them.

I met a woman at a grave. Her grandmother is dead. She is broken.

Jackie turned back to the beginning of the file, then past the pictures of the children. The woman on the last page of photos had sharp brown eyes and long black hair. Her mouth formed a slight smile. Beneath the photograph was a name in bold: Ariel Morrissey.

Jackie squeezed her fingers into a fist until she stopped trembling. David wouldn't reach the top of the waiting list until spring. Plenty of time. But Morrissey had to be told about her husband. What precisely could Jackie say?

What indeed.

"You must convince David to refuse the injection. If you don't, it will let loose a monster."

4

THE LAWN MOWER WAS HAVING a terrible day. David set it on its side and clawed leaves and grass from its innards, then stripped off a glove and wiped its lenses with his fingertips. The backyard was a mess of fallen leaves and small branches. The mower could handle grass – even soggy grass – but it plowed the leaves up as it moved and covered its own eyes. Not being very bright, it didn't stop but merely kept going until it ran into something. The leaves and branches needed to be raked and bagged before the mower's next foray onto the lawn.

David tapped the Home key on the machine's keypad; the mower wheeled itself around and rolled back to its little shed against the garage. The sun hung near the horizon, out of sight beyond the houses but casting a strip of red across the western sky. David straightened stiff legs and looked around. Uncle and Auntie's lawn didn't have trees in it, not like the massive cedar and two smaller maples here, close enough together that in the summer Ariel slung a hammock between them.

Wait: Uncle did have a hammock. It had come with a steel frame with arms that rose at head and foot, and the hammock's webbing hung between them.

I didn't write that in my journal, David thought. What else? He closed his eyes and struggled to hold on to the scene of Uncle's yard. The barbecue. The old man kept it behind the house next to the propane tanks, under a blue tarp.

Fire leaped across David's mind. He winced in the imagined glare.

David rounded the house to the door. He hung his coat on a free hanger in the closet, shucked his boots off, and headed into the basement. At the bookshelf in the library he eyed the gaps with disapproval. Two of his journals were upstairs. How could he have forgotten that?

On the shelf next to his journals lay his scrapbook, open like a Bible on a pulpit. The book jutted out almost far enough to send it toppling to the floor. The pages pasted into it had yellowed at their edges. David remembered printing them on the ancient laser printer that Ariel had, back when they met.

News clippings showed terror oozing through the ERIN years. In 2027 a doctor in Buffalo, New York, infected her ex-husband with a syringe of blood, knowing the courts would never award custody to someone who would have no memory of his children within a year. In 2029, General Roberto Marieta took power in Peru in the wake of a bloody rebellion and ordered all political prisoners dosed with blood plasma from ERIN patients. But Marieta miscalculated. Loss of memory in his victims made new memories all the more potent. Friends and relatives were more than happy to tell the victims how their lives had been deliberately destroyed. Four years later General Marieta died of strangulation in the presidential palace during an uprising led by his victims.

Less reputable arms of the press played the story of the illness for sensationalism and horror. Sanity prevailed in the end, when researchers at Johns Hopkins in Baltimore began to understand the illness's process. And of course there was Benjamina Shimmerman. Patient Zero – the first recorded case of the illness which for the next decade carried her name. The early news described how "experts" expected her to spend the rest of her life in an institution, incapable of readjusting to the world outside. "It's tragic," one psychologist declared, doing her best to look sympathetic in the photograph included with the article. "Her brain is fine; there is no indication of damage. But how can a human being function without a past?"

Damn well, thank you, Bennie seemed to say, five years after the illness struck her down. She had enrolled, at age forty-eight, in a psychology program at UCLA – calling herself Jem Shimmerson to keep reporters from pestering her. The world didn't learn of that until years later.

A passage from her second book, *Surge*, thundered into David's awareness:

> Memory is a story the mind tells to itself. Those of us who survived the illness have had our stories stripped away, shattered into oblivion.
>
> We must construct new stories and views of the world around us. But we are not infants. The childhood process of osmosis no longer functions – the brain has lost that skill because it no longer needs it. We cannot simply absorb. So instead, we must analyze and probe and reason our way to a new foundation of memory.

"Our stories do not grow organically and unconsciously," David heard himself say. "They are written into our minds through acts of will."

Why am I remembering this? he thought. It's all new – newer than memories of growing up with Auntie and Uncle. It's –

A clicking sound thrummed in his thoughts. A door opening. Light blazed.

"Davie, come out of there." Auntie stood in the doorway to . . . what? A closet. David huddled near the wall, his back pressed against a stack of cardboard boxes. Clothes hung on bars on left and right. A long coat brushed his side, leather against the skin of his arm. Then a thudding sound, though Auntie stood unmoving in the doorway. Not Auntie: the distinctive rapid pounding of Warren's boots, followed by Elizabeth's gentler footfalls.

I wanted to look up Uncle and the barbecue and the hammock, David thought, looking at the shelf where his journals stood, the rightmost book leaning against its fellows. Two of them were missing.

Upstairs, of course: I knew that.

Footsteps struck the staircase behind him. "Hi, Elizabeth," he said.

"Have you moved?" Her footfalls reached the floor – a dull sound, not the hollow echo of the steps.

David turned and followed her. In the rec room he found his daughter leaning over the chess table near the facing wall beneath the window. A separate wooden block made up each square on the board. White squares: yellow cedar. Black squares: rich, dark oak. The chess pieces were tall, carved into ornate and, in the case of the queens, somewhat erotic figures.

Of course, the game. Fifteen days into it. He had forgotten that also.

"Haven't moved yet. How is your friend?"

Elizabeth pursed her lips and tapped her knee against the edge of the table. Her mop of dark hair shook when she shrugged. "Joleen? Getting better. We studied. Mostly."

David caught the smile before it reached his face. "Mostly," he suspected, translated into "very little" in teen-speak. "She's going to pass math this time?"

"Yup."

"Got anyone else lined up?"

"Yup. A couple of possibilities. Shen is a deuce at bio, so probably him."

Elizabeth: babysitter's license at age eleven; running her own tutoring business since she turned thirteen, complete with online promo vids, website, and little temperglass business cards spit out by the maker in the den – cards that played her videos and testimonials the moment somebody picked them up. What are the odds I was like her at that age? David wondered. Low – very low, probably.

She had grown, he realized with surprise, as tall as her mother now. "Remembering anything yet?" she asked.

"Not much." David turned his attention to the chessboard, hunting for the Shape. Each game had one, a shifting form that implied a pattern to the game's movement of play. This particular game formed a hydra, sprouting new heads with each potential move, the largest being the best.

"Mom said you had a nightmare."

"Not really a nightmare." The Shape darted out a new head. Then another until it was a flurry of dancing, snakelike necks, jerking in his thoughts. David visualized one rising, thickening, morphing into the head of a horse. He reached for his king's knight and moved. "Checkmate in six."

When his hand came away from the piece, committing him, two of the hydra's heads turned and bit at the throat of the move he had chosen.

*****

Ariel sat at the den's desk reviewing her messages. The house had grown quiet. Elizabeth had gone into the basement to find her father. Warren had disappeared into his bedroom, probably to play that game which had obsessed him all summer. He spent more time alone than he used to, and she often found him hunching over his GameDome, thumbs twitching the controls while gazing at the little figures projected within, or wearing the Dome's visor.

That issue could be dealt with later. She tugged her thoughts back to the present. Two dozen messages in her work account scrolled down the screen, the new messages highlighted in blue.

Ariel sighed. "Nob. Select first new. Read."

"Katie Rabinovich, yesterday, November tenth," the computer said. "'Ariel. I need the file on the Bradley Building. Can you meet with Linley on Monday?'" Nob's voice was deep and rich, like that of a large, round opera singer. Ariel imagined Katie with that voice, Katie of the blonde coif and frustratingly slender build. At forty-one she still looked the way she had in college.

Bitch, Ariel thought, chuckling ruefully.

The Bradley file had, now that she thought about it, come across her desk about two weeks ago – on the morning David had called.

Ariel had been in her office on Commercial Drive, her chair swivelled so that she could use the desk facing the third-floor windows and downtown Vancouver's high-rises, when her pad chimed *Ode to Joy*, rendered hollow by the tiny speakers but still full of beauty and power. On the screen the Rabinovich-Morrissey Realtors logo – a sketch of a house made to look like a child's drawing – had a blue bar across it which read: "Bitwise Perceptual Technologies."

Ariel set the pad up on its legs and hit the Connect tab.

"Good morning, love." Ariel grinned. "No, I won't be late again tonight, and yes, I – "

David's head twitched. "Conference call with San." The Accept Conference bar appeared in blue across his face. David's eyes gazed at her above the bar, that unsettling stare he still used – even after twenty years of reeducation – when excitement or worry filled his thoughts.

One doesn't keep San waiting, Ariel thought ruefully. The last time she had ignored the doctor, she had found herself in Crawford Memorial Hospital with tubes sticking into parts of her she preferred not to think about, discovering she now had a synthetic tricuspid valve and a line of stitches that would become a scar between her breasts. Ariel touched the Accept Conference bar. The screen split down the middle, and David's face moved to the right. Dr. Santiago Nolan materialized at left. The thickset man looked relaxed. A good sign, Ariel thought – I hope.

"Good afternoon, Ariel. How goes your day?" His Trinidad accent came and went according to his frame of mind. It was strong and thick today. A disturbing sign.

David's eyes narrowed. "No small talk. Tell her."

Santiago sighed, a bit more theatrically than usual. "Very well. A colleague of mine in Portland has a patient waiting for a dose of beta ephemerase."

Ariel shrugged. David wouldn't see his until April. "So?"

"A week ago she suffered a mild ischemic stroke. She is on medication and has to be observed for at least a few weeks more. Until then, she can't receive the injection. By the time she is ready for it, it will have degraded past the point of usefulness."

"What does this have to do with – ?" Ariel blinked. "Oh. Sudden, isn't it?"

Santiago nodded. "I'm afraid it is."

"Wait. David isn't at the head of the list. Shouldn't someone else have dibs on it?"

David smiled faintly. "What I said."

"Commendable sentiment. But my colleague has tried reaching the others. We can't ship it out of North America without all manner of clearances; he can barely get authorization to ship it into Canada. There are two patients on the list ahead of David in the U.S.; Dr. Wiley can't reach either of them. His patient's dose reaches its 'best before' date this Friday; at that point it will be returned to Baltimore for disposal. If you and David agree, I can have the shipping flask couriered to my office. It'll be here by noon tomorrow, or Wednesday at the latest. David can have it Wednesday morning."

Ariel rubbed her eyes. "San, let me have a moment with David." She tapped the Lock key on the phone, cutting the doctor out of the call. "Love? We can't."

David's brow shot up. "Why not?"

"The fund. It doesn't mature until next year. I can't pull cash out of it, and even if I did, there won't be enough, not yet. And with the car payments and your new gear at work, we're strapped." Her heart thundered against her ribs. "If I go to a bank and ask for that kind of money, they'll laugh me out of the office. If I get a Quickloan online, the interest will be murder. And God damn it, David, with Christmas coming, there's no way – "

"It's paid for."

"What?"

"San and his friend are doing this under the table. The stroke patient's paid for that dose. We stick to the plan we laid out. April, when we have money, we wire it to San. He pays for my dose, couriers it to Oregon."

Ariel's throat felt as though it had shrunk. "You're sure about this?"

A nod.

"You're going to spend the next month with your brains curdling. What about work? You signed a contract – "

"Vanida can cope; she already runs the place. If we don't do it, this woman in Portland will have wasted all that money.

Have to start fresh. San didn't say this, but I don't think she's well off."

No one else she had ever known looked at the phone camera tucked above the screen. Most people looked as though they were speaking to your chest.

Smiling, she thumbed the button. "San, tell my husband to quit wasting my time. He'll be in your office on Wednesday."

*****

The sound of a footstep in the hall brought Ariel back to the present. Elizabeth appeared in the den's doorway. "Hey."

"Hey yourself."

"How long will Dad be a screw-up?"

"Don't talk about your father that way."

Elizabeth crossed her arms. Ariel had a flash of her in the kitchen at ten years old, cultivating her sullen look in preparation for her teen years.

Ariel turned her chair toward the girl. "Come on, speak."

"He made his move on the chessboard. His knight. Then he said, 'checkmate in six.'"

"Oh God. That's terrible."

"Don't make fun of me. He always does that. I mean, he always tells me how long till he wins."

"Why do you play if you always lose?"

Elizabeth gave her a you-must-be-an-idiot look. "I can see how Dad plays. He says things about his moves that stick in my head. About how he sees Shapes in the games." She bit her lip. "When I play at school, I almost never lose. Even against the older kids. I can almost see the Shape, the way he talks about it. And he always tells me how the moves will play out. 'Checkmate in six. Two choices. First: expend your rook to protect your king. But do that, and I take your queen and check you. Second: move your queen to protect the king – but I get you with my bishop and checkmate you sooner.'

"But, Mom, this time he's wrong. He put his knight in front of my queen. I can take it. And there is no way he can take me in six moves without his knight. It was a dumb play. Not a little dumb – *really* dumb."

"He's had a rough day. It's probably thrown his game off."

Elizabeth rolled her eyes as only a teenager could. "Maybe you remember the last time Dad played a crappy game of chess. I wasn't born yet."

5

MONDAY MORNING IN THE FLOW. A river undulating in thirty directions, tributaries pouring into hundreds of concepts illuminated in a myriad of shapes and colours. Neutrons and protons leaped into view, unravelling into individual shimmering, vibrating strands.

Only a handful of theoretical physicists had even a slight grasp of string theory. David smiled to himself; he likely understood it better than most of those who worked in the field.

When he let himself ride the flow, he could feel the changes it wove in his mind. The "perpetual revelation effect," a sense of unceasing flares of understanding, of binding pieces of ideas together into a cohesive whole.

The flow did not teach. It shaped capacity, grinding away at rigidity until you were able to absorb a foreign conceptual framework.

"Freeze," David said.

Vanida's voice filled his head. "Want to run it through from the start?"

David nodded. "Set for an auditory kinesthetic. Musical aptitude. With a skill set involving dance. Roll it."

He expected the jarring sensation of the rollback to the beginning, but even so, it unnerved him.

The flow rolled again, different this time: sounds thrumming in his ears, a scene before him almost dark. Protons danced and spiralled, joined by neutrons, all twisting into undulating cords, this time with a swell of bizarre music, sliding from one earpiece to the other, disorienting.

"Freeze," David said, gasping.

"Boss, you aren't focused," Vanida said.

"Not enough sleep. But I'm fine."

A touch on his shoulder. He looked that way, saw nothing. Then a touch to the side of his head.

The scene cut out. His lenses switched to transparent. Vanida Prem stood before him, brow pinching.

"Boss," she said. "I say this with love. Fuck off."

David lifted the headset free. He forgot the nose plugs, with their scent dispensers, and the tongue plate, so these tugged free with a sensation not quite painful but hardly pleasant.

Vanida winced in sympathy. "I mean it. You're useless today. We don't need *you* getting disoriented and throwing up in here; leave that to the paying clients."

"Your father would be appalled, hearing you speak like that."

Van gave him a mock scowl. "Dad would be appalled that I let you stay so long. Go home. Vamoose."

David rubbed his eyes. He hadn't slept for most of the weekend. Here, back at work, he couldn't think straight, couldn't feel the rightness or wrongness of the flow.

Usually he knew when it worked and when it didn't, even when the flow ran counter to his own aptitudes and sensibilities. But today he felt as though it were just tossing him like driftwood caught in rapids.

David handed her the headset. "Okay, you deal with it."

"Did you save the changes?"

No, he hadn't. David mentally cursed. "Better do that before you do anything else with it."

"I will," Vanida said with a smirk. "Thanks for the tip. In college I must have slept through the stuff about saving your work regularly, especially after slaving away at it for two hours."

"Why I'm the chief and you're the peon."

"Go home!"

"Yes, ma'am."

David collected his coat from one of the hooks near the back door and stepped outside. November's storms hadn't arrived yet. The sky poked through scattered clouds. He glanced up at the sign over the door. "Bitwise Perceptual Technologies" had picked up an annoying flicker during the yellow phases and needed tuning – desperately.

Come to think of it, the whole place could use a fresh wall spray. It looked almost as bad as it had when he bought the place. Bitwise had been one of the last shops in the region to actually repair computers. It had lasted into the late twenties, run by an old man with a ready smile and failing vision.

He could take care of the sign over the Christmas break. Resurfacing the walls would have to wait for spring.

He walked along Rumble Street, collar up against the chill. Traffic groaned past. His thoughts spiralled away, stealing concentration. Watling Street and home appeared, though he had no memory of the passage up Royal Oak Avenue. David pressed his thumb to the reader next to the front door and waited for it to flash green. The deadbolt clicked. He pushed the door open, then unzipped his coat and pried his shoes off. Yawning, he made his way to the bedroom.

Just a few minutes, he thought. Rest a little.

The world went away in a blink. He woke to footsteps – Ariel's distinctive stride, slightly heavier on her left foot. A glance at the clock radio told him he couldn't have been out for more than half an hour. She appeared in the doorway as he got to his feet. "Hey."

David frowned. "You're home early."

"Van called me." Ariel came to the edge of the bed and kissed him. "How about I take your coat?"

David looked down at himself, uncomprehending, certain he had hung his coat in the closet. Ariel eased it off his shoulders and hung it over the black railing along the foot of the bed. Unsettled, David lay down again.

*****

Ariel watched David burrow his head into a groove in his pillow. Then she opened his pants and tugged them down his legs, removing his socks in the process. He could sleep in his white polo shirt.

David's eyes opened, and his stare passed through her to something she couldn't see. When had David ever been forgetful – in any way at all? And when had he even left work early? Only twice, Ariel thought: the time the school had called to say Elizabeth had broken her leg sliding into home plate – Ariel had been at a Realtors' conference in Victoria. And when Santiago had called to tell him Ariel had been rushed to the hospital with a ruptured heart valve.

Ariel strode to the den. Katie hadn't been pleased to see her go, cutting out in the middle of their morning meeting, especially with the three condos in the Bradley Building going on the market. She would, Ariel knew, find a way to take some quiet form of revenge. At the eleventh hour of some house deal, a file would land unexpectedly on Ariel's desk and Katie wouldn't be around to help.

Nob sensed her and lit the screen. Warren must have changed the computer's background. The black kid who played Luke Skywalker in the *Star Wars* remake glared at her, glowing sword in hand. Behind him lurked the shadowy gray figure of Darth Vader. And behind them both . . . ick. According to the early reviews, the new director had improved on the original with a sharp script and dramatic visuals, but to Ariel, re-imagining the Death Star as a diseased kidney didn't seem a particularly welcome renovation.

My psychic powers tell me the little man would like to see this soon, she told herself with a mental chuckle, and turned her attention to the computer. "Log me in to the server at work. Page Katie and tell her I'm online."

"Yes, Ari," Nob said.

Ariel enjoyed working here rather than in her office on Commercial Drive. The window showed her the backyard with its lush cedar and bony maples jutting skyward, and the waist-high wooden fence. The neighbour's fat ginger-and-white cat wandered across the grass. This room had been Gran's office, too, though her desk – a heavy beast made of hickory – now sat in the rec room in the basement under a heap of children's toys.

Thank God the real estate agent Ariel had hired after Gran died couldn't sell sunblock in the Kalahari. The sign had sat on the lawn for months, battered by winds and whipped by rain, until David fell into her life, slamming down on her like a meteorite.

Nineteen incredible years. You gave me those, David. Two mostly wonderful kids – you contributed there also. And – oh yes, before all that, the mental breakdown. You pushed me into that. Thanks!

Thump. Ariel straightened in her seat. The sound came again. Ariel rolled her chair clear of the desk and made her way down the hall back to the bedroom.

David lay on his back, his eyes squeezed shut, the fingers of his left hand digging into the comforter. His right fist beat a steady rhythm, rising off the covers and pounding like slow heavy footfalls. His eyes never opened, never moved. Ariel stepped forward, then stopped. No. Better to let him sleep. If this could be called sleep.

The sound of David beating the bed into submission subsided. An hour later, Ariel came out of reviewing a not-very-exciting appraisal of a house in North Vancouver to find David in the doorway watching her through glazed and bloodshot eyes.

"Smell is gone. Mostly. I hear voices once in a while."

"Voices?"

"Memories of voices. I can't figure out what they're saying." His gaze drooped. "Ari. Things I've heard, or read. Not old things, not from before. New things. They hit me. Start playing in my head like a song I can't shake." His palm slapped against the side of his head, making a crack like a thunderclap. "Supposed to be quiet in here."

"David?"

His gaze sharpened and focused on her.

"Go back to bed. Can I get you anything?"

"Leaves," he said.

"Uh, you want leaves?"

"The kids. Need to clean up the leaves. Maybe when they get back from school, I'll take them out and rake."

"Okay, but go to bed. You need sleep."

David nodded, then came to her, bending and hugging her fiercely. "Love you."

"You're not so bad yourself. The bedroom's thataway."

Ariel fed the kids and chased them to bed early that night, then joined David. At one in the morning she abandoned the bed, easing her feet to the carpet while David rocked himself side to side, moaning something sounding like, "Mama." She hunted in the dark for her two books on the night table: one a murder mystery, the other Bennie Shimmerman's *No Inner Voice*. She took these to the linen closet outside the bedroom, dragged out a large purple comforter, and trudged to the living room to crash on the couch.

She woke to find *No Inner Voice* lying open on her chest and Warren peering down at her.

"You and Dad fighting?" he asked, dark green eyes blinking, birdlike.

"No, my little man. He just isn't sleeping well. Lying beside him is like being in an earthquake."

Warren relaxed. "Breakfast," he said.

"In the kitchen. Cereal."

"I want French toast."

"The frying pan lives under the stove top."

"Mom!"

"All right, all right. But you're helping. You can start by cracking four eggs."

Warren raced into the kitchen. Ariel struggled off the couch. The clock beneath the wall screen indicated six o'clock. She opened the book again and looked at the passage she had read last night.

> Suppose you have a fear of drowning. Water terrifies you; being immersed in it is unimaginable. What is the root of this fear? Perhaps when you were a baby, your mother left you for a moment in the bath while she answered the phone. Or perhaps when you

were still very young, your family took you to a pool and your brother pushed you under and held you for a few seconds.

Your childhood mind branded these sensations into your psyche. Now as an adult, the event itself is long forgotten, but the ancient fear still plagues you.

One of the hardest things for normals to understand about us is that we carry no plague of voices and feelings in our minds. We have no memory of pain and guilt, no nameless fears and anxieties. The popular press believe our lack of memory must be terrifying. But for us there is only peace and silence.

If David felt this way, she envied him. No buried fears, no guilt gnawing at the soul. Did the beta ephemerase shot mean David was really going to become a "normal"? Ariel snorted at the thought. BE might resuscitate memory of his first fifteen years, but the last two decades had made the man.

Ariel wandered to the bedroom and peered in. David lay on his stomach. His body jerked, and he mumbled something.

The opening bars of a waltz echoed down the corridor from the den, indicating that Elizabeth was up and at the computer. Ariel found her sitting at the machine with one leg tucked beneath her. Elizabeth rubbed sleep from her eyes. "Dad's still in bed."

"He's staying home again."

Elizabeth scowled. "Why does he get to stay home? How come the world revolves around him?"

"When you broke your leg and you were laid up for four weeks, the world revolved around you. Remember?"

"The good old days."

"Remind me to make up a 'No Bitching' sign. I'll post it in every room in the house. You can explain it to your friends when they come over."

Elizabeth pouted, staring at Luke Skywalker on the screen. "How bad is he going to get?"

"Nobody has ever been hurt by the treatment."

"But not many people had that disease in the first place. How do they know no one's going to be hurt? And why does he want to remember being a kid, anyway? I remember, no matter how hard I try not to."

Ariel laughed. "You still haven't gotten over us raising you in the linen closet?"

"The closet was fine," Elizabeth said, snatching at the dangling thread of absurdity. "But the cannibalism scarred me for life."

Ariel grinned. "Speaking of which, I'm off to make breakfast."

"Oh, yuck!" Elizabeth shrieked as Ariel walked away.

Warren ate breakfast at the coffee table, his left hand holding his fork and his right holding the little white controller for his GameDome. Within the Dome a blue figure raced over images of green hills.

Ariel eyed Warren, wishing he would tear his eyes away. He fed himself mechanically, fork shovelling into his mouth, his attention unbreaking on the Dome.

The kids left before eight o'clock, trudging out the door. Cool morning air filled the living room. Ariel bound her robe to her middle and peered into the bedroom. David gently snored.

In the den she tapped the phone's screen. "Nob. Call Katie's line at the office."

"Yes, Ari." A moment later Katie's avatar appeared. "Good morning, you have reached Rabinovich-Morrissey Realtors. We're not available at – "

"It's me, damn it."

"Please record your message."

"I won't be in this morning. David isn't going to work. He's not well. I'm playing Nurse Jenny." Ariel sighed and stared at the screen. "Katie, I'll be online all day. If there's anything you need me for, page me."

*****

David woke to the sound of the living room screen. The noise warred with echoes in his mind. Thoughts raced along at an impossible speed. He saw his journals in his mind, lined up like soldiers. They held the key; they had to. Now he needed to slot his memories into what his books had recorded, to find out where the images and sensations fit.

A throaty cartoon voice reached him, though the words were too low to be understood. That meant Warren had settled in before the screen. The light from the bedroom window cast an oblique strip of white across the wall, telling him late afternoon had come.

Ariel peered in. "Are you awake for real this time?"

"What's that mean?"

"You've alternated between staring at the ceiling, muttering to yourself, and bouncing on the bed. If you're going to tumble around, I'd like to be part of the fun."

"Did I say anything useful?"

"Nothing I could translate into English."

David struggled to sit up. His body ached. "Time?"

"After four. The kids are home."

"How long have I slept?"

Ariel's mouth formed a compressed O. "If we count everything you've done as sleep, more than twenty-four hours."

"Twenty-four – !"

"I think it's done you some good." Ariel smiled. "You look like you're thinking straight now."

David shifted his legs off the bed. His mind felt quiet. At peace. Maybe a day of catatonia was just what he needed.

His journals could wait, he thought. "The lawn mower."

"What about it? It's back in its hut."

"Going to drag the kids outside and rake the leaves before it complains again."

"Would you like something to eat first?" Ariel's nose twitched. "Or a shower?"

"Feel fine. Good. Clear. Work to do." David tugged his jeans and a sweater on. Moments later he walked into the living room where Warren and Elizabeth watched a Batman cartoon. He clapped his hands, and the explosion made Elizabeth jump.

"Leaves," he said. "The rakes are in the garage. I'll bag them."

From Elizabeth: "But Dad!"

From Warren: "Aw!"

"Out. Nobody does anything else till the yard is raked."

"Can't we just let the lawn mower chew them up?"

"No. Go."

The kids trudged outside like soldiers on a march. The day chilled David's cheeks. The breeze made the pine tree in the front lawn whisper to itself. David thumbed the reader next to the garage door and waited for it to slide upward. The lines of white lights in the ceiling glowed, revealing the cavern of the garage. The blue four-door Honda had parked itself in the centre, leaving ample space on either side. Racks of wire-mesh shelves along the walls overflowed with tools no one had used in months, green lawn chairs that wouldn't see the outdoors again until June, assorted jugs full and empty, and pieces of an old tent that hadn't survived the camping trip to Washington but hadn't made its way into the trash yet.

Looking dejected, the kids each collected a rake from the corner and set off around to the backyard. At four thirty in the afternoon, the sun lit the western sky. Warren stopped at the corner of the house. "Can we go see the new *Star Wars* this weekend?"

"I think so. Be a madhouse at the Plex, but we can live with that."

"Aces!" Warren said, and slung his rake over his shoulder.

"Hey." David beckoned to him. "Tell your sister, pile the leaves near the maples. I'll bag them and bring them in."

Warren raced off along the fence. David collected large paper bags from the shelf along the side wall, then followed the kids. Elizabeth, in her white jacket, had already begun scraping leaves toward the trees. She looked at him and rolled her eyes – a master at that, she was, and so much like her mother. David kept a smile from reaching his lips. Making that observation would only make Elizabeth snarly.

A smell of woodsmoke reached him, and he glanced about in surprise. Then the image unfolded in his thoughts: the camping trip to Washington, Warren and Elizabeth dancing around the fire. The scene twisted, as though projected onto a screen which rotated away from his view. His head swam.

"Stay here, Son; it'll be all right." A fireman in a long heavy yellow coat. A house with a tall brick chimney. Flames licked the sky.

Auntie Mel and Uncle Stuart had been in the house, asleep. He had escaped; he couldn't yet remember how. He recalled the hard cold seat of the bus stop bench across the street, the kindly face of the fireman, the sound of sirens, and the glare of the crimson lights.

Yes! he thought. I remember that. The fireman – tall, Asian – had a mole on his chin.

"Dad?" Elizabeth's voice flung him back to the now. She crouched beside him, hand on his shoulder.

David opened his eyes and peered at his gloved hands, pressed against the cool ground. "I'm fine."

Elizabeth had sat with him when he lit the campfire in Washington. The red sparker, a long narrow device which now sat on a shelf in the garage, had sent a yellow flame into newsprint tucked among wood fragments.

No, don't think about that, he told himself. Focus on the other. The house: that's a memory from before. Hold onto it.

David knelt, picked up a batch of leaves, and shoved them into the bag. His thoughts spiralled back. Auntie and Uncle's house had a fence around it, a wooden latticework as tall as Uncle Stu. A huge window dominated the front of the house; when he walked home from the bus stop and came through the front gate he often saw Auntie or Uncle in the living room, the television casting a blue glow against the white curtains.

Fire shot up in his thoughts. Even from across the street, the warmth of the burning house stole the bite from the early spring air. David shut his eyes and felt the heat on his face.

His gloved hands continued their work, mechanically lifting fistfuls of leaves and shoving them into the bag.

*****

Ariel watched David from the den's window. His body moved as though he were a puppet in the hands of a palsied puppeteer. He seemed focused intently on something no one else could see. Elizabeth tugged at her rake, looking angry at the effrontery of being told to work in the backyard. Warren dragged his back and forth, rocking from one foot to another, seemingly enjoying the job.

Ariel turned her attention back to the computer, frowning, and studied the photos Katie had taken of the Bradley condos. They were upscale, with cabinetry in the kitchens that must have cost upward of forty thousand dollars per unit. Ariel preferred selling houses. Houses were real, tangible, solid. The land under them typically formed part of the sale. But condos amounted to volumes of air. If a nasty quake hit, like the one that turned Tokyo into a parking lot three decades ago, even a building with earthquake protections could guarantee nothing. Few buyers seemed to appreciate that in most cases earthquake-proofing meant the building wouldn't fall over or pancake down on top of you while the earth beneath shook and rattled. It didn't mean the building wouldn't be condemned and torn down afterward, along with the owner's box full of air two dozen meters up.

Elizabeth materializing in the den's doorway didn't help. "Are you going to be on there all night?"

Ariel looked up. "Why aren't you helping your father?"

"He's bagging the leaves."

"And?"

Words came in a rush from Elizabeth: "We raked them up! Why do we have to do everything around here?" She flung her arms together and stood defiantly. Ariel ignored her. Deflated, Elizabeth pulled up the second chair from its place against the wall. "Dad's not going to get weird, is he? I mean, weirder."

"Is that possible?"

"I doubt it." The girl's face clouded. "He looks like he's on autopilot."

"We'll all have to live with that for a while." Ariel glanced at the window. David had vanished, likely dragging the bagged leaves around to the garage to await trash-and-compost day. Darkness crept across the lawn.

"How long?" Elizabeth demanded.

"A few weeks. Maybe a month."

Elizabeth's brow furrowed. "Can I go over to Joleen's tonight? I'm waiving my tutoring fees since she's helping me with physics. We're going to order pizza."

"Something wrong with my chicken stir-fry?"

"Nope. We just absorb knowledge better on pizza. Somebody did a study into that."

"Right. Okay, I'll take you in a bit."

"Thanks." Elizabeth got up, then slipped her hands into her pockets, looking like a little girl for a moment. "Mom? Can I have fifty bucks for pizza?"

An alarm flattened them beneath a wall of sound, jacking Ariel's heart rate into the stratosphere. Nob barked, "Fire detected. Contacting emergency services." The screen showed the house, a flashing scarlet gunsight on the garage.

6

"Shut off that damn alarm."

The computer must have heard, for the alarm cut out, leaving Ariel's ears ringing. She raced to the front door, barely taking time to ram her feet into her loafers before bolting outside. Flame flickered in the open garage. Behind her, Elizabeth swore. Ariel scrambled across the lawn toward the flames.

On the floor of the garage near the wall lay a mass of large brown bags. Two were full of damp leaves, and these lay split open. Around them were empty bags, enough to have done service for years had they not been ablaze. Fire licked at the wall, and the wood panelling of the garage had begun to darken and catch. The damp leaves refused to burn, but the heat from the flames had driven moisture from them, causing steam and smoke to billow up until an acrid haze filled the garage's mouth.

David stood within, his back to the light, a silhouette. He clutched the red barbecue lighter he had bought for camping, its long steel tip blackened. Ariel cringed. Then, aware of the kids beside her, she clamped her arm across her face to mask the smoke and stench, and stepped around the heap of leaves and burning paper.

David didn't move. She saw him in profile, his blank gaze upon the leaping flames. A smile cut across his mouth, showing teeth.

"What's happening?" came from Warren.

A cardboard box of camping gear lay at David's feet, and out of its open top jutted the little fire extinguisher he had bought. Ariel scooped up the extinguisher, pointed, squeezed its trigger. Nothing happened. Flames leaped. Panicked, she stared at the device and saw the steel ring on its side. She pulled hard. The pin caught, then let go.

The extinguisher sent a plume of white foam across the wall of the garage. Ariel aimed it at the floor and squeezed again. The flames dissolved beneath the blast, leaving a smell of ash and chemicals and a cloud of gray steam.

Ariel set the extinguisher in its box, then shook David by the shoulders. "You in there? Wake up."

His eyes wandered to her. "Pretty."

"Thanks, but now isn't the time."

A wobbling smile. "Pretty colours."

Elizabeth snorted. "Weirder and weirder." The girl's voice sounded as though it had gone through a cheese grater.

Ariel turned. Warren's mouth hung open. Elizabeth stood next to him with her arms crossed, trying for anger over shock.

Ariel said, "Your father and I need to talk. Take your brother inside."

"I want to know what – " Warren began.

"Go!" Ariel glared at him, then at Elizabeth. "And for God's sake tell the computer to call off the fire department."

The kids retreated, Warren's complaints receding into the house.

Ariel drew a deep long breath. "Love?"

David looked at her and blinked. His nose made a hissing sound as he drew a breath; he opened his mouth to let it out, drew again through his nose. His fingers let go, and the lighter clattered to the floor. His gaze followed Ariel's to it. In silence he knelt and picked it up.

"Decided to burn the leaves?" Ariel asked, keeping her voice light. "Or did you get sick of the garage?"

"Had a dream last night. The fire at the house where Uncle and Auntie died. I think. Remembered it, started thinking about our trip to Washington last year. Then I thought, simpler to burn the leaves. Just a fleeting thought, and I told myself that was stupid. Don't remember lighting the bags ... ." David's voice took on a childlike fragility. "I'm dangerous. Don't leave me alone."

"I'm taking Elizabeth to Joleen's. Come with us."

Warren stayed home. Elizabeth, in the backseat, was quiet. David gnawed at his knuckles, and at times his head flinched. His left hand rested on his knee. She reached for him, touched his fingers. He wrenched his hand away. Not the response she expected. After a moment he smiled at her sheepishly and entwined his fingers in hers.

Later he came with her to collect Elizabeth. That night Ariel checked on him almost hourly. He thrashed about, and his breathing formed whispered words she couldn't make out.

She worked in the den the next day, though he seemed better. He spent much of his time reading his journals. But Ariel found herself unable to focus on her work. Every sound coming from the bedroom or the basement – wherever David happened to be – put her on edge and sent her scrambling to him.

Early the next morning sound ripped her from sleep again. Ariel flung herself off the couch, found her robe on the carpet, and padded down the corridor to the bedroom.

The bed shook. David's head twisted from side to side.

"Love?" Ariel said softly.

In the dimness she could see David's left hand, balled into a fist, pounding at his side. His right arm lay across his stomach, fingers flexing.

Ariel knelt on the side of the bed where she usually slept. "Love, wake up," she said, then pondered whether this was the best course of action. Even in the throes of a nightmare, at least David slept. She envied him that. He cried out, his voice shrill and brittle.

She didn't see it coming. His right fist swung up in a wide fast arc and found her mouth. Pain exploded through her jaw. Ariel tumbled back and fell clear of the bed.

"Shit." She clutched her chin, moving her jaw gently with her hand. Her lips hurt, and the sensitive spot just below her nose burned. But her jaw moved as it should.

A thumping sound came from the bed. Then again.

Ariel fumbled for the switch on the lamp beside the bed. The glare stabbed into her eyes, and she winced.

David's eyes were tightly closed. His fist beat an even rhythm on the bed where she had knelt. Ariel picked herself up and stumbled into the corridor to make her way to the bathroom.

"Ugh," she told the face in the mirror. Blood trickled from her left nostril, and she could see more of it along her upper teeth. She washed with cold water, then found a ball of cotton in a bag in the drawer next to the sink. This she rolled into a cylinder shape and slipped it into her nostril, then she plodded back to the bedroom.

David continued to pound his oblivious rhythm on the bed.

"Hey," Ariel said. "Asshole. Wake up."

David made no response. Ariel rounded the bed to the side she slept on. With one hand she covered her mouth, and with the other she grabbed David's wrist and tugged on his arm. "Yo."

His eyelids fluttered. After a moment his eyes focused on the ceiling, then on her. "What?" The word sounded slurred.

Ariel dropped her hand from her mouth. "You were having a nightmare."

"Your nose – "

"You punched me."

That brought him instantly awake. "What?" He sat up. "I couldn't – I mean – "

"You were thrashing around. My face got in your way."

"Ari. I'm sorry. I – "

"Nothing broken." She smiled.

"Lips are bleeding."

"Go make chai." Though her mouth tasted of blood. Maybe hot liquids weren't such a good idea.

David wrapped his arms around her and hugged her. "I'm sorry."

"You didn't do it deliberately. What were you dreaming about?"

His gaze cast itself down. "None of it stays with me."

David sat on a stool next to the chess table in the rec room. Through the basement windows he saw Elizabeth's boots tramping schoolward along the sidewalk, followed by Warren's. David smoothed his gym shorts against his legs and eyed his journals. He had left three of them out, and they lay open on the chess table at the edge of the squares. His thoughts buzzed like insects. He picked up the remote for the basement wall screen and tapped the Phone tab. The screen glowed blue, and the time flashed in the lower right corner.

Santiago usually arrived in his office at ten.

Ariel glanced at David in the basement, to find him leaning over the table with one of his journals clutched in his hand. She crept back upstairs as quietly as possible and wandered into the den, where she tried to work.

Later she heard David's voice downstairs, probably calling Vanida. His footsteps resounded on the staircase up from the basement. Ariel turned to the doorway when he appeared.

He leaned against the doorframe and rubbed his eyes with his fingertips. "Need you to drive me down to Crawford Hospital; Santiago is checking me into the psych ward." Then he straightened and strode away.

"Jesus!" Ariel raced after him. "What did you say to him?"

David headed into the living room and lowered himself to the couch. "Told him what happened. I beat up on you this morning."

Ariel stood before him, her hand on her throat. The artery on the left side of her neck pounded against her fingers. "You didn't beat me. You were having a nightmare, I shook you, your fist shot out and hit me. It was an accident."

"Setting fire to the garage was an accident too." David fixed her with an unblinking stare. "I'm getting worse. Will I do something to one of the kids?"

"You had no right to do this without consulting me. I'm calling him back."

"No. I made the decision."

"And what, you think you're so damned competent right now that you can make up your mind for the both of us?"

"If I'm not competent enough to decide whether I should be put in Crawford's psych ward, that's a good reason to have me committed."

"God damn it, you had no business doing this. You don't need a hospital. We can take care of you here."

"How much sleep have you got in the last week? In four days I've had less than a decent night's worth. You're snapping at the kids like a shark. How many appointments have you cancelled so you could be here with me?"

"My work doesn't matter. Right now you're my job – we signed on for that together, remember? Quid pro fucking quo."

David let silence stretch between them.

Ariel grimaced. "Damn it. What am I going to tell the kids?"

"We'll both tell them. You don't have to take me down there till afternoon."

"You should have asked me."

"If I had, we'd have had the same fight we're having now, and then I would have called San anyway."

"You can be a real son of a bitch."

"I know."

"I hate it when you're right."

"Won't happen again."

Ariel laughed in spite of herself. "Liar." She slumped next to him. "God, I feel worn out." Her hand slipped into his. "I love you madly."

"Should pack some things. Love you more."

"Do not."

"Do."

"Don't forget your toothbrush."

*****

"Are you gonna be okay?" Warren asked.

Elizabeth rolled her eyes.

Ariel had insisted on telling them herself. She sat across from them on the black leather chair and looked from one to the other. "Your father will be fine. This is only temporary." David stood beside her, hands clasped together.

"How temporary?" Elizabeth demanded.

"We'll figure that out in a few days."

Warren eyed David. "You're not gonna be crazy, are you? I mean, not all the time?"

"Damn it, Warren," Ariel began.

"I'll be back in a few days," David said. "Maybe a couple of weeks. No more."

Warren shoved his fists between his knees. "So we're not seeing *Star Wars* on Saturday."

Elizabeth sniffed. "Don't be a deuce."

David's fingers twitched. He tapped on the glass of the car's passenger window, then on his knee. His eyes glanced furtively at the passing streets and lights.

"You really want this?" Ariel muttered.

"Want to be home in bed. Asleep. Sane. Not having dreams that make me feel like throwing up."

Ariel's jaw ached; her body had chosen David's side here. "I don't like hospitals."

David nodded. "Full of sick people."

A ten-minute drive brought them to Crawford Hospital. It looked like a castle. Towers like battlements featured helipads on their roofs; Ariel saw an air ambulance launch from one, visible only by its red, green, and white lights, its rotors pounding air.

Ariel remembered her room on the third floor, recovering from having her chest cut open. She shivered at the thought of her heart exposed to the air in a surgical theatre. The car wheeled itself into the roundabout that took them into sheltered parking near the entrance, and the vehicle's hum receded into silence. A stone wall split the entrance in half; one side led to Emergency, the other to the main lobby.

As they approached, the hospital doors whispered open. Ariel noticed narrow stripes embedded in the glass; they made her think of prison bars.

7

DAVID FIXED HIS GAZE ON the reception desk and the dark-haired nurse in green behind it. Time flexed like a spring. Each footstep became an arrhythmic motion. When had he spoken to Santiago? This morning? That didn't feel right. Then his gaze found Ariel beside him, and he felt something twist in his mind. She had her fists in her pockets, and the left side of her neck throbbed with the artery beneath the surface.

A vision swept over him of Ariel huddling in a heap of blankets and dirty clothes, her hair dishevelled, her face contorted in a scream.

She wonders if she should have been in a place like this, David thought. The revelation brought clarity. He slipped his hand into hers. Yes, just this morning he had spoken to Santiago. The doctor had told him to go to Crawford Memorial and check in at Reception. "Don't go to Emergency," the old man said. "The psychiatric people will look at that as an admission of a problem more serious than it really is."

David said something to the nurse at Reception, and passed his ID across the marble-like tiles of the counter. The suitcase he had packed made itself known, leaving him with a feeling that it had materialized in his hand. He had wrestled with whether to bring some of his journals, but had decided against it. They were too easy to lose here when he had no idea what the rules were going to be.

The nurse's mouth quirked as she read the two screens before her. She typed on a black keyboard. "Mr. Glass. Referred by Dr. Santiago Nolan?"

"That's right."

"Your address is still on Watling Street?"

"Yes."

"It says here you're scheduled to receive beta ephemerase."

Would finding out that Santiago had finagled him a dose of BE early cause problems for the doctor?

Ariel squeezed his hand. David glanced at her, smiling in reassurance.

"Right," he said.

"I need you to sign here." The nurse pushed a pad to him, and handed him a flimsy stylus.

Ariel intercepted it and turned it toward herself. "What's this?"

The nurse stood and leaned over the counter, eyeing Ariel. "This places your husband in our care for the next fourteen days. If he – if a problem arises, the psychiatric nurse can recommend an extension."

Ariel pushed the pad back and wheeled on him. "You won't be able to leave for two weeks? David, that's – "

" – necessary." David picked up the stylus and signed the line.

"This is supposed to be temporary."

"Two weeks is temporary."

"The psychiatric nurse will be down for you," the nurse said. "He will take you for your assessment."

"Assessment?" Ariel asked.

"The assessment group decides the category your husband should be placed in. Your family doctor has recommended category three, but the assessors must make that decision."

David heard a hum and turned to see the elevator door sliding open. A man slightly shorter but as thin as himself stepped out, followed by a woman and a hulk of a man, all in hospital greens.

"David Glass?" the thin man held out his hand. "I'm Ezekiel Crane, head psychiatric nurse. Call me Zeke."

David motioned at Ariel. "This is my wife, Ariel."

A look pulsed across the psychiatric nurse's face when he glanced her way: the look of someone disregarding her. "Pleased to meet you. Now, Mr. Glass, we'll take you upstairs. You'll have to come alone."

Ariel crossed her arms. "I'll wait."

Zeke turned his attention to her fully, a tenuous smile wandering across his face. "If the psychiatric assessment group permits, you can visit Mr. Glass tomorrow."

David turned to Ariel. "I'll be fine." He bent and kissed her mouth. "Not going anywhere, Ari."

She grimaced at that. David had hoped it would reassure her.

The trio led him – or rather surrounded him on his way – to the elevator. The door closed with Ariel standing there, shoulders taut, her hand on her throat.

David studied the buttons. Nine, each marked in red stencil on burnished steel. The fifth floor, he remembered, housed maternity. Elizabeth and Warren had both greeted the world here.

The label for floor seven read, "Category 3 Mental Health." Beside the floor 8 and floor 9 buttons was a thumb reader, and those buttons were labelled Category 2 and Category 1. Number three must include the more benign forms of mental illness. What qualified as category two? Delusions? Psychosis? If so, what was category one?

Zeke examined a pad, tapping buttons on it. The other two said nothing, although the large man spent a great deal of time scratching his stomach. Muscle, David thought. They're here to subdue me if I cause trouble.

"You're slated to receive a psychotropic treatment called beta ephemerase in April," Zeke said.

"My doctor may be able to get it early. That acceptable?"

"We're only here to assess you, Mr. Glass. I can't speak for the care your family physician provides."

David tapped the crook of his left arm. "Got it two weeks ago. Why I'm here."

Zeke cleared his throat. "Your medical records haven't been updated then."

The elevator door slid open onto a corridor with pastel-green walls and a smell of cleansers and scorched electronics. Before him stood a half-circle desk with a nurse behind it. She didn't look up.

Zeke led him to the left. In seconds they came to a small office. A man and woman sat behind a small white table. Zeke didn't introduce them. Instead he motioned to a chair and took one next to the man and woman. David studied Zeke's body language. Part of his attention pointed like a laser at the old man. The woman gave a nod to Zeke, but her awareness focused on the old man too. The man was short, thick in his middle, with graying black hair. He wore beige pants and a loose black turtleneck shirt. The woman wore hospital greens.

The two nurses or interns, the black woman and the larger white man, positioned themselves on either side of the door.

Zeke looked at his pad. "You've received beta ephemerase treatment. You've been having some disorientation?"

That got the attention of the other man, who unfolded a pad and began scrolling through it.

David nodded. "Haven't slept a full night in four days. Nightmares."

"You had encephalopathic reductive influenza."

"ERIN, yes. When I was fifteen."

"Why did you choose to take reclamation treatment?"

"Aunt and Uncle raised me till I was fifteen. Died before I was diagnosed. Have a set of journals to tell me about them. Nothing else, not even photos. Want to remember them."

"Your parents are listed as deceased as well."

"Died when I was a year old. Car wreck in Oregon. Don't know anything more about them."

Zeke stared at his pad. His thumbs tapped keys. David wondered if he'd ever read anything about the illness in his life. "Have you begun to recall anything?"

David thought of his image of Auntie Mel's hands on Ariel's throat. That wouldn't go well here. "Nothing that makes any sense."

"How have you been, emotionally?"

"Strung."

"Define 'strung.'"

"Haven't slept properly. Can't concentrate. Disoriented. Almost set fire to the garage. Apparently I punched my wife yesterday morning – "

"You struck your wife." Zeke's eyes narrowed. "Is that why she had you brought down here?" The older man leaned forward on his elbows, and the woman beside him matched the gesture.

"Didn't have me brought down. She doesn't even think I should be here; we had a squabble about it when I told her I wanted to be checked in here."

"And that's when you hit her?"

"No. Hit her in my sleep. I called Dr. Nolan this morning when Ariel told me about it. We argued because I called Santiago, told him I could be dangerous to my family."

"I see."

No, David thought; you don't. The air in the room felt chilly.

The older man appeared to be forcing himself to keep his face expressionless. David wondered if he knew how much he gave away.

"Why did you feel like hitting your wife?" Zeke asked.

"Didn't feel like it. Didn't do it deliberately. Didn't know I'd done it until I woke and saw Ari's nose bleeding."

"What do you do, Mr. Glass?" Zeke asked.

"My job?"

"Yes."

"Operate a perceptual-engineering company."

Zeke raised his brow. "I've read about that. Psychological manipulation. Aptitude adjustment." Distaste flickered across his face.

"Only with willing participants."

Zeke smiled uncertainly, glancing at his coworkers. "That must be fascinating, altering how people think."

"We change how well they are capable of understanding a topic. Used to be estimated that maybe a fraction of a percentage of those who learned string theory in university physics could understand it at a gut level, including the math. We turn that into fourteen percent." David smiled. "Need someone who can understand quantum computing? Give me a week and a plumber. Or a psych nurse."

Zeke's coworkers smiled at the barb. Zeke reddened. "I see. And what does your wife do?"

"Co-owner of Rabinovich-Morrissey Realtors."

"And your children. They're both in school, is that correct?"

"What does this have to do with this assessment?"

"That sounds hostile, Mr. Glass."

An old and not very effective trick: accusing someone of defensiveness could put them on the defensive. The older man's eyes narrowed at the edges. David smiled. "Apologies. Isn't meant to be."

That derailed Zeke. His gaze skimmed over his pad. "I have some standard questions for you. Please answer as quickly as you can."

"Go ahead."

The questions seemed random initially, but David soon noticed a pattern to them. Some probed his feelings toward his parents or his wife, while others were logically inconsistent – tests to reveal problems with reasoning, he guessed.

The gray-haired man, who might hold David's life and freedom in his hands, stifled a yawn, the swelling of his throat giving the gesture away. After seventeen questions he tapped his pad. David heard a beep from Zeke's. The psychiatric nurse glanced down, then at the other man.

"Well." Zeke's voice sounded strangled. "We're finished here."

The old man pushed his chair back. He met David's gaze, clearly satisfied.

Even more obvious: Zeke didn't like the decision made.

*****

Back home, Ariel stopped outside the front door and rubbed her eyes. With good luck, David had a room by himself where she could visit. With bad luck, he could be locked away from her for two weeks. Or more.

She drew a deep breath and let the reader scan her thumb. The door clicked and beeped.

Elizabeth sat at the coffee table, her netpad glowing.

"Dad's in the nut farm?"

"He'll be fine."

"Surrounded by crazies. Who wouldn't be?"

Ariel hung her coat on a hook on the wall and squeezed her shoulder blades together to work out the tension cutting across the back of her neck.

Elizabeth snorted, as though she had expected a reaction she hadn't got.

Ariel dug her phone from her jacket pocket. The message light blinked green. A tap on the screen brought up the caller's name and face: Jackie Olver, graying hair tied back. Ariel didn't recognize the woman, which of course meant the phone sent the call straight to voicemail after work hours.

Ariel wandered to the hallway. Warren had shut his bedroom door. These days he spent more and more of his time alone. She tapped on the door. Immediately a muffled, petulant, "What?" came through.

"Remember me? Your mother?"

"Just a moment."

Ariel heard feet thudding on the floor. The door swung open. Warren wore his blue sweatpants; a T-shirt hung dishevelled from his shoulders.

"Do you mind if we talk?" Ariel asked.

"'Bout what?"

"Your father."

"Sure." Warren pushed the door open and threw himself at his bed, landing on his backside with a thump, somehow missing the GameDome on his pillow. Ariel winced at the groan the bed made.

The room, since his last cleanup, had slipped back into chaos. From the ceiling hung a model of the Toulouse-Chen space station, an array of tubes and modules plugged into each other like pieces of plumbing pipe, with black square wings spread out from it on either side. Across the wall facing the bed hung the wide, hideously expensive 3-D mural Warren had insisted on getting for Christmas last year; it gave the illusion of a portal looking out from some currently fictitious settlement on Mars.

The window faced the backyard, though two potted plants blocked the view. Ariel remembered buying them three years ago, replanting them into larger pots and setting them up in the living room in an unfortunate attempt to brighten the mood of the house. After months of neglect resulted in yellowing leaves and brown stalks, she had set them outside to be thrown away. By the next day they were gone, which had made her think someone had stolen them for the pots. A week later she discovered them on Warren's windowsill, each showing signs of a healthy green hue. She had never asked him about them, had never mentioned them. Warren hadn't either. The orchid thrived, blossoming regularly into royal purple petals. The ivy had spread around Warren's room. He had set hooks into the wall near the ceiling to carry the vines.

Across the cluttered floor Warren had carved a narrow path among toys, gadgets, plastic models of spaceships, and discarded clothing to his bedside. Cringing, Ariel stepped through the mess and sat on the bed. Warren pulled his GameDome to him. The blue figure within swung a staff at a creature that looked like a cross between a Border Collie and a crow. Warren worked the control pad with his thumbs.

"Do you feel like talking?" Ariel asked.

Warren's gaze remained on the Dome. "Can we visit Dad tomorrow?"

Damn, always with the hard questions. "It depends on what the people at the hospital say. And can you look at me while we talk?"

"I'm at level 197. When I hit 200, I'll be a Priest in the Order of Sarandok. Then I can go into his new world."

"Um. What's a Sarandok?"

"A Jamaican. Sarandok's his character name. He got to godhood a few months ago. He's been making a new world ever since. In a few weeks he is going to let other players in. As soon as he opens the portal, he needs followers. With enough priests and worshipers he can keep his power over the creatures and physics and everything else." Warren's brow creased. "Dad isn't taking me to see *Star Wars* on Saturday."

"Maybe we can do that. You, me, and Elizabeth."

Warren said nothing, focusing his attention on the Dome.

"Tell me something. Your father was just a few years older than you when he caught the ERIN bug. What would you want to remember if you knew you were about to lose everything?"

Warren stared at her; apparently the thought had never occurred to him. "I dunno." He lowered his voice and motioned with his chin at the wall separating his room from Elizabeth's. "Probably wouldn't want to remember *her*. But you and Dad could tell me anything I don't remember."

"What if you didn't have us? What if we were gone?"

Warren's throat danced and his eyes darted to and fro. "I dunno."

Ouch, Ariel thought. I've hit a nerve. "Nothing's going to happen to us, little man. I'm just curious about what you'd want to remember. What would you write down if you knew in six months you'd have no memory of it all?"

"Hoshi," Warren said without hesitation. "I could ask him about things. He could tell me stuff."

"Okay, a friend. What else?"

Three monsters ganged up on the thin blue creature Warren controlled. His thumb touched a button on the controller. The figure blazed scarlet, and the three dog/crow creatures fell in masses of bones and ash. He ignored the carnage and squinted at his mother. "Maybe the camping trip. That was fun. I wouldn't write much about school. Maybe I'd put down that A-minus I got in Bio. I wouldn't write about the ass – the morons. Maybe about Mr. Rogerick in Science; he's fun to talk to."

"What about things that interest you? What would you write about them?"

Warren shrugged. "I'd say I want to go to Mars."

Ariel smiled. Soon puberty would kick in, and his obsession would shift to –

Don't go there, Mom, she told herself.

Warren turned back to his Dome. Ariel watched him play. "Get some homework done, little man."

Warren pretended he hadn't heard.

"Your father will be home soon."

"Good."

Ariel rose, sighing, and strode to the hallway. "Want your door shut?"

"Yeah."

"You're welcome."

Elizabeth's laughter echoed up from the basement. Ariel meandered into the den and slumped in the chair, then set her phone next to the computer keyboard. "Grab my messages."

"You have one new message," Nob said.

The woman on the screen had straight graying hair. Lines gathered around her eyes. In her fifties or early sixties, Ariel guessed.

"Uh, hello," she said. "I'm trying to reach . . . ." Her gaze flickered down. "Ariel Morrissey. I – My name is Jacklyn Olver." She paused, flustered. "I'd appreciate it if you would return my call." She recited the number – unnecessarily, since it glowed in a blue bar beneath her image. "I'm attending the medical convention here, so I'll be out till evening. Thank you." The screen turned black.

What the hell? She considered the image on the screen. An older woman, a doctor, in Vancouver for a medical conference. She could be looking at property. No, she wasn't looking for Ariel the Realtor; she would have called the office number.

"Nob, return the last call."

"Yes, Ariel."

The woman appeared on the screen instantly. Her skin glowed, too pristine, her mouth a study in symmetry. An airbrushed version of the real person. "You've reached Jackie Olver's voicemail. How can I help you?"

"Shit."

"Please restate your request," the avatar said.

"I'll leave a message."

"Excellent. You may record now."

"This is Ariel Morrissey. You called me earlier. You can reach me anytime this evening." Her thumb touched the button to break the connection.

She eyed the phone's black screen thoughtfully. "Nob."

"Yes, Ariel," the computer said.

"Google Jacklyn Olver," Ariel said.

A search list appeared, looking like a spider web with a thousand strands.

Actually, Ariel noted, more than that – Google said it had found 11,239 links with that name.

"Replay my last message," she told the computer. "Grab a still pic."

Olver appeared on the computer screen.

"Isolate the face and cross-reference with the previous search."

The computer showed a new list, this one reduced to ninety-six entries.

> Jacklyn Olver. Medical doctor. Chicago.
> Jacklyn Olver. Researcher. Johns Hopkins University.
> Mohammad Seraf, head of neurological research at JHU.

"What. The. Hell?" Ariel breathed. "Cross-reference with Mohammad Seraf."

The screen shrank to three references.

"First result. Show me."

The Johns Hopkins University *Gazette*'s title and logo filled a banner at the top of the screen in blue and black. Text filled the space below. Mohammad Seraf's roly-poly dark face with its familiar smile looked at her from the screen. And below it, a younger version of the woman who had phoned.

> **Mohammad Seraf**, Professor of Neurology, has received a grant from the Gates Foundation to continue his studies into the link between influenza strains and neurological conditions.
> **Jacklyn Olver** has been named Director of Research in the Department of Neurology.

Gooseflesh rose on Ariel's arms. David got emails from them several times a year and filled out the questionnaires they sent to support ongoing research into ERIN and its aftermath. She lived with a survivor of the illness. Why would someone involved in Johns Hopkins be calling her now?

She turned to her phone and touched its screen. "Put Jacklyn Olver on my white list. Any time she calls, no restrictions."

The phone beeped.

8

"HE'S BEEN MAKING THOSE SOUNDS ever since they brought him in." Two shadowed figures stood in the doorway, voices hushed. *"Have you ever seen anyone who had that disease? God, imagine what it must have been like, waking up . . ."* David turned over, shaking his head, wishing clarity would pierce the fog around his brain. Time skipped.

Consciousness came like an explosion. He sat up, gasping. With a hard-on to die for and his wife nowhere in sight.

And where did *that* observation come from?

The edges of his vision fractured. Hallucinating. That explained why Aunt Mel perched on the edge of the bed, hand on his knee. The bed turned over and dumped him onto the porch out back, Uncle Stuart sitting on the bench. The rumble of the old Chevrolet rolling out of the driveway: Aunt Mel had left to visit friends. David was twelve or thirteen. He couldn't recall.

Uncle Stuart: "Damn. A hard-on to die for and the woman nowhere in sight."

How had he responded? At that age, probably with a roar of laughter. Only the memory of the words remained.

Pain in his legs and up his back. As though he had slept in an awkward position. The bed felt both too small and too large: it seemed Ariel had always been there, slipping a leg over his, pressing her back or chest against him. The bedroom at home could swallow this room and two of its companions. A tall window cut the wall to his left. Last night, when he had been shown to this room, he had looked down at the hospital's parking lot and Kingsway Avenue, watching the glare of white streetlights and the opposing rivers of red and yellow vehicle lights along the street.

The reason for his erection became painfully apparent. Not arousal – just a desperate need to pee. David made his way out into the corridor, then stopped and looked down at himself. Black T-shirt and undershorts, enough to stave off an indecent-exposure accusation. His bladder motivated him to continue down the hall toward the counter where Ezekiel Crane and a female nurse stood in hushed conversation. They stopped when he approached.

"David, good morning." A perfunctory smile hopped across Zeke's mouth and vanished.

"Need the bathroom."

The nurse pointed.

"Thanks." David yawned and padded along the pale green corridor in that direction.

The washroom was a cubicle with a toilet and sink. A large sign next to the mirror read: "Did you remember to wash thoroughly?" David nudged the door shut with his heel. A small shower was tucked into the alcove behind the door. A shower would be wonderful. A hissing sound reached him, water flowing in pipes –

In an instant it was gone.

He sat. Ariel had seen him in that condition two years ago, hunching and bending his "morning woody" into the toilet. She had guffawed, asked if she could "borrow it" for half an hour, and then shared her observations with son and daughter – earning her a confused look from Warren and a shriek of horror and embarrassment from Elizabeth. Now his own laughter at the memory took care of the erection, and he managed to empty his bladder.

Ariel would be hustling the kids off to school soon. Warren would be a problem for the first minute or so. Elizabeth would wake herself up but be cranky at breakfast. If the weather was fair, Ariel would tell the kids to walk to the bus stop. Then she would duck into the shower. If David were home, he might join her, ostensibly to conserve water. He thought about lathering soap on her back, running his fingers over the bones of her spine as she worked her fingers through her hair. In his mind, she smiled and made that soft "hmm" sound she added to the ends of sentences when she was happy.

The image of Ariel morphed into Auntie Mel, standing with him in the shower, plump body towering over him. David flinched and tugged his undershorts up his legs. His head swam. He washed, then fumbled until he found the cold handle of the door and tugged it open.

A girl walked toward him, her narrow face wan. A bandage sheathed her neck. A pink stain marked the space over her throat. She had the same lean build as Elizabeth, but this girl had a mop of black hair, unkempt against mocha skin, hanging in tangles past her shoulders. Hospital whites covered her: a tunic, pants, and slippers all made of what looked like paper. The fingertips of her right hand twitched, running along her left arm from the crook of her elbow to her wrist, and back.

She drew her gaze away from her arm as she navigated around him and continued on. Beneath her bleak, dark eyes, he saw someone screaming.

Like Ariel, decades ago.

David followed the girl with his gaze. Strips of narrow tape held her bandage to the back of her neck.

Zeke's slippered footsteps, already familiar, padded behind him. "So, David. How did you sleep?"

David chewed over several responses. "Horizontally. That girl. Why is she here?"

"I don't think you need to concern yourself with her."

"Attempted suicide? Not common, doing the throat like that."

"No, it isn't."

"Keeps looking at the veins on her arms. Something wrong with her blood?"

"No. I think we should talk about you."

David shrugged and gestured toward his room.

Zeke had more questions, covering everything from his current emotional state to his sex life. Which turned his thoughts to Ariel.

That shifted his thoughts to the girl he had seen. A Shape grew in his mind, a form that captured the essence of her. He knew starfish were bloodless, but this one oozed scarlet through lesions in its twitching limbs.

*****

Ariel left her office at eleven in the morning and drove to Crawford Hospital. The hospital looked even more like a prison as she climbed from the car in the visitors' lot. What had David told them during his assessment? She had no idea. The thought made her stomach twist. She strode into the hospital and approached Reception.

In answer to her questions, the nurse typed on her keyboard, then tapped the screen before her. "He is in room 708. Go right up."

So he hadn't been locked away. Relief left her light-headed. When she reached the elevator she thought, what is security like in here, if they let me wander into the psych ward? Then she saw the thumb scanners for the eighth and ninth floors.

The psychiatric ward looked like any other floor in Crawford. Green walls. A smell of cleaners. She followed numbers beside doorways past a room with an old man snoring like a train, two empty rooms, another where a skinny girl with a bandaged neck slumped in a chair, until she found 708. None of the rooms had doors – probably to keep the crazies from locking themselves in.

Ariel found David sitting in a chair near a single tall window. The small brown suitcase he had packed lay open on the floor next to his bed, a narrow affair with rails along its sides. The muscles of his neck looked like ropes drawn taut. One fist beat a slow rhythm against his cheek. Ariel clicked her tongue against her teeth. The sound seized David's attention. He shoved himself back, turning the chair, swivelling his head to face her. He hadn't shaved today, and his eyes appeared to have receded into his skull. He looked like he hadn't eaten in days.

"Ari." David spoke her name as though it were new to him. "I really look that bad?"

Ariel tried to smile. "Worse."

David blinked, a rapid-fire strobe of eyelashes. "Something in this room makes a god-awful buzzing sound. Hear it?"

"No."

David's hands brushed his temples. "Did you ever meet my Uncle Stuart?"

My God, Ariel thought. "You and I met at the cemetery. Remember? Your uncle and aunt were already gone."

"What I thought. But it all runs together. I can see you and Uncle Stuart in the kitchen. And having coffee out on the back porch with Aunt Mel. It's all screwed up. I think Aunt Mel had large . . . ." He held his palms in front of his chest.

"Breasts?" Ariel grinned. "That's something a teenage boy would notice."

"House had a swing set out front. An orange-and-white cat used to come over from the neighbours; Uncle Stu was allergic."

"David, remember Steve and Zoe next door? They have an orange-and-white cat that goes through our yard."

David stared at her; then he rose and came to her, taking her in his arms. He hadn't showered yet today; his shirt smelled musky. Ariel didn't care. She slipped her arms beneath his and hugged him fiercely, pressing her ear to his chest.

David lifted her chin and studied the line of her jaw. "Bruise has faded. Or is that makeup?"

"I'm fine. Really."

A sound behind her caused her to turn, and there stood the psychiatric nurse in the doorway.

David let her go. "My shrink."

Zeke stepped into the room. "Ms. Morrissey. How – "

"How is your patient?"

"He has been fine so far. Last night's reports say he slept fitfully."

"That sounds familiar."

"He seems confused."

"Don't you medical people have technical terms for things like confusion? 'Inattentiveness syndrome' or something?"

Zeke smiled tentatively, as though he wasn't sure she was joking. "We try to avoid jargon these days. But about your husband – "

David waved his hand between them. "He's right here."

Zeke laughed, a sound too smooth to be genuine. "David, I need to speak to your wife alone. Do you mind?"

"No."

Zeke motioned to the corridor. "Please, come with me."

Ariel followed him. Zeke Crane slowed his step and fell in beside her. He led her farther along the passage and gestured at a room in the corner of the corridor's elbow. A kind of coffee room, though Ariel saw no coffee maker or cooking equipment. A gray spoon lay on the counter. It looked like rubber.

Zeke motioned to a table next to the wall.

Ariel sat. "David looks terrible."

"Ms. Morrissey – "

"Call me Ariel."

The psychiatric nurse nodded. Ariel studied his face, thinner than David's at that age. Twenty-seven, or thirty, perhaps. He pressed his lips together and drew a long breath through his nostrils. "Ariel. Has your husband assaulted you?"

Ariel snorted. "Of course not."

"He tells us he did." Zeke gazed pointedly at her jaw.

"Oh that. He wasn't conscious at the time; it was more a reflex than anything else."

"But you thought him dangerous enough to have him brought here."

"This was his idea. I disagreed."

"You have two children, is that correct? If there is any chance he is a danger – "

"That's what he is afraid of. But what he did wasn't deliberate. You know how sometimes your leg will jerk suddenly when you're almost asleep? That's what it was like."

Zeke eyed her carefully. "You're certain he didn't assault you? We can help you if . . . ." His words hung in the air, unfinished.

Ariel rested her elbows on the table and put on her sweetest smile. "Zeke. Have a doctor examine him. If my husband's testicles are still attached to his body, you'll know he has never tried to harm me or our kids."

The psychiatric nurse, to her immense satisfaction, turned a bright shade of scarlet. His Adam's apple bounced like a basketball. "Yes. Well."

"David isn't violent. Frankly I'd rather have him looked after at home. Can you find us someone who can do that?"

"We'll see."

"Is there anything else?"

"David did say your physician arranged for him to get beta ephemerase early. Is that correct?"

Ariel licked her lips thoughtfully. "It was arranged; let's just go that far."

Zeke nodded. "But it is true, he has received it."

"Almost two weeks ago."

"From a reputable source."

"Jefferson Labs in Baltimore. The only biotech lab approved by Johns Hopkins to produce the stuff. It's legit." Ariel rose. "I'd like to spend some time with my husband, if that's all right."

Zeke looked as though his mouth had more to say but he couldn't think of how to form the words. Finally he shrugged and nodded. Ariel wandered back to David's room. David had returned to his chair, but now he leaned forward, gazing out the glass. As soon as she stopped behind him he looked over his shoulder. His eyes didn't focus on her.

She knelt beside him and settled her hand to his arm. "We have some time. I can stay for an hour or so."

"Ari. No. Need to go inside myself, let this figure itself out. You're a distraction. And, you've got work to do. Been in your way lately." His fingertips touched her cheek. "Don't do that."

"What?"

"That thing you do with your eye." His thumb ran along the skin beneath her left eye. "I asked for this. Don't blame yourself."

"Damn it, don't do that!" Ariel forced herself to breathe, then kissed his mouth. "You want me to go."

"Please. Yes."

Ariel walked to the elevators, feeling as though she had been hollowed out and filled with sand. Her hand shook when she reached for the Down button. Then she noticed there wasn't one.

The nurse at the desk behind her said, "It's on its way up."

"Thanks."

He is right, she thought. You didn't make him take the damn drug. He wanted this. Give him a few weeks and he'll be back to normal.

As the door closed and the elevator trembled into motion, leaving her staring at its wood veneer walls, she realized she had forgotten to ask David if he had ever heard of Jacklyn Olver.

*****

The kids were home when Ariel arrived at twenty past five. Elizabeth read her pad on the couch with her feet up on the ancient oak coffee table, while Warren channel-surfed the wall screen.

Elizabeth looked at her, eyes narrowing. "Can we visit Dad?"

"Yes, but not right away. He needs to rest."

"Then when?"

"Next week, for sure. I'll make dinner."

Warren looked at his feet. "Can we have lasagna?"

Good, Ariel thought. Food distracted Warren from Elizabeth's questions. The girl rolled her eyes but said nothing more.

Ariel smiled at Warren. "Yes, little man. You can help."

Elizabeth vanished into her room, to be called out for dinner an hour and a half later. She took her plate into the basement. Ariel heard the rec room screen turn on. Muffled female voices. Warren took his plate into the living room and turned on the screen there.

"Dibs on the movie feed at seven thirty," Ariel told him.

"Aw!"

"Why don't you do some homework tonight?"

Warren gaped at her, appalled. "It's Friday!"

"Then go and play on the computer."

"Can I get a netpad? Then I could study online in my room, like Elizabeth."

"I'll ask Santa." Ariel filed away the conversation in her mind. Christmas was six weeks away.

"I'm too old to believe in Santa," Warren said.

"Then he won't be giving you a pad for Christmas."

Warren stuck out his tongue and fled to the den. Ariel found the original *Casablanca*, not only in 2-D but in black and white. She keyed it, adjusted the volume, and curled up on the couch. She tugged a cushion against her side, where David would sprawl if he were here, resting his head on her hip.

Just as Rick pondered how of all the gin joints in all the world Ilsa could have walked into his, her phone chimed. A box flashed in the lower left corner of the screen.

Jackie Olver.

Ariel threw her legs off the couch and tapped the phone. "Send the call to the wall-screen," she said.

The phone beeped once. Rick and the crew of *Casablanca* vanished, replaced with Olver's image. Ariel sized her up: professional, businesslike. But the woman's eyes darted right and left, and the bridge of her nose twitched.

"Good evening," Ariel said.

"Ms. Morrissey?"

"Yes. What can I do for you?"

"I'm calling about your husband. David Glass. Is he in?"

"No."

"When do you expect him back?"

Ariel shrugged. "Anytime." Anytime between now and two weeks hence.

The woman's eyes glanced down. "I knew your husband. A long time ago. I assume you know about his illness?"

"Somewhat," Ariel said dryly.

"I knew him at a clinic in North Vancouver."

Ariel stiffened. "The Shimmerman Clinic."

"You know of it."

"Of course. My husband spent two years there. Doctor, would you please get to the point?"

"Of course. According to your husband's file, he is on the waiting list for beta ephemerase therapy."

Ariel narrowed her gaze.

"I think he should reconsider."

What the hell? Ariel kept her voice neutral. "Why is that?"

"For at least a month he could suffer serious disorientation. We have evidence of effects lasting as much as four months. It would be best if he thought it over carefully."

"David and I have discussed this. You aren't telling me anything new."

At that moment Elizabeth stomped up the steps from the basement. Ariel waved her away. The girl rolled her eyes and headed for the kitchen.

"Beta ephemerase causes dramatic changes to the brain," Olver was saying. "To brain chemistry. The long-term consequences aren't – "

"In our basement David has a library with everything ever written on the subject. We've got all the reports on early ephemerase trials, including the work your friend Mohammad did before he brewed up the recipe for beta. David can recite chapter and verse of every study ever done. Believe me, there isn't anything we don't know about how beta works. David wants to remember his childhood. All he's had are his journals."

Dr. Olver's mouth curled. "Yes, of course. His journals. He kept those all these years?"

Ariel felt like laughing at the woman. David's journals were his only connection with his aunt and uncle; all else was ash. "You knew him before the illness, is that right?"

"Yes. A little. I managed the Patients floor in the clinic. I had David in my care for five months."

"Then he'll want to meet you."

Dr. Olver's mouth fell open. "No! I would prefer . . . I don't want that." Her voice took on a pleading tone. "Please, it would be best if David not take beta."

Klaxons rang in Ariel's mind. "Why have you taken it upon yourself to come all this way just to talk David out of taking the drug?"

"It would just be best if – "

Ariel held up her hand. "Wait." She reached for her phone and told it, "Take back the call." The wall screen flashed black, replacing the call view with a still shot of Rick in the bar. Ariel headed for the bedroom.

When the door thumped shut, she leaned against it and said, "David got the injection two weeks ago."

Dr. Olver looked like her head might explode. "No, that's not right. He's on the list." Pages rustled. "He won't get it till April."

"Well, don't ask how, but he has received it."

Jackie Olver paled. Her fist dug into the cloth of her white blouse above her heart.

Ariel wished David were here. He could read this woman, pick up a thousand subtle, telling cues.

"Does he remember anything?" Dr. Olver asked.

"Smells and sounds. Nothing more than that."

"How is he sleeping?"

"Badly."

"Ms. Morrissey, I think – "

"What is the matter?" Ariel murmured, forcing her voice low. "Talk to me."

"You have to understand, we never expected there to be a way to recover lost memories." The woman's voice cracked. "Back then we were sure Shimmerman's Disease – ERIN – destroyed everything you knew."

"What is wrong with my husband?"

Olver's jaw trembled. "David lied, about everything. His journals are fakes."

~

The boy sits in the dark of the closet with his back to a set of boxes full of Auntie's junk. The closet is special. Mom's soul hovers outside the door. Sometimes he can feel her in the air.

The door cracks open. The boy closes his eyes, wincing against the glare.

Uncle towers over him. The old man's hair is a fringe above his ears, aglow in the light of the afternoon sun cutting across the living room floor. The boy feels Uncle's eyes on him, though he can't see them in the backlighting.

"On your feet, boy. The woman wants you."

Uncle motions him out of the room. The boy scrambles to his feet, ignoring the buzzing sound that of late has grown loud in his thoughts. He considers telling Uncle and Auntie about the sound. For the thousandth time he changes his mind. The sound is his. No one else's. Like Mom's soul, drifting in the air outside the closet door. She is his alone.

~

Spring 2028

"Death Row."

9

While the man from Western Corrections Services inspected the isolation room, Jackie inspected him. He was tall, bald, running to middle-aged fat. He kept a camera clipped to the collar of his pale blue jacket, the way police on television shows did, with the camera eye positioned to view whatever lay in front of them. Gary Holmes glanced at the metal toilet, bent to push on the army cot, nodded to himself, and turned his attention to the terminal. "Get rid of that."

The terminal was built into a green steel case with a military-grade screen and keyboard designed to take a bomb blast without jarring a key loose. It could even survive patients in the throes of a psychotic episode, suicidal terror, or phase two of Shimmerman's Disease.

"The kid won't damage it," Jackie said.

"He is no kid, and that's not the point. Let him sit in here alone. Let him stare at the walls and think. Let him rot."

"My patients need social contacts. Keeping them isolated exacerbates the condition."

Holmes turned his gaze along the walls and stopped when he saw the black glass dome above the door. "Camera?"

"Yes. We can view from the security office."

"What about at night?"

"We dim the light. It's enough. I'll need his records."

"The kid has no records. Your security man. Is he alone?"

"We have a small medical and psychiatric staff here during the day. At night we have additional security people, and a duty nurse. We've been lucky lately – we have had only a couple of slideovers to deal with. Now, records are not optional. You must have a police report. And if this young man is an arsonist, there should be a psychiatric assessment."

Holmes glowered at her. "Fine. We can give you all that." He rubbed his cheek with his palm, leaving sweat behind. "Slideovers?"

"The first phase of the illness is what you've probably seen already, which is nothing. When patients slide into phase two, they begin to remember things. Vividly. Anything charged with emotion comes back strong."

"I thought Shimmerman just erased them."

"It does in the end. Before then . . . ." Jackie shrugged. "I had one patient break another's arm because he thought he was seven years old and horsing around with his stepsister." I didn't even know he had a stepsister, she thought, remembering the Lawyer's agonized scream and the sound of snapping bones.

"The kid will probably enjoy reliving the fire. I'll need to talk to your security man; then I'm done. Your guard is the only one on during the day?"

"There is the medical staff."

"One skinny little guard." Holmes smirked. "Oh well, your people are your business. Maybe he knows kung-fu."

"Believe it or not, some Asians *don't* know martial arts. George is here because he is immune to the illness, like the rest of us."

Holmes's brow rose. "Immune?" he muttered in a strangled voice.

"There's a bridging protein in the brain. Shimmerman's Disease depends on it. We don't – "

"The kid isn't contagious, is he?"

No, Jackie thought. But she had no reason to enlighten this arrogant goon. "I'd have to examine him."

To her satisfaction, Holmes's cheek began to twitch.

"I'll need names and phone numbers for David's next of kin," she said.

"Hold a seance. His only relatives were an aunt and uncle. His legal guardians. They were asleep when he lit up the house."

"No one mentioned murder."

"The fire crew found him on a bus stop bench across the street. He sat there with a bowl of popcorn in his lap, watching the house burn. It was a show for him. A God damn night at the movies."

*****

The next morning Jackie ran her passcard over the lock by the side door of the nondescript wood-panelled tenement that was the North Vancouver Shimmerman Clinic. She pushed the door open and wandered along the corridor. Along the way she tried the security office door. It didn't budge. George started at six, an hour before she arrived; he would be making his rounds.

She swiped her card over the lock beside her office door and stepped inside, propping the door open. Random file folders and sticky notes lay scattered across her desk. As part of her normal routine, she scowled at the clutter and promised herself she would clear it up when she found the time.

A small silver rectangle next to her keyboard caught her eye. She reached over her desk and picked it up. A memory stick on a metal ring. A plastic tag on the ring read: WCS. Jackie sat at her desk and slipped the stick into the slot on the side of her keyboard. The computer popped a window open on the screen. The stick held three files, icons gleaming sky blue: "Police report," "Psychiatric assessment," and "Medical." Jackie opened the first.

The boy in the mug shots had an angular face and sharp chin. A mess of brown hair crowned him. His eyelids drooped. He could have walked by her a dozen times over the past two years without drawing her eye.

    Name: David Harrison Glass.
    Age: 15.
    Offences: Arson.

No mention of murder. Perhaps they hadn't gotten around to putting that in.

Victims: Melanie Reed (aunt), Stuart Reed
(uncle).

Four pages made up the police report. David Glass had no prior record and no history of violence. The young man had admitted to starting the fire but refused to tell the police anything further.

Jackie opened the psychiatric file. It was crudely done – a few paragraphs in a document, not an official assessment form. The psychiatrist used words including "confident" and "self-assured." But David Glass had told him nothing.

She turned her attention to the medical records, scrolling through them until she found a note marked "GPT+" toward the end. The plus sign made it seem like such a positive thing. *David Glass, we can positively tell you that in about seven months, your life will end. You will wake up empty. You can anticipate a life of psychiatric help, or the care of your family if you have any. They can take you for walks, and you can look wide-eyed at a world you no longer recognize. By then you will never have known anything else.*

A tap of knuckles on the doorframe made her look up to see George Ross, his Chinese eyes narrower than usual.

"Good morning," she said. "I see our friend from Western Corrections delivered the new patient's records."

George beckoned to her. "He delivered more than that."

The security office had a row of screens bolted to the wall, and each one showed David Glass in the isolation room, sitting at the terminal's keyboard. He wore orange pants and a shirt that matched. Prison garments.

Jackie tapped a fingernail on one of the screens. "So, our firebug is typing. Can I see what he is doing?"

George leaned over his desk and worked the mouse. One of the screens shifted, and now showed a web browser window. "That's straight from his screen."

The window showed a website called WorldSearch, which Jackie had never seen. A row of links appeared in a column, and when the mouse pointer hovered over one, a box of text materialized. "Oregon. August 20, 2014. Massive thirty-car pileup on I-5." Another search box opened, showing a photograph of overturned vehicles and police cruisers.

The view shifted to a white box: a word-processor document.

George cleared his throat. "David asked me if he could create files on the computer. I set up an account on the server for him."

Jackie nodded. "Good." Perhaps David would tell her something about his past. He had been busy; the document already had a list of notes.

> Born in Vancouver
> School
> ~ South Burnaby (RECORDS)
> Aunt Mel
> ~ Fat
> ~ Cooking? (Yeah, right)
> Uncle Stuart
> ~ Quiet
> ~ Stereotype: strong and silent

As she watched, text appeared letter by letter.

> Mom and Dad
> ~ Car wreck
> ~ Oregon - pileup on the highway
> ~ Drunken idiot

Jackie winced. Two years in Chicago's Mercy Hospital working ER had left her with visions she had never shaken. Human bodies smashed by tons of steel and glass. But losing his parents to a car accident didn't justify murder.

"I checked the server logs," George said behind her. "He's been up since three this morning, searching all over the Net. Looking up Bennie Shimmerman and the disease."

"What's your impression of him?"

She heard the rustle of George's blue uniform jacket as he shrugged. "He didn't say much. He asked about saving files. And whether he could have things printed and delivered upstairs when he is done."

Jackie turned. "That doesn't sound like a typical patient. I guess I should say hello."

George rose.

"No, stay here." Jackie waved him back to his seat. "I want you to watch him closely."

"I can record this. We can see it later."

"He's not dangerous. He's nowhere near sliding over."

George hesitated and opened his mouth to argue; then he sat down. He plucked the long black flashlight he carried on his belt and held it out to her.

Jackie smiled. "Do you seriously expect me to pound him with that if he becomes a problem?"

George shrugged and set the light on the table. "Your call."

Jackie left the flashlight where it lay and set off to the narrow *L*-shaped corridor that housed the isolation rooms. The white walls here looked newer than the painted stucco of the main halls. Two cameras, tucked into black domes in the ceiling, monitored the corridor. Jackie imagined George leaning his elbows on his desk as he watched her. She swiped her card over the lock. The latch clicked.

The new patient sat in front of the terminal, hands poised over the keys. Initially he didn't move. Then he rotated his seat and lifted his gaze to hers. The boy's expression drained blood from her face, leaving a chill in her cheeks and cool sweat on her brow. His eyelids were flared back, one eyebrow cocked. A sneer twisted a mouth that might otherwise have seemed soft and warm. The effect froze her in place, hand still on the doorknob, locked in his brutal stare. The moment clenched her throat, cutting off her breath.

Holding her in the grip of his gaze, he spoke.

10

"WHAT MAKES YOU SPECIAL?"

"Wha-at?" The word broke up as it passed her lips.

"I said, what makes you special?"

"I don't – "

"The rent-a-cops knock. The nurse who brought me breakfast knocked. What makes you so damn special?"

Now the boy's voice carried a hint of whine, breaking the spell. Jackie caught a laugh before it burst from her throat. "You think I should knock before coming into your room?"

And yet he was right. The isolation room had a faint odour that implied the toilet had recently been used. Walking in on him then wouldn't have been a treat for either of them.

Dave eyed her, holding his glare. Then he turned his eyes back to the screen. His fingers fluttered past the side of his head as though brushing away insects. Disregarding her.

"Okay. Dave, I'm sorry."

"My name is David. Not 'Dave,' not 'Davie,' not 'Dee.'"

Silence. But his body language had changed. He didn't ignore her now.

"What are you doing?" Jackie asked.

David nodded at the screen. "I've been reading about the Shimmerman bug since Sherlock brought me in here."

"Sherlock?"

"Holmes. The cop wannabe from WCS."

"Oh. Of course. What have you found?"

"I'm going to die."

"It's not fatal."

"It's going to wring out my brain like a towel. Same thing. This place is Death Row. How long do I have?"

Jackie hesitated. "At least six months. Perhaps as many as eight. David, I understand, believe me."

"You've got this too?"

"That's not what I meant. I can understand. You're afraid. However, this will be painless." Jackie sat on the cot and crossed her knees. She reached to touch his arm, but the look he cast built a wall and she drew back. "David, when my older brother Jason was sixteen he contracted non-Hodgkin's lymphoma. Do you know what that is?"

"Cancer."

"That's right. It *should* have been treatable. But Jason reacted to the chemo. I watched him lose his hair and shrink to skin and bones. He died less than a year after his diagnosis. I was only thirteen and I had to watch my big brother die. So I know how you feel. This is not going to be easy, but it won't be painful. I promise."

David's gaze grew savage. "That story is supposed to be some kind of bonding bullshit, is that right? 'I lost my brother, you're losing your life, so we have something in common. And besides, bald skinny Jason went through horrible shit so you should feel lucky you get to die in your sleep.' Does that actually work on people?" He spun his chair back to face the screen.

Jackie stared at him, stung, unable to think of something more to say.

David spoke again. "Can I get out of here?"

"We can't let patients out of the clinic. This is a volatile time for you. You're much better off with us."

"I meant this room."

"Oh. We'll have to see about that." Holmes's words resounded in her thoughts: leave him here to rot.

Jackie rose and smoothed her pants. "We'll talk again later."

"Since you've introduced the rest of your family, any chance you'll tell me who *you* are?"

"I'm Dr. Olver. I manage the clinic."

"Badly, from the sound of it."

Jackie backed to the door and clasped the knob. An image of Jason lying in bed materialized in her mind, his skin stretched across his cheeks.

The kid's voice cut through her thoughts. "How long has Bennie Shimmerman been going to a university in California?"

Jackie choked on a startled laugh. "Where did you hear that?"

"RumourMill. Look it up – you may learn something. It's smart. It ignores mainstream news sites, deep-trolls the Net for anything weird. People have seen her at UCLA, sitting in psychology classes."

Bennie Shimmerman is in an institution in Tennessee, playing with toys. Jackie clamped down on the thought. "No, David, it isn't true. Some people believe things that have no foundation in reality."

Before he could say anything more she ran her card over the lock and pulled the door open. When it squealed shut behind her she stood, shaking, her skin feeling raw and exposed.

Jackie plucked her phone from her waist and tapped a key. "Hello Simon. Are you free right now? It's important."

The elevator opened on the second floor. The Recovery floor, as Simon called it. Jackie thought recovery was a stupid word for this category of patient. A stocky man with a graying beard wandered by, his body clad in loose white pajamas. His gaze passed over her.

Jackie almost blurted out, "Uri!" Uri Myrnovski continued on along the corridor, oblivious to her. She imagined him in his room downstairs: the slideover to phase two, his hands on his knees when he woke from his first rewind. She had placed her arm around his shoulder when she told him. Some patients cried or raged. But for Uri, the slideover was just another storm for the sad-eyed Russian sailor to weather. Three months later he slid into phase three, his memories coming and going like the glow of a light swinging on a cord.

Apparently Uri was the only patient awake. Relieved, Jackie made her way along the empty corridor to the open door of Simon's office.

Simon Markson had styled his office like a living room. He had placed two small couches next to an ornate dark wooden desk which, unlike hers, had no clutter. Bookshelves lined one wall, in dark reddish wood matching the table. On the opposite wall hung a reprint of the Mona Lisa; in garish contrast beside it was an Andy Warhol made up of four pastel graphics of an actress she couldn't remember.

Markson was tall and wiry. He wore khaki slacks and a yellow T-shirt with "Weregild Ale" across the chest amid artful red splashes.

Jackie spoke first. "I need to talk to you about David Glass."

"Oh yes." Simon motioned to one of the couches. He smiled. "And good morning to you."

"Sorry. Good morning. You didn't tell me David Glass is a murderer."

Simon's smile vanished. "An arsonist. He has no history of violence. There is a difference."

"But he is volatile."

"Volatile how?"

"Abrasive, sometimes vicious. He is going to push all kinds of buttons in the other patients. I can't afford that. Where can you put him besides downstairs?"

"He is a fifteen-year-old boy. Your people can handle him. You'll only have him for seven months. I only spoke to Western Corrections two days ago. How could you have concluded he is going to be a problem so quickly? Has he done something to one of the patients?"

"No, he is still in isolation." Jackie thought back to what he had said about Jason. But Simon wouldn't accept that as a reason. Was that all that irked her about the kid? Willpower kept her face expressionless; that thought needed to be considered more carefully.

Simon pursed his mouth. Jackie had the impression the man was examining her.

"You moved Quentin Draper out when he got violent," Jackie said.

"Quentin Draper had to be placed in a psychiatric hospital. I had meant him to be there just long enough to stabilize. He took his own life by strangling himself with a shoelace."

Jackie recoiled. "You never told me that."

"I didn't think it would do any good. I had intended for him to go back to you once we had him sorted." The old man took on a faraway look for a moment. "You have had surprisingly few losses or incidents, Jackie. I've been passing your reports on to others across the country, as examples." Simon smiled. "What did this boy do to make you so uneasy about him?"

"Besides killing his aunt and uncle? He is extremely brutal verbally. I can already see him taking strips off the others. People are as comfortable and happy as they can possibly be down there while living with a death sentence. The kid read somewhere that Bennie Shimmerman has recovered and is going to college in California. It's ludicrous, but that's the kind of thing the other patients will grab hold of. I can't afford . . . ."

Then she saw the wide-eyed expression on Simon's face, and laughed. "Yes, that's what I thought. It's ridiculous."

Simon moistened his lips with his tongue. "How did the lad find out about Saint Bennie?"

"You mean *it's true?*"

"Not exactly." Simon rubbed the stubble on his chin. "Jackie, we've been noticing changes in recovering patients this past year. Saint Bennie is the latest. I think it takes longer for older patients like her."

Jackie loathed Simon's nickname for Bennie Shimmerman. There were times when she wanted to say, She was no saint! All she did was catch a previously unknown illness. "What takes longer?"

"After two years – sometimes as long as three – something wakes up in them. It happened to Saint Bennie almost a year ago."

"Simon, their memories are gone. Obliterated."

"They aren't recovering *per se*. If Saint Bennie were getting her life back she would be going back to being a journalist, not studying psychology. Right now she is just auditing courses – she isn't officially a student. She moved to California with the help of a psychologist at UCLA. She insisted on using a false name to avoid the press."

"*She* insisted?"

"Yes."

"These people have no lives anymore. I'm sorry if I sound like I have no compassion for my patients, but when I hand them over to you, they're human robots with no operating system."

"Nevertheless, something wakes up in them. I've been seeing it with my long-term patients here also." He eyed her thoughtfully. "Do you remember Lily and Peter?"

"Vaguely."

"I think you came here after they had slid into phase three. They've been in my care for almost two years. They have no family. We got them assigned to BigBurger on Lonsdale for the work experience project."

"Slinging fast food."

"It does them good, associating with normals." Simon made a dismissive flutter with his fingers. "They went through the usual training – which amounts to an hour of being shown which buttons to push on the screens. The orders appear on displays in the kitchen. Anyway, they were into their third week at BigBurger and nobody had any complaints about them. Then last Tuesday, an hour after the place opened – in the middle of the breakfast rush – the computers failed."

"Ouch."

"Not ouch – no, not at all. When the computers went down, Lily and Peter kept taking orders. They told the manager to pass them on to the kitchen staff."

"I suppose they're not used to the technology, so they adapt to paper and pencil more quickly."

Simon hesitated. A gleam appeared in his eye. "This was the breakfast crowd, Jackie. When Peter and Lily took charge, the manager was so shell-shocked she had no idea what else to do, so she let them. Peter and Lily took orders, perhaps a hundred or more over three hours, took money, and gave out correct change. The store didn't get a single complaint. The manager claimed most of the customers weren't even aware the computers were down.

"And no, Jackie, they didn't write anything down. Nobody told them there were handheld calculators under the terminals, so they crunched the numbers in their heads for change. For dozens and dozens of customers."

"Oh come on. That's not possible."

Simon lowered himself to the opposite couch and rested his arms on his thighs. "Jacklyn, we've always assumed these patients are never going to amount to anything. It's true their previous lives have been wiped away, but their psyches are intact, their intelligence unaffected – to borrow your analogy, perhaps the operating system is still there despite the erasure of the data. I'm beginning to think they aren't as helpless as we expected."

"Why haven't I heard about this?"

"Why would you? This is too new; no one has talked to the press about it. Everybody is too afraid of getting it wrong and looking like a fool." Simon grinned. "But things are happening to these people. Incredible things.

"And no, I won't move David Glass elsewhere."

11

THE PATIENTS FLOOR – JACKIE'S DOMAIN – had fourteen patients. Four were in phase two, and she was glad there weren't more. With just a handful routinely dancing with memories that wound them back to some of the most emotionally potent moments of their lives, the security men were busy enough. George on the day shift and the two at night had to check both the patients who had slid over and those who had been here at least two months, since they were close to the line also.

Jackie made a point of reminding the staff regularly to keep everybody calm. Upsetting phase two patients almost guaranteed they would have an episode.

Security men, nurses, and interns made up the ward staff. The interns came from the University of British Columbia and were usually studying psychology or psychiatry. Jackie found one of them talking quietly with the Lovers in the infirmary. Carmen, one of the Lovers, lay in bed while Virgil held her hands. Jackie stood in the doorway watching them. The pair had come to the clinic together, each having been infected by the same source, or one having infected the other. Nobody knew how Shimmerman's was transmitted.

She kept her nicknames for the patients to herself. Thinking about Carmen and Virgil as the Lovers, or Maureen as the Fat Woman, or Fred as the Carpenter, allowed her a certain detachment from them.

The intern broke off from them and strode to Jackie.

"How are they taking it?" Jackie asked in a low voice.

"Better than I thought. They have each other to lean on."

"What about . . . ." Jackie turned her gaze to the Fat Woman in the next bed over.

"She has been quiet. I'm more worried about her than them. Can we have the new patient watch her?"

Jackie thought the intern was talking about David Glass. Then she remembered Switch, and chuckled. "I think he would scare Maureen half to death."

The young woman smiled. "Switch is a nice man when you look past the tattoo and the bear paws. He has been asking for something to do around here. He says he can cook. How about we put him on lunch and dinner detail? He is at least two months away from slideover."

The word brought the attention of the Lovers and the Fat Woman, their heads swivelling toward Jackie.

Jackie smiled at them in reassurance and lowered her voice. "Don't use that word in here; it pushes buttons. I'll talk to Switch."

Jackie found him in the common room. Switch looked like he might have come here from prison. He wore black jeans torn at the left knee and a tank top that showed off hairy biceps. A tattoo of a rattlesnake started with its tail on the back of his left hand and wound around his arm to his shoulder, where it entered a skull's base and emerged from an eye socket, its teeth bared. Switch wore his hair bound so tightly in a ponytail that it cut lines across his head. His face hadn't known a razor in a week.

Switch looked up from his coffee, his grin a lopsided monster showing a hint of broken incisor.

Jackie strode to his table. "You're looking for a job."

"Yup." The man's voice rumbled up from his paunch. Two gold loops jangled in his left ear.

"You can cook?"

"Yup."

"Good. But first I have something else."

"What can I do?"

"You can look mean."

Switch leaned against the bookshelves when George brought David into her office. Impeccable timing, Jackie thought. David had had a day in isolation with only guards and a nurse for company, and then only sporadically. Now, in late morning, the common room had filled up with most patients talking, playing cards, watching the corner television, or using one of the terminals against the back wall. The din of activity carried down the hall. Maybe David would notice and feel a need for human contact.

The kid looked Switch up and down. Switch did something with his pectoral muscles that made them dance and bulge against his shirt, which caused David's throat to move the same way.

"Sit down, David," Jackie said.

David dropped himself into one of the chairs. George stood near the door.

"Did you have a good night?"

"Good enough." The kid's hands kneaded his armrests.

"That's good to hear. David, this is just a casual conversation. We want you to join the rest of the patients, but right now we don't know anything about you. So if there is anything you'd like to say, you're welcome to speak up at any time – "

"You sound like you're trying to be my shrink, or my mother."

Jackie's voice faltered. Time for a different approach. "Why don't you tell us about yourself?"

"What do you want to know?"

"Tell us about your aunt and uncle."

"We got along like a house on fire."

Switch's knuckles cracked. Jackie cast him a sharp look. "David, we need a little cooperation from you if we're going to release you to join the others in this clinic."

"Then quit saying my name every time you talk." He looked away, his gaze wandering to the filing cabinets. "My lawyer advised me not to answer any questions that might have a bearing on my trial."

Was that what bothered the kid? Jackie smiled. "Dav – Sorry. When you leave here, you'll be free. You're in the clinic's care at least until you turn eighteen. Dr. Markson has told me you were never formally charged, and your record will be expunged."

"What if someone comes up with a treatment that stops it before it wipes me out?"

"That's extremely unlikely, David."

"University of Helsinki. They're testing a serum on advanced Shimmerman's cases. Success rate is twenty-two percent."

Jackie felt her smile freeze in place.

David pressed on. "So, if I blurt out something to you that you can use in court, what's to stop you from telling it to the judge if something comes along that keeps the disease from nuking my brain?"

"We have something called doctor-patient confidentiality here."

"I'm not *his* patient." David jutted his thumb over his shoulder at George. "Or his." Motioning at the huge man.

"Fine. George, Switch, could you step outside?"

"No, George and Switch; stick around. I'm not going to say anything worth a cat's ass anyway."

Jackie studied David's face. He met her gaze evenly, though she sensed he was struggling to keep his eyes locked to hers. Perhaps he wasn't as self-assured as he wanted her to believe. "All right then. We won't discuss your aunt and uncle, or anything to do with the fire. You can at least tell us about your life before then. Start at the beginning. You lost your parents when you were very young."

"Shit happens."

"In a car accident. Is that right?"

David stopped breathing. Shock crossed his narrow face. Then his mouth grew hard. "Don't you have that in your report on me?"

"We have been looking into your past, yes."

David made that odd gesture Jackie had seen yesterday, as though brushing something away from the side of his head. "Not a car accident. This is hearsay, since I was just a little bastard then – barely past the diapers and barfing stage. But

Uncle Stu liked to share this story so I wouldn't forget the details.

"Once upon a time, Mommy got pissed off at Daddy. So Mommy found Daddy's shotgun and blasted him a new asshole, from the back of his head down. And since Mommy didn't have anyone to whine at anymore, she decided to redecorate the living room with her own brain matter. The end.

"When Auntie and Uncle moved into the house they tore out the carpets and painted the walls. But in the ceiling next to the lights you could see where Mom's blood splattered around. Of course, you can't now since the house is a pile of – " He stopped speaking abruptly and looked down at his lap. His hands gripped the armrests and tugged at them, knuckles turning white.

Jackie watched him. Impressive, she thought, coming up with a ridiculous story like that on the spot. But she couldn't let it pass. "David, I think we've heard enough." She motioned at George. "Take him back to isolation."

George stepped forward. Then David wailed "Mama!" and yanked his chair sideways.

Jackie rose. At the same moment, David toppled to the floor. He wrenched himself back and forth, hands clenching his chair. His voice rose in a wounded animal's howl.

12

"WHAT THE FUCK?" CAME FROM Switch.

George was crouching next to David. "He's sliding over."

"That's not possible." Jackie rounded her desk. "He's – "

He is what? she asked herself. Faking?

"I thought he just got here," Switch said. Jackie looked up at him. His voice had turned smooth, free of its roughness. His face was white. "It's hit him already. That's – you said it would be three months."

Jackie shook her head. "Switch, it never comes early. Never."

"But he – "

"Calm down and let me handle this." She shifted her gaze back to David. He lay on his side, tears pouring from his eyes, his head and body shaking back and forth.

Jackie clutched his head and turned him toward her. "David. Happy birthday, David. Happy birthday." Forcing lightness into her voice. "You're four years old today."

David's face grew slack. Then a grin broke across it. "Prezzies?"

"Yes, David. That's right. Come on, get up. Happy birthday."

David struggled to sit, cradling his left arm. "Hurts."

"That's okay, David. I'll look at it." Jackie took his arm and ran her hands along it. Nothing broken. He would have a bruise.

Jackie looked back at Switch. The man had pressed his back to the bookcase. He shook his head, sweeping back and forth, unable to cope with what he had seen.

"Switch, listen carefully. This isn't going to happen to you, not now. Not for a long time."

"How the fuck do you know?" the man hissed. "That kid —"

"Think, Switch. You had an infection a week ago, right? Sneezing, coughing, aching? Your doctor tested you and told you you'd contracted Shimmerman's Disease, right?"

The big man blinked.

"That's when you got it. Last week. And the next stage never comes early. We know this."

"What about him?" Switch stabbed a dubious finger at the boy.

"He has had it at least three months. He should have been in here with us for all that time. Somebody screwed up." And I think I know who, Jackie thought.

"Tell them to stop," David whined.

Jackie cursed inwardly. David was dragging her attention back to him, but it was the big man who needed to be dealt with now. She glanced at George, saw him gripping the flashlight he carried and gazing uncertainly at Switch. The big man looked like he could snap George in half.

"David, be quiet. You're fine. Happy birthday."

"Why do you keep saying that?" Switch growled.

Good: make him think about something else. "In this state he is very suggestive. I'm keeping him focused on something good."

"What if his birthdays all sucked?"

I won't be using that trick on you, she thought.

"Tell them to stop it," David said again, leaning back against her desk. He thumped his head back. "They're making too much noise." He made a gasping throaty sound. "Auntie sounds like she's dying. And Uncle Stu sounds like one of Uncle Ray's pigs."

"What are they doing, David?" she said softly.

David's face glistened bright red. "I'm not supposed to say. Their bed, it's thumping." Pointing at the ceiling. "Upstairs."

Switch barked surprised laughter. "Kid, sounds like your aunt is a screamer." Jackie glanced back at him. A broad grin brightened his face.

She caught a laugh of her own before it emerged. "David, you shouldn't be telling strangers that."

David giggled. "I won't tell, Auntie."

Jackie lined up a bed in the infirmary for David. Then she wired him to the EEG and watched spiking lines crawl in blue across the screen, the distinctive serrations of a patient in a phase-two flashback. She swore, wishing David had been putting on an act.

She took Switch aside. "I'd like to put David in your room. I can't isolate him when he is like this; it just makes things worse. Could you watch him, help us keep him under control?"

Switch looked dubious.

"We can't have the patients here getting upset; it just pushes them over more readily. If David is a problem, it would be best to get him away from the others. Do you understand?"

Switch's eyes flared. "What about me? Will I get pushed over?"

"Not for several months. Now I'd like to put you on the dinner detail in the common room."

That seemed to shift his gears. "Can do. Who should take the shopping list?"

"What list?"

The big man grinned easily. "I'm not doing burgers here. You want food, you'll get the real stuff. Prawns tonight, with Thai rice."

Jackie laughed. "Fine. Give me your list. I'll see what I can do."

She headed back to her office and shut the door behind her. Two phone calls later, she had Gary Holmes of Western Corrections on the line.

"Mr. Holmes, when exactly did WCS get David Glass?"

"Why is that important?" the man asked, guarded.

"I called Trent Mueller. He is the psychiatrist you took David to for his assessment, remember? He says WCS officials brought David to his office in early February. I checked with the Attorney General's office. Private corrections firms like yours are required to give new inmates the GPT. Do you know what that is?"

Silence.

"It stands for 'Gentry Prion Test,'" Jackie said. "A positive means Shimmerman's Disease."

"Look, we can't – "

"From what I've seen, you had David in your facilities for at least two months. I'm looking at his medical file. You tested him only last week."

"He had some kind of seizure. Started wailing for his mommy. We figured someone had given him drugs."

I could end this man's career, Jackie thought. With a phone call I could end it.

"That was a phase-two slideover. It only hits after three months." Jackie could hear Holmes's breathing grow laboured. "I don't care whose fault this is. Someone in your company didn't do his job, but I still need to do mine. And my job involves keeping David Glass safe until the end. I need your help to do that."

Holmes's breathing changed. His voice took on a gritty edge. "What do you want?"

"David has given us two stories about his parents. One: they died in a car wreck. Two: they died by murder-suicide – his mother killed his father."

"Half the kids I deal with blame their mothers. It's bullshit."

"That's irrelevant. I need you to find out whether his family really was involved in a murder-suicide."

"And just how am I supposed to do that?"

"You must have connections with Vancouver police. Ask them to check their records. It must have happened about fourteen years ago. David's parents were Isabelle and Harrison. Maybe there is something about his aunt and uncle too – Melanie and Stuart Reed. David told us about another uncle also, an uncle Ray. Find him. Perhaps he can tell me what's in store for David in the next few months."

Holmes was silent. Finally he asked hoarsely, "Anything else?"

"That will do. The sooner you get me some background information on David, the better it will be all around. Have a good afternoon, Mr. Holmes."

Jackie hung up, heart pounding. She drew several long breaths, shutting her eyes. Then she turned to her computer.

A window opened to reveal the assorted accounts on the central server. FredB, MaureenJ, DavidG.

She clicked on the folder marked "DavidG." A single file appeared called README.

Why had David keyed information about a car pileup in Oregon, if his parents had not died that way? What was truth here?

She clicked the file. It opened to reveal a single sentence:

Quit looking at my files, cunt.

13

JACKIE WAS IN THE COMMON room two days later when her phone buzzed. George said, "Gary Holmes is here."

"Good. Put him in my office."

She found Holmes standing near her filing cabinet, arms crossed. Trying to look imposing or intimidating, Jackie decided. He held a bottle of iced tea with a white straw jutting out of it, which short-circuited the tough-guy effect.

"You found something?" Jackie rounded her desk and sat.

Holmes hesitated, then lowered himself into the chair opposite.

"You did find something?" Jackie pressed.

"The kid's mother is on record; he wasn't bullshitting. It wasn't her first attempt either – she tried a few years before with pills. As for the more recent one, murder-suicide." Holmes smiled unpleasantly and plucked his phone from his belt. The camera he wore clipped to his jacket's breast pocket seemed to glare at her. He laid the phone on her desk. Its screen, about the size of the palm of her hand, glowed and filled with scrolling text.

"August 24, 2014. Isabelle Glass," Holmes read. "Victims: husband Harrison and son David."

"David wasn't a victim."

"He survived, but he was there. I'll get to that." Holmes thumbed a scroll button beneath the screen. "Here's a good bit. She apparently came up behind the light of her life with a twelve-gauge shotgun. Took most of his head."

Jackie stifled a grim smile. Holmes obviously thought he could punish her for leaning on him. Let him play. "So she shot her husband, but let her son live. Anything else?"

"She didn't 'let' him live." Holmes tapped a button on the screen. A handwritten page. "Ugh. This is before the force started using tablets." He leaned forward and studied the mess of text. "Look here. The date, August 24, is the date of discovery. The coroner estimated the actual murder happened on August 21."

"That's an *estimate?*"

"Nobody reported the shots. A courier delivering a parcel smelled something. Called the law. The uniforms on the scene found our boy Davie in a walk-in closet, tied to his high chair."

Jackie's throat felt as if it had shrunk to the width of the straw in Holmes's iced tea. "Tied up for three days?"

"Almost dead from dehydration."

"So his mother tried in her own way to spare him."

Holmes arched his left eyebrow, a smile playing on his lips. "You want to believe his mother was a sweetheart, don't you? Have a chat with someone at Provincial Children's Services sometime."

"She tied David up in a closet. Obviously she didn't have the stomach to shoot her own son." Jackie struggled with an image in her mind: a child crying and tugging at cords around his tiny arms. "She took her own life then, is that right?"

"Nope. Davie boy was tied into his chair, but the chair was leaning sideways; he must have rocked it side to side and tipped it over."

"Trying to free himself."

"Sure. But he started right away, probably as soon as Mommy shut the door." Holmes wiped his mouth with the back of his hand. "There was a blast hole in the door about the size of my fist, and a buckshot pattern on the back wall. She fired through it, both barrels, dead centre. The kid had rocked himself sideways; that's the only way he came through it alive."

The image swelled in her thoughts, filling in colours and sounds and a stench of sulphur. She thought of David rocking his chair violently, gripping the armrests as though he couldn't let go. Then the fall. And the screaming. She had thought it was the pain in his arm that had made him cry out like that.

"Wait; it doesn't make sense." Her voice sounded thick. "He must have been crying. His mother would have known he was still alive."

"Ever hear a twin-barrel shotgun go off? Your ears ring like crazy." Holmes's breathing had become rough. In another context the husky timbre of his voice might have been sexual. The thought made Jackie's belly clench, as though someone squeezed her stomach in a vise.

Holmes clicked a button and selected another page. "David's aunt and uncle had come to town just a couple of months before. The police interviewed them."

"That can't be a coincidence, so soon before the . . . deaths. They must have known something was wrong." But what? Post-partum psychosis? David was a year old by then. Could it have been as simple as depression? Perhaps his aunt had learned something, heard his mother on the phone voicing frightening thoughts. Suicides often telegraphed their intentions – giving away their possessions, or talking about "after I'm gone." Was that enough for David's aunt and uncle to come to Vancouver and stay for two months to be with her? "So we know David's mother really did go off the deep end. Fine. Do you have anything else?"

"Raymond Reed. He moved out from Mississauga a couple of years before Mel and Stu headed west. Had a patch of farmland out in the valley. I tried contacting him, but it turns out he died six years ago. Colon cancer."

"What about Melanie's side of the family?"

"What do you mean?"

"David's aunt, Melanie. Didn't anyone from her side of the family drop in? Parents or brothers and sisters?"

Holmes shook his head, but the look on his face told her he didn't mean "no." It was a mocking gesture. The man spoke as though he were addressing a child. "Who told you the kid's aunt and uncle were husband and wife? They were siblings."

~

When Auntie beckons the boy to the bed, Uncle moves to the wicker chair in the corner beneath the windows. He sits with his tartan bathrobe open, legs apart, a warm smile on his face.

Auntie moistens the boy's small fingers in her mouth, then moves them down her body past her breasts, and gently coaches him in how to touch her. When she squirms and moans in response, he feels loved, and strong in a way he has never known.

Later Uncle takes him into the living room and sits him down on the couch. "You have to get a few things straight, boy. We aren't like other people. Outsiders don't understand us. You mustn't tell them anything about what we do here when we're alone. You understand?"

The boy looks up at Uncle and nods.

"This is real important." Uncle kneels and places his massive hands on the boy's shoulders. "If anyone finds out, they'll take you away and they won't let you play with us anymore. You understand?"

"Yes, Uncle," the boy says, trying to look serious while recalling the angel-like expression on Auntie Mel's face.

~

Autumn 2051

"Sometimes I hear things."

14

CHAIN YOUR BRAIN TO A thought and hang on, David told himself. His mind skipped from one image to the next, too fast to follow. Sounds overlapped like too many voices in a crowded room. Where was Ariel right now? At home watching something on the living room screen, or in the den rattling computer keys. Damn it, all she had to do was lose a little sleep, that was all, but instead she had him locked up here in the psychiatric wing, and *just who was Crawford anyway and why did they name a hospital after him*?

Ariel didn't put you here, he told himself; you did this. You almost set the house on fire, and you belted her in your sleep. Don't think you can guilt her over this.

Along the corridor most of the ceiling panels were dark; every fourth glowed. Zeke had the night off. Good. The man's questions had begun to grate. The clock on the wall across from the nurses' station said 8:40. Warren and Elizabeth would still be up. David stepped to the counter. "Is there a phone I can use?"

The woman sitting at the station pointed at an alcove beyond the elevators.

"Thanks."

David found a bank of four phones with little screens. What am I doing here? he thought. Oh yes, phoning Ari and the kids. He tapped the nearest screen.

"Name, please," the phone said.

"David Glass."

"I have three numbers on record: Ariel, Elizabeth, and Warren."

"Ariel."

The call chimed. Then Ariel's avatar appeared. "Hello, you've reached Ariel Morrissey of Rabinovich-Morrissey Realtors. I am not available at the moment – "

David tapped Disconnect. Probably it hadn't occurred to her to put the hospital on her phone's white-list.

"Try Elizabeth," he said.

Seconds later the phone clicked. "Hello?" a bored teenage-girl voice answered.

"Hello, love."

"Dad." The screen blinked and showed his daughter, the image jerking slightly, thanks to her handheld phone.

"Let your mother know I've called, and shake your brother free of whatever he is doing."

A sigh that only a long-suffering teenager could utter issued from the phone. "Mom is out. Some woman called, and she took off in a hurry." Then Elizabeth bellowed, "Warren! Turn on your phone; I'm putting Dad on conference."

At that moment a shadow crossed the floor. David's gaze followed it. The girl who had tried to slit her own throat shuffled past. A starfish Shape hovered above her, translucent. Lesions in its limbs oozed black fluid.

Warren's voice, far away. "Dad?"

"How are you?" David asked, staring at the girl's back as she passed out of view. Anguish pulsed through the Shape, waking memories of Ariel huddled in the garage half a lifetime ago, screaming at him, swearing the house wanted her dead dead dead.

"Who are you talking to?" Warren asked.

David snapped his gaze back to the screen. The display had split, Warren on the right. The reading lamp beside his bed rendered his face ghoulish in the glow. "You."

"I'm doing homework. Sort of."

"How is school?"

"Fine. Boring." Warren paused. "When are they letting you out?"

Elizabeth cleared her throat. "Yeah; when can you come home?"

"Soon. This isn't jail; I can leave whenever I like. It's just not a good idea right now." David swallowed, remembering a trickle of blood in the corner of Ariel's mouth. "Definitely not a good idea."

Warren's gaze darted about. "Are you remembering things?"

Fire danced in David's thoughts. "Some. There's a pretty nurse here. Hoping I recall someone like her."

"That's what I'd want to remember too."

David laughed. "You're only twelve. Get your mind out of the gutter – crowded enough with your mother and me down here."

"But you are remembering stuff?" Elizabeth asked.

"Sometimes I hear things." And see things, David thought, picturing the starfish. But that was normal. What did the girl's starfish mean, with its dark blood and gore? Usually he knew when the Shape came, had some sense of it, beyond the picture in his mind.

"Voices?"

"What voices?" David asked, confused.

"You said you hear things."

"Oh. Yes. But not voices, really."

"So no one is telling you to become an axe murderer?"

"If they do, I promise I won't listen."

"Don't be too hasty, Dad. You could visit some of my teachers – "

"Not getting out of homework that way."

Mock groans erupted in stereo from the kids.

"Need to go." David's temples throbbed. "Tell your mother I called."

Silence. Then Warren: "Good-bye, Dad."

David touched the End tab. Then he rose, clasped his hands across his middle, and went in search of the girl. He found her in her room. She lay on her side on the narrow bed, her hip and shoulder forming hills with her middle a valley. He could only barely make out the Shape. Not enough. Not yet.

David backed away. In the corridor he wandered to his own room. The starfish walked with him in his thoughts.

*****

In other circumstances, Ariel would have felt at home in the restaurant of the Hyatt Regency Hotel. Her table had a white lace tablecloth and white napkins. The place served coffee in an ornate cream-coloured bowl. If she were clad in her black suit and her emerald blouse with its mandarin collar, and her hair bound behind her head, she could walk into a meeting and draw the eye of every male over thirty – and quite a few under. Radiating covert sex and overt money had helped her close more than one real estate deal.

But now, in jeans and a faded peach-coloured sweater, and hair that suggested she had trimmed it herself with garden shears after four bottles of Zinfandel, she felt as if any moment the hotel manager would peer into the room and demand, "Who let in Frumpy Woman? Throw her out before the guests see her."

Ariel tried to picture the woman before her twenty years ago. The lines around those eyes had come with age. Would she have worn her hair short, or would she have had that long, anachronistic ponytail even then?

Olver had talked for almost an hour, all the while plucking at the cloth of her teal-coloured turtleneck above her breasts. Ariel listened while a voice in the back of her mind said, This bitch is insane.

"Holmes told us what happened with the mother," Olver was saying. "Of course that's how we found out about his aunt and uncle and their relationship."

"Incest." The word burned in Ariel's mouth. She couldn't remember ever feeling so numb. She understood what Olver had told her this evening, but she felt nothing when she should be howling at this woman to get out of her life, to leave David alone.

Olver nodded. "Holmes looked into it further, but we didn't find out much more. We confronted David about it sometime later. He refused to talk. Holmes did learn that Isabelle Glass had run away from home at fourteen. The family lived outside Mississauga, out east – "

"David's family is from Nebraska. He put that in his journals."

"He made that up. I think he wanted to be sure that if he tried finding out the truth later, he'd be looking in the wrong places."

If that was true, it worked. Elizabeth was two, and Warren unborn, when David announced he wanted to visit his family's hometown. They rented a camper van, drove down the Interstate from Blaine, Washington, for two weeks in July. The drive took them to Lincoln, Nebraska. Ariel toured the city with Elizabeth while David raced between the library and City Hall.

"An Isabelle Reed lived here in 1948," he told her one evening at the motel. "And a Stewart Reed in 1989; spelling of 'Stewart' is wrong. Nothing else comes close."

David's journals implied his aunt and uncle were married. He never mentioned his aunt Melanie's maiden name – which didn't necessarily mean she didn't have one.

"We suspected her family had provoked Isabelle to run away," Olver said. "They probably started with her. Their sister."

"Started?" Ariel put her coffee cup down. "You're suggesting their . . . relationship didn't finish with them alone. And this is what David is going to remember."

The woman nodded, a single almost imperceptible movement of her head.

The son of a bitch is a murderer, Ariel thought. And he's been lying to you for twenty years. Part of her mind clamped down before that line of thinking got momentum. For all she knew, this woman was a psychopath.

Ariel set her elbows on the table, made a fist, wrapped her left hand over it. "Do you have any proof of what you're saying?"

Olver stiffened. "I'm a doc – "

"Doctors can lose their minds as easily as anyone else. Maybe you're a mental patient who has got it into her head to prowl after my husband. David is delicate right now; this could ruin him." Ariel shoved her chair back and rose. Her chair rocked, balancing on its back legs as though debating whether to right itself or topple backward to the floor. Like her.

Petulance and desperation duelled in the woman's voice. "I'm not lying to you."

Turn and go, Ariel thought. Walk away and forget you met Jacklyn Olver. "Don't go anywhere near him."

"He was my patient."

Ariel held up the ring finger of her left hand in a parody of a rude gesture and pointed at the gold loop encircling it. "This gives me jurisdiction here." She dropped a ten-dollar coin on the table. "For my coffee."

The restaurant's doors were heavy oak. She pushed the pair of them open and stepped out beneath the awning. Traffic crept along Burrard Street. Rain had begun in earnest. Ariel plucked her phone from her belt and called the car's number.

"Hello," the tinny mechanical voice said.

"Where the hell did I park you?"

"Home," she told the car moments later when she flung herself into the driver's seat. The Honda beeped, complaining about her lack of seat belt. Ariel strapped in, swearing. The car began to move, then stopped when she beat the steering wheel with her palms.

"Do you wish to drive?" the machine asked.

"No." Ariel leaned her forehead on the wheel.

The car navigated the parking lot toward traffic. The radio quietly played a satellite station. Drums and violins bloomed, and a male voice wove through the sounds. The song crept into her awareness, and Ariel found her thoughts drawn into it.

> I know what you call heaven
> And I know what you call hell
> And I know where you're at 'cause I've been
> there myself
> And I know what you want to say when you
> can't find the words

You're walking that path again
Between madness and earth

Shit. Ariel thumbed the volume knob and the sound cut out, but the song played on in her mind.

David's friend Switch, she thought, remembering the snake tatt winding around his arm. How had Olver known about him?

Easy: she had met the man. Ariel straightened up. "Not home. Take me to my office."

The car beeped in acknowledgement and wheeled onto Georgia Street, heading east.

Hadn't David's journals always seemed idyllic, his aunt and uncle too perfect? Of course, a fifteen-year-old kid writing to record his life probably wouldn't devote his time to writing about misery. Wouldn't he rather remember the good and lose the rest? But if they were as awful as Olver suggested, how could he have written about them with such love?

Windshield wipers fought the rain. The sweeping sound grated. She shut them off and watched a blurry rain-soaked world pass beyond the glass. Minutes later the rain cut out as the car eased into the parkade beneath her office building and rolled into her spot.

In minutes she strode along the third-floor corridor. Lights glowed beyond the glass door of Rabinovich-Morrissey Realtors. Ariel slowed a moment, then gritted her teeth and marched on. She pushed the door open.

"Hello?" a voice called. Katie, in her office.

Ariel wanted to race past. Instead she slowed at the doorway.

"You're in late," Katie said. "What's up?"

"Nothing." Damn; she hadn't meant to sound so curt. "I mean, I just have some things to look up in the database."

"God, Ari, you look terrible." Katie's forehead rumpled. She could be striking at times – times like this. She had dyed dark streaks into her hair. Lenses gave her aquamarine eyes. She wore a black suit jacket and skirt with a blouse beneath it which matched her contacts. Katie had the kind of form which even in her early forties caused teenage boys to turn their heads.

Ariel rubbed her cheeks with her palms. "I'm fine. Well, actually I'm not. My husband is in the psych ward, my kids are bitching because their father isn't around, and I'm exhausted."

"And snarky."

Ariel forced a grin. "That too."

"Why don't we go downstairs? The cafe is – "

"I really do need to get some things done tonight." Ariel gestured at her office across the hall.

Katie cocked her brow, then shrugged. "Fine. I'll leave you to it."

Which meant it wasn't fine. Ariel sighed and crossed the hall to her office. She sat at her desk. A tap on her screen lit it up. Ariel picked up the bud and plugged it in her ear. "Search LandGrab."

On the screen the real-estate database appeared, an innocuous blinking icon that looked like a house sitting on a roadmap.

"Location?" the computer said in her ear.

"The Fraser River Valley."

"Search criteria?"

"Owner's name. Raymond Reed."

"Time frame?"

"Let's see: 2005 to 2015. Search for variations in name spellings. Include initials."

"Initial search year exceeds maximum range for this database. Would you like to access government land records also? There is a fee of – "

"I know, I know. Yes, look in the government records."

The screen displayed a large hourglass. Ariel heard the hiss of sand in her earbud. "Shit."

"Please clarify," the computer said.

"Fuck you." Ariel tugged the bud from her ear and flung it onto her desk.

The kids should be brushing their teeth by now or at least thinking about the steps involved in going to bed. Elizabeth would yell at Warren in the basement to get his butt into his room. There would be a stream of invectives from him, followed by insults from Elizabeth. Then she would vanish into her room, and moments later Warren would retire to his. There would be cursing when one or the other made it to the bathroom first.

David must have been Elizabeth's age when he set fire to his aunt and uncle's home.

"They found him outside the house, watching it burn," Olver had said. "Eating popcorn."

Ariel pictured him in the garage days ago, standing near the bags of leaves he had set alight. The burn on the garage wall would be permanent. They could paint it over, but it would still be there under layers of paint. Much like David's memories.

Damn it, David, you're supposed to be the cool and collected member of the team, Ariel thought. I'm the boneheaded one.

Chaos never seemed to touch David. One Saturday morning when Elizabeth was nine and Warren seven, Ariel heard the muffled sound of popcorn popping in the microwave. She drifted in and out of sleep until she realized she had been hearing that sound for almost an hour. When she reached the kitchen, the kids had popped most of a box of twenty bags of the stuff and had laid them all unopened on the dining table.

Ariel felt herself winding up for a thunderous conniption when David came up behind her and settled his hands on her shoulders.

"Kids?" he said gently. "What are you doing?"

Ariel leaned back against him, knowing that having him there was enough to keep her from exploding.

Elizabeth peered out of the kitchen, her voice thick with solemnity. "It's a scientific experiment."

Warren strode out from behind her. "We're determining the opt – optimal – "

"Optimal," Elizabeth prompted.

" – the optimal settings for the nuke. For popcorn."

David kneaded Ariel's neck. "You do know there's a button on the microwave marked 'Popcorn'?"

Elizabeth's cheeks bunched. "Dad, it never gets all of it. There's always a handful that don't get popped."

"Mind if we have a bag?"

The girl picked up one and peered at it. She had scrawled a number three in black on it. "Take this one." She passed the bag to him, then picked up a plastic bowl and wrote the number on its side with a thick black marker. "Here. We need the kernels. We have to count them."

David took the bag and bowl, and steered Ariel back to the bedroom.

"Do you know how much that cost?" Ariel said when David shut the door. "And we'll have to clean up that mess."

"We've put away thousands of dollars a year for their education – never mind what we spend on school supplies and books. They want to do lab experiments in the kitchen, great. They're learning something and all it's costing us is a box of light butter-flavoured corn."

"That's not the point."

"They finish, they'll remember that they learned something through reason and smarts. Go in there and yell at them, they'll remember how they got slapped down for being imaginative." David grinned. "Enough room in the pantry to stack up all the popcorn the kids crank out. Only have to live on the stuff for two weeks."

"*Only* two weeks?"

"Not making gunpowder, at least." David's fingers ran lightly over her throat, prying her fingers from her neck. He slid the cloth of her robe off her shoulder.

"Ah. I'm pissed off, and you're going to screw my brains out so I'll forget about it."

"Your point?" David moved her robe lower.

Memory of his touch made her shiver.

The hourglass on the screen ran out. A globe appeared and the image zoomed in on North America, then the west coast, narrowing down to cottage country in the Fraser Valley east of Vancouver and its suburbs, settling at last on the town of Hope. A white box popped up on the right.

Ray Reed
Lot 34, 332 Mulligan Way
Hope, British Columbia
Purchased: March 23, 2009
Ownership transferred by order of executor to
M. and S. Reed: June 7, 2022
Sold by estate: August 20, 2029

Coincidence, Ariel said to herself resolutely, her fingernails sinking into her palms.

Right, pure coincidence; this Ray Reed just happened to have relatives with initials M and S, came a retort uttered by a voice she thought she had long ago banished from her mind.

15

ARIEL FELT THE BED MOVE beneath her. She opened the one eye not buried in her pillow, and found Elizabeth's denim-clad knee carving a valley in the mattress. "It's almost eight," the girl said.

"Damn! Why didn't you wake me?"

"I did just now."

"Why haven't you gone already? You can walk, you know."

"It's raining outside."

"Aw, crap. Are you and your brother ready?"

"Yeah."

"Then go. I'll be out in a moment."

Ariel grabbed her jeans from the heap next to the bed. She still wore her sweater and bra. The bra itched.

Warren was sitting in the front seat when Ariel raced out. Elizabeth was in the back, knees against her chin. The sky's ugliness from the previous night had carried into today. Rain fell in a drizzle.

The car purred to life. "The bus stop," Ariel said. "Get us there."

The car beeped and rolled back.

"Can we see Dad today?" Warren asked.

Ariel remembered with painful sharpness why she had forgotten to set her alarm. Dr. Olver, and all she had said about David. Lies, Ariel thought. She wasn't talking about my husband. It was all a fantasy she dreamed up.

"Maybe. It depends on how he feels."

"We won't have to hang out with the other crazies, will we?" Elizabeth muttered.

"They might not let you out," Warren piped up.

Elizabeth started a retort.

Ariel thumped the steering wheel. "Enough. You can bitch at each other on the bus; I'm not in the mood for it here."

Blissfully the kids said nothing during the two-minute wait for the bus. Four other students – all older than Elizabeth – were huddled in the glass shelter. One boy seemed underclothed, clad in an orange padded vest and black sweatpants.

The bus rolled up. The driver – chaperon made a better job description – had a book open on the steering wheel. Warren picked up his pack from between his legs and pushed the car door open. He waited for Elizabeth, then trudged beside her to the bus. Ariel rolled her window down and waved. Her sleeve darkened under the onslaught of rain.

"Holmes found out about his parents," Olver had said.

Incest, murder, and suicide. Great family you had there, David. Shimmerman's bug must have been an improvement. Ariel bit her lower lip. "What if she's right?"

There, you've said it, she thought. Out loud. So what do you do now?

Find some answers, that's what.

And then? The question danced about in her brain.

She found her phone tucked into the car door's pocket, and plucked it out. The screen flickered and steadied under her touch. She tapped the tab for her office. Moments later, with the Rabinovich-Morrissey logo blinking on the screen, the office computer responded with its cheerful greeting.

Ariel cut it off. "It's me. Katie, I won't be in this morning. If it's important, call me. I have an errand to run. A house to check out."

She drove downtown and told the car to find a spot in the public library's lot. At almost nine in the morning, the library was, to quote Gran, "locked up tighter than a bull's arse in a blizzard." Ariel grimaced and marched up the slope out of the parking garage amidst a smell of dust and mildew. She set off down the street to the BigBurger a block over, stooping her shoulders against the rain and cursing the umbrella hanging in the closet at home. She took a corner table and watched men and women in suits, scrambling for a morning coffee or a muffin before heading off to work. Quietly smouldering, she spent the next hour checking messages and making notes on her phone's screen with the little stylus she had broken months ago and had repaired with an adhesive that had left a large, uncomfortable lump halfway along the stylus's shaft.

At ten o'clock she strode back along Robson Street. Vancouver's library looked like a coliseum in the final, crumbling days of the Roman Empire. Pushing through the turnstile, she made her way up the escalators, sidestepping her fellow riders who stood waiting for the moving steps to carry them to the next floor.

In the periodicals section Ariel found a collection of desks, screens, and keyboards, pressed together with narrow aisles between them. She strode to the Information desk. A woman with a long blond braid and too many silver loops in her left ear glanced up, casting a suspicious look.

"I'm looking for old records," Ariel said. "Newspapers, that sort of thing."

"We have those on the terminals," the librarian said. "Just follow the menus." She turned her gaze back to the screen before her.

Ariel shook her head. "I need records going back to 2014."

"Then you'll have to take the pedway to the Archives offices next door. Local periodicals are in the basement."

Ariel had never been in the Archives section of the library. Ironically it was the newest part of the ageing structure. She descended in an elevator and found herself in a lobby. A rotund man who looked like Santa Claus after a full head shave looked up from his desk and smiled broadly.

"How may I help you?"

"I need to look at news records from 2014. Where would I find the terminals for those?"

The man somehow managed to expand his smile. "We have those on DVD."

"On what?"

"Old-style disks." The man led her along a corridor to a room with rows of white drawers tucked into the walls. "Do you know the time you're looking for?"

"August 2014," Ariel said immediately.

"*Sun* or *Province*?"

"What?"

"The newspapers back then were the *Sun* and the *Province*."

"Oh. Uh, which would you recommend?"

"The *Sun*." The librarian tugged one of the drawers open and brought out a small white box. He led her farther down the corridor to an alcove. A boxy machine sat on a desk. The man thumbed a green button under the screen.

They say time travel isn't possible, Ariel thought. But what century have I plummeted into here?

The ancient computer purred, then made a hideous grinding sound. The librarian brought out a gold-colored disk, then reached down to push a button on the box beneath the screen. A tray large enough for a coffee mug slid out.

"Just place the disk here. You'll have to wait a few seconds for the computer to read it. These machines are quite slow."

The librarian showed her how to use the crude search tools. "You can go by names, places, dates. Just type into the box here."

Ariel sat and stared at the screen. Finally, she tapped the buttons.

Jackie Olver had said David's parents died late in August. That much appeared true, according to David's journals. But his journals described a pileup on the I-5 in Oregon, fog coupled with a drunk driver in a heavy rig speeding through a dozen slow-moving cars; his parents were among the casualties. He had looked up the accident decades ago.

She typed "David Glass" into the search box, and found nothing. She inserted a new disk in the drive, and found references to a lawyer called David Glass. Of course, it had to be a common name. Damn.

Then she thought: would they have mentioned David's name in the news? Or his parents'? She tried "Isabelle Glass." Nothing. Then she tried the two words without quotes. The computer found forty-seven references to articles which included both "Isabelle" and "Glass." She added "murder" and "suicide" to the list, which reduced it to twelve. She clicked a link to each article and viewed the articles in question.

An unsolved murder of a woman called Isabelle, whose father had committed suicide a few months before.

But what if the articles about Isabelle Glass attempting to kill her own son didn't include the words "murder" or "suicide"? This relic – it didn't deserve to be called a computer – wasn't bright enough to use similar words and phrases, like "slay" or "took her own life."

Ariel backtracked and looked at the list of forty-seven articles. She skimmed the headlines. One was dated August 25.

Couple Found Dead in South Side Home

This could be about anyone, she told herself, fingertips drumming the keyboard. There were plenty of homes on the south side.

A husband and wife were found dead yesterday afternoon in their home in the 700 block of Marine Drive. According to police, both victims died of gunshot wounds.

The 700 block of Marine must have had at least eight homes then. Ariel rolled the mouse's scroll wheel.

Police say 31-year-old Isabelle Pamela Glass shot her husband, Harrison, in the family's living room before turning the weapon on herself.

Their one-year-old son has been placed in the care of relatives. According to police, this was not Ms. Glass's first attempt to end her life;

in December 2010 she swallowed sleeping pills
and was placed under psychiatric observation.

Ariel breathed slowly, borrowing David's rhythm: in through the nose, out through the mouth.

*****

David feigned sleep until the psychiatric nurse stepped back and his footfalls receded down the corridor, leaving David alone with his thoughts. Rotten meat. Buzzing insects. Woodlands fleeing past a car window. His uncle Stu, pushing him on the swing out back of the house. A clear image rolled into consciousness. Lying on the ground facedown, brown soil pressed against his cheek. Then his uncle's big hands grasping his shoulders, turning him over. "Quite a flight there, boy. You need a parachute."

And then Uncle Stuart's face twisting into rage, and his aunt, Ariel, her grandmother – looking just like the pictures he had seen – gathered round him, bellowing, raving. And David himself, rolling into a ball, arms clutched about his head.

David heaved himself off the bed. He tucked his fingers into the waistband of his gym shorts and wandered into the corridor and past the nurses' station where a pretty blonde nurse glanced at him with a professional smile. The corridor smelled of cleansers, recycled air, and scorched electronics.

He walked farther, to the room assigned to the girl who tried to kill herself, and looked in. Empty.

Voices reached him from the end of the corridor. David turned in that direction, stopping at the doorway. The girl sat at a small square table, flanked by a man and woman. The girl's hair hung thick and tangled to her shoulders. Her coffee-and-double-cream skin glistened. The man and woman were both dressed well – he in a black suit, she in the female equivalent but brown. The girl sat with her arms crossed, her gaze on the tabletop, jaw fixed in place. The man and woman had their backs to him.

He imagined the girl's hand on her throat, a blade glinting.

David strode in. The girl glanced up; then the eyes of the couple shifted to him. Silence.

The room featured a white counter and sink. David opened the cupboard door on the left. Plates, firm but flexible to the touch, like soft plastic. He tried the next door. Here were cups, all of them made of the same soft material as the plates. David picked up a cup and filled it from the faucet; then he turned and set off back toward the door. His gaze swept across the couple. The man glanced at David, then at the girl. For an instant the man's eyes found the bandage on her neck. David saw a tightening in the man's left arm, tension pulsing in his neck.

The girl's starfish Shape flexed its torn limbs. When the man looked at the bandage on the girl's neck, his body responded viscerally. The woman eyed it, and her face showed fear, pain, guilt – but no raw physical reaction.

The Shape flailed, its limbs bursting outward. Then it calmed, its tentacle limbs entwining the girl and the man who must be her father.

Understanding rocketed across David's brain, unfolding like a scene in a film.

The girl stands (sits?) in her bedroom (bathroom?) gazing at a mirror. The blade in her hand is short and dull – a sharp blade would have carved through flesh and spilled her life from her throat too quickly for rescue. Her hand trembles when she presses it to her neck. She tugs hard and fast, feeling it bite and tear. Blood weeps from the wound. Not enough. With bleak determination she aligns the tip of the blade and drives it in again.

A voice reaches her. "Honey?" Or perhaps there is the sound of a shoe on the floor outside the room. The door swings open as her blood falls, and her father gazes in mounting shock.

He is on her in an instant, cradling her head and carrying her to the floor. He presses the fingers of his left hand against the wound while his right fumbles with his phone. He speaks frantic words to the 911 operator, his voice driven staccato by the thump of his heartbeat.

David's fingers squeezed the cup. The starfish illusion trembled, and instead of the girl, he saw Ariel, her face contorted in a scream – not the bellow that came to him in his twisted visions of Auntie and Uncle. This was Ari, huddling beside him, hands pressing against her head as she wailed, "Stop doing that, just stop it!"

A new Shape formed, a connection between Ari and this girl like a guitar string growing taut. A high harmonic note thrummed, ringing through his visions of Auntie and Uncle. They shattered like a wineglass, and his mind grew clear and sharp.

16

A FAMILIAR FOOTFALL. ZEKE STOOD in the doorway. He glanced at David, then smiled and walked to where the family sat. David watched the girl's eyes turn blank, as though she had withdrawn still deeper into herself. Zeke bent and spoke briefly to them. Then he straightened and, pained smile fixed to his cheeks, came to David's table.

"Put on street clothes." The psychiatric nurse motioned to the corridor. "We're going on a little trip."

"Where?"

Zeke's smile became wider, though more pained. David sensed a Shape in him, a dog tugging on its leash, trying to keep its master from dragging it out the door.

"Home," Zeke said.

David looked up at the building dubiously.

"In other circumstances I'd take you to the house where you grew up," Zeke said, slamming the door of his little Hyundai shut and clipping his phone to his waist. "This will have to do."

David was glad for his heavy coat. Aside from it, all he had for outdoor clothes were his jeans and black T-shirt – the garments he had worn to the hospital. Rainwater ran along the curb, adding to the background noise of the drizzle.

"Been here before. Nobody knew me, even when I was a patient. And I do remember the Recovery floor. What's this supposed to prove?"

"Do you remember the Patients floor?"

"Not yet."

"Then we have something to work with." Zeke drew a folded sheet of paper from his jacket's inner pocket. He looked out of place in street clothes: beige pants, a white long-sleeved shirt, a black leather jacket with padded shoulders. "Here we have a map of the floor plan when the place was called the North Vancouver Shimmerman Clinic. Let's play a game. We'll go in the front door, and you tell me what we'll find."

David pointed at the sign. "Old people."

The building that had once housed the North Vancouver Shimmerman Clinic had become the Angela Deveraux Seniors Home. The outside had been repainted in a cheerful cream colour, an improvement over the green building David remembered. The steps were wider than he recalled. Rather than the wooden steps and railing the place once had, there were now concrete steps and a long gentle wheelchair ramp that formed a *U* shape to the left, joining with the main staircase at the top. The entrance lay to the right side of the building.

"Won't someone complain?"

Zeke started up the steps. "I called ahead. I explained your situation. The manager is an understanding man."

David walked along the wheelchair ramp. Zeke held the door at the top. David stepped inside. An air of wrongness about it struck in an instant. "Two doors back then, inner and outer."

A wide hall stretched before them. Along each wall were brass lamps with white shades over the LEDs. Whoever had designed the renovations had tried to make the place feel warm and homey.

"Brighter then," David said.

"Maybe your eyes have changed. They lose sensitivity over the years."

An empty hall greeted them. David heard a clinking sound of metal on ceramic. The double doors at the end of the hall were open.

One closed door on the right, two on the left. On the nearest was a white sign with red letters: "Infirmary." Windows were set into the left corner where the entrance hall branched into a corridor.

Zeke touched his shoulder. "Wait here. I have to check in with management."

An image coursed through David's mind: striding into the hall, arms handcuffed behind his back, surrounded by too-serious men in blue jackets. The ridiculousness of the scene made him chuckle. Of course I felt like a prisoner here, he thought.

Zeke returned moments later. "All set. Shall we explore?"

David nodded and trudged to where the corridors branched off from the main hall. Zeke eyed him expectantly. When they reached the cafeteria, David peered in. A dozen tables filled the room, large round tables covered in white tablecloths. Breakfast dishes rattled. Several faces, lined with age, turned his way. Some sat in wheelchairs, but most were in high-backed white seats. Windows faced south, and David saw a wall of apartment buildings across the street.

"Too big. Common room was smaller."

Zeke held up the paper in his hand. "So far you're on the mark."

"Not memory." Pointing at an outline in the wall farther down. "You can see where the doors have been filled in."

The nurse frowned. "You're using observation and logic. Any chance you can turn that off and just go by what comes to you?"

"Don't see how." A scene of an office unfurled. Ancient filing cabinets, a gunmetal hue, on the right. His temples began to throb. A woman sat at the desk, a white tabletop with black legs, utilitarian and impersonal. She had long straight blond hair.

"A woman ran the Patients floor. Had an office down there." David pointed the way they had come.

Zeke's eyes widened with excitement. "That's good, David. Keep going."

"Happy birthday, David."

The voice came from the woman in his mind, seated at her desk. Then the film shifted and she stood over him in bed, watching him unwrap the game his aunt had given him. It came on a black disk that went into a machine, not the thin wafer used by Warren's GameDome.

"'Happy birthday'?" Zeke echoed.

"Think I remember my birthday here."

"You were born in September, is that right?"

"Yes. Oh. No way I had a birthday in this place. Upstairs, in Recovery. But not here."

In the common room an old man in a wheelchair was parked next to a paisley couch, its cushions clad in soft blues and greys. He snored quietly. On the wall, a television showed some kind of nature program. Two computer-generated dinosaurs, a Tyrannosaurus Rex and a brachiosaurus, were locked in mortal combat, the predator's jaws gripping the brachiosaurus's long neck. The sound had been turned off; a block of closed caption text filled the bottom quarter of the screen.

David tried to imagine the room back then. "Nothing."

Zeke gripped his left shoulder from behind. "Think. Focus."

David stepped back from the room and let his gaze sweep left and right.

"I remember more doors."

"Where was your room?"

"Don't know."

David remembered having a room to himself, with a bulky terminal in it and a single bed. He winced. Not a single room; he had confused Auntie and Uncle's house with the clinic. His room here he had shared with another. Whom? An image flickered into being like a photograph in his thoughts: Switch. The big man had the lower bunk.

Zeke came around from behind and peered at him. "Take your time, we have all day if you like."

"It's the stuff before this place that I really want to remember."

"What do your journals say about it?"

"Nothing. No point to writing about the clinic."

The nurse took him to lunch at a soup-and-sandwich place up Lonsdale Avenue. David chose a table near the windows. The long slope of the avenue reached down to the blue-green waters of Burrard Inlet. The Lions Gate Bridge spanned the water. The Richard van Damme Tunnel had long ago replaced it, leaving the bridge a relic. Freighters plied the bay beyond, their hulls painted black and red.

His thoughts gravitated to Ariel. "Borrow your phone?"

Zeke eyed him with something between thoughtfulness and suspicion. Then he plucked it from his belt and handed it over.

*****

It's true, Ariel thought. Everything Olver said.

No, she couldn't be sure of that just because the names and dates fit. Maybe Olver was very, very clever.

Ariel shook her head as she strode between the book-sensor panels and out to the common area beyond the library's entrance. Starbucks beckoned. A smiling young man in a green shirt asked her what she wanted.

"Coffee. Just a regular damn coffee."

The man filled a ceramic mug. Ariel held out her phone for the VISA scanner and picked up the mug, setting it down some distance away on a little green table with a pair of rickety chairs facing it. Ariel placed her phone next to her cup, struggling to ignore the hiss and din of chatter around her. Too many people.

Isabelle Glass, formerly Isabelle Reed, had been unstable – one suicide attempt and a murder-suicide attested to that. And David's aunt and uncle were intimately involved. Ariel looked at her notes on her phone's screen.

> ~1997 – Isabelle Reed (age 14) runs away from home (just guessing at the year) (and Olver said this. Trust her?)
> ~March 2009 – Raymond Reed buys land in valley.
> ~December 2010 – Isabelle Reed/Glass attempts suicide.

> ~June 2014 – Mel & Stu came out west.
> (According to Olver.)
> ~August 2014 – Isabelle kills husband Harrison,
> almost kills David.
> ~2022 – Ray Reed dies. Cancer. (According to
> Olver.) Land sold by gov't in 2029.

Did David's younger self know that his uncle and aunt were siblings? He had clearly known about his parents' deaths and had lied about that in his journals; he certainly wouldn't have mentioned incest.

Incest. Ariel wrote the word on the screen and circled it.

David's journals didn't mention the ages of his aunt and uncle, but she remembered him guessing they were in their sixties when he was fifteen. That put them in their late forties or fifties in 2014, when David's parents died. The newspaper report said Isabelle Glass was thirty-one.

Ariel's heart thumped. If the entry she had found in the land title database referred to David's uncle Raymond, then he had bought land in the Fraser Valley less than a year before David's mother first attempted suicide. And Isabelle had snapped only months after his aunt and uncle came west. So the monsters followed her, seventeen years after she fled. First her eldest brother Raymond, then Melanie and Stuart. Did it take that long for Isabelle's twisted family to find her? If they and their brother Raymond had victimized Isabelle to the point where fleeing across the country was the solution, what might they have done to the child handed over to them after their sister's death?

Her phone played a rapid-fire stream of tones. Ariel flinched, then dropped the stylus and thumbed the Answer button. David appeared on the screen, dark sacks beneath his eyes.

Ariel forced a grin across her face. "Hi, love. You look – " *Awful.* Ariel bit back the word. The bar along the bottom of the screen read, "Ezekiel Crane." "Where are you?"

"Escaped from the nut farm. On the run."

"Right. And you stole your nurse's phone."

David winked. "Up on the North Shore. Zeke brought me here to see the clinic. It's a home for old people now." His smile vanished. "You don't look well, love."

"I didn't sleep last night."

"Called in the evening; you were out."

"A client phoned. She works until late, and she wanted to see the house on the east side."

David's eyes grew steady. Your nose is growing, Pinocchio, Ariel told herself. Hastily she tried a change of subject. "Did seeing the clinic help?"

"Layout is different; they did renovations over the years. Not much help. Are you coming to the hospital today? I'll be back there later."

"Yes. I will."

"The kids want to visit me."

"Is that okay with Zeke?"

Ariel heard a muffled conversation. "Yes. As long as visitors are supervised."

"I'll bring them as soon as they're home from school."

David's face brightened. Ariel smiled back and disconnected.

Her notes replaced him on the screen. She read them over again. Then she thought: what if David or one of the kids borrowed her phone and found this? Shit. Perhaps she could finally figure out the password feature.

Which of course would prompt David to ask why she had locked it. She shook her head and tapped the Delete tab.

David shut Zeke's phone and pushed it across the table. Zeke tugged a little green plastic sword out of his club sandwich and laid it next to his plate. "That sounds healthy. Seeing your kids."

"We're close."

"That's good."

David tuned Zeke out and focused his thoughts on the conversation with Ariel. She had said nothing more than that she had a client last night. Her eyes, her flickering smile instead of that steady dimpling around her mouth, the tightening of the skin around her nose – all of it fell together into a single sharp revelation.

Ariel had lied.

17

ARIEL SPENT THE AFTERNOON AT her office, unable to concentrate. She left early, made a light dinner of sandwiches, and drove to the bus stop to collect the kids. When they approached the car she lowered the windows. "We're going to visit your father."

"Aces," Warren said.

"Shotgun." Elizabeth reached for the front passenger door.

Of course it couldn't be that easy. Warren settled onto the couch at home with a sandwich in one hand and his game controller in the other. When Ariel told him they were leaving in five minutes he muttered, "Level 198," as if that explained it all. Ariel watched him, her heart heavy. Warren withdrew into his room in the evening, a normal occurrence these days. His world revolved around the game. When he spoke, Panthea was the topic.

Where had the boy she had known for twelve years gone? Vanished into that Dome, turned into a thin blue elf with a staff that glowed white and green. The boy he had been was a short, pale memory wandering through the Saint Patrick's Day parade crowd, his hand in hers. That was what – six years ago?

A journalist for *NetNews Vancouver* had been working the crowd, stopping people to ask mindless questions. The wide-eyed child with his family looked like an easy target. The man pushed his microphone at Warren's face as the fat cameraman looked on. "Hi, son. Are you enjoying the parade?"

"Yeah."

"Are you Irish?"

"Nope."

"But you're out celebrating St. Paddy's Day?"

"Yeah."

"You're not wearing green. Green is the colour of St. Patrick's Day."

Warren cocked his head, pouting.

Ariel started pulling him away, but the man with the mic wouldn't stop. "Son, tell me something exciting you did today."

Warren looked up into the lens of the camera and announced to the viewing audience: "I farted."

The journalist blinked. The man with the camera choked. Ariel shoved her knuckles in her mouth while David simply raised an eyebrow and Elizabeth cowered behind him in embarrassment. Warren looked downright serene.

"Um," the journalist said. "Back to you, Frank."

Ariel chuckled at the memory, then sighed. That version of Warren had disappeared from her life, changed into this creature somewhere between boy and man. Losing himself in a fantasy world.

David's voice played in her thoughts – not something he had said, but words which fit his temperament. "How do you know it's even a problem? Ever tried the game yourself?"

*****

David and Ezekiel sat at a table in the centre of the tiny lounge in the psychiatric ward. David had put on his gym shorts and a gray sweatshirt. Ariel had seen Zeke's full name in black on a brass strip next to an office door near the elevator. "Ezekiel Crane," followed by two other names she didn't remember. She had begun to make an effort to think of him as Ezekiel rather than Zeke. "Zeke" sounded like a hillbilly.

David and Ezekiel were engrossed in conversation. David's gaze swung to Ariel and the kids, and his face broke into a grin. He rose, leaving the psych nurse looking on.

"Dad!" Warren cried and raced to hug his father.

Elizabeth was as usual more circumspect. Her gaze flitted about the room; Ariel imagined her looking for any school chums or other teenagers. Satisfied that no one who mattered might see her, she stepped up and embraced David also.

"When are you coming home?" Warren demanded. "Can I get a Coke?"

"No, just water in here." David grinned. "Do you good."

The kids followed him to the sink where he began to fill cups.

Ariel dropped herself into the chair across from Ezekiel. "How is he?"

The psych nurse cocked an eyebrow. "Has he ever talked in his sleep before? He does that regularly here. I haven't told him." Zeke lowered his voice. "Can I talk to you in private?"

Ariel glanced at David and the kids. "Let me get them settled."

The trio returned to the table, Warren and Elizabeth each sipping water. Ariel rose. "I'll leave you three alone for a bit."

Zeke followed her. Behind her came a guffaw from Warren in response to something David had said, followed by Elizabeth hushing him.

"How has he been?" she asked. "Was the trip to the clinic useful?"

"I think he knew the place – I mean the Patients floor, though he hadn't seen it since they moved him up to Recovery. However." Zeke stopped in the corridor and leaned against the wall. "I think he is holding a lot back from me."

Jacklyn Olver's tale skittered through her mind. "Like what?"

"I'm not sure. The night nurses have kept notes on what he says in his sleep. He has made incoherent comments about the fire. I assume that's the fire that killed his aunt and uncle."

"That doesn't sound like he is holding back. Disorientation is normal for patients who get a BE shot."

"After he phoned you, when we were having lunch after the clinic, he seemed lost in thought. When I asked him what he was thinking about, he refused to answer."

"David is like that. He is still putting things together in his mind. He doesn't like to open up with half-formed thoughts."

Ariel smiled faintly. "It only takes twenty years to get used to."

When Ariel returned to the lounge later, she hung back at the door and watched. David had his back to her, Elizabeth slouching in her chair on the left, Warren on the right. David's hand twitched against the side of his head. That gesture was new to his repertoire of mannerisms. It seemed like a response to . . . .

To flies buzzing around his head. Olver had mentioned it. Ariel swallowed and wandered to the table. Warren's face lit up at her approach, and David turned in his chair and grinned.

"How goes it?" Ariel asked.

"Dad said, 'I'm not crazy and neither am I,'" Warren told her, beaming.

Elizabeth rolled her eyes.

Ariel smiled. "You both have homework to do."

Warren fussed about that. Elizabeth sat quiet and sullen.

Later in the elevator descending to the main floor, Warren asked, "Can we come back tomorrow?"

"We'll see how your father feels."

Clouds had thickened in the western sky. Warren raced ahead to the car and stood next to the front passenger-side door, looking a challenge at Elizabeth. His sister made no argument.

Warren started chattering as soon as the car moved. Ariel keyed it to autodrive, then listened as Warren hummed happily to himself.

"How was your visit?" she asked, peering at Elizabeth in the rear-view mirror.

"When are they letting Dad come home?" Warren piped up.

Elizabeth scowled, her face to the window. "He's not getting better. They're not going to let him out."

"Yes, they are!" Warren shrieked.

"They don't let crazy people out."

Ariel stared at Elizabeth's reflection in her mirror. The girl's throat moved as though she were chewing and swallowing something hard with jagged edges. "All right, what happened?"

Elizabeth glared at the traffic and passing streetlights. Ariel remembered seeing that look only once before. Her hand leaped to the spot on her chest where her surgical scar lay beneath her sweater. David had brought the kids to see her in the hospital after her surgery. Warren seemed fascinated by the gadgets in the room, and David had to follow him around for fear that he might turn something on or push a button that could bring the nursing staff down on them like hawks.

Elizabeth stood with her arms crossed, her mouth narrowed in a pout, glaring at her mother. But below the veneer of her anger lay something more.

"You're going to die," she accused. Anger, it seemed, had evolved into Elizabeth's response to fear.

"Bethie, I'm going to be fine. They just needed to fix my heart. That was the problem. It's gone."

Now Ariel saw that same look. "What happened, Elizabeth?" she said again, more softly.

Elizabeth met her gaze in the rear-view. "He called me 'auntie'."

*****

David looked at the elevator doors long after they had closed on Ariel and the kids. Thoughts spun through his mind like insects, tugging at his concentration.

He thought of the girl, and his thoughts slowed, sharpened. He turned and made his way to her room.

The girl sat with her back to him, her feet up on the sill of the tall window. She tilted the chair back, balancing on its hind legs. The fingers of her right hand touched the bandage around her neck, creeping over her left shoulder like mice. David kept his mouth wide so that his breathing made no sound. When her fingers tightened on her neck, her shoulders hunched. She grunted, a sound that seemed to try for laughter and derailed into embarrassment. The starfish Shape flexed its limbs in the air above her, the tips quivering. Her shoulders were hard. He remembered her in the lounge with her parents, that rippling effect across her shoulders: bravado and humiliation tangling about each other. The recollection dictated his approach. He crossed his arms and leaned against the doorframe. "How incompetent does a person have to be to screw up her own death?"

The effect was swift. The girl pushed off and almost tumbled over backward, catching herself with her hands on the sill and pivoting the chair on one leg. She gazed at him, shifting from a stare to a glare and back.

David tensed the muscle in his right cheek, forming something he hoped was more smirk than smile. "I'm David."

The girl flickered a grimace across her face and stammered, "I'm Lake."

David snorted. "Your name is Lake?"

"You think my name is funny?"

"I think drowning would have been more appropriate."

Lake's eyes widened. A smile crept into the corners of her mouth and darted away as though unsure of whether she should laugh or spit.

David met her eyes, willing her to break the stare. "Didn't answer my first question."

"Deuce." Lake's throat danced, and she looked away. "What are you in for?"

An obvious effort to change the subject. David shrugged and let it go. "Don't remember the first fifteen years of my life."

"That's a problem?"

"Have you heard of ERIN?"

"Erin who?"

"Shimmerman's Disease?"

The girl's brow furrowed. "I saw something on TV about that. It screws up your brain."

David gestured about. "Look where I am."

Lake's gaze absorbed him. David recognized interest, curiosity, a superficial bluster worn like a mask – and beneath them all a palpable sense of yearning.

He touched his neck. "Bet that hurt."

Lake's eyes flickered down. David watched her gaze march along her left arm. "Didn't hurt much." She squeezed her fist, flexing it until the arteries grew prominent beneath her skin. Then she looked up at him again. "It just bled. A lot."

Euphoria glimmered in her eyes.

*****

The kids fled in different directions when they reached home: Warren to his room and Elizabeth to the basement. Ariel made her way to her bedroom. Her heart thundered.

I'm going to lose him, she thought. It will all come back, everything they did, and he's going to remember watching them burn when he had finally had enough. That's going to plow like a crashing aircraft through everything he thinks he is. And what then?

A snake coiled itself around her spine.

She stepped from the bedroom. Near the door to the basement she heard the muffled sound of the television in the rec room. She walked to the front door and slipped her shoes and jacket on.

The sun had set. Streetlights glared. She moved down the steps and along the side of the house to the garage, and pressed her thumb to the lock. The door hummed and rolled upward. Ariel ducked beneath it before it could open fully, and tapped the button to close it. The garage lights came on automatically, white LEDs burning in the ceiling. She slipped past the car. The Honda still carried rain droplets. The burn scar on the wall of the garage looked like an eagle claw.

Tools and a trouble light hung on the wall, camping equipment sat on racks near the ceiling. Ariel heaved down a blue sleeping bag. She sat on the cold concrete against the wall and wrapped the sleeping bag tightly around her. Then she leaned back. Within a minute the motion sensors shut the lights off and darkness enveloped her like a second blanket.

Ariel huddled in a silence without peace. Then a gasping sob struck her belly like a punch.

It's not fair, she thought.

No, maybe it is fair. Maybe this is all the time you get with him. Maybe this is how fate punishes you: with twenty wonderful years. You change, become something good – then when you think you're settled, it all gets torn away.

Kismet is a bitch.

~

"Your ma was weak," Uncle says. "Killed your da, blew her own brains out, tried to blow you away, too. Could have been special. No guts, though. Just like one of them." Gesturing at the wall. The others live out there. Masses of them. Like rats. Just as important as rats.

But rats are dangerous. Better to keep your distance.

The boy avoids the closet now. Ma tried to put a hole through him here. He still senses her soul lurking outside it. But he is done with her.

~

Spring 2032

"What do you have to do?"

18

Even standing around in a cemetery beat holy hell out of staying home. Grass sprouted across the grave but didn't yet match the surrounding lawn. The funeral director had told Ariel a headstone should wait a year for the earth to settle, and it had been only six months since Gran's funeral.

Something had come apart in her when Gran died. Details she never paid attention to before now seemed vital. Why did Gran call her ancient computer "Hal"? And why did she nickname the paper shredder next to it "Enron"? It felt like Gran had never bothered to mention whole chunks of her life. Not deliberately, of course, but so much had never come up in conversation. Gran had lived almost eight decades. She had buried her husband long before Ariel was even born.

How did Granddad die? Ariel wondered. You can't answer that, can you? You lived with Gran for nine years and you still didn't know her.

In the months that followed the funeral, Ariel found scrapbooks full of photos; apparently Gran and Granddad had travelled in Western Europe early in the century. Before that, there were heavy books with photographs pressed into plastic sheets. Ariel's grandfather was stocky with shaved head and a goatee protruding from the tip of his chin. Leaning against him, her arm around his waist, was a young version of Amber Morrissey. Mountains rose behind them. They wore what had to be mountain-climbing gear: helmets, boots, metal rings, fasteners.

Gran hadn't kept secrets. She hadn't withheld anything. Ariel knew about the investments – she could do nothing at all for years if she chose. Gran had often spoken of her travels; Spanish and French phrases littered her speech. But Ariel had assumed her grandmother had gone to Europe for a few weeks at a time, staying in hotels, sunbathing on beaches, playing tourist.

Amber. It was a name she associated with bubbly teenagers in television sitcoms, not the graying woman who smiled at her when she came home from school and invariably said, "Tell me something you learned today."

The old woman had turned seventy-eight last August. Still spry, still enjoying her life. Somehow, she managed to jog five kilometres each morning, while Ariel struggled to get out of bed. Like Gran had on that last morning.

Ariel pushed her thoughts away and looked around, absorbing the view of Hillview Cemetery. As cemeteries went, this one had plenty of greenery but few tenants.

Nearby stood a boy. Thin, clad in a burgundy jacket which would have looked more at home on a ski slope than in Vancouver in the spring. The plots before him were partially dug up. Heaps of earth lay next to each.

Some kind of accident, if his parents both went at the same time. Tough luck, kid.

No graves for her own mom and dad. Their vacation in Greece ended with a plunge into the Mediterranean along with pieces of a 777 and hundreds of fellow passengers.

Ariel kicked into the side of her other boot, savouring the pain. Better that than the creeping emptiness in her.

The kid glanced her way. His face was slack, his mouth loose and open. Shell-shocked.

Is that how I looked at Gran's funeral, listening to all those old farts mutter about how sad they were to hear she'd passed on?

The kid shifted his gaze back to the overturned earth before him. For an instant she felt a tug of compassion. She set off toward where she had parked Gran's car, on the street beyond him.

No, *your* car. It's yours now; you took all the papers down to the Department of Motor Vehicles and got the car put in your name and then the insurance rates shot way, way up because you're twenty-one. Remember?

The kid looked at her when she neared. Empty eyes.

"I'm sorry." The words popped out of her mouth, surprising her.

"Pardon?"

From a distance he had seemed small. Yet here, up close, he stood over her by almost a head.

"I'm sorry for your loss." All those old bastards at the funeral said that. Did it help? No. But at least she hadn't fallen apart and bawled like a baby, like that Mr. What's-His-Name with the big ears.

"It's all right." The kid spoke with a stronger, smoother voice than she expected. "Don't remember them."

"I know how you feel. I felt that way when Gran – my grandmother – passed away. I couldn't picture her face for weeks afterward."

The kid looked as though he were ready to shatter. He drew his right hand from his pocket and pointed at the ground. "Nicer when it was green. They didn't need to open it."

"You'll remember them. The good things, I mean." Right; like Gran in bed that morning. *"Honey, I can't move my legs."*

"That's not how it works."

His choice of words struck her as odd. The kid sounded shut off, flat-lined.

"How did it happen?" Ariel asked.

"The house burned down."

"I'm sorry."

"Four years ago."

"Four years?"

The kid nodded.

Ariel gazed at the overturned soil. She squeezed her hands into fists, feeling like the butt of some colossal practical joke. "You're only burying them now? Aren't they getting a little ripe?"

The kid looked at her this time, really looked. His gaze locked onto hers. He didn't blink. He seemed to have stopped breathing.

"What?" she said.

"No bodies. Not burying them. Want a place I can come to. To honour them. That's what people do, right?"

"So you're spending thousands of dollars on graves for your parents, and they won't even be buried here?"

"Not my parents. Aunt and uncle."

"Whatever. Are you some kind of mental case, for chrissake?"

"Yes."

"Huh?" Ariel wanted to boot this smartass in his crotch. "What the hell are you talking about?" She didn't wait for an answer. Instead she pushed past and continued toward the car on the road.

"Am a mental case."

Ariel stopped and turned in surprise. The kid touched his temple with two fingers. "Shimmerman's Disease."

The memory plague. Ariel recoiled, her arm across her face. "Jesus. Don't breathe in my direction."

The kid's arms hung at his sides as though he had forgotten about them. "Don't have it now."

Ariel motioned with her chin at the empty graves. "You really don't remember them."

The kid nodded.

"You *do* remember them?"

"No. I don't."

"Then this is a waste. They won't even be down there." She pointed back at Gran's grave. "At least my grandmother is over there in a box, turning leathery." The instant she said it, the image made her cringe.

The kid turned his gaze to her, unblinking. "Why do you come here?"

"To pay my respects."

"Do you have to remember her to do that?"

The kid watched her in silence. Seconds passed. Ariel stared back defiantly until her eyes stung. She blinked on tears. "No, I guess not."

"Like to have supper with me? Small restaurant four and a half blocks down Elm Street."

The question caught Ariel off guard. *This kid is asking me for a date?* she thought. *In a cemetery?*

"Why?"

"We can talk."

"Why would we want to do that?"

"We're talking now. And it's suppertime. We go to the restaurant, we could talk and have supper."

Ariel laughed at the simplicity of his answer. "I don't even know you."

"My name is David Glass. My birthday is September 17. I live in North Vancouver at – "

"Jesus. I get the point." Ariel tugged her phone from her pocket and glanced at it. Almost five thirty; she had planned to be home by six. But hell, she wasn't gainfully employed or going to the university anymore. And here was something a hell of a lot more interesting than another evening in front of the TV or Gran's clunky old computer. Or curled up on the floor of the garage.

"What the heck. I'm Ariel." She held out her hand.

The kid took it and held it firmly, didn't let go. He fixed his stare on her again. Not the brightest bulb on the Christmas tree. Ariel pulled her hand free and started toward the street. David fell into step beside her. He glanced around constantly as they walked.

When they neared her car, Ariel mulled over whether to walk or drive. On one hand, they'd be walking five blocks. On the other, this guy might be a nutbar. He could have a nasty knife under his jacket – though he didn't seem like he could figure out which end to use. Laziness won the debate. She brought out her key chain and thumbed the button. The black Plymouth Duster beeped twice and popped its locks.

"So, you live in an institution?" she asked when she slipped behind the wheel.

David stepped gingerly into the machine as though he thought the seat might poke his butt with a wayward spring. "Used to. Now I live in a house. I have roommates. Patients like me."

"They had the disease too?"

"Yes. Carmen and Virgil and Switch came out of the clinic when I did. Simon set up rooms at the halfway house for us."

"How did you get it?"

"Don't remember, but probably the same way everyone else does. You cough a lot."

Ariel had seen the masses of students at the university who scrambled along the corridors with blue breathing masks on their faces. Even Katie kept one in her purse. "If you don't remember your aunt and uncle, how do you know about them?"

"Journals. Wrote them before the disease erased me."

Imagine remembering nothing, Ariel thought. Nothing about Gran in her bed, calling out for you. Nothing about –

She bit her lip until pain clouded the image of Corey's face.

The cafe David had mentioned looked like a converted shack tucked between a closed furniture store and a Chinese grocery. Ariel had never set foot in this place before. The woman at the counter looked Indian. She wore a broad smile like Gran's and an apron that matched the burgundy colour of David's jacket.

They took a booth. David slid into the seat opposite her and tugged a pen from his pocket. He pressed its top, and the "pen" unrolled into a flat panel. Ariel eyed it, impressed. Most of the phone's surface was a colour screen with a tiny set of flashing buttons.

The woman brought two menus and placed them on the table. "Anything to drink?" Her voice carried a thick accent.

"Coffee," Ariel muttered.

The woman retreated.

The menu was two pages tucked into clear plastic sleeves, bound in the middle. Soup, sandwiches. Boring food. Ariel put the menu down. "It must be tough, having no life."

"Getting used to people is the hard part. I'm doing well. Simon says it's up to me to decide when I'm ready to leave."

"Leave? They're letting you out?"

"Want an apartment. Simon says – "

"Who is Simon?"

David's voice slipped into a monotone. "Simon Markson is the director of the North Vancouver Shimmerman Clinic. He also oversees all patients who have moved out of the clinic, to ensure that they integrate back into society with the utmost – "

"I get the point."

The woman returned to the table, note pad in hand.

Ariel pointed to the turkey club sandwich. "I'll have one of those."

"Smoked salmon sandwich," David said. " Entrée number six. And a glass of water. Please."

The woman picked up the menus, smiled, bowed, and shuffled away.

Something nibbled at the back of Ariel's mind as the' woman retreated. Then realization struck: David hadn't looked at the menu.

"You come here a lot?"

"Once."

Ariel began to speak again when a jangling sound interrupted. She looked at David, then at his phone.

"Yours, not mine," David said.

Ariel sheepishly reached for the phone in her pocket and swiped it with her thumb. Damn; *Kate Rabinovich* blinked on the screen. "Hello, Katie."

"So you've crawled out from under your rock at last."

"Sorry I haven't gotten back to you. I've been busy."

"Doing what?"

"Stuff." Ariel scowled at the phone.

"Can you break away from your 'stuff' this evening? Laurier is picking me up, and we're meeting Shay and Tyson at the pub in half an hour."

"I'd rather not. I'm busy tonight."

"More 'stuff'?"

"Yes."

Hesitation. "I worry about you. Ever since your Gran died – "

"Damn it, Katie."

"Chrissake, don't jump on me. Look, if you need to talk about, well, anything, call me. Okay?"

"Sure. I'll call."

"Why don't you come over some time? We could rent awful movies."

"I'm about to have dinner. I have to go." Ariel closed her phone. Her hands shook. She looked at David. Again he greeted her gaze with a stare that stretched too long to be comfortable. Like a cat watching a bird. Ariel took her time fumbling with her phone and returning it to her pocket.

"Why don't you want to see your friend?" David asked.

"She's going to be there with her boyfriend, and Shay and Tyson will be together. I'll just be a fifth wheel."

The woman padded up to the table and placed plates before them. The smell of fish from David's selection made her mouth water, leaving her wishing she'd ordered that instead.

"You don't have a boyfriend, but you want someone to go with you," David said.

Corey's face leaped into her mind. "Don't you start, damn it."

"I could go."

"You?" Ariel choked on a corner of her sandwich and swallowed. "I appreciate the offer."

"Simon says I need to meet people, to spend time with them. It will help me if I go with you."

Again the long stare. Ariel looked away, discomfited. Shay will love this guy, she thought. She'll have him for dinner and spit out the bones. "I don't want to go."

David watched her eat.

"Don't stare at me. You don't even know them."

"Simon says meeting people is important." He looked at the tabletop. "Hard to figure people out. It's the hardest part of learning how to live again." Ariel was sure the kid's mouth quivered.

'Kid'? she thought. He must be at least eighteen.

Ariel plucked her phone out. For an instant her own number flickered across the screen; then the contacts menu appeared. This is a stupid idea, she thought as she tapped the button to call Katie back.

19

ARIEL LIKED SCREWDRIVER'S PUB, THOUGH she had no idea who the hell "Screwdriver" was supposed to be and the painting of a grinning bearded man holding a Phillips didn't help. The picture hung above the bar where a succession of slingers of drinks had come and gone. The latest was a bone-thin woman with dark mop-head hair and a snug pink tank top which made her nipples noticeable.

Ariel smiled at her, keeping eye contact while David passed under the brilliant light overhanging the doorway. David probably wasn't old enough to be in here, and that spot under the lamp was where the bartender was most likely to see him clearly. She led David past the bar and into the main room.

The pub occupied the second floor of a glass-and-concrete monolith on Seymour Street near downtown. Inside, the place was meant to look English. The timbers making up the ceiling had been designed askew, suggesting the building had begun a slow collapse after centuries of patrons. The place had, Ariel knew, been built just two years ago. Built to look old.

Two figures sat at the booth in the back corner. No sign of the boyfriends. Katie, as usual, looked immaculate. Ariel had gone to school with her, though they hadn't become close until they met again at the University of British Columbia. In high school, Katie had made the common teenage assumption that more of everything – more lipstick, more blush, more mascara – equalled more attractiveness. There had been days in high school when Katie looked like a mannequin or a junkie. Since then she had evolved from a hack to an artist.

She didn't look as though she were made up now; mascara accentuated her eyes, if you knew to look for it, and a hint of blush gave her a healthy glow.

Shay followed Ariel's creed: if you don't need makeup, don't wear it. She kept her crimson hair cut nearly to her scalp.

David stood beside Ariel, hands in his jacket pockets. She motioned him to follow and strode across the room among the tables.

Katie was the first to notice Ariel. She smiled, then looked at David and replaced her smile with surprise.

"Hey," Shay said – her customary minimalist greeting. Her gaze fixed on the young man beside Ariel.

"This is David. Where are the guys?"

Katie and Shay swapped glances. "Laurier had to work tonight," Katie blurted. "And Tyson thinks he's getting a cold."

Ariel's bullshit detector trumpeted.

David lowered himself into a seat. After a moment's hesitation, Ariel sat next to him.

Katie eyed him. "We didn't know you were bringing someone."

Ariel was glad she had now. Her friends had obviously ditched the guys for the evening, hoping to talk to her alone. Right now the thought of having a heart-to-heart with anyone made her belly twist into unbelievable contortions.

"So, David." Katie put on her most winning smile and pressed her chest forward. "How long have you known Ariel?"

Ariel opened her mouth, but David responded first. "Thirty-seven minutes."

Katie and Shay glanced at each other. "How did you meet?"

Again David spoke before Ariel could intercept the question. "Cemetery. We had supper at a cafe. You phoned. We came here."

"David had Shimmerman's Disease four years ago," Ariel threw in at last. "He doesn't remember anything before that."

Both women rocked back in their chairs. This little gem guaranteed that Katie and Shay weren't going to ply her with questions. David now dominated their attention, and Ariel felt confident it wouldn't shift for the rest of the night. Katie looked like she wanted to dive into her purse for her breathing mask.

David's unnerving stare swept between them. "Not contagious."

Shay and Katie shared a look. Katie shrugged. "So you, what, don't remember anything since you were born?"

"Right."

"What was the last movie Jackson Reeve starred in?"

"Don't know."

Shay caught on. "Who is the president of the United States?"

"Jeffrey Blake. Born May 4, 1976. Got his law degree at Cambridge in England before returning to the U.S. and taking economics at Harvard. Married his childhood sweetheart. First elected governor of – "

"Enough," Katie said. "Who was the first person to walk on the moon?"

"Neil Armstrong, July 20, 1969."

"Who created Mickey Mouse?"

"Don't know."

Ariel studied the kid's face while Shay and Katie tossed questions at him. David Glass had close-cut brown hair and a narrow jaw. His green eyes looked vacant.

Katie said: "Who is, um, Elvis Presley?"

"Don't know."

"Bill Gates?"

"Bill Gates created Microsoft in 1975, retired in – "

"Batman," Shay threw in.

"The person who looks after bats at a baseball game."

Shay howled at that and added, "Superman."

"Don't know."

Katie: "The vice president."

"Stephanie Thornberg, born in 1971, studied genetics at – "

Shay: "What was it like waking up with no memories?"

David's gaze fixed on her. "Got nothing to compare with. Remember realizing I understood what Simon was saying. Remember the tests – they started testing me two weeks after I woke up. Coordination. Spatial acuity. Intelligence."

"What's spatial acuity? How well you see?" Katie held up three fingers: "How many fingers do I have?"

Ariel huffed. "There's nothing wrong with his eyes."

At the same moment, David said, "Eight."

Stunned silence. Then Shay snickered.

Katie laughed out loud. "Three. I'm holding up three." Waving her hand in front of his face.

"Not what you asked."

"But that's what I meant." Katie grimaced. "And besides, I have *ten* fingers." She held up her hands, fingers splayed.

David pointed. "Thumbs."

"God. They tested your intelligence too?"

"Yes."

"How did you score on that?"

"Eight-six."

Shay shrieked with laughter. "An eighty-six IQ? At least you beat the male average."

Ariel chortled. David stared at her in silence.

She spent an hour and a half at the pub, during which Katie and Shay pried David's life story out of him. He had, according to eight notebooks, been raised by his aunt and uncle, who died in a house fire months before the Shimmerman bug wiped his hard drive. He spent more than a year in a clinic until his psychiatrist or counsellor (David didn't seem to know what Simon Markson was) decreed he could take baby steps out into the world. He now lived in a halfway house in North Vancouver.

Ariel sensed Katie and Shay's interest in David beginning to wane. "We'd better go," she said. "I have things to do at home."

Shay gripped her arm. "It's only eight o'clock."

"What do you have to do?" Katie demanded.

"Just things." Ariel shook Shay off and rose. "I've got things to do on account of Gran's will. There's still stuff to be settled."

"After six months?"

"I have to deal with lawyers. They always take their time." Ariel eyed David. "Coming? I can drop you off at Waterfront Station."

Ten minutes later, Ariel stopped the car at the corner of Seymour and Cordova. "There's the Waterfront Seabus terminal. You'll be all right?"

David nodded. "I've taken it a lot. Got change."

Ariel rolled her eyes. "Goodie."

David turned to her and fixed her with that too-long stare.

"What?"

"Could have supper again," he said. "Or coffee. Or something."

"I'm flattered. Sure."

"You free tomorrow?"

"Sure. Call anytime." Which, she thought, will be a problem since you don't have my number.

Ariel parked in the driveway. At the front door, swallowing, she squeezed her eyes shut before sliding the key into the lock. Then she grit her teeth, twisted the key, and shoved the door open.

Gran spoke in her mind. "I can't move my legs."

Then a ghost of Corey's voice, on the ancient answering machine on the table next to the couch. "Sweetie? If there is anything I can do, anything you need." He had paused then, as though expecting her to pick up. Her hand had hovered over the phone.

"Fuck off." Ariel beat her palms against her temples. The walls flexed, breathing around her.

Ariel flung her coat to the floor and fled to the basement, pounding down the stairs and past the laundry alcove. The door at the end opened to three steps up into the garage. Blankets she had found in Gran's closet lay scattered about, with laundry she should have done weeks ago. The garage held its shape, as though disconnected from the spirits in the rest of the house.

Ariel kicked her boots off. The concrete floor chilled her feet despite her socks. But the blankets were enough. She plunged into the mass of heavy wool and grimy shirts and jeans. She wrapped herself in them, only the light from the hall illuminating the garage. She tucked an old gray sweater under her head as a pillow and lay back in her nest.

Sleep took its time.

*****

A distant jangle of notes reached her. She ignored it and closed her eyes. It came again later, barely louder than the sound of her own heartbeat in the utter quiet of the garage. A glare reached her from the bottom edge of the garage door. Morning.

Ariel struggled up, back aching, and headed for the open door into the house. It breathed around her, but quieted during the day. She made her way to the kitchen.

She didn't remember setting her phone on the dining table. It jangled once again. She scooped it up, scowling – and blinked when she saw the message list.

Six messages from the same number, an unknown caller. Every fifteen minutes since eight o'clock. She typed her passcode to retrieve her messages and put the phone to her ear.

First message: "Hello Ariel. This is David."

Ariel's spine grew cold.

"Need to look at tombstones today. Hope you can help me. Guess you're not awake yet. I'll try again later."

"Next message, eight-fifteen," the phone's mechanical female voice said. Then David's voice came again: "Hello again, Ariel. Must be still asleep."

Third message: "Hello." His voice sounded frayed. "It's important that I have someone to help me look at tombstones for my aunt and uncle, Ariel. Good-bye."

Fourth: "Maybe you're busy. Don't know. But, need help. Looking at tombstones. Bye."

Damn it, he's yanking your pity chain, Ariel thought.

Fifth: "Ariel, it's me again. David. Need your help. Tombstones. Bye."

Ariel squeezed the phone, wishing she had her grip on the asshole's throat.

Sixth: "Hi Ariel. Hope you're awake. Can you help me look at tombstones? You need one for your grandmother's grave too. Simon says I should go with someone who can make sure I'm not being taken advantage of. You said you're free this afternoon. I'll call later. Bye."

"Shit." Ariel tapped *Disconnect*. The phone rang in her hand. "Damn!" Rattled, she tapped its screen again. "Hello!"

"Ariel. Hi."

"Jesus H. You've been calling and calling."

"Yes."

Silence.

"Um. I thought I forgot to give you my number."

"You did."

Silence again. Ariel stared at the living room carpet. It desperately needed vacuuming.

"How did you get it?"

"It appears on your phone when you turn it on."

"When did I – ?"

"When you called Katie back. At supper. At the cafe."

Ariel replayed the previous day in her head. "You couldn't have seen it for more than a second." And upside down.

"Got a good memory."

Ariel laughed, shaken. "I see."

"Said you'd be free this afternoon."

"I did, that's right. And you want to look at tombstones."

"Yes."

Damn it. "All right. Where do you want to go?"

"Requiem on Main. Pick me up at the Main Street Skytrain Station?"

"Okay. Give me an hour. I need to get changed." Ariel disconnected. At least she had an excuse to get out of the house again.

Her previous excuse lay where she had left it. Gran's photo album, open on the coffee table in the living room. Ariel sat and hunched over it to peer at the photos she had been looking at the day before. A picture of herself and Gran in the backyard standing before the old charcoal grill. That picture had prompted her to visit Gran at the cemetery. Ariel remembered balancing the camera on the windowsill, hoping she had the angle right to catch the both of them along with the massive trunk of the cedar tree.

The loss of her parents at eleven had made her lash out at Gran. Gran's death just left her hollow.

Not just hollow. And you're not just pissed off. You're scared.

Ariel shook her head.

What's the matter? the voice said. *Not willing to acknowledge that? Too much a coward to admit you're alone and terrified?*

Shut up, she told the voice.

No time for breakfast. She would eat out. Anything to get away from the house.

She dressed in her bedroom. Gran's door was shut, as she had left it when the ambulance came and took Gran to the hospital. The day Gran died.

"Honey? Can you call an ambulance? I can't move my legs."

The house breathed around her. She tugged her jeans to her middle and buttoned the fly. Then she collected a sweater from her dresser, ignoring the assortment of bras lying cast off on the bedroom carpet. Let the girls flop around, she thought; the moron isn't going to notice.

Ariel pulled into a "taxis only" spot outside a building across the street from the Skytrain station. Two trains passed on the elevated track. Ariel watched the white railcars pull into the station and spill a mass of humanity down the steps. She fiddled with the radio and got static, then remembered seeing the satellite bills in among the papers on the dining table, unpaid since Gran –

"Shit." Ariel pounded the car door with her fist. Then she smoothed her jeans on her legs. Her knee-length black coat used to be her mother's, Gran had told her years ago. Ariel remembered her parents in the kitchen of the apartment in

New Westminster, east of Gran's house. Arguing again. The memory tied the muscles in her shoulders into knots.

David descended the steps from the Skytrain station. Ariel watched him glance about, his head jerking like a bird's. He began to jog, long even strides, toward her. Apparently he remembered her car, picking it out in the parking strip.

"Welcome," Ariel said when he pulled the passenger door open.

"Hi."

"You have an address for this Requiem place?"

David buckled himself into the seat, then plucked his phone from his shirt pocket. It unrolled in his hand.

"I thought you'd have it memorized," Ariel muttered.

"I do." David held up his phone. Its screen showed a map of Main Street, a green arrow pointing at the block between Twentieth and Twenty-first Avenues. "Go there. Please."

Ariel eased the car into Main Street traffic.

"Why don't you have a stone for your grandmother yet?" David asked.

"The ground is too soft after a burial. It has to settle before they put the stone in. That takes about a year."

"What will you put on it?"

"I haven't thought about it."

"What do you think I should put on Uncle and Auntie's stones?"

"How should I know?" She rolled her eyes. "I guess 'In Loving Memory' won't work."

David clasped his hands together and stared at traffic. How mouselike.

Ariel's mouth grew hard. "All right, what do your books say about them? Find something in those."

"They were good to me. After my parents died."

Ariel's gaze found her hands on the steering wheel; her knuckles had turned white. "How did they pack it in?"

"'Pack it in'?"

"How did they die?"

"Car wreck. In Oregon. In fog. A man driving a rig. Drunk."

Ariel pictured the man at the door, speaking in hushed tones to Gran. He had "cop" or "civil servant" written all over his cheap black suit. Then Gran telling her to sit down, they had things to talk about. "You were lucky."

"That I wasn't with them?"

"I mean, that you don't remember."

"Better to remember."

"How would you know?"

"Must be good things to remember about your grandmother. Wouldn't hurt so much if there weren't."

"God damn it!" Ariel beat the wheel with her fists. "Don't talk about her. What I feel is none of your business."

"Don't people feel better when they talk about things?"

"You're not my therapist. And if I needed one, I'd get one. I wouldn't blather to some retarded bastard with the brains of a nine-year-old who shoots his mouth off whenever he . . . ."

Ariel shut up, her teeth snapping together. David wore his usual stupider-than-thou look. The car ride grew silent.

A minute later David pointed. "There."

"What?"

"The tombstone place."

"Right." Ariel pulled in across the street, behind a silver Ford Capek. "Stupid name for a car. What the hell is a 'Capek' anyway?"

The place was austere, a single-floor building painted dark gray. The sign above the double glass doors read, "Requiem: Memorial Tablets and Funeral Stones," engraved in an elegant calligraphic script. David was quiet as they approached. It looked like an indoor cemetery. The proprietor, a tall man almost as thin as David, had a silver loop in each ear and gray hair that looked like a toupee. His black dress pants and a blue button-up shirt looked more downtown than grave site. When he approached, Ariel pointed at David with her thumb. "He's the one you want to talk to."

The man turned to David. "How can I help?"

"Two stones. For my aunt and uncle."

"I'm sorry for your loss."

Ariel snorted. "Believe me, he's over it."

The man looked at her again, chillier now.

"They died four years ago," David said. "I want stones."

"I see. Did you have a price range in mind?"

"Want to see what I can get."

The man led them to a tall marble stone. An angel perched on top of it, wings outspread.

Ariel cleared her throat loudly. "Someone could knock those wings off with a rock."

David glanced at her, nodding.

"Well then, we have a line of simpler stones . . ."

David's question now plagued her. What *would* she put on Gran's stone? Beyond the obvious, *Amber Morrissey, 1953 – 2031*, she couldn't think of anything that fit Gran. Maybe something poetic.

Here one day then gone in a flash,
Pucker up world and kiss my ass.

Her head began to ache. The voice in her mind returned: *Maybe bawling your eyes out till snot runs down your face would do you good.*

Shut up, she told it. Her stomach rumbled, reminding her she had skipped breakfast. She turned her attention to the annoying hollowness in her belly. It gave her something better to think about.

Later she led David to a Blenz coffeehouse across the street. David selected a steamed almond milk. Ariel ordered an Americano and a cheese scone from the girl behind the counter, then motioned David to a table. "Have a seat."

When she joined him with drinks and food, David had his phone laid out in front of him, puzzling over something on its screen – the tiny graphic looked like a green car.

Ariel pushed his mug in front of him. "Have you come to any decisions?"

"Small stones. Simple." David gave her his classic stare, holding it longer than was comfortable.

"How come you can afford tombstones?"

"Government is holding Aunt and Uncle's money. I get some each month. The rest when I'm twenty-five. Or when Simon signs a paper saying I'm okay."

"So he doesn't have a problem with you wasting money on headstones for empty graves?"

David's brow pinched. His tongue darted out and moistened his lips. "Why are you getting a stone for your grandmother?"

"There is a body down there."

"Is that really your grandmother?"

"Her body."

"But not her."

"If you want to get religious, fine; if there are such things as souls, hers has buggered off."

"Then no one's in her grave. Just a box full of meat and hair. And clothes no one would wear anymore."

The bones in Ariel's shoulders turned to ice. "God damn it! Don't talk about her that way." Her knee banged the bottom of the table, spilling her coffee. "Now look what you did." Wiping the spill with the sleeve of her coat. "Shit." Mom's coat.

David watched her in silence. Then: "In 1920 a playwright named Karol Capek wrote a play called *Rossum's Universal Robots*."

"Huh?"

"The Capek was Ford's first model to come with autodrive as standard instead of optional. It's why they named it after the playwright."

Ariel stared.

"Forty-six minutes ago you asked why Ford called it the 'Capek.'" David tapped his phone. "Looked it up on the Net."

"Great. Trivia. Drink your milk." Ariel bit into her scone and tore a mouthful free.

David lowered his gaze to his cup and lifted it with both hands.

Ariel forced her voice to soften. "What are you going to do? How much did you inherit? You can't live on that for the rest of your life. Can you?"

"There's a work program. They want me to wash dishes. Or make fast food. Don't want to do that."

"Then, what?"

"Good with computers. Look after them at the house. I like that."

"What do you mean, you look after them?"

"I fix them."

"You?" Mr. IQ eighty-six?

"Learned by myself. You can find manuals and tutorials on the Net."

"You taught yourself to repair computers." Ariel eyed him with new respect. "So you're some kind of savant?"

"Don't know that word."

"It's like – " Like what? Those stories of autistic kids – barely functional, but sometimes brilliant musicians and artists? Was that a side effect of Shimmerman's Disease? "Never mind. I'm impressed you managed to learn that stuff."

"It's easy. Started by reading everything I could find. Made a shape in my head, how all the parts work together." He wrung his hands, as though shaking the words free of his body. "Had to make sure I really got it. The house had a broken one in a closet. Thought if I can make it work right, I'll know I understand it."

An effort of will kept her from patting David's head. "Maybe I should have you fix mine. It keeps crashing."

"What kind is it?"

"A Neurion Seven."

"Socket 1730 or Intelligent Module?"

"I have no idea what that means."

David's voice lost inflection, as though he were reading something from a textbook. "Socket 1730 is a zero-insertion force socket, while Intelligent Module is the new standard, permitting a motherboard to support multiple modules, each of which is in essence a dedicated – "

"Forget it, okay? What do you want to do now?"

David glanced at the green pastel walls. Paintings and framed photographs hung on them. "Want to look at the pictures."

"I meant, what do you want to do this afternoon? Assuming you don't want to hang around the tombstone place for the rest of the day."

David stared at her, unblinking. "Your friends said we could watch a movie at Katie's place."

"'We?' Why do you want to spend time with them? They were . . . ."

They were rude and obnoxious, Ariel thought, especially Shay. But don't kid yourself, Ari; you were no angel either.

David waited. Then he said, "Simon says I should spend more time with people. People from outside the house. People like me make too much sense."

Ariel set her mug down. "What does that mean?"

"Everybody at the house is like me. Except for Simon and Dagmar. Need to spend time with people who've had real lives. We don't have all the stuff in our heads normals do." Tapping the side of his head with his palm. "Quiet in here."

No shit, Ariel thought. "That's not a bad thing."

"Why don't you call your friends?"

"You're pushy." Plucking her phone from her pocket. "Give me a minute."

Katie answered on the second ring. "What's up?"

"Do you guys want to do a movie tonight?"

"I have an exam tomorrow."

"Oh, hell. What day is this?"

"Wednesday."

"How about Friday, then?"

"I'll text Shay. I don't think she has any plans."

Ariel licked her lips. "David wants to come along."

Katie was quiet a moment. "What can we rent that's going to appeal to him? *Tommy the Tank Engine*?"

"I don't think we need to worry. He wants to spend time with people. He says it's educational."

David stared at her as she spoke.

Ariel heard Katie's breath against her ear. "Why are you spending time with him, Ari? I don't get it."

"This is my good deed for the month. What time should we show up? Seven?"

"Seven is fine. See you then."

Ariel disconnected.

"Good." David grinned and bobbed up and down as though his head were coming loose. He jumped to his feet, startling Ariel, and turned to the wall across from them. On it hung a painting of orcas, their dorsal fins tall and grand, jutting up from white-capped ocean. The girl behind the register watched him through narrowing eyes. Ariel sipped her coffee, wishing she could duck under the table and disappear. Periodically David leaned in close, his nose less than a finger length from the scene.

Tommy the Tank Engine might be too highbrow for him, she thought.

20

ARIEL WOKE IN THE GARAGE on Thursday, with a burden of resentment at the moron for railroading her into Movie Night At Katie's tomorrow. She waited and listened near the door to the basement. The house slept. Ariel smoothed the white sweatshirt and pants she had dug from the pile of laundry scattered on the floor, and headed for the stairs. Lunch was microwaved noodles flavoured with a little envelope full of spices and too much salt. She gingerly carried the hot bowl by its edges into Gran's office. The computer woke to the touch of its black power tab and settled into its customary hum. Of late it had added an occasional grinding sound to its vocabulary, an unnerving tone that made her imagine flames bursting out from behind it. Bending over the keyboard, she looked down at herself and grimaced. Her sweats reeked of . . . well, sweat. She had spilled coffee down her middle at some point, leaving a disgusting stain that looked like she had shit herself. In front.

She could always call Katie to say she couldn't make it to movie night tomorrow. David probably had already forgotten about it. No; he would say something like "You must be too busy for me," and her pity gland would flare up again. Damn him.

Ariel touched the Menu square in the upper left corner of the computer's screen, and chose Email from the list of services. Nothing new in her Inbox. She closed the email window and woke a browser. Picturing David kneeling before a tombstone in the shop on Main Street, Ariel tapped the

Google tab on the screen, then typed "Shimmerman's Disease" in the search field. A list of links materialized. The topmost read, "The Truth About Shimmerman's Disease." Ariel tapped the link.

"Does Shimmerman's Disease Make You Psychic?" read the headline. The logo of the site in the upper right corner read, "The Brodksy Report." A tabloid. Ariel shrugged and read the first paragraph.

> Researchers at MIT have discovered that Shimmerman's Disease, the plague that wipes away the memories of its victims, can grant its sufferers extrasensory perception.
> Neuroscientist William Shut, who has studied over one hundred victims of Shimmerman's Disease for four years, says –

Right, Ariel thought, noting the next three articles on the site's table of contents column.

> Sasquatch spotted in Seattle Park.
> Are space aliens watching us through our phone cameras?
> Noted theologian says Second Coming is due next year.

With a yawn, she hit the Back button and chose another Google link. Conspiracy Theories ("Did the CIA create Shimmerman's Disease?"), religious nutters ("God's way of purifying unclean souls"), tasteless jokes ("Shimmerman's is a wonderful disease – you can hide your own Easter eggs!"). She ignored them, her gaze tracking down the list until she found: "Biochemist announces link between Shimmerman's Disease and the flu." She clicked it. A scientist named Mohammad Seraf theorized Shimmerman's Disease didn't just *look* like the flu, it was a bizarre mutation. The rest of the scientific community theorized Mohammad Seraf was a flaming fuckup. Seraf had even dreamed up a cute name for it: ERIN.

Ariel scrolled down the list of Google links:

Evolution of personality in Shimmerman survivors.

J. J. Sebastien sux!

Shimmerman's Disease and intelligence.

Shimmerman's Disease and the death penalty.

Pattern and structure recognition in survivors of Shimmerman's Disease.

Bennie Shimmerman: official home page.

Ariel eyed the link at the bottom, then reached over and tapped it on the screen.

Bennie Shimmerman really did have a website. It looked like the kind of self-indulgent stuff school kids liked to build, full of diary entries and photos of their cats. The page was white, with a picture of the woman in the top left corner. Ariel skimmed the page. Some journalist was researching a new book about her. Shimmerman had left the halfway house where she lived for the past few years. It sounded as though she hadn't lost quite as many head points as David. She had a job, though the site didn't say what. Pushing a broom somewhere, the kind of work David would end up doing.

He thinks he'll get a job working on computers, Ariel thought. Sure. A guy whose shoes have Velcro instead of laces.

You're one to talk about work, the voice in the back of her mind whispered. *"Oh Mr. Kettle, there's a Ms. Pot on the line."* *You're not getting by on an IQ of ninety – but you're a bigger waste of space than David. You can't even talk to your ex.*

Ariel's fist thumped the desk, sending the mouse clattering against the monitor. Goddamn, Corey isn't my ex! We're on hold, that's all. I'll call him. We'll talk. Things will go back to where they were.

Yeah. Right.

On Friday evening Ariel left the car in the driveway and took the Skytrain to Granville Street. Vancouver had a long history of downtown parking that swung between exorbitant and nonexistent. She found David crouched near the entrance to the Skytrain station, his back to the wall. Ariel smirked at the sight of him. If he put a cap on the ground, he could make his bus fare in loose change in no time.

David looked up at the sound of her footsteps. Ariel pointed across the street. "We need the number 22 bus. Katie's place is out in the West End."

"Expensive," David said.

"What's expensive?"

"The West End. Renting."

"Yes, very. Her boyfriend is auctioning his testicles on eBay to cover the rent."

David gave her his famous blank look.

"Don't tell them I said that; it was a joke. Understand?"

They walked across Granville and stood waiting for the next bus. Ariel glanced at the masses of people moving back and forth along Granville. She used to enjoy the pace of downtown, but now the crowds seemed to press in on her. Downtown buzzed with traffic and too many clashing conversations. People gathered to catch the bus. Ariel sank her gloved hands in her pockets and stared at the ground. When she looked up, she found David watching her. The bus rolled up, making a hideous squealing sound as it stopped.

Ten minutes later they stepped out on Denman Street. The bright little shops and cafes were alive with people. Ariel clutched David's sleeve to lead him across to Katie's apartment building.

Why the hell am I here? she asked herself. *I should go home and . . .*

And what? demanded the voice in her mind. *Channel surf? Moon about Corey? Masturbate again?*

She found Katie's call number on the intercom board and jabbed the button.

Laurier answered. "Hello?"

"It's Ariel."

The door buzzed.

They were alone in the lobby. Ariel led David to the elevator. "Try not to say anything embarrassing."

"Like what?"

"I don't know."

David fixed his gaze on the elevator door. Ariel glanced at him and shook her head, discomfited by the sensation that he watched her still. She looked at the elevator – and blinked. David's reflection stared at her from the metal.

The door slid open. David peered into the box, then stepped in. He turned and held the bar along the back wall.

"Never been in an elevator before?"

"Once. Unconscious."

"Unconscious?"

"At the clinic. When I reached phase four. Taken in an elevator up to the Recovery floor."

"That doesn't really count." Ariel tapped the button. The elevator lurched and began to move.

David bent his legs, straightened. "Heavier."

The fifteenth-story corridor smelled of cinnamon. David followed her to the open door of 1525. Ariel took her shoes off. David matched her movements, bending as she bent, tearing his Velcro strips free when she tugged the bows of her laces.

Katie stepped out of the kitchen, her boyfriend behind her.

"Laurier, this is David," Katie said.

Laurier stuck his hand out and smiled. "Hello, David."

David shook it. His gaze drifted past Laurier. He wrenched his hand away and raced into the living room. Ariel scrambled after him in time to see him staring out the glass overlooking the balcony. He fumbled with the handle, slid the glass door open.

"He's not a jumper, is he?" Laurier asked.

"I'll tell you in a couple of minutes."

Night had fallen on the city, leaving a sliver of sunset in the west beyond the high-rises along the shore of English Bay. Ariel stepped over the lip onto the concrete of the balcony. David stood at the railing, leaning over, peering straight down. His gaze swept up, taking in the lights of the buildings nearer the waterfront. Laurier and Katie didn't have the most spectacular view you could find in the West End, but between the nearby high-rises they got a slice of English Bay. Four freighters lay at anchor, discernible only by their cabin lights.

"Uh, David?"

His eyes glittered. "Never been in a building like this."

"No kidding."

Clouds had broken overhead. He pointed. "A star."

"Great. I'm cold. Come on inside when you're done gawking."

Ariel stepped back into the living room and slid the door shut. Laurier and Katie stood watching.

"It's his first time in a high-rise."

Katie shrugged. "Shay and Tyson are on their way. They're picking up a couple of flicks."

"Any idea what?"

Laurier laughed, his potent baritone utterly unlike David's voice. "We'll know when you know."

Katie and Ariel went into the kitchen and filled bowls with potato chips. Katie began a monologue about her university classes in environmental chemistry. Ariel tuned her out, throwing in the occasional "um-hm" to imply she was listening. Minutes later she heard the balcony door slide open. Laurier asked David something about Shimmerman's Disease. The intercom buzzed. Katie strode to the panel in the hall and tapped the button. Shay's voice sounded metallic.

The apartment's cleanliness appalled Ariel when she thought about her own home. Here wineglasses hung from a rack under the cupboards, though she had never seen either of them drink wine. The coffee maker next to the sink looked as if they cleaned it after every use – unlike Ariel's, placed to hide a stain on the counter.

Katie returned to the kitchen and resumed her monologue. Ariel tuned her out again and picked up the bowls of chips. She took these to the living room and set them on the black wooden coffee table. Laurier's right hand seemed pre-programmed to reach for them. He didn't look at them or interrupt what he was saying to David as he collected a fistful of potato chips and shoved them in his mouth around his words.

"Where are you going to live?"

David stared. Narrow empty eyes. "I don't know. Haven't started looking for an apartment. Not ready yet."

The conversation sounded familiar. Ariel was sure David had used the same words with her.

Shay's voice. "Evening."

Ariel glanced at the hall. Shay and Tyson stood side by side, hands clasped. Tyson was shorter than Shay and built like a brick. Knowing Shay, she would have someone new in a couple of months.

"We got two funny ones." Shay held up the disks. "We figured you could do without something depressing. One is British, and the other is wall-to-wall fart jokes. Guess who picked that one?" Nodding in Tyson's direction.

"Lovely." Ariel joined David on the smaller of the two couches.

"Oh – introductions," Katie said. "Tyson, this is David. David, Tyson."

David rose, held out his hand, shook Tyson's.

The movie, *Something in the Water,* was even worse than Shay's description implied. That led to Tyson and Laurier and the women chatting through it and trying to engage David in conversation. They were more interested in hearing from him than from Ariel.

Thank God, she thought.

Ariel felt like leaving when the film ended, but Katie beckoned her into the kitchen to pour glasses of Pepsi for the others. Ariel returned to the living room in time to witness Shay and Tyson necking on the couch. David stared at them in fascination. Ariel glared, hoping to catch his attention, but he never looked away from them until they broke apart.

She thought about Corey, kissing her on the sofa at home before Gran came home. Corey, tentatively unbuttoning her blouse. They had their first time together there, with Gran's comforter beneath them.

Enough. Ariel shook her head to drive the image away. Usually Shay mentioned seeing Corey at the university. He hadn't crept into the conversation this time, thank God.

The second movie, *Holland Park*, was a sweet romantic comedy about an American woman becoming involved with an aristocratic British architect half her age. Ariel loathed it. David asked why the cars drove on the wrong side of the road, which prompted Laurier to expound at length on automobiles.

Shay and Tyson stayed behind when midnight neared. David joined Ariel at the door.

"You can stay if you like," Ariel told him. "You don't have to follow me."

"It's late. Want to sleep."

Ariel shrugged and slipped her shoes on. "Whatever."

Katie hugged her. "Don't be a stranger, okay?"

"Sure."

"How about we do this again next week?"

"Um."

Katie squeezed her shoulder. "Just say yes. Or I'll nag you for the rest of the week."

"Okay. I'll see."

The corridor lights seemed brighter than before. Ariel zipped her coat up and tucked her fists in the pockets. David followed her to the elevator and tapped the button. As usual he eagerly looked at everything. His head twitched as he glanced from one light bulb to the next above the elevator door.

"Did you like this?" he asked, shifting his gaze to her.

"What?"

"Being with your friends."

"Getting out? I guess."

"Good."

Ariel's lip curled. "You could learn a little discretion."

David's brow pinched.

"If Shay and Tyson are going to paw at each other, you don't have to stare like you're watching live porn."

David's brow seemed to wrinkle even more. "Wanted to be watched."

"Huh?"

"People kiss and touch each other differently when they think they're alone. But when they're in a room with other people they . . . ." David wrung his hands. "It's different," he finished, looking helpless and confused. "Like people in movies. They act."

"Just because they're putting on a show doesn't mean you have to stare."

The door ground open and they stepped in. David said nothing until the elevator trembled and began to move. Then: "Shay starts it; Tyson never does."

"And you're entitled to gawk at them?"

"Only does it when you're in the room."

A muscle in Ariel's neck began to throb. "Shay's an asshole."

David grew quiet again. Moments later the door slid open and Ariel marched across the lobby. David had to scramble to catch up as she slammed the double glass doors apart. People of all shapes and sizes and colours wandered back and forth on Denman Street. The masses of bodies pummelled her with a chaotic buzz of conversation.

David spoke up again. "Why is she your friend?"

"Who?"

"Shay."

Ariel's fists clenched. She thought of pushing him into a gap between the buildings and dropping a few choice words on him about not exercising his short-loaded brain late at night, but the bus stop with its dented metal and graffiti-stained glass loomed and David slowed to a stop. A black couple stood waiting for the bus. David grinned like an idiot. The woman smiled back. The man nodded, almost formally.

Ariel felt like saying, Good evening, I'm just out for a walk with the village idiot.

Damn it, David kept shooting his mouth off, and what business was it of his if her friend was a callous bitch who –

Except he's right, dumbass.

Now that she considered the situation, Shay was Katie's friend, not hers. While Ariel had known Katie since high school, Shay hadn't come into the scene until she and Katie shared a study group at the U. And lately Shay alone mentioned Corey, as though she enjoyed digging an emotional corkscrew into Ariel's flesh and giving it a twist.

Minutes later the bus pulled in. Ariel followed David to a seat at the middle of the vehicle. When the bus rolled up to the stop on Granville Street, her mood had shifted. David stepped off behind her.

"Will you be all right?" she asked.

David nodded. "Can take the Skytrain to Waterfront Station and ride the Seabus." His gaze narrowed. "Never answered my question."

"About Shay? I have no idea." Ariel scowled, then softened. "Hey, call me. We'll look at more tombstones. Or something."

David's mouth fell open. He stared at her as though she had sprouted bat wings from her ears.

Okay, sure, Ariel thought. I can be nice to you once in a while. Just don't get used to it.

21

April passed into May. To her surprise, Ariel found herself enjoying David's company. She took him to Katie and Laurier's the next week, and twice more with the whole crew to Screwdriver's Pub. The boys didn't mind; David even drew Tyson out of his shell for a while by asking him about the scar along his arm from elbow to wrist, courtesy of a bicycle accident. Shay maintained a steady stream of veiled barbs which sailed past David, unnoticed.

David bothered Katie as much as he did Shay, and when he went to the pub's washroom Katie asked Ariel why she brought him along.

"The doctor who runs the halfway house says it's good for him to be out among people who aren't like him. David talks about this Simon person like he's God himself."

Shay was more forthright. "The guy is a poster boy for euthanasia. Feeling sorry for him isn't a reason to tow him around with you like he's your kid in a stroller."

The following week Ariel joined her friends at the pub without David. Shay and Tyson put on a happy-couple performance. Ariel eyed the seat next to her, wondering if the regulars were asking themselves what happened to her "boyfriend." At least she looked like part of a couple with him.

David Glass had a talent for prying her out of the empty house with just a few words. Only once did Ariel refuse to pick up the phone when he called. She watched the numbers blink on her phone screen, then saw the voicemail icon flash. When his number vanished, she tapped the Messages tab.

"Hi, Ariel. David. Guess you're too busy. Wanted to ask if you could have lunch with me. But if you have too much to do, that's okay."

Ariel sat on the couch and surveyed the living room. The carpet desperately needed vacuuming. The papers she had dug out of Gran's filing cabinets while hunting through her records months ago now lay stacked in four piles beneath the huge single window. Dishes from breakfast three days ago sat on the dining table.

Yes, you've got plenty to do, she thought. You could clean up this dump. But are you going to? No, you're going to mope and whine and count spots on the ceiling. What is wrong with you, Ari? People lose their parents and grandparents all the time. Why do you have to drag out the histrionics for months?

She called him back. "I was in the bath when you phoned. So you want to do lunch?"

"Thai restaurant on Granville Street. It's called Ayutthaya. Named for Thailand's ancient capital."

Ariel wondered if he learned everything he knew from Trivial Pursuit cards. "I figured you for a burger and fries type."

"Boring."

"No kidding. What's the address?"

David recited a street number. Ariel wrote it on the pad on the end table and tore off the yellow square of paper.

"See a movie after lunch?" David said. "There is one called *The Lazarus People.* It's about vampires."

"I've heard of it."

"Matinee. At two forty-five. At the Capital Six."

"Sounds good. I'll see you at the Thai joint in an hour or so. I need to slip into the shower first."

"You just got out of the bath."

"I forgot to wash behind my ears."

A sign with fake Asian lettering spelled out "Ayutthaya: Authentic Thai Cuisine" across the restaurant's glass door.

Ariel tugged it open. A smell of a dozen spices she couldn't name hit her.

Inside, she spotted David at a table. Across from him sat a hulk. The man had no hair on his head except a pair of thick grey eyebrows. A snake tattoo crawled up his left arm and vanished into the sleeve of his black T-shirt. Ariel could see one of his knees, jutting out from beneath the table. His jeans were worn and faded. The man sat with his elbows on the blue tablecloth, his gaze fixed on David. David was talking, and the man stared like an animal watching prey.

David was too dumb to know who he shouldn't talk to.

When she neared the table, the man's eyes swivelled to her like searchlights. Ariel willed herself to stare back.

David followed the man's gaze. "Ariel. Hello. Sit. This is Switch."

The monster watched her as she lowered herself into the chair next to David.

An enormous hand with jagged fingernails jutted at her. His voice rumbled. "Good afternoon, Ariel."

Ariel glanced at his hand but didn't shake it. Instead she set her phone on the table in front of her.

"Switch came with me from the house," David said.

Huh? "He's like you?"

David nodded.

"Oh. I . . . ." She held her hand out. "I thought . . . . Never mind."

Switch put on a goofy smile. Then he picked up her hand with more delicacy than she expected, and shook it. Her fingers vanished into his massive grip.

Is he that big all over? she wondered. And let's shove that thought into the sewer where it belongs.

"So. Switch. What do you do?"

"Depends."

"On what?"

"The time of day."

"Uh, right."

David spoke up. "Switch is moving out of the house. Wants an apartment. Has a list."

Switch tapped a button on his phone. Ariel watched a list appear on the screen. Addresses. Handwritten – badly.

David piped up again. "Teaching Switch to play chess."

"Good for you."

Switch's version of The Stare was creepier than David's. Like he was sizing her up for a barbecue. "David is good. He's lost seven times."

That didn't sound "good" to Ariel. "How many did you play?"

"Twelve hundred sixty-two."

"Huh?"

"Simon taught me. Been playing for twenty-one months. With some old men at the library. They have tables in the foyer."

"I meant how many did you play today."

"Four," Switch said. "David won." He pointed at her fingers, drumming away on the table. "That means you're nervous. David says so."

God, he's just like David. Big mouth, no goddamn brains. Ariel clenched her fist. "Well, I'm not."

Switch's gaze tracked up her arm and fixed on her eyes. "Are you going to say something nasty now?"

"Huh?"

"David says when someone tells you something you don't like, you say something mean. It's – "

Switch's mouth snapped shut with a sound of teeth on teeth. He stared at David. David stared back.

"What?" Ariel's throat felt as though it were coated in sand.

"Like sauteed Thai noodles?" David asked.

"Well, yes."

"Chicken, beef, or pork?"

"Um, chicken."

David gestured at the small Asian man at the counter. The man came to the table, smiling, and David blurted out what sounded like a string of random syllables. The man nodded with approval. Switch thumped the table and somehow didn't spill the cups.

"You speak Thai?" Ariel muttered.

David gestured with his jaw in the direction the man had gone. "Told me how to pronounce everything in the lunch menu. He's my friend."

They're just overgrown kids, Ariel told herself, and sometimes they don't know when to shut the hell up. Her heart slowed. She sensed that something had passed between David and Switch, something she couldn't grasp.

Fifteen minutes later, Ariel thought: This must be how he feels when I'm with Katie and the crew. David and Switch were talking about apartment-hunting, and she was no longer included in the conversation. The man who had filled their cups brought three plates, one balanced in the crook of his arm, and placed them on the table. Then he set chopsticks down beside each and retreated to the back of the restaurant.

Corey used to say, "I get offended when I go into an Asian place and they assume I can't use sticks."

Ariel choked at the memory. The conversation between David and Switch ground to a halt.

"Hot pepper," Ariel muttered.

"Oh." Switch resumed his chatter about apartments.

Half an hour later, they split the bill three ways and stepped out onto the sidewalk. Switch said good-bye, shook Ariel's hand again, and set off toward the waterfront. Ariel noticed people scrambling out of his way as he approached them.

"I need a book at Chapters," David said. "Got an hour before the show."

"You read books? Paper books?"

"Yes."

Ariel shrugged. "Lead on."

They walked along Granville Street. David peered at her from the corner of his eye. They turned at Robson and made their way west to the bookstore.

The place was a huge anachronism, rising three floors. Ariel loosened her coat when they stepped inside.

"Going to the Computers department." David pointed at the escalator. "Meet here in twenty minutes?"

"Sure."

"Wander. Look at books. They have lots."

Ariel watched him stride away, shoulders hunched. She fought the urge to laugh. With a sigh she set off in an orbit of the place, glancing at the signs above the racks. History. Psychology. Sexuality. Cooking. After all these years, people still bought books on paper – or whatever they were printed on now. She glanced around once more and turned toward the escalators. The Fiction sections were –

Corey Hewitt stood between her and the escalator.

22

Several things registered at once. First, Corey wore the pale blue shirt of a Chapters employee, white name tag pinned above his heart. Second, he had cut his hair; it no longer hung like a mop to his shoulders. He looked like a professional. And third, she was staring like he had just beamed down from the mother ship.

He smiled, a flicker at the corners of his mouth. "Hi."

Ariel gulped. "Hi, yourself."

"Long time no chat."

"I thought you'd be at the U."

"We had finals two weeks ago."

"Oh. Right."

"Didn't Katie tell you I'm working here over the summer?"

"No." She hasn't talked about you, Ariel thought. She hasn't uttered a word.

"How have you been?"

"Great." I feel like a bomb went off next to me, and now I'm watching myself bleed to death.

"Have you sold the house?"

"Not yet." It's a prison.

Silence. Corey's prominent Adam's apple moved.

"I can't talk now." He crossed his arms, uncrossed them, glanced at his shoes. "I have to get back to work."

"Yes."

"Want to talk? I have a break in half an hour."

"Okay. No! I can't. I'm with a friend. Can I call you? Tonight? We could catch up."

Corey's face fell. "I guess." He made a vague gesture over his shoulder. "I have to go."

He hesitated. Then Ariel saw the moment when he made the choice; he stepped to her and slipped his arms around her, hugged her to him. He pulled away.

Ariel clutched at his arms. "I'll talk to my friend. I don't have to go."

"Can you meet me in the coffee shop, then?" He gestured at the Starbucks across the room.

"Yes."

"Good."

Ariel stared at his back, unable to breathe, as he walked away.

She found David wandering the bookshelves on the second floor, lugging a heavy tome titled *Modern PC Repair: Twelfth Edition*. And, bizarrely, a skinnier book called *How We See: The Psychology of Perception*.

"David. I can't go to the show with you."

"Why?"

"I ran into a friend. We need to talk."

"Oh." David stared. "Talking to a friend is good."

"Look, if you want to see the show, go. I have to wait till he's free. He has a break in half an hour. This is important."

"Okay. We can see the movie tomorrow."

Not likely. "Yeah." Ariel touched his arm. "Thank you."

"Welcome."

In the coffee shop on the main floor she sat at a corner table, her fingers drumming the side of her mug. She remembered dropping her photo of Corey in the bottom drawer of her dresser, unable to look him in the eye. The phone had rung; he had left another in a long parade of messages on Gran's answering machine.

He had been a mainstay in her life since she entered UBC. Like her, he studied the sciences, though he leaned toward organic chemistry rather than genetics. Corey was a loner. She asked him to lunch after a Chemistry 171 tutorial. He looked amazed that someone wanted to spend time with him. Ariel soon found that behind that insecure brow lived a sparkling mind. Corey could keep up a stream of conversation about virtually anything. When she invited him over to the house one afternoon, she felt sick at the thought of Corey and Gran meeting. And yet they talked so intently that Ariel felt ignored.

Gran understood how things were going long before Ariel twigged.

"So, have you and Corey started wearing out his mattress yet?" Gran asked over dinner one evening.

Ariel's mouth opened, tried saying five things at once, and closed around her forkful of pasta. "No," she mumbled through the mouthful.

It was true, she berated herself. Those spectacular things he did with his fingers four nights ago on the couch didn't count. She squeezed her legs together and pushed the thought away.

Gran's gaze narrowed. "You're due for a new ring."

When Ariel turned fourteen, Gran sat her down and explained to her in no uncertain terms that (a) as a teenager she was stupid enough to get knocked up on general principles, and (b) sex could be lethal without appropriate precautions.

"Now I'm not going to tell you not to. God knows I was rolling in the bushes with Brent Thackery at sixteen, and I still can't convince myself there was anything wrong with it." Grinning, she added, "However, my dear, you are getting your HIV vaccines and any other shot that'll keep you from getting dead on account of your glands. And then you're getting a ring planted in your butt cheek."

That was long before she met Corey. On the day when Gran confronted her about him, Ariel's voice squeaked with embarrassment. "I started peeing blue last year. The doctor gave me a new one." After almost five years, the ring's contraceptive payload had run low. At that point it released a blue dye. Ariel had yelped when she looked into the toilet and saw that colour coming out of her.

"Good. You're learning." Gran turned her attention back to dinner. "More Parmesan?"

Gran, I miss you, Ariel thought. And Corey, I'm sorry I pushed you away. I can fix that now, at least.

Time stretched out before her. Then Corey stood at the counter ordering something and smiling at the woman behind the register. He picked up his white disposable cup and came to the table. She watched him, letting her eyes soak up his form as he settled into the chair across from her. He squirmed a bit, sipped his cup.

His ring was on the left side of his butt. The image of him slipping naked out of his bed stormed into her thoughts.

"So," he said.

"So."

"How have you been?"

"Getting better. It's been hard."

"Katie said you've quit the U."

Ariel turned her gaze to the dark walls, swallowed. What to say? I came off the rails, but I'm better now.

For the first time she believed it.

"Gran's dying threw me. I had all that legal stuff to deal with. And . . . I needed time to get used to things."

"Well. If you need to talk, don't hesitate to call me."

"Thanks." Silence. "What have you been up to?"

"Studying. Job hunting. I got lucky getting work lined up so soon after classes ended. Some of my buddies are still pounding the pavement." He smiled. "It doesn't pay a hell of a lot, but it'll get me through."

"Good." Ariel's gaze absorbed the shape of his mouth, the dimple on his right cheek. His mother's parents emigrated from Hong Kong. His father was a WASP from West Vancouver. The mixture of genes gave him a permanent tan, narrow eyes, and an Irish nose.

He was beautiful.

"I've given up on selling the house for the time being. The Realtor was a prick."

Corey nodded. "There's more than one out there."

Ariel drained the remains of her coffee. "So. Are you free tonight?"

Corey's gaze narrowed. "What did you have in mind?"

"Dinner? I'll throw something together at the house; you could come over." The words poured out of her in a flood. "We could talk, get caught up."

Corey shook his head. "Wing bought a new chair. It has a massager thing in it. I promised I'd help her set it up this evening."

"Wing?"

Corey voice grew hushed. "I thought Katie or Shay would have mentioned her."

A cloud settled over the table. "You're seeing someone." It had only been five months, for chrissake.

"You never returned my calls. It seemed obvious we were finished."

Her life had officially become a soap opera. "You're seeing someone named Wing."

"Yes."

"Jesus. *Wing?*"

"It's Chinese."

"Did you meet her before we came apart, or after?"

Corey's gaze hardened. "I met her a month ago. Do the math."

"You expect me to believe that?"

"What you choose to believe has nothing to do with me." Corey picked up his cup. His hand shook. "I thought you knew. Katie has seen us together at the U. Even talked to us."

And she had kept Shay on a leash ever since, Ariel realized. Damn them both. "You couldn't have waited?" The brittleness in her own voice appalled her.

"Waited for what? The last time we spoke, you said, 'Don't waste my time.' It sounded like we were done. I left messages but you didn't call back."

"So it's my fault, shithead?"

"Ever since your Gran died, this is how all our conversations have gone." Corey's voice cracked. "It didn't have to be like this."

"Actually it did. Fuck you."

He rose, picked up his empty cup, crushed it in his fist. "Good-bye, Ariel." His eyes sparkled. "Don't call me."

Ariel sat trembling. Her stomach began to ache.

I should have told him I'm seeing someone too; that would have nailed him where it hurts. I will not cry. Gran didn't get that and he doesn't deserve it. I will not.

Ariel rose and fled. She found herself on the sidewalk outside the bookstore. A chasm yawned within her.

It would have been so good to curl up next to him on the couch tonight. Her crotch felt warm. She glanced about to ensure no one watched, then wrapped her coat around herself and slipped her hand down the front of her slacks. Heat. Wetness. She hooked her finger, brought it up between her labia. Shivered when the tip of her finger touched her clit. The sensation collided with her mood.

You left David hanging for nothing, the voice in the back of her mind said.

David. Ariel pulled her hand out of her slacks, fumbled for her phone. She tapped the button and held it to her ear.

"Hello, Ariel."

"Hi. David."

"Talked to your friend?"

"Yes." And he's moved on. It's about time I did. "I'm free now. Where are you?"

"Behind you."

Ariel spun around. David stood near the doorway, phone in his hand. A yellow Chapters bag swung heavily against his side.

"Your voice sounds funny," he said.

"We've missed the show you wanted to see."

"Yes."

"Can I make it up to you? Would you like to see my house? Gran got *The Lord of the Rings,* the 25th Anniversary release. On Hyperstream."

"Sounds good."

Don't do this, Ari, she thought. He's got the brains of a nine-year-old.

David fell into step beside her. They walked toward Granville Street. David's arm brushed against her shoulder. For a second her voice refused to work. "What will happen if you don't go home tonight?"

David turned his gaze to her, gave her a full-on dose of The Stare. "You want me to stay with you?"

"I have a spare room. We could watch videos, and stay up late. It'll be fun."

He will sleep in your old room, Ariel told herself. Or give him Gran's room. Nothing is going to happen. You just don't want to be alone, not now. That's all.

"Carmen is answering the phone this evening," David said. "I tell her I'll be out all night. That will be okay."

Of course, Carmen was like him. Dumb as a brick.

"Good. Call her."

David took his phone from his shirt pocket, then stopped and gazed at her. "I could work on your computer."

That's not all you can work on, she said to herself. She squeezed her eyes shut to drive the thought away.

~

Uncle is out. The boy is glad. He likes being alone with Auntie. Auntie shows him how to make her cry. Not in pain, or as though she is hurting inside, down in her soul. It's a different kind of cry. A call to God.

"Come with me." Auntie's voice is hushed. The way it is when she shows him how to use his fingers. She holds her hand out to him. He takes it, and she leads him to the bathroom. She lets his hand go and reaches for the faucets in the bath. The water sprays, too hot and full of steam. The sound in the pipes changes, the stream slows and speeds up as she adjusts the silver knobs.

Satisfied, she lifts her dress over her head. Then she smiles at him and kisses him on his forehead. "Take off your shirt." That husky voice that sends electricity through his belly.

She takes his hand again when she steps into the spraying water.

"Here." A light pressure on his shoulders. He lowers himself to his knees.

"That's right," she murmurs. Then later, she screams, and he feels angels watching.

~

Autumn 2051

"Happy birthday."

<h1 style="text-align:center">23</h1>

Light blazed, blasting memory away and thrusting Ariel into the present. The garage's concrete floor chilled her bottom. For a moment she saw David in silhouette in the doorway to the house. She cringed. The illusion collapsed into Elizabeth's slender frame. Ariel had a vision of herself huddled against the wall, the sleeping bag tucked around her body, tears leaving channels down her cheeks.

Her daughter's face was empty, a blankness carefully fixed in place. Too much like her father. "So it's really bad, isn't it?"

"What?"

"This stuff that's happening to Dad."

"No, it isn't. He is going to be fine."

"And that's why you're hiding out in the garage." Contempt oozed into Elizabeth's voice. "Crying. Warren thinks you're in your room. Good thing he didn't start looking for you first."

"I said everything is fine."

Elizabeth glared at her, then turned and marched back into the house.

It has to be hard, doesn't it? Ariel thought. As she rose she ran her arm over her face, blackening her skin with wet mascara. She drew several breaths, tamping grief down into her belly, and followed. As she neared the stairwell past the laundry alcove and began to climb, she heard the waltz that played when Elizabeth logged in to her account on the computer. Ariel stopped in the bathroom and washed mascara from her cheeks, then followed the girl into the den. She found her slouching in front of the screen, chin resting on her left palm.

After a long moment the girl looked up at her mother. "What?"

"I'm sorry you had to see me out there."

Elizabeth sniffed.

Ariel leaned against the doorway, steeling herself for another battle. "What exactly did your father say to you at the hospital?"

Elizabeth fixed her eyes on the keyboard before her. "He started talking about this girl in the hospital. Then he called me Auntie."

"Maybe he was joking."

"I know what he looks like when he's kidding. He wasn't."

"He's confused. His memories – "

"Do you listen to him? He keeps saying, 'It makes no sense'. It's like what's in his head won't fit together. There's no Shape."

"It's been twenty years since the bug wiped his brain. Now he is trying to figure out the person he was when he was a teenager." Ariel laughed gently. "Look at us – imagine yourself in my head, trying to figure you out."

Unexpectedly Elizabeth guffawed.

Ariel smiled, praying it looked genuine. "Your father is going to be fine."

Elizabeth rolled her eyes. "Who are you trying to convince, me or you?"

Damn. David asked questions like that.

"That woman who's been phoning. Who is she?"

Ariel froze, her smile locked in place. "What woman?"

"Yesterday evening. Afterward you left in a hurry."

"She's . . . ." A client? An old friend? Selling raffle tickets? Ariel's thoughts sped through the options and settled on the truth. "She was an old friend of your father. From before. She thinks she can help."

"Dad doesn't know about her yet. Why didn't you just tell him?"

Because she is going to tell your father he spent years getting raped, and then torched his relatives when he grew sick of it.

"I don't want to put too much on him. He's vulnerable."

"How can seeing an old friend be a problem for him?"

"It just is." Ariel turned from the room.

"Geez. Shoot me for asking questions," Elizabeth muttered behind her.

Ariel hesitated, chewing on several responses, none of them good. Instead she headed for Warren's bedroom. A tap on the door brought forth a mumbled, "Come in."

Warren lay on his stomach on his bed, oblivious to the chaos of clothing and objects around him. Ivy vines hung in great arches of green leaves along the wall near the ceiling. The game glowed in its Dome beside him.

"How are you?" Ariel asked softly.

Warren put the controller down. "Elizabeth's being a deuce. Can we bring Dad home and leave *her* in the hospital?"

Ariel settled her hand on his arm. "Little man, your father is going to get through this. As for Elizabeth, you know she's a worrier. In a few weeks we'll all be back to normal. "

Warren eyed her with suspicion. Ariel fled.

The den was empty when she stepped out of his room. Elizabeth's voice issued from the basement. Probably on her phone. Ariel nudged the door shut with her toe and tugged her own phone from her belt. The Messages LED blinked.

Olver appeared on the screen in response to her tap. "Ms. Morrissey, I think we ended on the wrong foot last night. If there is anything I can help with, please contact me."

At least here was some connection with David's true past. Perhaps Olver really could help. Soon enough, David would realize his memories didn't mesh with what his journals described.

She tapped the phone's Return Call tab. Olver's too-pristine avatar appeared. "This is Jackie. I'm not available right now. Would – "

Ariel hit Disconnect and glared at the avatar's frozen image. How to tell David he burned alive the two people he had most loved?

A broken sleep. The next morning, aching and tired, Ariel put on her white robe, stumbled down the hall, and told Nob to warm the house a few degrees; then she made her way into the living room and asked for the television. A talking head in a navy-blue suit jacket and perfect hair smiled at her. Ariel lowered the volume and sat on the couch, hugging her robe around herself, giving part of her attention to the morning news. A shooting in California. Peace talks between Austria and Germany had broken down again, thanks to a car bomb in Vienna.

It would help if you had someone to talk to, she told herself. But who? Dr. Olver? Santiago? San at least could be sympathetic, but he had his own agenda: David was his patient first.

What was Zeke's agenda? Three days ago he had been ready to accuse David of abusing her.

And what's your agenda, honey? a voice in the back of her mind demanded.

I want David home. I want to wake to the smell of chai, and feel his lips on my brow and hear the sound of my fat marble mug on the night table. I want to make love with him and know the expression on his face is ecstasy, not the pain of remembering something his aunt and uncle did to him. I want to feel his hand on my knee as we drive. I want him to rub my neck after I've sat too long in the den.

A light glowed from the hall. Ariel heard the bathroom door close. Rain rattled the living room windows. She rose and padded to the kitchen to make breakfast. Pancakes from Gran's recipe: eggs, milk, sugar, baking powder, a pinch of cinnamon. Slices of pink ham went into a pan before she turned her attention to pouring from the bowl of batter. Warren wandered out of the bathroom, his Dome tucked under his arm. He set it on the dining table, then drifted into the kitchen. Saying nothing, he reached up into the cupboard and brought down a blue glass, which he filled from the jug of berry juice in the fridge.

Ariel squeezed his shoulder. "Pancakes are pending."

"Yum."

She had a vision of David striding through the doorway. His contribution to the family lexicon: that one word in the morning whenever she made pancakes or French toast.

As though reading her mind, Warren said: "Can we see Dad tonight?"

The response came more sharply than she expected. "No."

At that moment Elizabeth wandered in, hair going in thirty directions, white pajamas hugging her body. She cast a tired scowl at mother and brother, then brightened at the sight of breakfast in the making.

"Yum," she said.

"We're going to see Dad tonight," Warren told her.

That got Elizabeth's attention. "Aces."

"No, we aren't!" Ariel barked. "I've got too much work to do and I've missed days already thanks to – " Ouch. Don't say "your father." " – all that's happened. Your father isn't exactly having fun right now. He doesn't need you two harping at him."

Silence.

Warren fixed his gaze on the wall across from the stove, his juice glass in his hand, knuckles turning white. Ariel followed his gaze to the faint indentation where a flung coffee can had left its mark. Her thoughts recoiled from it.

Warren turned his eyes back to her. "Dad was going to take me to Star Wars."

"Damn it, Warren, I don't – "

"I'll take you," Elizabeth said. Ariel blinked in surprise.

"But – " Warren began.

"Do you want to go or not? We can see it tomorrow. Saturday matinee."

Warren glared at his sister, then shrugged. "Okay. Let's." With that he turned and wandered to the living room.

Elizabeth folded her arms. "I need a shower." At the kitchen doorway she turned and gave a thumbs-up sign.

Once in a rare while, her daughter could surprise her.

*****

Auntie, holding him down, her mouth contorted in a scream –

Uncle Stuart on the patio. Sound of the car pulling out. Uncle smiling and unbuckling his belt –

Ariel, kissing him hard, pushing him onto the bed, his head against Auntie's thigh –

Part of David's mind seemed to have detached itself from his emotions, idly watching the badly cut film roll past. That part of him wondered at how little he felt about the images. They seemed unreal, devoid of pain or fear.

The film in his mind skipped. He pictured a park, dense with woods near a lake. Aunt Mel lay on her stomach on a gray blanket, dark green sweatpants and a pale green T-shirt covering her. When Davie caught her eye, she smiled at him. Uncle Stu sat nearby, his back to an arbutus tree, a book open in his lap. The arbutus grew lush above, but much of the old bark had peeled from its trunk, leaving it bare and smooth.

"Snake trees." Auntie laughed. "They shed their skin."

Davie had been playing with a girl about his age, six years old, at the base of a concrete slab where a carved bust of a man's head had stood, though the bust had been shattered so that only the chin, part of the nose, and the leftmost half of the forehead remained. The girl had a silver dog bot that whined and walked in a drunken kind of way, and rolled over on the grass, mechanical paws clawing at air. Her name was Elizabeth.

No, not Elizabeth. Something like Danielle. Or Danica.

Later Auntie and Uncle walked him back to the parking lot along a path beneath maples dense with leaves larger than his hands, even with his fingers spread as wide as they could go. He talked about wanting a robot for his birthday – not a dog, but something like those metal monsters on *Killerbots*, on TV.

"What do we do when it tears up the living room?" Uncle asked.

David shrugged. "Auntie says we need a new couch anyway."

Now he leaned back against his pillow, aware he had stopped breathing. When he shifted his feet off the bed to the floor, pain stabbed his ankles. He lifted each foot and flexed his toes.

A quiet cough. Zeke stood in the doorway, nodding a greeting. "Good morning. Has anything fresh come back to you?"

David described the park he remembered. The psych nurse listened and, for a change, didn't interrupt. When David wound down, Zeke said, "That's good. I'm impressed you remember that child's name."

"Not sure about that." Then a dream from last night stormed his thoughts. "I think I remember the clinic." Forgotten until now, the dream unfolded in his mind. "And Carmen. Awful seeing her like that. Started writing in my journals like crazy, because I knew that was going to happen to me."

"Carmen?" Zeke's eyes narrowed. "Who was she?"

"Knew her in the Recovery floor, and at the halfway house. But, dreamed about her, from before the illness wiped us."

"What do you remember?"

"Slideover to phase two. Half a dozen of us went over at once. Place went mad."

"You also?"

"Yes. All of us, in the infirmary together."

Zeke appeared content to let his silence prod David to continue.

"That's all. Wish it would just start at the beginning and roll right on through to the end."

"That's too much to ask; the mind doesn't work that way." The nurse smiled. "I'm glad your wife brought your children here. You looked happy."

"Don't I look happy most of the time here in the nut house?"

Zeke chuckled, a throaty sound carrying a timbre of relief and rue. "I'm running out of reasons to keep you here. You're still confused, but your sleep is improving. That's a good sign. Your wife asked about having someone care for you at home. We can arrange for a home-care nurse."

In David's thoughts, flames licked the wall in the garage. Remember yesterday with Warren and Elizabeth? he asked himself. You could have sworn you saw Aunt Mel.

Sleep deprivation, he answered his doubts. I've been hallucinating. That's all.

Later in the morning, voices stirred him. He stepped to the corridor and watched Lake's parents stop at her room. They didn't set foot within. He watched as Lake joined them, leading them past him toward the lounge at the bend in the passage. He followed when they vanished, and paused at the entrance. They had taken a table near the right-hand wall. David filled a glass at the sink and strolled to a table beyond, against the tall vertical windows. He plucked a copy of *Time* from the rack and laid it on the table. Reflected in the window, David saw Lake's back and the faces of her parents.

David drank lukewarm water and turned to an article about a bombing in Hong Kong, ignoring the text, casting a glance at Lake. Her shoulders stooped, as though she were sinking inside herself. David listened, stretching his hearing to the whispers and low tones of Lake's parents.

" – tomorrow," her mother said.

Her father spoke: "I'm sorry. I have to go. This meeting. But we'll be back, by Wednesday."

Lake's head moved in response.

Her mother said something else too soft for him to hear.

He felt a twist in his mind. The Shape materialized, the starfish twitching. Two of its limbs shrank into itself, leaving three. One touched her father's temple. The second hovered above her mother, avoiding the woman.

The limb kneading Lake's neck looked torn and bloody.

When the trio rose and wandered into the corridor, David closed the magazine. Shadows lurked in the back of his mind and moved before he could fix his gaze on them, clouding his thoughts. But the Shape, for all its hurt and all its wrongness, bound his thoughts together and held the chaos back. He rose and followed, in time to see them outside the elevator doors. Her father hugged her, then her mother did the same. They spoke to the nurse, who touched something on the desk. The elevator doors slid apart and swallowed them, leaving Lake alone with the Shape wrapping its limbs around her. She turned and caught his eye, and for a moment the limbs of the starfish opened. Then she looked away, and they closed about her.

David followed her into her room. She lowered herself to her bed, unaware of him, fingers coiled in her lap.

David grunted. The girl looked at him with vacant eyes. Her shoulders were like stone. "What?"

"Need an ear?"

"Nope."

"You do." David lowered himself to the floor and leaned against the wall beside the doorway.

The girl's voice carried no inflection. "You're a deuce."

"Am I?"

"Yes."

"Then say it with conviction."

Lake turned her gaze to her lap.

*****

At nine Ariel headed for Crawford Hospital, letting the car choose a parking spot. In the elevator she stood with her back against the wall, her vision pointed at her shoes. When the doors parted, she drew a long breath through her nostrils, letting it hiss out over her teeth. Then she walked past the nurses' station toward David's room, nodding at the woman behind the counter.

She didn't reach it. Instead she saw David inside another patient's room, his back to the wall next to the doorway. He wore his shorts, T-shirt, and slippers. When her shadow fell across him, he looked up, a soft smile on his face.

"Ari."

On the bed sat the teenage girl Ariel remembered from yesterday's visit, a fresh white bandage on her neck. She glanced once at Ariel, then looked back at her hands.

David rose by sliding up the wall. His arms opened. He hadn't shaved lately, and Ariel felt his bristles against her forehead.

"Busy?" she asked.

A glance at the girl. "No." He led Ariel from the room.

Down the corridor, she jutted her thumb back the way they had come. "What was that about?"

"Her name is Lake. She's broken." David's jaw twitched. "Had a good memory this morning. Remembered my aunt and uncle and me in a park under an arbutus tree." He stepped into his room, hand in hers, gentle pressure on her palm and fingers. "Confusing. All of it, confusion. Random pictures and scenes."

Ariel squeezed his hand. "I think I've found someone who can help. Do you remember Dr. Olver?"

David stopped moving, became still as a corpse.

"She looked after the clinic when you were young."

"Dr. Olver." His hand released hers. He sank back into the chair before the tall window and gripped the chair's arms. "Dr. Jackie."

"You do remember her."

David's chin sank down against his chest. Oblivious to her, he began to rock his chair side to side. Then his head jerked back. His eyes gazed through her at something only he could see. His shriek made her ears ring. "Mama. Mamamamama!"

No. Oh no, Ariel thought. She clasped his arm hard. "David, stop. Look at me."

His gaze met hers for an instant, and she felt some part of him struggling to hold himself here. The expression in his eyes sucked itself in like a breath. He tore free from her grip, lurched and heaved himself sideways from her, tumbling to the floor. The room echoed with his howls.

24

HER HUSBAND LAY ON HIS side twisting in his fallen chair, shrieking. His head rocked seizure-like, colliding with the floor in a steady rhythm.

"David, stop it!" Ariel grabbed his shoulder. "Damn it, you're the sensible one. Don't do this to me."

Then Ezekiel appeared beside her, crouching. "What happened?"

"I don't know."

David's legs kicked at empty space.

Zeke elbowed Ariel aside. Over his shoulder he barked, "Sedative."

Ariel staggered back out of the way. Two female nurses had followed Zeke. The blond woman brandished an injector like a television cop wielding a pistol. Zeke lifted David under his arms and flung him onto the bed. David broke free momentarily and shoved him back. Ariel tried shutting her eyes, which made it worse. "Mamamamama!" The black nurse caught David's wrists. She held them against the bed. His droning shriek went on and on. "Mamamama. . ."

That's not David, Ariel told herself. That's a child who remembers his crazy mother trying to shoot him before blowing off the top of her own head. Dr. Olver described him falling over in her office, wailing as he slid down, his mind dialing back to childhood horror until she pulled him back from it by flinging him into another memory.

"There's a trick we learned for getting them under control . . ." Olver had said.

From a distance Ariel heard her own voice. "Happy birthday, Davie. You're four years old."

David's eyes locked on hers. "Auntie?"

"That's right, Davie. Happy birthday."

His face broke into a wide grin. "Prezzies?" He clapped his hands together and laughed.

Zeke glared at Ariel in confusion. The blond nurse had the presence of mind to kneel and press her injector pistol against David's shoulder. He flinched and looked at his arm, then back at Ariel. His breathing slowed. Before all feeling bled from his eyes, Ariel felt sure she saw betrayal roll through them.

With spectacularly useless timing, the thick-necked crew-cut Marine sergeant of an intern arrived, shoes pounding the linoleum.

Zeke beckoned him over. "We need this man upstairs."

The intern nodded.

In spite of the drug, David could walk. The guard and the two female nurses led him toward the door. The girl David had been with stood in her doorway, peering at David as the intern gripped his arm and marched him to the elevators.

Zeke turned on Ariel, his voice hushed and jagged. "Why did you say that? 'Happy birthday.'"

"The staff in the clinics used it to get patients under control when they slid over."

"'Slid over'?"

"When patients slide into phase two of Shimmerman's – ERIN – they get suggestive. So you can give them something good to focus on, something pleasant." Ariel almost laughed at her own voice. Smooth and professional. How did you spend your morning, Ms. Morrissey? Well sir, I watched my husband's mental clock wind back to one year old; had to trick him into thinking he was four, because that wasn't quite as awful.

The elevator doors slid apart. David groaned as the intern muscled him inside.

Zeke looked from David to her, then shook his head. "I'm putting him in isolation. Don't leave; I'll be back in ten or fifteen minutes."

As the doors closed, Ariel saw her husband grin at her. A line of drool crept from the corner of his mouth.

The number above the door jumped to "8" and stopped. Category two mental health, she remembered from the panel in the elevator.

Ariel stood waiting, then turned, dazed, and walked back along the corridor. She found herself near the tiny room down the hall from the nurses' station. The black nurse stood at the counter, pouring juice from a bottle. When Ariel entered she placed the bottle back in the small fridge and flung the door shut. She pushed past Ariel without making eye contact.

Wife of the crazy guy, Ariel thought. Don't look at me; it might be contagious.

Ariel sat on a hard chair amid a smell of pungent antiseptic. The sound of padding footsteps reached her from the hall. The girl with bandages on her throat wandered in, dragging her feet.

Water hissed in the faucet. The girl had a brittle voice. "They took him upstairs, huh?"

"Yes."

The girl touched her throat. "They'll buckle him down. Give him drugs."

Ariel stared, unable to take her eyes off the bandages. "You've been up there?"

"When the ambulance brought me in."

"What's it like?"

The girl's voice was the auditory equivalent of a twitching corpse. "White rooms. They have cameras in the ceiling; someone's always watching. When I pulled my bandage off, they were in my room right away. Shot me full of something." The girl paused and drank. The bandage on her throat swelled.

She reminds David of me, Ariel thought, touching her own neck. "Why did you do it?"

The girl turned. A wall grew behind her eyes. She threw her half-full glass into the sink. "None of your damn business."

Ariel watched her back as she marched away into the corridor.

Ariel drifted the halls before returning to David's room; she stood at the window staring at the apartment buildings and office towers, barely visible through her own reflection. She imagined David strapped to a table, wires plugged into his head, an insane doctor who looked a lot like Ezekiel cranking a huge switch.

"Ms. Morrissey?"

Ariel turned from the windows. Ezekiel stood in the doorway, arms crossed, mouth in a narrow line.

"I have some questions for you." The psychiatric nurse gestured at one of the tables and sat. Sweat darkened his armpits.

"What have you done with him?"

"He is comfortable. Asleep." The nurse's eyes narrowed. "I need to know what happened before he collapsed."

Ariel lowered herself to a chair, watching the man as her mind turned the question over. The cold and uncaring part of herself felt as though it had taken charge. "A doctor called me. Her name is Jacklyn Olver."

"I know that name. She ran the North Vancouver Shimmerman Clinic."

"She came up from the States for some sort of convention."

"How long have you known she was here?"

"A day. Or two."

Ezekiel watched her as though expecting her nose to grow. "So this Dr. Olver called you. What does that have to do with David's collapse?"

"He was fine until he heard her name."

"Mentioning her triggered it."

"I think so."

Zeke looked thoughtful. Then his gaze hardened. "Your husband hasn't told me everything. Is there anything *you* haven't told me?"

"If David has been holding back, there's nothing I can do about that."

"I wasn't talking about a lack of honesty. Perhaps there are things he can't understand or articulate. But you could have told me about Dr. Olver yesterday."

"I needed to confirm some of the things she said."

"Such as?"

"Everything David believes about his past is wrong."

There, Ariel thought. I've said it. I can't claw it back from the air or this man's mind. Why does it feel like I've given up on my husband?

Zeke gazed at her as though waiting for the punch line. "Go on."

It all poured out: David's hallucinations, Dr. Olver's tale about the fifteen-year-old arsonist and killer flung at her by the corrections company, her discovery of an article from that time describing Isabelle Reed.

You have given up.

When she finished, Zeke laced his fingers together; they shook at the tips. "Well, then. Is there anything else you haven't considered important till now?"

Ariel stared at him mutely.

He glanced at the wall clock. "I have another patient to attend to. I'll need to speak with Dr. Olver on Monday."

"She's staying at the Hyatt. Can I see David?"

"He won't be lucid for hours. The best thing you can do is go home and try to get your mind off all this. If you like, I can give you something to help you sleep."

"I'm not going to drug myself up."

Zeke rose. "Suit yourself." At the doorway he stopped and turned. "I'd hoped to send your husband home. But we can't give him the kind of treatment he needs. All we can do is keep him from harming himself and try to stabilize him well enough for a proper therapist to take him on. Do you understand?"

Ariel nodded, unable to speak.

25

AN EXPLOSIVE SOUND FAST-FORWARDS through a stench of old flesh and sulphur, hurtles into a vision of Ariel huddling amid a collection of grimy sheets and faded T-shirts, her arms clutched across her chest, "No, please, just go," terror drawing the blood vessels in her temples into sharp relief. Her body shrinks, and in an instant she is Lake, hands gripping her neck, eyes vacant and still.

The images collide: Ariel, then the girl too thin and fragile, then Ariel again, hands raised like claws. The girl sprawls in a pool of her own blood. Above her the starfish Shape hovers, a maze of lacerations.

David gazed at a white ceiling. Lake's face filled his thoughts. He squeezed his hands into fists. His heart wound up, walloping against his ribs, clearing his mind.

Interesting, he thought. The drug is a sedative. But if you force your heart into gear, let adrenaline run loose, you can think again. But *stop wasting time; it won't last.*

David lifted his head and gazed down the length of his body. Thick black loops encircled his wrists. He tried shifting his feet and felt resistance.

Piece it together, he said to himself, drawing an even breath through his nostrils. No, hyperventilate – drive your system hard. Now think. A padded room. They believe you're dangerous, to yourself or someone else. They will be watching.

He searched the walls. A door across the room. No window. Video then. There: hidden in the grill where a circular fluorescent bathed the room in light. If they could see in here, they would probably want to hear as well.

A smell crept up from the hard bed beneath him: rot and brimstone.

David filled his lungs and howled. He thrust himself up, tugging against the straps on his wrists. He flung himself right and left, pulling on them, cursing, flaying his fingers apart as he fought the straps.

The door flew open and Zeke scrambled in, the heavyset intern behind him.

David laughed. "Good, you're here."

Zeke held a syringe pistol. He placed one knee on the bed. "Just calm down, David. You're going to be fine. This will help you sleep."

"Shut up and hear me." David felt the injection thud against his shoulder. His right arm grew cold. "She's going to do it again."

Zeke's brow rose. "Your wife? What is she going to do?"

The chill reached his shoulder, then his neck. His tongue felt like raw fish. "Idiot. Not Ari. Your patient – Lake. She's going to do it again. Tonight."

The white ceiling became gray, framing Zeke's face. The nurse's mouth formed a stunned *O*, and darkness ate him.

*****

Ariel stared at the vehicles and shops on Kingsway Avenue as the car rolled along. Her eyes wanted to close, to carry her into sleep. The display in the dashboard said 2:52 p.m. Watching David's collapse had drained years of life out of her. When she reached the house, she dropped her coat on her shoes and wandered into the den. She sat and rubbed her eyes. The book she had flipped through earlier lay open on the desk, a pen serving as a bookmark.

A hum reached her from the living room. The vacuum cleaner had rolled out from under the couch and now navigated the house.

The image of David on the floor of his hospital room, wailing like a child, scrolled through her mind in an endlessly repeating loop. Ariel beat her temples with her palms. Do something, she thought. Anything. Just get your mind off all this. Off David going crazy and wailing for Mama.

A sob broke from her throat. She shut her mouth and wiped her eyes with her sleeve.

On her feet again, she wandered unsteadily along the hallway. Warren hadn't closed his bedroom door. Ariel peered in. The squat vacuum cleaner would choke on the first pair of well-aged socks it encountered. She made her way around the room, gathering up socks and undershorts and T-shirts. Warren had left the last batch of clean clothes in two neat stacks next to the door. Ariel built a heap of dirty laundry on the bed, then picked up one of the clean stacks and carried it to the chest of drawers. Warren kept his socks and underwear in the top drawer, T-shirts and sweaters in the second, pants and shorts in the third. The very bottom of the chest was open, intended for shoes and boots. By dumb luck some old sneakers had found their way into it; they had to fight it out for space with a blue stuffed rat Warren had won at a fair years ago, three portable electronic games that now bored him silly, and a dozen or more grimy socks.

David, screaming for his mommy, tumbled through her thoughts.

Shit. An effort of will forced her attention back to Warren's laundry. She emptied her first armload of clean garments, dividing it appropriately among the three drawers. Then she turned, sighing, and reached for another.

Warren had tucked his GameDome against his pillow, its visor beside it. Ariel sat and picked the Dome up. This was the boy's obsession, and she knew so little about it. The thought left a cavernous sensation in her belly. She found the power tab and turned the little device on.

Icons floated in the Dome. Panthea, his favourite game of late. Its lightning-bolt logo flashed. A Settings logo blinked. A Recent Views graphic – a tiny spinning folder – drifted about.

Curious, she worked the controller and found the pointer that moved within the Dome. The controls were remarkably responsive and simple. The pointer shot across the Dome and lit up the folder.

Words filled the Dome in red: "Locked to visor."

With a shrug she picked up the little glasses and fitted them over her ears. The earphones dropped down into place. The display awakened and the Recent Views folder hovered before her. She hit the button.

The visor filled her vision in 3-D. It filled her brain with a long jagged moan. The display was so realistic she felt as though she were standing beside the swimming pool watching the couple.

The woman knelt astride the man. Her dark braided hair looped over her right shoulder. Her back arched, forming a shadowed line of backbone. The man's penis, thick and hard, jutted up inside her. She ground down on him, her voice rising into sharp little cries.

Thank you very much, Warren, Ariel thought. I could have done without this little revelation. Couldn't you have waited till you're really a teenager before turning into a teenager?

She fumbled with the controls, then noticed that touching the controller brought up a display of the device, overlaid across the video clip of the cavorting couple. One button was marked "Folder Contents." She tapped that and found a list of video files with revealing titles. She gulped and picked another.

A blond woman. She lay on her back on a blue couch, breasts rounder and fuller than nature made them. Her arms were above her head against the cushions. The man had a lean, muscular body. The woman's belly jerked as he plunged his cock into her.

David, I have enough trouble with our daughter. I had to explain the finer points of her time of the month last year. Couldn't you deal with this? Can't Warren go back to being that little boy I used to carry on my shoulders?

All right, you're not here. So be it.

Another: a woman crouched on hands and knees, her head twisted back to gaze at the camera lens and through it into Ariel's eyes; the man behind her leaned to the side so the camera could see his erection buried inside her. And another:

a muscular blond man suckling a woman's left breast. She wore a black one-piece swimsuit, pushed down around her waist. The cloth covering her crotch hid the man's right hand. She cradled his head, smiling.

You know what David would say, Ariel thought. Put away your biases and see what's really there.

She hopped randomly through the videos. No hint of violence, brutality, pain. The couples even looked like they were enjoying themselves. Considering how awful porn actors typically were, they sure as hell couldn't be faking.

Ariel hunted for the video she had started with and selected it. Then she tugged the visor from her head, breathing hard. My God, she thought, don't tell me you're getting horny looking at your son's porn collection.

I miss you, David. You have no idea.

"Little man," she said aloud, "we'll have that conversation another time."

She strode out of Warren's room to the living room and flung herself down on the couch. She picked up the TV remote and tapped the Phone key. Hesitation. Then she called Olver.

"Hello," the doctor said, eyes narrow.

"An hour ago I watched my husband throw a tantrum and scream for his mother."

"That sounds like . . . ." Olver pressed her lips together, then moistened them with her tongue.

"Slideover," Ariel said. "Yes. And you were right. I found out about David's mother. She did kill his father and herself."

Dr. Olver's gaze softened. "I'm sorry."

"They've put David in a padded room."

"What happened exactly? Was he violent?"

"Remember what you told me about him sliding over? I used your 'happy birthday' trick to get him under control."

"I've never heard of that being used on someone who had the recovery treatment."

"I told David's psychiatric nurse about you. He'll be calling."

The woman's gaze narrowed. "What have you told him?"

"Everything. He'll be calling on Monday."

Olver raised her brow. "I'd like to see David before then. If that's possible."

Ariel shrugged. "Are you free tomorrow morning? I can take you to the hospital."

When Olver disconnected, Ariel stared at the blank screen. Her thoughts turned to the cemetery and the kid standing before two empty graves. Then later, sitting with him in a cafe blocks from the cemetery, listening to him describe the illness that had stolen his life. She had felt no sympathy for him, no pity.

What, then? she asked herself. Say it. Contempt. You got involved with your future husband because you thought he was a moron. If there's a God, he has a hell of a sense of humour. Twenty good years and two lovely kids, all because you were such a shit that when someone who looked weak-minded and pathetic came along, you pounced like a cat.

~

Uncle tells the boy to sit in the wicker chair. The boy tucks his legs under himself, the way the Buddha that Auntie keeps on the fireplace mantel sits. Auntie smiles at him from the bed.

Uncle peels her, each bit of clothing dropping to the floor. Auntie watches the boy as Uncle climbs onto her, grunting like an animal. Auntie makes a sound in her throat, almost a growl. Then a shriek. She stares into the boy's eyes, and he knows this isn't pain that provokes the sound. This is the kind of scream he can draw out of her with his fingers and mouth.

Uncle looks at him, the old man's face cracking into a grin. The boy sits quietly, watching Auntie and Uncle on the bed. He imagines himself leaping on Uncle's naked hairy back, clawing at the old man's throat until his head comes free in a spray of blood.

~

Spring 2032

"What did you tell Simon?"

26

Corey has a new girlfriend. Who the hell would name their kid Wing?

Ariel tried to focus on driving. One of those rich-dick cars that drove themselves would be great right now. Then she wouldn't have to worry about losing her concentration and running the car into the oncoming white five-ton. On the other hand, causing a multicar pileup on Kingsway Avenue half an hour after Corey dumped her would be a good way to kick him in the balls.

Getting herself killed to spite him. Brilliant.

And he didn't dump you, a voice in her mind said. *You dumped him. Months ago. And then you expected him to hover over his phone waiting for you to get off your ass and change your mind.*

Ariel winced, pounding the wheel with her palms.

David spoke. "Never been in this part of the city before."

"Then you're in for a treat," Ariel muttered.

Bad idea, she told herself. On the heels of the thought came Corey's face and their last conversation, playing in an endless loop. Maybe he loved Wing.

The car lurched. Ariel wrenched it back over the yellow line. "Shit."

The buildings along Kingsway changed from shops to high-rises and the Metrotown Mall, to more shops and Asian restaurants. Ariel veered the car onto Royal Oak Avenue, passed the Skytrain station, slowed down, and let the Duster glide past rows of tract homes. Anonymous neighbours. Gran knew them, and Ariel remembered a few names. Some of them had come to the funeral, wandered past Gran's coffin, made pointless murmurings of sympathy.

Ariel saw the driveway almost too late and slammed the brake pedal to the floor. The move flung them against the seatbelts. She stopped the car with its nose touching the garage door. "We're here." Shoving her door open.

David stepped from the car. Ariel watched him over the roof. He made a complete rotation, took in the house, the "For Sale" sign, the street, the rows of homes on the opposite side. If the fact that her lawn was the only one unmowed registered in his childlike mind, he said nothing. David waited for her to approach the house, then followed her up the steps to the front door. From her coat pocket she tugged her key ring with its mass of keys, most for locks she no longer recalled. David watched her fumble for the steel deadbolt key.

The door swung inward, bottom hinge squealing. David's boots thumped on the steps behind her.

In the living room moments later, Ariel watched his gaze absorb the couch and jump to the black leather chair and the coffee table. The television and speakers hung on the wall. His gaze lingered on the piles of papers she had pushed into the corner near the standing lamp. A flush of embarrassment burned in her cheeks.

"Bright," he said, eyeing the shaft of afternoon sun across the carpet.

"Sure. Bright."

His gaze returned to the coffee table. The photo album lay open where she had left it. David sat, hands kneading his thighs as he stared down at the faces in the photos.

"You look like them," he said, his tone free of emotion. "Your folks?"

"Yes."

"Died when you were eleven."

"How did you know – ?"

"Katie said so. I asked questions."

"Well don't."

David turned the page, studied the photo of Ariel when she was ten. Months before Mom and Dad boarded the plane to Europe and never came back.

Ariel reached across David and slammed the book shut. He looked up, unfazed. "Watch the movie now?"

Ariel needed a moment to remember what the hell he was talking about. "Sure."

She found the box in the bookcase near the lamp and cued the movie up on the player, then strode into the kitchen for a bag of barbecue-flavor potato chips. She emptied them into a bowl and crumpled the bag, her fist clenching it.

We're just two people watching a movie, she told herself. Nothing else. Nothing is going to happen here.

Ariel flung the bag into the trash can under the sink and fled to the living room, bowl in hand. David sat watching her, his face empty. She set the bowl down and scooped up the remote. In an instant, *The Lord of the Rings: 25th Anniversary Special Edition* filled the screen.

The first time she had seen this was with Gran almost a year ago. The old woman had come home and stood in the kitchen, grinning and saying, "Look what I found."

Just a month before Gran died, Ariel had watched it with Corey. Gran had gone out to a friend's place down the street and had made a point of saying, "I won't be back till eleven."

Corey put his arm around her and held her against him. Later he lay on the couch with his head on her thigh. And later –

Maybe that's what he's doing with Wing right now, Ariel thought. She tried to lose herself in the swordplay and magic.

Halfway through the film, she phoned Burnaby Pizza and ordered two mediums: one Chef's Special and one Mediterranean Delight. When the delivery man arrived she paused the movie and set out plates and napkins.

For a while as the film played, she eyed a slice of Mediterranean Delight, with its layer of feta cheese. Mom and Dad had died in the Mediterranean. Boom. Weeeeeeeeee-thud. Crash.

Credits rolled.

David turned to her, grinning. "See the second one?"

"I've had enough."

"Fix your computer now?"

Ariel eyed the carpet. Green and beige spirals. David sat with his head canted to the left, waiting for her to speak.

The back of her throat grew dry. "I have a better idea."

"What?"

The inside of her lower lip stuck to her teeth. "Let's play a game."

"Chess?"

She turned to him then, soaked up the shape of his face. A red welt along his jaw showed where he had probably cut himself shaving. He is old enough, she told herself.

"Not chess. Come with me."

David followed like a puppy. She led him down the hall to Gran's room. She hesitated, staring at the cream-painted door, then bit her tongue and pushed it open.

The room smelled slightly musty. Gran's bed was a huge beast of wrought iron. A dark green quilt covered it. Five white pillows, untouched for months, leaned against the looping black metal struts of its head. Ariel remembered the ritual of heaving the sheets into the washing machine in the basement, dragging them from the dryer later, and slowly and methodically making the bed. Gran had gone to the hospital hours before and hadn't come home. Ariel had expected to sleep in this room. Before the house began to breathe.

She pivoted on her heel to David, driving back memory. "Kind of skinny, aren't you?" Corey had been broad-shouldered, with the sort of build that suggested he would have a potbelly later in life if he wasn't careful. Good.

Ariel sat down on the bed. David stood still as she freed the single button at the top of his fly and undid the zipper. She tugged his jeans and undershorts down his legs. His penis flopped around at half-mast. Nothing to brag to Katie about. When she reached for his shirt, he lifted his arms, as though used to someone changing him.

My God, what are you doing?

Another part of her mind slammed down on the thought.

"Lose the socks," she ordered. He perched on the edge of the bed to slide them off. She unbuttoned her shirt and flung it aside, then slipped her pants off.

Down to panties and bra, she hesitated. David watched her. Gritting her teeth, Ariel released the clasp between her breasts, shrugged her bra off, and slid the panties down her legs. Then she put her hands on her hips and parted her legs to give him the full effect.

No hunger in his eyes, no anticipation.

Asshole, she thought. "Stand up."

David rose.

"Touch me."

His fingertips settled on her cheeks, touched her lips.

"What the hell?" Ariel took his hands and set them roughly on her breasts. He raised his left eyebrow, pursed his lips, and began to make circles around her nipples with his thumbs. Annoyed, she took his right hand and held up his index finger. She moistened her lips, then drew his finger into her mouth. It tasted like feta and mushrooms.

She brought his wet finger to her crotch. "Touch me here."

His fingertip worked through her hair, probed her folds. She could feel him moving it like a hook. For a moment he slipped into her.

"Yes, like that," she breathed against his ear.

His fingertip touched the knob of her clitoris. She flinched. "Good. Like that."

All the while he touched her, Ariel forced her face against his chest, imagining his eyes on her: vacuous, uncomprehending.

Her body shuddered. She pulled his hand away from her groin and sat on the bed. "Use your mouth down there." Lying back.

David knelt. Ariel watched him press his lips against her. She could feel his tongue probing, missing the spot.

"Stop staring at me, for chrissake." She reached to cover his eyes with her palms. But then his tongue did something that jolted all the muscles along her spine. She gasped. Her back arched.

"Beginner's luck," she mumbled. Then David's tongue hit her again and her fingers dug into the green quilt.

Fast learner, she thought with her last dose of clarity. His tongue sent waves through her, sucking her into the sensations of her body. She pulled him onto the bed, his cock slick with his own fluids. She gripped him, guided him into her. Joy filled his smile.

Ariel ground herself against him, eager to see pain in his eyes.

Not the best sex she had ever had – David hadn't even come. But it beat brooding over Corey.

Ariel listened to David's gentle breathing for several minutes. Then she turned over. The clock on the nightstand said 2:47. David lay on his back. In the bluish light from the window, Ariel could make out the movement of his eyes beneath the lids.

REM sleep, she thought. But – Jesus.

David must be dreaming about a tennis game, with the players jacked up on meth. His eyes swept back and forth. For an instant they opened, gazed at the ceiling, closed again. What could he be dreaming about?

A smile played across his mouth. Soft. Like a child's.

Ariel swallowed. He was nineteen. An adult. Past the age of consent. *An adult with a child's mind.* No, she told herself. He taught himself to fix computers – he said so. And he's a genius at chess.

That other voice returned, louder now, bleeding contempt: *Ah, that clinches it. There's never been a nine-year-old chess prodigy before.*

Her stomach filled with acid and rusty nails. Sweat burst up from every pore on her body at once, leaving an icy sheen on her skin. David moaned something in his sleep. Ariel sat up and lowered her feet to the carpet. Gran's gray robe was on the other side of the bed, slung over the chair next to the dresser. Ariel rose, then crept around the bed and slipped the robe from the chair, careful not to sweep anything from the dresser onto the carpet.

David's eyes danced beneath his eyelids.

Ariel cinched the robe around her waist. A knot formed in her throat as she slipped out of the room.

You know what happened last night, don't you?

It's not the same, she told the voice. He's a *guy*.

Her head throbbed. She clutched her arms across her chest, stumbled down the hallway to the basement steps.

Her body refused to move. *You aren't running from me now*, the house said. Her legs moved on their own, steering her past the stairway, on to the living room and into the black leather chair. Her hand found the lever that slanted the chair's back. She pushed it flat, then lay down and shook.

Suppose a man did this to a Shimmerman's victim. David's friend Carmen, for instance. The guy says he didn't know she had the brains of a child, and they put her on the stand and she giggles and says, "He told me we were going to play a game. It was fun." You'd demand that they lock him away, wouldn't you? And why?

Say it.

Ariel squeezed her eyes shut until they hurt.

Rape.

27

WHAT WOULD COREY THINK? Getting herself into the sex offender registry would show him a thing or two. Right. If her family weren't all dead, they would each take a turn kicking her ass to the Moon.

Footsteps echoed. Ariel lifted her knees and huddled in the chair, listening to the bathroom door open and close, its bottom hinge squeaking. Minutes later, light glared into the corridor from the bathroom. Then darkness. A tentative step, and another, receding. She heard the door to the den close.

Ariel rose and wandered along the hallway. Through the den's door she heard a clanking sound, metal against metal. David muttered something. She clasped the doorknob and twisted. The glare made her wince. David sat lotus-style with Gran's computer in front of him on its side. He had taken one of its panels off, exposing its guts. A stripe of dust lay across his left thigh. His flaccid penis rested on the heel of one foot.

He looked up. "Video fan."

"What are you doing?"

"Machine is old. Uses cards instead of modules. See that?"

Ariel leaned over and peered into the box. She recognized dust, but nothing else. The part David pointed at was a square green board with a large black block on it. He touched the edge of the board. "Video card. Little fan on it doesn't work. Why your computer crashes."

"You got up in the middle of the night for this?"

David picked himself up and stood before her. "I woke you?"

"No. I was awake." Ariel's gaze flickered down his body.

David followed her eyes. "Want to screw again?"

"Last of the romantics, you are."

She spent the last few hours of the night curled up in the leather chair. David went back to bed in Gran's room. The house felt as though it were towering over her, glaring down at her.

On cue the voice returned. *What do you do now, Ari? You were an utter shit to Gran when Mom and Dad died. Then you messed up with Corey. You've been a fuckup for almost a decade.*

But this, this is way beyond that. This is serious – lawyers-and-jail serious.

No, Ariel told herself. Call Katie today, get your mind off this stuff. Maybe you can get some perspective, figure out what to do next.

"Stuff"? Raping a retard is just "stuff" now?

David came out of the bedroom at eight o'clock. "Towel? Want to shower."

"Get a clean one from the linen closet. Outside the bathroom."

The bathroom door closed, followed by the hiss of the water. Ariel huddled in her chair, staring at the carpet. She could hear him moving, the scrape of his feet on the bottom of the tub.

David didn't believe in long showers. He appeared less than five minutes later. "Go for breakfast? Downtown."

"We aren't going for breakfast. I don't feel well."

David tilted his head and scrutinized her. "Simon is a doctor. Come to the house; he can look at you."

"Don't you have things to do? Is someone expecting you to show up and play chess at the library?"

"You sound funny."

Ariel put her hands between her knees and said nothing.

"Library opens at ten."

"I know when it opens. We'll go around nine. It'll take an hour to get down there, what with morning traffic and all."

"If you feel better later, we could have lunch at Ayutthaya."

"Maybe."

"I'll get a fan for your computer downtown."

"Whatever."

"Did your grandmother say that?"

"What? What did my grandmother say?"

"'Whatever.' Figure of speech in the 1980s. I read a book about English three and a half months ago."

An image flashed through her mind: in the kitchen, telling Gran she planned to visit Corey tonight. "Whatever, honey. Have a good time."

Have a good time. Gran knew what she and Corey were doing. Gran had insisted on the contraceptive ring in her butt cheek. Gran was broad-minded about sex.

How about rape, Ari? What would she think of that?

David sure as hell didn't look like a victim.

Oh, that makes it all better, doesn't it?

David knelt next to the chair and gazed at her.

Ariel wanted to push his face away. "What are you staring at?"

"Look like you want to cry."

"Don't be so goddamn nice to me. Don't . . . ."

Don't what? "Don't waste your time here, you'll only get screwed over like everyone else." Too late for the warning now.

Ariel heaved herself out of the chair. "Let's go. There's a cafe near the library."

"Getting dressed?"

"Of course I'm getting dressed."

Almost an hour later, Ariel stopped the car in a bus lane outside the library.

David turned his stare on her. "Call you later."

"Great." Ariel looked at her hands on the wheel, unable to meet his eyes. He pushed his door open and climbed out.

*****

Shattered clouds lay across the sky. Ariel drove to the cemetery. She parked along the curved street and stumbled out of the car. The path took her past the plots where she had met David. Two small stones now stood at the head of the empty graves.

MELANIE REED   STUART REED
LOVING AUNT   LOVING UNCLE
1976 – 2028   1974 – 2028

"Pathetic. He should have asked me."

He did. You couldn't be bothered.

David had said nothing about the gravestones since the visit to the tombstone shop on Main Street.

Why do you care? You didn't give a flying fuck about it for more than a month.

She reached Gran's grave and sat on the cool grass, her hands clasped in her lap. "Gran, I'm in trouble."

Somewhere below, Gran rotted away in peace.

The house was pissed off. Ariel felt it as soon as she stepped over the threshold. She struggled to ignore the movement of the walls as she made her way to the kitchen to retrieve two slices of leftover pizza from the fridge.

She carried her plate into the basement and on up the short staircase out to the garage. She ate curled up in her reeking nest of laundry.

Her phone rang. Ariel fumbled amid heaps of grimy clothing until she found where she had dropped it. David's number blinked on the screen. Ariel lay back, trembling, for several minutes – long enough for David to leave a message – then she thumbed the Messages tab and put the phone to her ear.

"Ariel. Hi. It's me. Guess you're busy. Call me when you're free. Good-bye."

"Maybe your lawyer can convince the judge you didn't know what he is," she said aloud.

Oh, that's brilliant. The prosecution will put Shay on the stand, and she will say David mentioned his eighty-six IQ points the first day you met.

The motion-sensitive light cut out. Sleep refused to come.

He didn't pop his cork, she told herself. *Maybe he'll forget about that night.*

But maybe he'll remember anyway. Maybe his buddy Simon will ask some question like, "What did you do last night?" And David will say, "Got screwed by Ariel."

Then someone with a badge will come to the door.

In the morning, body and mind numb, Ariel stumbled back to the living room and spread out on the carpet, a pillow against her cheek. By afternoon, the walls seemed to have stepped three paces inward, and Ariel fled back to the safety of the garage. David left messages. Katie left an invitation to Screwdriver's. The voice in her mind refused to shut the hell up.

You do this every time. First the colossal screw-up, then guilt that chews away your stomach. Maybe it's time to break the habit – except now it's too late. This is the one you don't bullshit your way through and then congratulate yourself for being smarter than everyone else.

In the evening she ran the bath, lowered herself until water covered her head and wondered how long it takes a person to pass out and drown. She came up gasping.

The third day followed the same track as the second. David left messages. "Hi, Ariel. Guess you're out. I'll call later."

When the doorbell rang on the afternoon of the fourth day, it came almost as a relief. Ariel lay trembling in the garage, the sound of the bell echoing through the house. A moment later it rang again.

The car is in the driveway. It's obvious you're home.

The weight of four days without sleep settled on her neck. Ariel wandered through the basement to the steps. The house waited quietly. Even the third ring of the doorbell didn't wake the house and bring its walls a step closer to her.

Ariel peered through the vertical panel of windows next to the door. David stood alone on the concrete slab of the step. "Shit."

He turned as though hearing the sound of her voice. Ariel flinched, then twisted the knob and tugged the door open.

She tried a smile. "Hey." Feeling like vomiting.

For a moment he stared at her, unblinking. Ariel couldn't meet his eyes.

David spoke. "Talked to Dr. Markson this morning. About us. Wants to meet you."

28

THE WORLD CANTED. ARIEL GRIPPED the edge of the door to hold herself up. "He sent you alone?"

"Didn't tell him I was coming for you."

Off to jail, she thought. "I have to get changed. You may as well come in and wait."

In her bedroom she rooted around in her dresser for something clean. This wasn't a day for a halter top and push-up bra – show up looking slutty and old Simon would call the cops without a second thought. She opted for jeans and a dark blue pullover with a thick turtleneck. When she sized herself up in the mirror above the dresser, she wondered what she would say to the doctor. "I didn't know" wouldn't cut it. Maybe his eyes would roll as he reached for the phone to call the police. The room swam around her.

David stood where she had left him. Did he even understand what was happening?

"Come on," she murmured. He followed her onto the step, and she deadbolted the door. Then she turned and thumbed her car's remote. The Duster's lights blinked and the locks popped.

"No," David said.

"What?"

"The house's parking lot is always full. Never find a spot. Worse than downtown. But the number 128 bus stops right outside it."

"Fine. Whatever." Ariel thumbed the remote again, then set off with David trailing behind her toward the Skytrain station.

Maybe I should have called Gran's lawyer, she thought. Maybe I should . . . .

Maybe you shouldn't have messed with him in the first place.

Minutes to walk up Royal Oak to the station, barely aware of David's footsteps. More minutes waiting for the westbound Skytrain to roll in.

The train ride gave her time to think – which was worse than driving. David sat beside her, toying with his damn phone. A chessboard lay across its screen. He dragged a pawn with his fingertip.

Her own phone sat on the dining table where she had left it days ago. Damn.

He called Carmen at the house, Ariel told herself, fingers digging into her knee. Carmen okayed him staying out all night. If this Dr. Markson clown gets pissy, I can always point that out.

Oh, that'll make a great excuse. "It's his own fault, Your Worship." And the judge will ask him what happened, and David will describe how you told him to . . . .

Then? "Ladies and gentlemen of the Jury, have you reached a verdict?" "We have, Your Worship, we think the bitch in the docket should be locked up with a couple of psychopaths for roommates, thank you very damn much."

"What did you tell Simon?"

"We screwed."

"Jesus. Did you put it like that?"

"Yes. Everyone at breakfast got really quiet."

The train shot past the stadium and down into the underground, squealing to a stop in Granville Station. When the doors slid open, David took her arm and led her into the crowd on the platform. Ariel wanted to scream. He guided her until she stepped onto the escalator with him and felt the metal stairs carry her upward.

On the street, a smell of fast food assaulted her. A middle-aged white man in a black business suit glanced her way. Ariel looked at her feet, imagining accusation burning in his eyes.

"Georgia Street." David pointed.

They walked half a block south and turned the corner.

"Fifteen minutes."

"What?"

"Have to wait fifteen minutes."

Ariel wiped her forehead with her sleeve and shivered. David stood expressionless, hands in the pockets of his burgundy jacket.

Too late to take it all back. You always want to change things after the fact, when you have no choice. Corey. Gran. Mom and Dad.

David nudged her. "The 128." The bus halted before them.

The route took them from downtown high-rises north into Stanley Park and up onto the mighty Lions Gate Bridge. Traffic crawled. Ariel sat near the window, peering down at the water. Along the shoreline lay the construction site where work on the new tunnel under Burrard Inlet had started. Maybe it would be finished by the time she got out of jail.

The bridge angled down and spit the bus out on the north shore. Minutes later, the vehicle lurched onto the shallow slope of West Fourth Avenue.

David pointed. "The clinic. There."

The bus rolled past a nondescript green tenement building. Balconies. White trim around the windows.

"Was there eleven months. In the Recovery floor. And five months before that in the Patients floor."

Ariel braced her legs against the seat in front of them and hunched down. David got the message. He shut up for the rest of the trip.

Several blocks later he reached over her to pull the cord. "We're here."

They stepped from the bus onto a sidewalk along a cute residential street. Well-tended houses lined each side. Mowed lawns. Plum and cherry trees in front yards. A sign saying "No parking" stood at the corner, an arrow pointing in the direction of a fire hydrant.

"Nowhere to park, huh?" Ariel muttered, waving at the empty street.

David motioned at the house across from them. "The halfway house. The lot is in back. Only four spaces. Always full."

"Whatever."

"The bus passes at ten after and twenty to. Going downtown."

You won't be leaving by bus, the voice said.

The halfway house had two stories and a tall peaked roof. A small square window in the peak faced the street. A wide staircase led up to a small patio overlooking a well-tended lawn. The house was yellowish white, the steps and railing dark chocolate. The steps creaked. Her legs refused to stop until she stood beside David on the deck. A screen door hung on old hinges. The wood inner door was open, and Ariel saw a hallway. David opened the screen door, stepped in, and held it behind himself for her. A din of conversation reached them.

"Forgive Carmen," David said. "She's experimenting with metaphors."

"What?"

He strode ahead without responding.

The hall opened into a living room. Two couches – white, old, and showing wear on their arms – faced a cheap round coffee table with a black metal top and struts on wheels beneath. A young woman with dark skin sat on the nearest couch; a good-looking young white man lay with his head in her lap. An older white woman, large and round, sat on the rug lotus-style, her face blank. An old boxy television in a wooden cabinet sat in a corner, its sound turned low, showing a movie she didn't recognize.

The conversation ceased. All eyes fixed on Ariel.

David must have told them all. Ariel wished her heart would explode and leave her dead on the carpet.

"Ariel!" a voice boomed, wrenching her attention across the room to where Switch stood beyond the couches. He pointed at her and bellowed: "That's David's girlfriend!"

The couple on the couch bolted to their feet and hustled to her. The large woman heaved herself up and joined them. Ariel felt like picking a corner of the room and cowering in it.

Switch lumbered toward her, a childish grin cutting his face in half.

David pointed at the young man from the couch. "This is Virgil. And Carmen." The woman who had sat with him. "And Maureen." The middle-aged woman.

Switch leaned close to Ariel. "You okay? You look funny."

"You look like you shit your pants and now you hope no one will notice," Carmen offered.

A shriek came from beyond the couches, and a woman in white tore through the room.

"Carmen, be quiet!" The woman came to a panting halt in front of Ariel.

"But she does. She's carrying shopping bags under those eyes."

"Enough!" The woman turned to Ariel. "I'm terribly sorry. These people never know when to stop. We're trying to teach them, but for some – " Glaring at Carmen. " – it's one step forward and two back. I'm Dagmar Watts. It's a pleasure to meet you."

Ariel tried saying a dozen things and settled on, "Yeah."

"Where is Simon?" David asked.

Switch grunted. "Downstairs. I'll get him." The corridor echoed with the sounds of the huge man's footfalls. Ariel swallowed, aware of the pounding of her heart.

Dagmar poked David's shoulder, smiling. "You could have warned us you were bringing a guest."

Huh? Ariel thought.

The woman turned back to her and frowned. "Um. I won't put it as crudely as Carmen did, but are you all right, dear? You look like you've been through something dreadful."

Ariel's throat felt as though it were filling with cement. "I'm fine. Thanks. Really." David hovered behind her. She sensed his gaze boring into the back of her skull.

Switch's tread echoed in the hallway. In that direction Ariel saw a green railing replacing a section of wall, and a flight of steps down to a basement. A skinny man with gray hair followed Switch up.

The man spoke with an accent. "Ariel Morrissey, I presume?" Irish or Scottish, Ariel guessed. He shoved his hand at her. "I'm Dr. Markson. Call me Simon – that's an order." Eyes brimming with warmth. "We're very informal here."

"Informal" didn't begin to describe the man. He wore frayed khaki shorts and an orange T-shirt with *Manchester U* in large letters across it. His hair needed garden maintenance. Darker stubble encircled his mouth. His feet were tucked into leather sandals which looked like they'd been handed down from the Bronze Age.

Revelation coursed across Ariel's brain: David hasn't told them anything.

But no, he must have. He didn't have enough brains to lie.

Ariel shook the man's hand.

"Talk to Ariel alone," David said. "Dagmar's computer doesn't work. I can fix it now."

Dagmar shook her head. "Oh, don't worry about that. You have a guest."

"Simon likes talking to visitors." David's gaze shifted to the doctor. "Show her around?"

Markson nodded. "That's an excellent idea." Smiling at Ariel. "Do you mind if David disappears for a bit?"

"Yes. I – No. Fine."

"Good."

"Simon, you moved yet?"

Simon Markson's eyes gleamed. "Oh, hell. I'm still pondering that bishop you put in the way of my rook. I could take it, but that's rather obvious. You're up to something, I can feel it."

"Bishop's not the problem. Look at my queen." With that, David turned to the stairwell, Dagmar following. Switch stood grinning like a fool.

Markson gave him a patronizing look. "You can find something else to do, can't you?"

"Sure." The huge man clumped away.

The doctor grinned. "You likely know David has become quite obsessed with chess. He has roped everyone into a game at least once. Right now he has six ongoing: one with me, another with Switch, and four more with a rolling roster of players." Pushing the door next to them open, Simon added,

"David mentioned you this morning. I didn't know he meant to bring you here today."

Nothing had gone according to expectations. Jesus, Ariel thought, giddy with relief.

"David said he told you about us and you asked to see me."

Markson laughed, a rich pleasant baritone. They stepped into the room that served as his office. "That isn't quite what happened. He brought you up in conversation and asked if we would like to meet you. I said, 'Yes, we'd love to.'" Dimples marked his cheeks. "I must say you impress me. Survivors of Saint Bennie have difficulty making friends. One of the hardest things to do is to learn how to relate to normals. David has done better than most. I keep telling him he is ready to strike out on his own." The doctor shrugged. "He insists he isn't. I'm not entirely certain why."

"Um, Saint Bennie?"

"Bennie – or Benjamina – Shimmerman was the first documented case of Shimmerman's Disease. Hence its name."

"Oh. Right. I knew that."

Ariel looked around. Two loveseat-style couches faced a coffee table identical to that in the living room. Books overflowed three bookcases. Under a row of windows sat a long narrow table with a row of six chessboards.

Markson followed Ariel's gaze. "David's, of course. Come look." He led her to the table and pointed at the first of the boards. "This is my weekly humiliation. Perhaps with your help I can survive past the twenty-move mark."

"I don't play. I mean, my Dad taught me years ago, but I don't remember now."

"David will change that – or drive you mad. Let me see if I can put the slaughter off a bit longer and *oh, bloody hell!*"

Ariel recoiled.

Markson laughed and reached for a white bishop, moving it across the board. "He's boxed me in. Queen, knight, pawn. I can't move my king. Alas, the end is nigh. Shall we talk?" He gestured at the small couches. "May I call you Ariel?"

"Sure. I guess."

"Ariel, are you ill? You look exhausted."

"I'm fine. I just haven't slept very well lately." Ariel moved to the couches, chose the one facing the door. "Uh, what has David told you about me?"

Markson sank into the couch opposite. He stroked the stubble around his mouth. "You lost your grandmother several months ago. I'm sorry."

"Yeah. Thanks."

"And he mentioned that you've taken him to visit friends. I must say, that's wonderful for him. He's quite taken with you."

"Sure." I've treated him like dirt, raped him four nights ago, and he has a crush on me. Great.

A warm grin spread across Markson's face. "I think I must apologize for him. He mentioned that you and he have become, shall we say, intimate. Believe me, that was a conversation stopper at the breakfast table."

Time ground to a halt.

The doctor leaned forward. "Please don't be upset. Survivors of the illness don't understand tact, I'm afraid. So please – " His mouth fell open. "Oh. Oh, my Lord. I see."

Markson rose and strode to the door. Ariel stared at his back. Her right leg began to shake. Markson pushed the door shut, then wiped his hands on his shorts and made his way back to the couch.

"You said you hadn't slept in days." The doctor seated himself on the armrest. "Is this the reason why?" Markson shook his head, cutting her off before she could babble a response. "I understand, believe me. I can't condone the fact that you and David were clearly unprotected, but I think I can set your mind at ease. First, there is no chance you're pregnant. Of course human physiology makes it somewhat harder for a woman in that situation to notice that a man is protected than vice versa, but if you see David from behind . . . . Well. I implanted his ring myself. As for disease, David has been inoculated against all the major HIV and hepatitis strains found in North America. Ariel, you could do far worse than to become romantically involved with a survivor of Saint Bennie."

"Ro – we're not – I mean . . . ." Ariel wanted to cry and laugh. "It isn't a problem then? Us?"

"Of course not. Why would it be?"

Ariel drew a long breath. The pressure on her chest lifted. "Well, David – he's not the brightest lighthouse in the bay."

The doctor's smile vanished. "I have no idea what do you mean."

"Um. He told me about his . . . ." Ariel tapped her forehead.

His eyebrows rose and fell. Maybe Doc Simon couldn't rub two brain cells together either.

"David has an IQ of eighty-six."

Markson drew back in amazement. "Whatever gave you such a ridiculous idea?"

29

"RIDICULOUS? WHY IS IT RIDICULOUS?" Ariel stammered. Her voice came out with an embarrassing nasal whine. "David said so."

Markson rubbed his stubble-covered chin. "Now why on Earth would he do that?"

"He said you started testing him two weeks after he woke up in the clinic. My friend Shay asked him how he did. He said eighty-six."

Markson held up his palms, grinning. "I think I understand. David answered the question you asked, not the one you thought you asked. He probably did score eighty-six on his first intelligence exams. But a patient just waking up after the phase-four coma can barely speak or walk. It's astonishing he managed even that."

"So he's not . . . ." Ariel's voice trailed off. The floor felt as though it were tilting beneath her.

"I must say, it's incredible that you could believe he was so limited, considering how much he reads, and his hobbies. He's been keeping our donated computers running with paper clips and duct tape for more than a year."

"I thought he was a savant."

"Oh, no. Shimmerman's Disease recovery involves adaptation to lack of memory. The brain itself isn't damaged. We do know their brains function in fundamentally different ways from those of normals, but they aren't mentally challenged. David's intelligence averages something like 171. We have students from UBC administer tests regularly, but I don't pay much attention to the results. The numbers are purely for research."

The doctor, she thought, could probably hear the thumping of her heart. "David is a genius."

"Absolutely not. Genius doesn't begin until 175 on our scale."

"He's four points short."

Markson rubbed his hands, holding his fingers together as though in prayer. "Ariel. I must tell you, I find it disturbing to learn you became involved with David believing he was mentally impaired."

Blood leached out of Ariel's face. "He . . . ." He tricked me. He has played me for almost a week.

But why would he do that?

Ariel pictured him beneath her, his cock jutting up inside her.

Why else? she thought. He's a *guy*.

Markson waited. Ariel's gaze skipped away from him. He sighed. "Well then. That's between you and David. I want to show you something." The doctor rose and motioned her to the chessboards on the table beneath the window. "This is as close to savantism that David and his ilk become."

"What, chess?"

"Not the game." Markson picked up the white bishop from the first board, then laid his arm across the board and swept the remaining pieces off in a clatter. Ariel blinked. Markson placed the bishop back on the dark wood square where it had stood before. "That was my move."

"Uh . . . ."

"Give me a moment." The doctor moved to the next board and repeated the process, plowing the chessmen off onto the table. He cleared each; then with a wink, he strode to the door. In the hallway he called out, "David, could you come up, please?"

David came bounding up the steps in response. Markson beckoned him into the room. "I moved, but I'm afraid we had a bit of an accident."

David had gotten rid of his jacket. He wore black jeans and a pale gray T-shirt. Ariel tried glaring at him, but his gaze fixed itself on the table. He placed his palms on his hips and moved to it, blocking her view of the first two chessboards.

Welcome anger crept along Ariel's spine. She had always pictured it as a wolf spider climbing her back, scrabbling up her skin until it reached the base of her scalp to fill her brain with venom.

"Checkmate in three," David said, to a clicking sound of wood touching wood.

Markson smiled. "My, I didn't think I was doing that well."

"Not you." David picked up a black pawn. Ariel heard another sound of wood on wood as he set the pawn down.

The spider stopped climbing her spine. Ariel stepped beside him and stared at the board. Seven chessmen. David picked up a white rook and set it on the board. Eight. Ten. Thirteen – the queen in the middle. Fourteen. The last were the kings, all returned to where the had been before Markson swept the board clear.

David moved to the next and picked up a pawn, placing it on a white square. When the pawns were in place, click click, he moved on to knights, then bishops, then rooks. Then queens and kings. Nineteen pieces this time. To the third board. Twenty-eight pieces. And the fourth board: sixteen. The fifth: twenty-seven. The sixth: nine.

Unsmiling, David turned to the doctor. "Knight takes queen. Watch your own knights now."

Markson looked at the first board. "Damn."

"I'm still busy downstairs." David turned to Ariel. "Join me. When you're free." Before she could clutch his arm, he was past her.

Markson cleared his throat, looking like a parent who had just watched his brat nail the ball over the outfield fence. "When Shimmerman's Disease appeared, we were certain those like David would never leave institutions. Without memory, how could they live? They don't have a mental library to call on, the way we do." He motioned at the chessboards, his face a maze of laugh lines. "But they adapt. While they have lost memory, the brain remains intact. David will tell you he doesn't recall where the chess pieces go. Instead he visualizes the shape of each game. It's like knowing how to find your way home. You don't remember a particular route, but you have an understanding of where your home is relative to the countryside. You can find it even by walking a route you have never taken before."

"Great," Ariel murmured.

"The brain is a pattern-recognition system. Without memory, it has no set of records to depend upon, so it starts piecing patterns together, looking for meaning, striving for understanding."

"I need to see David."

A sad look passed over Markson's face. "Ariel, I hope you understand, he is a remarkable young man. You are fortunate to know him."

Ariel glanced back at the chessboards. "Well. I'm glad we talked." The fury spider began to move again.

By the time she reached the bottom of the narrow staircase the muscles along her shoulders had grown hard. Anger boiled, bringing welcome heat. Over the years she had cultivated two types of rage: the sharp, shoot-from-the-hip type she had turned on David more than once when he said something that dug into her; and another kind she didn't use often, the kind where she knew the clash was coming and worked out in advance the words to be swung like a whip. Once, Corey refused to speak to her for days because she had said something in the middle of a fight. She couldn't remember the words, but that crumpled look on his face made it worthwhile.

No one plays me like a fiddle, she told herself.

The basement looked like an office. Three old desks, the kind made of veneer and chipboard, sat in the middle of the room, positioned to form a square with one side missing. On each sat a computer, old box types like hers. One of the machines lay open, and David's hands worked within. Carmen stood beside him, peering in. Maureen sat before the computer on the left, and Virgil hunched over the third machine.

Ariel's rage reminded her of an all-night study session before her biology midterm at the university. She'd emptied a bag of chocolate-coated espresso beans down her throat and used a box of powdered mini donuts for a chaser; she'd been so wired that she couldn't sleep, had walked into the exam in the morning vibrating. Had squeaked through with adrenaline and caffeine fighting like rabid dogs in her backbrain.

Maureen lifted her gaze from the screen before her and stared at Ariel. Ariel almost gasped at the look on the woman's face – no, the sheer absence of anything that could be called a look. An instant before, the woman looked alive. The moment her eyes met Ariel's, her face drained. Carmen glanced at Ariel, then straightened and stood still as a mannequin. Her face echoed the void of expression on Maureen's. Virgil leaned back in his chair and looked at her also, eyes dead as a corpse.

Welcome to the home of the Pod People, Ariel thought.

David looked at her then, his face empty.

Ariel put on her warmest smile. "Can we go somewhere and talk? In private?"

"No," David said.

The word jolted. Ariel opened her mouth to respond and caught the halogen glare of three pairs of strangers' eyes.

David sounded like he was reading a script. "You're trying to convince yourself that your four days of stewing in your own guilt are my fault. But if you had been right about me, if I were as stupid as you thought, then you would be guilty of something dreadful. Something you couldn't live with.

"You believed I was slow; you were comfortable with me then. You liked believing it. But your actions were based on your own choices. If I had been sitting in a wheelchair when we met and you pushed me down the Granville Station escalator, seeing me jump to my feet and save myself wouldn't make what you chose to do okay. You met me in a cemetery standing before two fresh graves and you joked about it. You destroyed what you had with Corey because doing that amused you. And when you got a chance to set things right at the bookstore, you chose to attack him instead. You even hurt Gran because you thought you'd feel better after what happened with your mom and dad."

Ariel's heart tore at her chest. *"How dare – "*

"How dare I judge you? I'm not. You are. I haven't said anything you haven't told yourself. Now leave. The bus arrives in ten minutes." David switched his attention back to the open box, ignoring her as though she had ceased to be.

Ariel shook, impotent in her fury, hunting for something to say. The others gazed at her, eyes empty – or seeing through her, like David. Sweat beaded on her forehead, running into her eyes like someone else's tears. She turned to the stairwell.

The sun glared brighter than she remembered. Six-thirty approached. A bench with a blue BUS STOP sign on a metal post marked the stop. She leaned against the pole, drawing shallow breaths. An Asian couple walked toward her. They stopped and sat on the bench to wait.

Ariel imagined David wilting before her, crumbling the way Corey had. The way Gran had when news of the crash came and Ariel had sat on the couch glaring at her as the old woman said her parents weren't coming back.

How had David known about Gran? And Mom and Dad?

Maybe Katie was free tonight. Ariel reached for her phone in her jacket pocket, and remembered it sitting on the dining table at home. The bus crested the hill. An overweight white man in a blue track suit came puffing across the street in front of the bus and staggered to the bench. A door slammed behind her, barely registering in her thoughts as the bus squealed its brakes. She joined the boarding procession, stepped up onto the platform, flashed her student pass at the driver, made her way down the aisle to an empty seat. She dropped into it and braced her knees against the seat in front. The bus rolled forward. Ariel ran her fingers through her hair. When she felt a tangled knot, she tugged at it until it came painfully free. Then she took in the faces around her: the Asian couple, two old black women, the fat guy. And David.

The significance of the sound of a door slamming behind her at the bus stop boiled into her thoughts. He sat across from her, his phone on his knee, the little finger on his right hand dragging something across its screen.

What are you doing here, Idiot Guy?

Ariel watched the trees along the avenue roll past. The bus crossed the boundary between North and West Vancouver, then slowed and stopped to pick up half a dozen giggling teenage girls. Ariel's fingers quivered. David was like a fart in an elevator; he just wouldn't go away.

The bus reached the series of on-ramps pruning five lanes of north-shore traffic into two on the Lions Gate Bridge. The waters of the Burrard Inlet were blue and dead calm. A tugboat crawled toward her on its way to open water. The intangible spider clung to her back, just between her shoulder blades, ready to latch itself onto the base of her skull. She tried glaring at David, but his gaze refused to leave his phone.

Asshole.

The bus rolled through Stanley Park into downtown. When it reached the Georgia Street stop, David strode to the midpoint of the bus and out the folding doors. Ariel joined the procession of passengers and followed. As soon as she reached the street she glanced right and left. David was gone.

Relieved, she set off to the corner, veered right, and walked to the broad steps down to the Granville Street Skytrain station.

The escalator. Imagining David sitting in a wheelchair at its top, her foot shoving him down. Then David next to her bed, her fingers hooked into the waist of his pants . . . .

Too many people passed her. The sounds of overlapping conversations bore down on her like a weight. She reached the platform, tugged her pullover lower around her hips, pulled the sleeves over her hands. The train arrived in minutes. Half an hour to home. She dropped herself into a blue seat facing forward. The train played its familiar three-tone arpeggio, and a figure darted through the doorway ahead of her as the doors slid shut.

David. He dropped his ass into a seat and tugged his phone from his jacket pocket.

The train shook.

Do I have a stalker now? she wondered, fingers clenching the bar on the seat ahead of her. Sure, I screwed you and felt like hell afterward. But you should count yourself lucky someone spread her legs for you, you pathetic brain-dead bastard.

The spider climbed a little higher, and stopped. How did he know about Mom and Dad?

He seemed unaware of her, intent on his phone. She tried pushing him out of her thoughts, turning her eyes to the windows – only to see his reflection in the glass.

The spider slipped down to the middle of her spine.

Ariel couldn't remember the last time her rage had just burned itself out. Once, she had carried it home from school after a fight with someone she couldn't remember. The moment she was home, she tossed her jacket on the floor and picked up the green vase Gran had bought at a yard sale, flinging it and watching it explode against the wall.

But here, fury had nowhere to go. She sank down in her seat and stared at her lap.

The spider lost its footing. Fell.

He's right about you. The thought exploded fully formed into consciousness. And the walls and windows and seats of the train began to breathe around her.

30

ARIEL GASPED. NO, HE CAN'T be right. He doesn't even know me.

The train slowed into Broadway station. Six stops to go. Too many; the train shrank until she couldn't fit in her seat, too close to butting her head against the ceiling. Then it sucked in a breath and swelled around her, and the heat of its brutal exhalation made her choke.

Mom and Dad in the kitchen. "This is your own damn fault, Lance, and you know it."

"Don't dump this on me. Let's take this outside, no need for Ari to listen in."

"Fine."

Don't think about that, think about David. He had no business telling me I've been vicious to him. If he has no sense of humour, that's not my problem.

Humour, dumbass? You met him in a cemetery and you joked *about his aunt and uncle getting ripe. Bet you would have loved to hear old what's-his-name at Gran's funeral mumble, "You must be glad the old bitch is rotting in that box now."*

It's not the same. I thought David was slow; he wouldn't have got it.

Ariel straightened and thumped her palms against her temples until pain dialed back the volume of the voice.

If you want to argue that point, how do you justify fucking his brains out? You used him because *you believed he had a dim bulb. You wouldn't have given him the time of day if you'd thought he was halfway intelligent.*

The train rolled into Patterson station. Two to go. Ariel fixed her gaze on the red lights along the elevated rail and began to count them. *One, two, three . . . four, five . . . .*

The voice in her mind laughed. *Not enjoying this? Rather not think about it? That makes sense. Nothing's ever your fault. You're an angel, baby.*

Oh, but wait – Mom and Dad are dead dead dead. Remember the airport when they left?

Her stomach lurched.

Ari is eleven, standing with Gran in YVR, watching Mom and Dad stride toward the security gates. She wipes Mom's kiss from her left cheek, shoves her fist back into her pocket.

Dad calls the airport "YVR"; he picked it up from the website where he booked the tickets to Athens.

Gran waves. Ari looks at the checkerboard floor.

"I hope they never come back," she says.

"You don't mean that, dear."

"Yes, I do." She is eleven.

Gran is silent during the drive home.

The video skips, and Ari is in the living room channel-surfing, remembering the call from Greece the night before. Mom and Dad sharing a phone in their hotel room.

Ari remembers Mom's voice. Like warm butterscotch for the first time in years. No longer like breaking rocks.

The bell rings and Gran opens the door. Ari sees her back, hears the whispers, sees Gran kind of slump against the doorframe. Gran closes the door and turns to Ari, face gray like ashes.

Ari remembers the words she said at the airport.

She wiped her eyes with her knuckles. The Skytrain had vomited her out into Royal Oak station. She ran across the avenue past the little convenience store. The voice taunted her. She fled past the church, past a lawn sign declaring "Yard Sale." There: Watling Street. She turned the corner. A black fringe grew at the edges of her vision. Finally, thank God, the house.

The house knew all of it – but the door to the house would let her through to the garage, and safety. At the top of the steps she fumbled for her keys. They slipped from shaking fingers.

Someone caught them and flung them up between himself and her. They rose, cartwheeling. At eye level they stopped, and for an instant she stared into David's eyes through sparkling steel and brass. His fingers shot in among the keys, caught steel for the deadbolt, brought it down and jammed it into the lock. The bolt thumped back. He pushed the door open and stepped clear.

Ariel scrambled ahead of him. Where did he come from? Oh yes, the bus. The train. Both.

Welcome wrath blazed to life again. A thought scudded across her mind: A single word and I'll rip you a new one.

Silence. For a moment she thought she had imagined him. Then the door closed. When she turned, he unzipped his jacket and let it fall. The house held its breath as though waiting for the explosion.

One word. Just one word, asshole.

David couldn't do a good goddamn thing right. He stood staring at her unblinking, like a cat.

"Say something!" Ariel bellowed, and her voice played back in her ears in an instant: no hint of welcome rage. Instead, the cold keen edge of panic.

She pounced, fingers like claws going for his eyes. At that moment David stepped toward her, closing the distance between them faster than she expected. He swung his arms around her, held her against him.

"What are you doing?" she screamed, and fought to pull away. He followed her until the dining table pressed against her back.

Ariel dug her nails into his shoulders, then clenched her fists and pounded him. "Let me go, let me go – "

Then an abrupt sense of wrongness, something about the press of his body to hers. It slammed against consciousness like a punch: he wasn't gripping her, refusing to let her go; his hands ran along her spine, down to her waist, and he held her as he would if they were dancing: gently, without force. The revelation led to a second: in spite of her beating on his back and raking his skin, it was she who held him, clutching at him as though she were drowning.

Clarity fractured and broke. Later she remembered a sound, like someone being strangled, then released to draw breath, then strangled again. Endlessly. And she remembered David wore a light gray T-shirt, except for one shoulder which grew dark and wet against her cheek. And later still she remembered thinking, when he led her to Gran's bedroom and lifted her sweater off, that whatever he wanted to do with her now wouldn't be undeserved.

He unhooked the front of her bra, and knelt. Her body quaked. He settled his hands on her hips and somehow his touch was enough to settle her heaving belly. He unzipped her fly and slipped her pants down her legs, bringing her panties with them.

He could use her however he saw fit, and if it hurt, even better. If it tore her up inside, it couldn't be as awful as the agony searing the skin of her mind.

He pulled the blankets back and held them for her, and she tumbled naked into bed.

"Sleep," he said.

The ceiling light died. The bedroom door whispered shut. And she found herself alone with her thoughts. Not what she expected.

Worse. Much worse.

~

It is the boy's first day at school. He takes a desk at the back of the room, where he can watch the others. Kids. He is different. But it's important to keep the differences secret.

He knows how to keep secrets. These kids are wimps. Chattering away like animals. Not real people. Not like Auntie. And Uncle.

These kids don't matter.

~

Autumn 2051

"The worst of it was yesterday."

31

Ariel was glad Dr. Olver opted for silence during the drive to the hospital. It gave her time for memories of her breakdown to wash through. She winced as she remembered huddling in her nest in the garage, David standing over her, silhouetted in the doorway like some kind of horror movie demon.

Think about something else, she ordered herself. Any of the hundreds of tiny, funny, stupid little moments with David. After all these years, the rest of the world had become an in-joke. A stranger's remark about the weather could trip thoughts of that time, before Elizabeth was born, when they had camped in the mountains beyond North Vancouver. The first day, still near the city, they had made love in a coppice off the trail – only to be accosted by somebody's German Shepherd out for an afternoon stroll. Ariel had shoved her fingers into her mouth to keep from howling with laughter. "Get back here, Barto, you stupid animal!" its owner bellowed. Unfazed, David hadn't even withdrawn from her when the dog found them and started yelping. If the man had followed and discovered two naked strangers amid the maple leaves, even the dog would have been more embarrassed than David.

That is all you really have with someone, she thought. A thousand moments, strung together like beads on a necklace.

Ariel watched Dr. Olver smooth her pants, then squeeze and release her knees. What would David make of that? He would glean significance from it, piece together subtle cues from the way her smile quirked to the left, to how she rubbed her right shoulder partway through a conversation, to the way she clutched the cloth above her left breast.

When did I start noticing that kind of thing? Ariel wondered. I must have been doing it for years, absorbing David's way of seeing.

The car rolled into a parking spot. Ariel shoved her door open. The doctor climbed from the car with a tense gracelessness.

"Nervous?" Ariel asked.

A strange look sketched itself across Dr. Olver's face and vanished. "I haven't seen David in twenty years."

"He turned out well. We are . . . ." The sentence refused to complete itself.

What happens now? Ariel thought, leaning on the car door. An institution? Weekend visits with a raving lunatic, or a shell of a man drugged into a stupor to keep him from hurting himself or burning the place down?

Dr. Olver looked at her. Ariel grimaced, certain the expression looked ghastly. "You'll be more useful to David than the psych nurse."

"My training never included psychiatry."

Ariel tossed her phone onto the car seat and slammed the door. "You knew him. And you've dealt with Shimmerman's cases before. Ezekiel is a dead loss on that front."

In the hospital, the elevator slid open on the seventh floor. Ariel led the doctor to the counter where the nurse named Jean sat.

"We need to see the psychiatric nurse on duty," Ariel said.

Jean glanced from her to the doctor. "Mr. Crane is upstairs at the moment."

"I thought he didn't work Saturdays."

The nurse's gaze flickered away to the corridor and back, tension cutting creases into her forehead. "We had a problem with a patient last night."

Ariel's voice cracked. "David?"

"Oh no, your husband is fine. I'll page Nurse Crane. You can wait for him in the room at the end of the hall."

Ariel shoved her hands in the pockets of her coat and nodded. Dr. Olver followed along the corridor. The old man who talked to himself had a quiet conversation going. Farther on, the room where the girl with the bandage on her neck had slept was stripped of its bed and chair. A mopper rolled back and forth, wet cloth sweepers spinning against the tiles. In the clear plastic bucket on the machine's side, amid the soap suds, the water had a reddish hue. An ammonia stench wafted out the doorway.

This was the room the nurse glanced at, Ariel realized, hastening on. The sitting room had drab off-white tables and chairs. She sat. Dr. Olver lowered herself into a chair opposite; her fingers tugged at the cloth above her breasts.

*****

Synthetic leather gripped David's wrists, ankles, and chest. A heavy gray blanket covered him. When he lifted his head from the foam pillow, the white room spun and the walls caved in toward him. His right shoulder ached. He remembered Ariel crouching next to him, holding him.

Aunt Melanie sat on the edge of the bed, fingers on his cheek.

You're gone, dead when I was fifteen, he told her. My son's name is Warren. My daughter is called Elizabeth.

His nose itched. He reached to scratch it, felt straps on his wrists, remembered the restraints. What did you do to get locked in here? he wondered. Punching Ariel in the mouth got you a suite in the psych ward; what did it take to earn this rubberized box?

Oh, God – what did you do?

"Hey, layabout. Couldn't you find something better to do with your time than go batty?" Ariel, her left eye swollen. Her jaw hung slack, as though the bones within were shattered, held together by skin alone. She lifted one leg over him and straddled his ankles. "We should do this more often. I like having you tied down." Her fingers ran across his chest, made a circle around his belly button, continued down until her hand wrapped around his erection.

"Zeke will complain," David breathed.

Ariel's left eye blinked in its bloodied and ruined socket. "Shh." She lowered her mouth to him. Her tongue played along the underside of his penis. Where had the blanket gone?

"Take your time," a thick deep voice said. David twisted his head sideways to gaze at Uncle Stuart. The old man grinned. "That's it, Ari. Slow and steady."

David's belly tightened. "This isn't real," he said aloud, shutting his eyes, squeezing his fists until his arms trembled. He wanted to scream when the door swung open, wrenching him back to himself.

Zeke and the big intern strode in. "Good morning." The psychiatric nurse glared, then his gaze scuttered away.

David plucked a memory out and held it in his thoughts. "Lake. She is all right?"

Zeke's eyes flared, eyelids tight with . . . fear?

"Alive," David said. "But you did nothing to stop her."

Zeke rounded on the other man. "Who has been talking to him?"

David looked the man over, peering at the name tag clipped to his breast pocket. Randy McAllister. Randy's face looked set in stone but for a brief curling of his lip.

"You." David locked eyes with the intern. "You did something. What?"

The man regarded him with surprised awe. "I talked to the night staff. They said they'd watch her."

David leaned back, aware he had been straining against the straps.

Zeke's anger was palpable. David imagined a crimson corona about his head. The psych nurse sat stiffly on the side of the bed. "She told you what she'd planned. For God's sake why – "

"Didn't tell me. I saw it." The starfish Shape filled his thoughts, twitching when he recalled how the girl had closed in upon herself when her father said he would be away. "How did she do it?"

The psychiatric nurse scrutinized him, unblinking. David met his eyes and waited, knowing what to expect. At last Zeke shrugged, disregarding the matter for the moment. "Well. Let's talk about you, David. How do you feel this morning?"

"Need to go to the bathroom."

Zeke glanced at Randy, then worked the strap across David's chest, loosening the buckle. David noticed a shift in shadows from the open door where at least two more staff stood outside. A shuffling of feet.

The straps free, David sat up cautiously, rubbing his wrists. "How did she do it?"

"That isn't any – "

"How?"

A look passed again between Zeke and the intern. Randy spoke up. "She bit her wrist. The duty nurse on graveyard said she laid it under her blankets in bed. She must have thought she would bleed out before anyone noticed."

Blood. Agony. The images fed into the Shape. It thrummed with anguish, keeping his own chaos at bay. "Where is she now?"

Randy motioned with his chin at the wall. "She's your neighbour."

"Didn't need intensive care?"

"It wasn't a bad cut. She's in restraints."

"Violent with the night crew?"

"Uh, no."

"Drugged now?"

"It should wear off in a few hours."

"Wait a minute," Zeke said brusquely. "David, we're discussing you."

"Put her back in her room."

The psych nurse's eyes widened. "She belongs up here until she stabilizes."

"Back in her room," David breathed. Auntie Mel and Uncle Stu crouched near the wall, speaking in whispers. Fire grew around them. Flame blackened the wall. Still they huddled together, cupping their hands and whispering in each other's ears, their words lost in the crackling and spitting of the flames.

Zeke's voice dragged him back. "David?"

Lake, David thought. Focus on her. Desperate to die? No: desperate for control, for power over her own life – choosing when it ends, not waiting for inevitability.

The revelation fed the Shape, driving the images of Ariel and Auntie and Uncle back against the walls of his mind, pinning them there.

"Move her to her room now. You screwed up once; don't do it again."

Randy and a pair of equally large female nurses led him to a washroom down the corridor. The women stood outside while Randy discreetly faced the wall and let him pee. They led him back to his padded room.

The straps had vanished, tucked into compartments in the walls. David peered, looking for the outlines. He found them, each shaped like a letter U, like a backyard swing, like the swing seat Uncle had assembled on a steel frame. It had a green canopy. Chains held the long seat, big enough for two with a back made of metal struts and strips of thick cloth like canvas. Uncle Stu liked to read out there; Aunt Mel used to send David out to collect the books the old man had left behind. David felt certain he had written about the swing in his journals.

A memory. Images, smells, sensations joined together and formed a solid whole. David leaned against the padded wall and let the film of his early life roll through him. Uncle and Auntie, out on the seat. Auntie's laugh filled the air like a song.

The sound of the door opening tore him from his thoughts. David turned. Jean, one of the nurses, stood with a breakfast tray in her hands. Behind her stood Randy, arms crossed.

Rage blossomed as his mind clutched at the vision. "What makes you special?"

The nurse set the tray down on the cot. "Excuse me, Mr. Glass?"

"The interns knock. Even Zeke knocks. What makes you so goddamn special?"

32

ARIEL HEARD A THROAT CLEAR in the corridor. Zeke stood in the doorway looking as though someone had booted his gonads up past his tonsils – not her problem, unless David had done the kicking.

"This is Jacklyn Olver," she said. "The doctor I mentioned."

The psych nurse almost snapped to attention at the word "doctor." "Yes. Good. I meant to contact you next week."

"I wanted to see David sooner than that. I'm only here for a few more days." Jackie rose and shook his hand.

Zeke's voice brimmed with forced authority. "You knew David during the primary phases of the illness?"

"He was in my care for five months."

"I'm glad you're here then." Zeke's posture said he was anything but happy. "We can use your help. He's a fascinating case."

My husband is a "case," Ariel thought.

Ezekiel glanced at Ariel as though assessing her presence here, looking for a graceful way to tell her to leave. Dr. Olver didn't give him a choice. She sat once more, motioned at the chair beside her, and launched into a description of what she had told Ariel. Ariel's mind refused to focus on their voices. Her gaze circulated the room, absorbing tables, tall windows, the counter with its white cupboards, the odour of lemon.

"You allowed him to forge his own past," the psych nurse interrupted Jackie. His back stiffened, as if he expected a fight.

Jackie squirmed, then shrugged and met Zeke's gaze. "That was his choice. At the time we didn't think a Shimmerman's victim's memories could be recovered. There was no down side. Not then."

"But now we do have to deal with it." Zeke subtly emphasized 'we'. Jackie's mouth quirked. She ignored Zeke's gibe and instead dived into describing David at the clinic.

"He spent most of his time in isolation when he reached phase two. He remembered some events vividly. That was the most hazardous stage, since acting out was common."

She isn't talking about David, Ariel told herself. She is talking about Ezekiel's fascinating case. Not my husband.

Katie has gone through four husbands, two fiances, and countless boyfriends. David and I got it right the first time. What the hell did we do?

"We have him in isolation right now," Zeke was saying. "He has recently begun to show signs of obsession with another patient."

Ariel's mind reeled back into the conversation. "What patient?"

Zeke glanced at her. "You've probably seen her. David has spent time with the young woman. If he has been sexually molested as a child, he may find aspects of his childhood – "

"My husband is not going to molest one of your patients."

Zeke put on a grim smile. "My patient is fifteen years old. Your daughter is that age, isn't she?"

A need to break the man's nose with the palm of her hand thrust itself through her, until an effort of will drove it down. "I want to see him."

"At the moment David is volatile – "

"I brought him out of it last time. I can do it again." The bluster sounded false to her own ears.

Zeke leaned back and shook his head.

"Do you have a video feed in his room?" Jackie said.

"This is a modern facility. We've been recording him since he was taken up there."

"Then it will be helpful if we can watch Ms. Morrissey interact with him."

Ariel saw a hint of uncertainty in Zeke's narrowing eyes. The psych nurse wasn't used to saying no to a doctor.

Jackie continued as though Zeke had already agreed. "Whatever you do," turning to Ariel, "I recommend you don't tell him I'm here. I think that's what set him off yesterday."

The elevator doors slid apart. "Normally we don't have visitors up here," Zeke said dryly. "You can understand why."

Ariel chewed on her knuckles, wishing she could choke him.

A station made up of a half-circle desk harboured a female nurse. The marine-sergeant intern leaned on the desk, straightening when he saw Zeke. The walls here were gray, not the pale green of the floor below. No pretence of warmth to comfort the sick. This place held the hardcore crazies, the people so far from reality that they didn't care whether the place felt like a mausoleum.

Crazies like David, Ariel thought, biting her lip. Then she remembered the row of buttons in the elevator. Category 2: Mental Health. David's meltdown earned him a room here. What did he have to do to reach the top floor?

The psych nurse led them to the round desk. Ariel saw a keyboard and a single long, curving screen set into the desktop's surface. Ezekiel bent and spoke in whispers with the other nurse. The woman whispered back. The psych nurse straightened. "You can speak to David through there." Pointing at an open door. "Randy will be there with you at all times. We'll call him when it's time to end the session."

Randy, the intern, stood at the doorway, waiting. For the first time Ariel noticed the phone bud in his left ear. She stepped past him into the room. He tugged the door shut and gestured to a small round table in the centre. Four chairs were bolted to the floor around it. The big man crossed to a door opposite.

Ariel sat and tucked her hands between her legs. The walls were dull gray like the corridor. Light came from two circular panels in the ceiling, and between them in the centre was a black dome. A nurse whom Ariel didn't recognize came in via the door the intern had used and stood to one side. Her gaze took in the floor and the walls but skipped over Ariel.

Moments later the door swung open again, and there stood David. They had taken his clothes away, his shorts and T-shirt. He wore a white hospital tunic, pants, and slippers. His hair looked like a worn-out broom. He looked thinner than she remembered.

His face broke into a smile. "Ari."

"Hey. How have you been?"

"Not so well. You all right? Look like you need sleep."

Ariel opened her mouth and realized she had no idea what to say next. The intern leaned against the wall. He looked like he wanted to be anywhere else but here. David approached Ariel and opened his arms. She hugged him, clutching his arms and back.

"You feel good," he whispered against her ear, and Ariel wanted desperately to cry. "Warren and Elizabeth?"

"Worried about you."

David stepped back and squinted at her. "Told them about this? Me, getting moved up here?"

"No." Ariel screwed a smile onto her face and bolted it down. "They're going to the new *Star Wars* flick this afternoon."

David's jaw moved side to side. "Told Warren I'd take him. Damn." His eyes grew blank. "Not good. Not working in here." He tapped his head above his right ear as he sank into one of the chairs. "The wires are wrong."

Ariel sat and gripped his hands. "It's okay. Elizabeth said she would take him today."

David grew still, eyes locking into hers. "Elizabeth. Taking Warren. To *Star Wars*."

"She amazed me, too. Our girl is growing up."

David looked ready to say something, then snapped his mouth shut. His head tilted and he stared into his lap, wringing his hands. Ariel recognized the gesture. His mind was reaching out, piecing together a Shape.

"Our son has a hobby," Ariel said, keeping her voice light. "He's started collecting pornography. On his gaming gadget."

Life returned to David's face, spreading across his cheeks in a wicked grin. "Any good?"

"Some."

"Talked to him about it?"

"That's your job. Let's have this conversation when you're out of here."

"Yes. Walls have ears. Eyes, too." He pointed at the dome in the ceiling. "Zeke said I had some kind of seizure. What did I do?"

"You started wailing for your mommy."

"Less than a year old when she died. Retrievable memories are not ready to form then. Usually." Rubbing his cheeks with his fingertips. "Been trying to figure it all out. Fit it together in my head."

"What, exactly?"

"Remembering two different things. Some of it fits, feels right. Like walking in Aznar Park with Auntie and Uncle. Used to go there in the summer. Statue in the centre. Uncle called it the Busted Bust. Vandals ruined it. And when I was twelve, we drove out to the other side of Vancouver Island. I remember Long Beach now – really remember it. Smell of seaweed. Uncle lost his sunglasses in the ocean – " David flinched, brushing his fingers against the side of his head. Then he tucked his legs beneath himself like a child. "Hear that?"

"What?"

Ariel had a sense of vertigo, as though David were mentally spiralling away from her and wrenching himself back.

"One part is that stuff about Auntie and Uncle and the park, and Long Beach. But the other part . . . it's like watching a movie, only all the frames are just random pictures. A montage."

"When you're watching the movie, what do you see?"

David shivered. Ariel placed her hand on his leg, squeezed in reassurance.

"Auntie Mel. She's got no shirt on. And Uncle Stu. He's smiling, and touching me."

The sheer matter-of-factness in his voice made Ariel's throat lock.

"You're there too. Sometimes we're making love, and Auntie and Uncle are . . . cheerleading." A tremor ran through his body. "Hear them now?" His eyes drifted from her once more. "Their bedroom's right next to mine." His voice grew shrill, childlike. "Sometimes I hear them doing it. Auntie is loud." His mouth became slack. "I can hear them. Through the furnace pipes."

"What do you hear?"

His eyes snapped back to her, narrowing in confusion. "What do you mean?" His eyes grew sharp, losing the question as though it had hovered in his peripheral vision and he could no longer see it. "Went driving into the valley. Remember a small house. Red tile roof. Think we stayed there once, when we went on vacation in the summer."

This time Ariel saw the moment when David's mind flipped over. His eyelids fell, as though he were about to fall asleep in his seat, and his mouth hung open. His voice deepened. "Yes, Davie. Your fingers. Like that."

Randy pushed himself away from the wall and took a step toward the table. "Ms. Morrissey. It's time to go."

The intern's voice sent a tremor through David. Something old and familiar and unshakable filled his eyes. He pinned Randy with his gaze. "Lake."

"A lake?" Ariel said. "What – "

"Tell them they'll lose her if she doesn't go back downstairs. It's important."

The intern took another step toward them. The nurse behind him surreptitiously plucked a syringe pistol from her belt.

Ariel forced her attention back to David. "Who?"

"Lake."

"Who is Lake?"

"The girl who cut her neck. She reminds me of you."

David's obsession, according to Zeke. "How does she remind you of me?"

"She's a complete fuckup."

The words were knives through Ariel's belly. "David – "

"Couldn't kill herself properly and she knows it. Everyone is so nice to her. Going to ruin her." David noticed the intern and nurse then; he rose and stepped clear of his chair, eyeing one then the other. His hands balled into fists.

"Mr. Glass, just relax." the intern said. The nurse stepped to one side. Randy reached for David's arms, drawing his attention as the nurse moved out of his peripheral vision. David moved back and left, surprising the nurse, catching her by her wrists. Randy surged forward. David spun the shrieking nurse about, blocking the intern with her body as he pressed thumbs into her wrists. Her fingers opened, dropping the syringe. The device fell, and he caught it just as Randy's hand reached past the nurse, clutching for David's arms.

A sideways twist carried David out of reach. He tossed the syringe in a lazy arc at the intern. The man fumbled for it in confusion.

David turned back to Ariel. "Zeke has to get the girl out before she wakes up." He spoke with a baritone of raw inviolable command, of irresistible purpose.

The intern, syringe pistol in hand, caught his arm. David spun free in a movement that took him nearer the man. The pistol jabbed air past his arm and spat fluid. David caught the handle of the door through which Randy had brought him and flung it open.

"Shall we go?" he said gently.

Randy froze. Then, his face contorting, he shoved David's back in a way that should have toppled him to the floor. Instead it set David striding through the open doorway. The nurse scrambled after them, rubbing her wrists.

Alone, Ariel tried willing her heart to slow. She palmed sweat from her face, David's insane dance with the intern and the nurse winding through her mind.

Behind her, the door leading back to Zeke and Jackie clicked.

33

THE MAN ON THE VIDEO screen bore only a superficial resemblance to the photos in the file Jackie had brought with her. Perhaps with a shave and a trim of the mop of hair sprouting around his ears, he might look like the man she had imagined him to be now or the boy she remembered. The psychiatric nurse hovered over her, answering questions she hadn't asked and being a general annoyance. Jackie tried to ignore him, leaning over the counter to listen to the speakers in the desk, weighing David's voice in her thoughts. It lacked the bravado she remembered, the rawness, the sharp edge that could slice through defences.

Jackie's fingertips twitched. The bottle of Vaxodin felt heavy in her pocket. She leaned back and touched it through the cotton of her pants. Her edginess eased.

The camera view was from above and to the right of David. His wife sat before him, her hands on the table. David rubbed his thighs and touched his face. Sometimes Ariel took his hands and held them.

David mentioned eyes in the walls, and glanced at the camera. His gaze met Jackie's through the screen, and pain stabbed through her left breast. She crossed her arms, her breath catching.

Zeke spoke, sounding as though he was quoting from a website. "Usually these things come to the recovering Shimmerman's patient in a more straightforward manner. Most victims are disoriented, not disturbed by their memories. It should have been obvious he wasn't a standard case." It would have been obvious the nurse had never seen a Shimmerman's victim before, even if Ariel hadn't told her.

Zeke started speaking again, and Jackie held up her hand. "This other patient he talks about. What is she in here for?"

"Attempted suicide."

On the screen, the nurse approached David with a syringe, and David turned so quickly he caught the injection pistol and plucked it from her hand. Jackie gasped, at the same time as the nurse. Jackie began to rise, ready to bark an order, when the man on the screen casually tossed the injector at the big intern.

Show-off. Pure David. That and telling his wife she was screwed up. Jackie pushed the chair back from the desk. The animal she had known really had come back.

Ariel emerged from the room where Randy had led her. Her hands made fists in her coat pockets. "Well? What do you think?"

Jackie looked Ariel over, eager to take her mind off the man she had watched on the screen. "I think you need to go home and get some rest, Ariel. We'll handle David."

"I can stay. It's not ten in the morning yet."

Jackie frowned. "How much sleep have you had lately?"

Lines grew around Ariel's eyes, joined by a curl in her lips. As quickly as they came, the anger softened into bleakness. "Not enough. Damn. If anything comes up, call me. Please. Anything at all."

"Your husband is in good hands," Zeke said.

Ariel glowered at him. "Thank you."

"The elevator will be here in a moment." Zeke stabbed the button on the desk and gestured at the metal doors.

Jackie sat again. "You have recordings of David?"

Zeke nodded. "Since we brought him up here."

"I'd like to see them. From the beginning."

The nurse leaned over the desk and tapped buttons. The screen went blank, then showed a row of green icons with times and dates next to them.

Palms thumped the counter. Ariel had returned and now stood over them, shoulders firm. "The suicide girl."

"Lake Waldridge. What – "

"Put her back in her room," Ariel said, then turned and bolted to the open elevator.

"Why is it that I have patients and their wives telling me how to run my department?" Zeke muttered.

That, Jackie thought, is your own problem. She rose, muttering about the bathroom. Zeke motioned at the corridor. "To the right. Three doors down."

Jackie found the room and locked the door. The pill bottle came out. She twisted the top and watched it rattle across the metal sink. Two tablets dropped into her hand. Beside the mirror was a black tube with small paper cups. She tugged one free and filled it from the faucet, then tossed the tablets into her mouth and downed a cup of water. Vaxodin jolted her, a momentary pulse of joy. Then the heavy thudding of her heart slowed. She reached for the bottle, her hand steady now that the drug had sucked tension from her. Her gaze took in the little orange bottle, its screw cap still resting in the bottom of the sink.

You have a patient again, she thought. This isn't research now; you aren't dealing with people who just have questionnaires to answer and time to spend in an MRI so you can map their brains.

When had she begun to take the drug during the day? Weeks ago, she realized. She had started with a single tablet each night to help her sleep. When that didn't work, she doubled the dose, then tripled it. Then when panic struck and stabbed into her in the middle of the day, one or two helped settle her without making her drowsy.

Then came that first burst of rapture when the drug hit her belly. Addiction.

Jackie shut her eyes and shook her head. Enough. She turned, pushing her hands against the edge of the gray counter, and dumped the bottle into the toilet. Tiny pills swirled in the water. She slapped the lever on the side of the toilet and watched them spiral down.

She glanced at the pill bottle. It was unmarked. She tossed it into the trash can under the sink.

*****

Ariel slumped in the driver's seat and rested her forehead on the wheel. Her temples ached. The car beeped a questioning sound.

"Home."

The machine rolled out of the hospital parking lot and crept into Kingsway traffic. Ariel rubbed her eyelids, wishing she could wipe away images of David alternately confused and focused.

"Wait."

The car beeped and slowed.

"Take me to Aznar Park."

"Yes, Ariel." The screen on the centre console displayed a map, zeroing in on the south side of Vancouver. The car began to roll again. Ariel let the seat ease her back and stared at the ceiling. Why am I going there? she wondered. Hoping to find a big sign saying, "Your husband isn't a whack job"?

The drive took almost half an hour along rain-drenched streets. Aznar Park was an oasis of greenery surrounded by houses. She began to stroll, picking a strip of concrete walkway that led to a stone block in the centre. The morning rain had become a drizzle, which suited her mood. As she neared the block, it resolved into a slope of pale stone, with what had once been a carved head upon its top. After two or three decades, the Busted Bust hadn't been repaired. Ariel slowed. The head looked as though a cleaver had sheared away its right side, taking it from the centre of the skull to the ear. The bust was made of the same yellow-white stone as the block on which it sat. Beneath it was a brass plaque, bolted in place. Upon it was a name: Henry J. Aznar. Time and weather had taken the luster out of the metal.

Beneath the plaque, raised letters in the sloping stone proclaimed:

<pre>
            In mer ory
        ary Ju ez /   ar
      w   se hu nit)   nd
    cour,   sa'   37:   ives
          d, ng   Tc   )
        eart, jua   of ∠ 23
</pre>

Ariel touched the ruined stonework. Something heavy with a flat end had been taken to it, hard enough to crack the raised letters. The stone felt rough against her fingertips, though worn by age and weather. She traced the broken words, then the untouched numbers. The Tokyo quake hit that year. Aznar apparently did something special. David would have been ten.

Ariel tried to picture him here, peering up at the ruined head. Perhaps there were times when his aunt and uncle were good to their nephew. When they weren't violating him.

The park was little more than a lawn with a pair of cedar trees towering up, and farther on, an arbutus, perhaps the very tree David had mentioned. His home had been on Marine Drive, about thirty blocks from here. Ariel turned, surveying the land. Her foot lodged in something and she tripped, flailing at the stonework to break her fall.

You've been coasting along on adrenaline, she told herself. Now that Dr. Olver is looking after David, there is nothing more you can do. Go back to bed. The kids will be out at the matinee; you'll have peace for a few hours.

There was a wrongness here, as though she were sensing one of David's Shapes but couldn't put it together. She glanced once more at Henry Aznar's broken head. Something began to gnaw at her thoughts.

34

"THE QUESTION, THEN, IS WHAT do we do with him now?" Ezekiel Crane mused. "In his current state, I don't see simply telling him he made up his life."

Jackie looked up from the video screen, fingers lacing and unlacing from each other. In the past hour she had watched David's first evening in the padded room, strapped to his bed. The image gave her a perverse jolt of pleasure. "There are institutions for him."

Zeke snorted. "In this province? With the government we've got?"

"Canadian politics isn't my problem. What David is going to remember involves years of abuse. He will need treatment. You have staff psychiatrists?"

"We don't deal with patients for more than a month. Our job is to stabilize them so we can send them for counselling. All I can do is keep David from hurting himself. Once he is through the worst of it . . . ." He held his palms up in a shrug.

"You have him in restraints here," she said, hoping to push Zeke back to the immediate issue. She motioned at the screen.

The nurse peered at the rolling video. "Yes. He was well enough to be released from them when I checked on him this morning."

"Here he says your patient Lake is going to attempt suicide again."

"David isn't exactly well balanced."

"But he was right." Jackie tapped the Forward button. The video surged ahead, hours passing in seconds. David's night had, from the look of it, been uneventful.

Morning. On the screen, Zeke and an intern appeared. Jackie listened. "He knew you hadn't taken him seriously. I've heard about this. Hypersensitive intuition."

Zeke coughed. "I thought you'd have more experience with cases like this."

"I've managed studies on these patients. Nothing involving treatment, aside from my time at the clinic." She nudged the button. The video surged.

For a period David had the room to himself. He prowled it, then sat on the bed and peered at something to his right. The door burst open, and one of the other interns stepped in, with the pretty nurse Jackie had seen earlier.

David's voice, half an octave higher: "What makes you so special?"

Jackie's heart skipped. She thumbed the Rewind tab and listened again, then again.

Zeke breathed on her, a blend of mint and coffee. "Something wrong?"

Jackie let the scene play on. David's voice issued from the speakers: "The intern knocks. Even Zeke knocks. What makes you so goddamn special?"

An ethereal knife stabbed Jackie's breast, and she gasped.

"Doctor?"

"Reassign your female staff. None of them should go in there with that – "

Monster. Jackie caught the final word before it reached her lips.

~

Uncle Ray is older than Uncle Stu. Frailer. Smaller. Less painful.

The boy doesn't mind the pain. Pain is easy. It's the watching that's the worst. Auntie is his. Not Uncle Stu's. Not Uncle Ray's.

His alone.

So when Uncle Ray takes Auntie, making the boy watch from the stiff plastic chair in a corner of the bedroom at the cottage, the boy feels a nugget of hate in his belly.

~

Spring 2028

"Rewind."

35

Starting up her computer at the clinic the morning after Gary Holmes's revelations about David and his family, Jackie found an email from Simon with the kid's school records. She combed through them, tiling the files in white windows across her screen. The kid really had attended Burnaby South Secondary.

> David is a bright and creative boy . . .
> . . . shows a tendency toward introversion . . .
> . . . skill with language beyond his years . . .

Jackie looked for anything that could tell her what to expect. Her gaze shifted to the filing cabinet, its lowest drawer open and forgotten. Within: rows of green and red file folders, each bulging with paper, photographs, memory cards, discs – the lives of her patients in tangible records. The Priest's folder alone was more than an inch thick, with photos of himself as a toddler wrapped in a blue blanket asleep in his mother's car, himself with his two brothers all dressed in little black suits and ties outside a church in Victoria, himself at his high school graduation with a blond girl in a red dress. Then there were the recordings she had made of his parents, which her computer dutifully transcribed into pages of text. She was prepared for his slideover. Red highlights on the pages indicated the trouble spots: the bully he had to deal with in school, the time he ran into the back of his father's car while pushing a wagon and needed four stitches in his scalp.

And David's records? Five pages of psychiatric exams, a police rap sheet, and school report cards. Where were the people who knew him? The friends and family who could tell her the stories, the powerful events in his life that his mind might gravitate to as the second phase of the illness took him?

Jackie tapped the keys that sent the files to the laser printer. While the machine grunted and hummed she rubbed a kink from her neck.

Her phone beeped. She flipped it open to find a text message from George Ross. The guard had sent, "dg rwnd rm." Jackie translated it as "David Glass is rewinding in his room."

It seemed to Jackie that this past week she had had no other patients except David. She muttered a curse and fled her office, slowing her stride in the corridor when she saw the Fat Woman meandering to the common room. She tossed a brisk smile at the woman, hoping she looked friendly and reassuring ("No trouble here, Maureen, none at all.") and continued past to the men's corridor with its half dozen apartments.

George waited inside the doorway to room 105. "In there." A gesture toward the bedrooms.

"Are they decent?"

"I don't know them that well," the guard said dryly. "They *are* wearing clothes."

"Get the hell out!" came a child's voice, shrill and trembling. She followed George to the bedroom with its six youth-hostel-style bunks for beds.

Switch sat on the edge of a lower bunk, arms crossed, a scowl on his face. "The kid tried crawling into bed with me. I used your 'happy birthday' line on him. That's what we got."

Jackie turned to the corner of the room. David huddled behind the bunks, his back pressing against them. Metal squeaked and rattled.

Switch made a growl in his throat. "He thinks I'm his uncle."

"Don't want to talk to you," David muttered, pushing on the bunks.

"Know anyone called Suki?" George asked, looking at Jackie. "He's been muttering about her for five minutes."

"David," she said gently. "Happy birthday."

David's eyes flared. "It's just supposed to be us. No one else." He stabbed a finger at Switch. "Uncle wants me to bring her."

"Who, David? Suki?"

The kid's arms crossed. "Yes. But no one else is supposed to – "

"Who is Suki?"

"From school."

Jackie's heart flipped over. "I see."

"Uncle wants to bring her home to play."

Jackie cringed. "George. Switch. Out. I want to talk to David alone."

George looked ready to protest, his mouth opening and closing, considering whether challenging his boss with a patient looking on was a good career move. He shrugged and motioned Switch to the door.

Jackie lowered herself to the bunk where Switch had sat. "David, how old are you?"

He looked at her over his arms, resting on his knees. "I'm eleven. It's my birthday." His face clouded. "Uncle picked me up at school."

"I see. That was nice of him."

David looked at his feet, his toes curling over the edge of the cot. "Yeah. Sure."

"Didn't you want him to pick you up?"

Sullenly: "Yeah. But." David began to rock. "It's my birthday. My day. Mine."

"You don't want her to come over?"

David's voice grew husky and raw. "No one else is supposed to play with us."

"Okay." Jackie held her hands together to keep from shaking. "Davie, have we ever brought other children over? To play?"

"No! There's not supposed to be anyone else. It's a secret. You said it's just us."

"That's right. Just us."

David pushed himself away from the wall and marched back to the cot. He sat, scratched his left arm, looked at her through narrowed eyes. "Want to play?"

"No, Davie."

He leaned against her then, ran the tips of his fingers over her thigh.

"Davie, no." Pushing his hand away.

David's face darkened. "You don't want me."

"It's not that, it's – "

"You want Uncle Stu to bring Suki home. You hate me."

"Of course not."

David plucked at the white cotton of her blouse's sleeve. When Jackie pushed his hand away, David glared like a little boy who had had his toy taken away from him. When he reached back to her and touched her right breast she rose. "That's enough, David."

The kid tucked his legs beneath his body and glared at her.

"Enough. I'm not your aunt."

"It's my birthday."

"David, I am Dr. Olver. You are in the North Vancouver Shimmerman's Clinic."

His head wobbled and his gaze met hers. "We're supposed to play. It's my birthday."

Jackie couldn't remember seeing such hatred in her life. Not in the junkies who came through Emergency at Mercy Hospital, not in the patients who had formed a steady stream through the clinic and had to live day after day with the worst news of their lives.

As she turned toward the door Jackie's gaze passed the windows. This early in the morning they were dark, reflecting the room within like mirrors. Jackie could make out David's face in profile, contorted with rage.

In the fraction of a second when she faced the door, she heard a double thump of feet striking the floor. Then something struck her from behind. Hands dug fingers into her neck. Jackie stumbled and collided with the wall. Agony shot through her shoulder, the combination of pain and the weight of the flailing boy driving her down. She heard herself scream as David tugged her shoulder, twisting her onto her back. A finger slipped into her blouse between buttons near her waist. A tug sent them flying like pearls.

The boy's right hand came down on her breast, clenching.

~

Uncle Ray looks worn out. The boy has heard whispers from the air vents at the house: Auntie Mel and Uncle Stu upstairs talking about the doctors, the chemo, the operations, the medication. The boy hears Auntie and Uncle's car pulling out of the cottage's driveway. He is to spend a week here at the cottage with the old man.

Auntie Mel told the boy the old man needs help facing his brush with death. The boy can do this with his body. But the hate calls out, even as Uncle Ray gasps before slumping against the boy's back.

It's a simple thing, in the end, to crush some of Uncle's pills and drop them into one of his whiskey bottles. The meds say, "Do not use with alcohol." The boy puts the bottle back in the cabinet and goes to Uncle Ray's bedroom. He smiles at the old man, who beckons him in.

It'll probably be a month or so before Uncle Ray gets to that bottle. The cancer has retreated. He might live a long time. Long enough to drink the whiskey.

~

Autumn 2051

"I can still bleed."

36

JACKIE FOUND HERSELF ALONE AFTER telling Ezekiel Crane about David and the clinic. She sensed satisfaction in the psychiatric nurse, suggesting she had told him something he expected or wanted to hear. For a while afterward he had hovered as though waiting in line for the restroom and getting desperate. When a patient in one of the other category-two isolation rooms began to wail, he moved her to one of the offices down on the seventh floor. The room was a white box with a white metal desk, a white monitor, and a white keyboard which she hadn't touched. The computer had isolated each of David's verbalizations, drawing a list of time stamps in light blue against a black box. Two video windows occupied the space next to the list of times. The upper one, with a border in green marked "Live," showed the view straight from the camera. David sat with his back to the wall of his padded room. The lower one held her attention. It showed the segment of the video record from David's two days in isolation.

The drug in her system made her nerves sing.

Jackie listened to David rave to himself for more than an hour. The video record followed no predictable progression: David alternated from weeping like a child to howling for his mother to murmuring about "Auntie" and "Uncle," to snapping at the nurse who brought him food.

"Repeat," she told the computer. "Go back ten seconds."

"What makes you so special?" the man on the screen said.

Agony lanced through her breast. She wound through the spot once more anyway.

"Next item," she told the computer. It jumped to the next time marked in the list in red, and the video display box shifted to a view of David huddling on the floor of his room, crying. The pain in her breast receded. Jackie leaned back against the stiff padding of the chair.

David would need a therapist, someone to pull the pieces of his life back together, to make him confront the person he was.

Zeke Crane appeared in the upper window, followed by an intern. Jackie nudged the volume slider on the screen and tried to listen to his conversation. David's voice grew firm and confident when he spoke of his fellow patient Lake. She turned the volume down, shaking her head. This version of David was irrelevant, soon to drown beneath the weight of his history.

Her mind wandered back to dinner at the hotel restaurant last night. Lamb and pasta. She had paid her bill and moved over to the bar. After the fifth Budweiser she stopped counting her beers. The barman couldn't have been older than twenty-seven. She had flirted with him – a pathetic gesture.

Cougar, she thought. Cradle-robber. Junkie.

Admittedly he did look more appealing than Edwin – Baltimore police detective, fitness freak, rabid fan of celluloid westerns. For almost seven months she had shared his company and bed. It ended weeks before her flight to Canada. An amicable finish: Edwin wanted to rekindle things with his ex-wife.

Willpower slewed her attention back to the present. Where to find a therapist for David? she wondered. Twenty years ago she might have been able to answer that question here; now the only therapists she knew were in Baltimore or Chicago. If only she knew a local doctor.

"Nolan," Jackie said to herself. Ariel had mentioned that name. Her family GP. Jackie tapped the phone icon on the screen, waking up a new video box.

"Call Doctor something Nolan," she said.

"I have no listing for that name," the phone replied.

"Stupid phone."

"Please restate your request."

"Search. Surname: Nolan. Physician. Um. If you can access patient records, cross-reference with David Glass."

The phone beeped. A listing appeared: Dr. Santiago Nolan, GP.

"Thank you. Please call," she told the phone.

The machine buzzed. A friendly voicemail avatar in a navy-blue blazer appeared. She looked Asian, her hair long and straight and dark. "Good morning, Dr. Nolan's office."

"I'd like to speak with the doctor."

"I'm sorry, this office is closed on weekends. If you'd like to leave a message, please record now."

Jackie held back a curse. "Record then."

The screen shifted to a logo marked "Recording" in green, the word fading in and out.

"My name is Dr. Jacklyn Olver. I'm calling about a patient of yours, David Glass. We are looking for a therapist with experience in ERIN, and I'm hoping you can point us in the right direction. You can reach me through the psychiatric department here. Ask for the head nurse, Ezek – "

The recording logo vanished, replaced by the avatar. "Please hold. I'm trying to reach Dr. Nolan now."

Jackie blinked in surprise. "I thought – "

"I've found Dr. Nolan. Have a good day. I am connecting you now."

A dark-skinned elderly man appeared. "Who am I speaking to, please?" His voice had a Caribbean accent she didn't recognize.

"I'm Dr. Olver. Jackie. I mean, Jacklyn. I – are you working this weekend?"

Santiago Nolan had laugh lines around his mouth and a fringe of grey-white hair on his temples. "I'm at home. But I've put David Glass on my alerts list. You mentioned him. Now what is this about? You're calling from Crawford, I see."

"Um, yes. David is in an isolation room here."

Nolan leaned his elbows on the desk before him and peered at her with that slightly off-centre look of someone staring at a screen below the camera eye. Like a slow-witted politician reading a teleprompter. "Why on earth does he need to be in isolation?"

"Well, it started when he assaulted his wife at home – the reason he was placed in – "

"David never assaulted Ari. There was an incident at home where he struck her accidentally while enduring a nightmare. David himself asked to be placed in the hospital's psychiatric wing. That wasn't the fundamental issue; his concern was that, in his state of mind, he came close to setting fire to his home."

"Well. I don't know about that. I do know he suffered a seizure and became violent with staff. He is now in an isolation cell."

Nolan opened his mouth. Jackie plowed on before he could speak. "Doctor, we need a therapist to care for David. We can't keep him in Crawford for longer than a few weeks."

The physician's eyes narrowed into suspicion. "You're calling from the psychiatric wing of a major hospital and *you* need *me* to help you find a therapist? One would think you wouldn't have required an outside number for that."

"We would like someone with direct knowledge of ERIN. Someone capable of dealing with their unique needs."

"Someone familiar with the illness."

Jackie nodded.

"I can think of only two local experts, and one is indisposed at the moment."

"Thank you. I'll need their names."

The doctor smiled shrewdly. "You know them already. David Glass and Ariel Morrissey."

Jackie stiffened, annoyed. "Doctor, this isn't a joke."

"I'm not making one. I've been Ms. Morrissey's physician since she was a teenager, and Mr. Glass's since he was twenty-five. They have read everything you will ever find about the illness. Ms. Morrissey has lived with a classic ERIN survivor for twenty years."

"We need a professional, not an avid hobbyist."

"Any professional you find will envy David and Ariel's library. And really, how many ERIN cases has Crawford or any psychiatric facility had to deal with? These are the sanest people alive."

Jackie bit back a retort. "Thank you for your time, Doctor."

"Just a moment. As his physician I – "

"As you said, this isn't your field of expertise." Jackie thumbed the Disconnect tab. A still picture of Nolan's shocked expression hovered on the screen before the phone program cut out. The view of David's cell returned.

Zeke had left the room. David now paced back and forth, rubbing his scalp and face with his palms.

"Rewind," Jackie told the computer, and watched the scene back up. Zeke tugged his phone from his waistband and headed for the door, the two interns following. Jackie wound back further to find David obsessing about the girl again.

A scuffing of a shoe on linoleum and a slight shift in how light fell through the doorway behind her made her turn. A familiar narrow face peered at her, crowned with short dark hair laced with blond highlights.

"I'm looking for my dad," the girl said.

A round face pushed into view around the girl, half a head below hers. "Me too," the boy said.

"And who is your dad?" Jackie asked, annoyed at the interruption.

The pair stepped into the room. The girl began, "He is – "

Then the boy pointed. "Him." Jackie followed the line of his finger, past her shoulder to the screen where David Glass huddled in two video windows in an isolation cell.

The girl surged forward. "Yeah, that's him. Where is he?"

Oh, no. Jackie rose and stood in front of the screen. "You shouldn't be in here. Please. Now, go talk to the nurse about – "

"I know you," the girl said curtly. "You called my mom."

"Did I?" Jackie said.

"We want to visit with Dad."

"Yeah," the boy added.

Jackie reached for the phone icon on the screen. It flung a box up, blocking the view of David's cell and cutting out the sound. "Let me find someone who can help you."

A voice, neutral and emotionless, spoke then from beyond Jackie's view. "They took him."

"Where?" Elizabeth demanded. She and Warren turned and were gone from sight. Jackie kicked her chair back and followed.

Lake Waldridge stood in the corridor, arms hanging loosely. "Upstairs," she said. "They put him in a rubber room. They had to drag him. He went crazy."

"I need to call a nurse," Jackie said. "Don't go anywhere, any of you."

No one inhabited the nurses' station. Jackie bit down on a curse and stormed back into the office.

"Phone Zeke Crane," she told the computer. The phone icon on the screen flared.

Footsteps receded behind her. She looked back to see the kids wandering away down the corridor of a major hospital's psych ward with no staff bothering to intercept them and ask what they were doing here.

Jackie shook her head. Zeke Crane appeared on the screen, his eyes dull, glancing away – walking and talking with his phone on video mode at the same time. "Yes?"

"You have a problem," Jackie said crisply.

37

Peace and quiet. Ariel napped on the couch, glad the kids had gone out this morning to catch the matinee. She could think.

And brood about David. She sat up, her heart racing. Soon he would ask himself hard questions about what had come back to him. Soon he would find the Shape of it and come to the only conclusion that made sense: his journals were lies.

"Shit."

Movement outside the living room windows. The lawn mower had made its way around the house and now worked along the edge where the sidewalk met the driveway slab. Only a few days ago, David had been out in the backyard with the kids, having them rake the leaves, almost bringing the fire department down on them.

If only she hadn't figured out how to pay for beta ephemerase. If only Olver had gotten in touch with her sooner. If only Santiago hadn't managed to get the dose months early. If only . . . .

If only she hadn't been so awful to David in the beginning, maybe karma wouldn't demand its pound of flesh and slice of spirit. Did she even believe in karma? She considered this and shook her head. David would say the whole concept was irrelevant. All those years together were born in who she had been then and the man he was becoming. She had looked for someone weak. He had wanted someone to fix.

Chimes played. The sound tumbled from a pleasant trill into cold sense: the damn phone at her belt. She took the phone in hand. "To the wall screen," she told it.

"Santiago Nolan" appeared in blue.

Ariel rubbed her eyes. "Phone. Local view."

The screen obliged, showing her the scene from its own camera. Her own face stared back at her, hair in a stringy mess. What the hell – San had examined her with her legs in the air, had inserted a contraceptive ring in her butt cheek every five years for the past twenty-five, had watched her ass soften and widen as the years passed. He could stand to see her hair in a tangle.

"Answer."

Santiago materialized on the screen. "Good day." His accent was thick. "What's this about David in isolation at Crawford Memorial Hospital?"

Ariel had a feeling of having been caught doing something she shouldn't. "How did you find that out?"

"I spoke with a Dr. Olver moments ago. She is looking for a therapist for David." His mouth pursed. "She tells me David became violent."

Again hovered unspoken in the air.

"What else did she tell you?"

San's thick brows pinched in at each other. "There is more?"

Ariel felt her face crumple. "Oh, my God, San. It's all going wrong."

The story spilled out. David's journals. His aunt and uncle. The bloody deaths of his parents. The unwinding of his sanity.

"Take it slowly, Ari," Santiago said as she wiped her face on her sleeve. "Let me see if I understand this."

The phone chimed again. "Crawford Memorial Hospital" scrolled across the bottom of the screen.

"San, can I put you on hold? The hospital is calling."

Santiago nodded.

Ariel stabbed the remote's buttons, routing in the second call. Ezekiel Crane's face appeared.

"Ms. Morrissey. We – "

"What's happened? Is David all right?"

"He is fine. I'm calling about your kids." Zeke's eyes flared. "They dropped in for a visit. You need to collect them."

The car bitched. "Ariel, my speed exceeds permissible limits, please reduce to under fifty kilometres per hour."

"Where are the kids?"

The car beeped in acknowledgement, then a map of Burnaby appeared. "Warren's phone is in his bedroom. Elizabeth's phone is at Crawford Memorial Hospital on the seventh floor. Your speed is currently sixty-three kilometres per hour."

Ariel said nothing, concentrating on managing the steering wheel and the pedals while telling herself: when was the last time you actually *drove?* Last year? Getting killed is a hell of a way to cope with the kids – and what the hell were they thinking?

She wheeled the car into the roundabout outside the hospital entrance and shoved the door open.

"This is not a legal parking location," the car whined. "I cannot move to a designated parking spot without a licensed driver on board. Please return to – "

"This is an emergency," Ariel barked into the car's interior. The machine stopped in mid-sentence, beeping. Ariel flung the door shut and raced into the hospital. Her phone rang. She tore it from her belt and stared at it. "Santiago Nolan – home."

I left him on the line, Ariel thought. "Fuck."

The nurse at the Reception desk looked up, glaring. Ariel powered off her phone, then thumbed the elevator button and waited. Numbers counted down above the doors. Four. Three. Two.

This was Elizabeth's doing. Warren wouldn't have planned this and missed his movie for it. Elizabeth was the devious one. Like her father.

The elevator door slid open. Ariel stepped into the empty box, stabbing the button for the seventh floor.

When the door opened, Ariel found Jackie Olver standing near the nurses' station counter. Ezekiel Crane stood next to her. He motioned with his chin. "They're in here. I told them we'd called you. They refused to leave. I don't need them upsetting our patients."

Where the corridor bent in an L-shape, two interns and a nurse, all in green, hovered at the doorway to the little coffee room. Ariel glowered at Zeke. "You let my kids wander in here, surrounded by crazies and suicides." She pushed ahead down the hallway, shouldering past the men.

Elizabeth and Warren sat at a table next to the tall window, Lake across from them, her slippered feet up on the edge of her chair and her elbows on her knees.

Elizabeth met Ariel's gaze with contempt. Warren slouched and didn't look up from the tabletop.

"On your feet," Ariel said. "The car is outside."

Elizabeth was first up. "You didn't tell us Dad is in a rubber room."

"I never said you could come here without me either."

Elizabeth's mouth opened. Ariel shook her head, a single sharp twist that cut off the girl's retort before it began. "Go. We'll talk about it at home."

Warren scooted past her toward the elevators. Elizabeth stood her ground, casting a glance at the suicide girl. "You could have told – "

"I said we'll talk about it at home. Get in the goddamn elevator, little girl. *Now!*"

Elizabeth's eyes flickered to the doorway. She scowled and stalked past. Ariel began to turn. Then her gaze found Lake watching her with impassive eyes.

"What? Do you have something to say? Or have you said enough already?"

"Ms. Morrissey," came Zeke's voice behind her, with all the muscle and authority of a dead fish.

The girl set her hands on the table, palms down, fingers splayed. She looked at them in silence.

Ariel wanted to fling herself over the table at the girl. *She reminds David of you*, a voice in her mind taunted.

This reminds David of me? she thought. This skinny little thing unable to speak, to even look at me?

Ariel's voice came out in a whisper, too low for the men behind her to hear and too fast for her own thoughts to intercept. "David was right. You *are* an utter fuckup."

Regret came boiling in behind the words. Stupid, Ariel thought. Oh, God, I said that to a kid who tried to kill herself – twice.

Lake's gaze leaped up from her hands. Her eyes grew wide. Her mouth slammed shut until it formed a tight scarlet line.

"Listen," Ariel said, struggling for something to say. "I'm sorry. I – "

The girl came at her, hands balled into fists. "At least I have the guts to choose when I go. And I'll go while I can still bleed. Can you, you icy bitch?" With that her right hand leaped to her wrist and tore the bandage away, revealing a jagged line formed of black thread and torn flesh. She bit her wrist, teeth tearing. Blood sprayed her tunic. Her voice rose to a screech. *"Can you bleed?"*

Chaos. The room filled with people shoving past her and pouncing on the wailing girl. Ariel stumbled against a table and backed out of the room. Zeke was muttering as he pushed by her. Lake flailed as though in a seizure while one of the interns held her arms and the other crouched on her legs. Zeke knelt, frantically tugging something silver from his tunic's pocket.

Ariel felt a hand on her shoulder. She spun, to find Jackie Olver beside her. "You need to go."

Jesus, what have I done? Ariel thought. The elevator door was open. Elizabeth and Warren stood within the metal box, staring. Ariel fled. Elizabeth let the door go, letting it close on a scene of Dr. Olver quietly contemplating the contorting form of Lake Waldridge.

Jackie watched the interns. The female nurse scrambled down the hall to grab a gurney. She wheeled it back to the room. The interns lifted the girl off her feet and held her down on it, fumbling for straps along its sides. The drug had turned the girl's screams into catlike mewlings.

"Back upstairs," the woman said, casting a sidelong glance at Zeke. The psychiatric nurse wiped sweat from his face with his palms and followed the men with the gurney.

"What's the issue with her blood?" Jackie asked.

Zeke stopped beside her, his mouth hanging open. "What?"

"She said 'I'll go while I can still bleed,' and 'Can you bleed?' Is something wrong with her blood?"

Shock skittered through Zeke's face.

"What's the matter?"

He looked away, gaze flickering to the floor. "David asked the same thing when he first arrived." Revelation appeared to course through Zeke's mind. He turned back to the interns wheeling Lake toward the elevators, catching the railing of the gurney's side. The other nurse glared. Zeke's voice shook, but he stood his ground. "She is my responsibility. Put her back in her room. Let her sleep it off. In the meantime, fix those bandages." His gaze shifted back to Jackie and grimaced. "We need to run some tests."

38

Warren raced wordlessly to the Honda. He flung the rear door open and scrambled in. Elizabeth strode a few paces ahead of Ariel, back almost painfully straight, and climbed into the front passenger seat. Ariel rounded the car. She dropped herself in behind the wheel and thumbed the starter. "Take us home."

Ariel stared at the Honda logo in the centre of the wheel as the car began to move. She imagined herself huddled on the couch at home, David beside her turning pages on Gran's photo album. He was inside her mind, crawling around, waggling the wires. She hadn't understood what he was doing then – still didn't.

Memories of the person she had been before her breakdown made her belly clench. Her head throbbed with the scene of the girl in the hospital wailing as the men held her down.

That could have been me, she told herself, but I'm not going to be that again, I'm not going to slide back. David needs me.

If David hadn't compared her to Lake, things would have been different. Yes; David had hurt her. Being in the hospital didn't excuse it. He had lashed out at her because he couldn't deal with what was happening to him.

No, that was silly. David never uttered a word that didn't have a sharp-edged purpose behind it.

Something nagged at her about this thought but refused to climb up to awareness.

"When were you going to tell us?" Elizabeth's voice slammed against her mind.

"Eventually."

"Right."

Ariel looked at the rear-view mirror. Warren stared at the back of her seat.

Elizabeth's voice became breaking glass. "Dad isn't coming home."

"Of course he is."

"They only stick you in a rubber room when it's serious. When you've lost your mind and they need to dope you so you don't hurt anyone."

"You father is going to come home. He'll be fine. Good as new."

Her daughter made the word ooze. "Right."

"He will be. All he has to do is get through this."

"Right."

"Stop saying that."

"Sure."

Ariel shivered. She shut up and let the car roll.

At home Warren bolted ahead to the house, the lock reader flaring green under his thumb. He pushed the door open and ran in, followed by Elizabeth. When Ariel reached the door, he was already pounding down the basement steps. Elizabeth was taking her time with her boots. She flung her jacket at the closet. "What now?"

"What do you mean?"

"What happens to Dad now?"

Ariel forced her face to remain impassive. "He is getting the best care available."

"That sounds like bullshit."

"Don't use that language with me."

"If that nurse at the hospital said it, you'd think it was bullshit too. Did they even give him the right memory drug?"

"Of course they did."

"Then what has he remembered?"

Hell, Ariel thought. That's what he remembers.

The din of the basement television thrummed up through the floor.

The tale poured out of her: Dr. Olver, Ariel's research at the library, David's memories that refused to make sense. Her daughter listened, her face unchanging, rage and fear carved into lines along the bridge of her nose. Elizabeth sank onto the leather chair's footstool. Ariel spoke as gently as she could. "There you are. Your father is going to remember setting fire to the house where he grew up. He is going to remember his aunt and uncle doing terrible things to him. His journals are nothing but lies."

Elizabeth was quiet. After a minute she spoke, her voice gritty. "He said his memories made no sense. He couldn't fit them together. This is why, isn't it? They have no . . . no Shape. Not the Shape he expects. He is trying to make his memories fit his journals. But they won't. They can't."

"Some things seem to fit." A weak smile tugged at Ariel's cheeks. "He has good memories. A few."

"Like what?"

"Going to Long Beach on Vancouver Island. He remembers his uncle losing his glasses in the ocean. And his uncle pushing him on a backyard swing."

"He wrote that stuff in his journal. What about . . . what they did to him?"

Ariel shook her head. "He remembers that. But it doesn't seem to hold together. There are memories he didn't put in his journal that have come back to him. But the clear ones are all good ones. He remembers a park his aunt and uncle took him to. Aznar. There's a broken statue – "

"Right, the busted bust."

Ariel straightened. "What did you say?"

"Never mind. What else does he remember?"

To Ariel it felt as though the world had leaned over and she was tumbling toward a precipice she couldn't see. "Please, Elizabeth. What did you say? The busted what?"

The girl rolled her eyes in classic teenage style. "Remember when I broke my leg and Dad stayed home to look after me? After a few days I think he couldn't stand to hear me whine. He said we should go out, so we drove around and found the park. But you're changing the subject."

A thought loomed, though lost in a haze of chaos. David had never mentioned Aznar. He had mentioned taking Elizabeth to a park, but hadn't given it a name. "I'm not changing the subject." Ariel felt the side of her neck begin to thump. "Tell me about the busted bust. Is that some kind of nickname you heard at school? Something the kids call it?"

Elizabeth's eyes narrowed. "Dad made it up. So what?"

"Damn it, Elizabeth!" Louder than she had intended.

The basement television swelled in volume. Warren, of course, trying to drown out the growing fight.

"I mean it," Elizabeth said. "Dad just made it up. We were looking at the broken head, and Dad blurted it out. It was funnier when I was nine. That's all. Jesus."

She heaved herself up and marched to the kitchen. Ariel stared at her back. It wasn't possible. ERIN was a barrier between old and new memories. Without the drug, there was no way for memories to cross. But something had managed to leap that chasm.

No, Ariel thought. Beta ephemerase is a translator, giving the disease's victim access to both languages: new and old.

"Elizabeth?" Her voice cracked.

The girl peered at her from the kitchen. "What?" She spat the word into the space between them.

"I need your help."

"Search," Elizabeth told the computer. "Henry Aznar. Vancouver. Park."

A list filled the screen. Ariel peered over her shoulder. "Twenty-two thousand references? We need to narrow it down."

"No kidding. Additional search terms. Bust. Park."

The list shrank to seventeen thousand.

"Can't you just go into the city maps site and tell it to find the damn park?" Ariel asked.

"You want to do this instead of me?"

Ariel was about to retort when the screen shifted to the maps page – the computer apparently had heard. The view now showed southern Vancouver, focusing on Henry Aznar Park. The address appeared in a little yellow balloon.

Elizabeth shrugged. "Okay, cross-reference the street address with the word 'bust.'"

A fresh list of search items appeared, this time reduced to a mere nine hundred. The first said, "Japanese Society dedicates park to Henry Aznar."

Ariel pointed. "That one."

The view shifted to a rendering of the page. An image of the bust – whole and unblemished – appeared in a window, rotating in three-dimensional glory. Beneath it were the raised stone letters, unbroken.

In memory of
Henry Juarez Aznar
whose humanity and
courage saved 371 lives
during the Tokyo
earthquake of 2023

Ariel read the text below. Aznar was a Peruvian freighter captain who sailed out of the Tokyo harbour to get away from the quake which had flattened huge swaths of the city. On the deck of his vessel and tucked into its belly were as many Japanese as he could take aboard in a hurry when the quake struck. Aznar risked the life of his crew doing it and sailed his black-hulled ship triumphantly into Vancouver's English Bay – only to die four days later of heart failure.

"2023," Elizabeth said. "How old would Dad have been?"

"Ten."

"What are we looking for?"

"I don't know. Something." A thought niggled at the back of her mind, refusing to take form. "It takes time to procure land, to commission someone to build a bust." The thought opened like a flower. "My God."

"What?" Elizabeth demanded.

"When was the park actually created?"

Elizabeth blinked, uncomprehending. But the computer had overheard the question and scrolled through pages of documents. It bordered a block of text in green. Elizabeth leaned her elbows on the desk. "2025. So Dad was what, twelve?"

"Search again. Same site. The bust was vandalized. When?"

The screen flickered and steadied. Now it showed two photographs: the bust before it had been ruined, and after. Ariel's gaze leaped to the caption below, where the date lay.

Elizabeth stared at it, then spoke. "Mom, that's messed up. When did Dad get Shimmerman's bug?"

"2028."

Ariel read the date again. August 6, 2030.

"There's no way Dad could remember his aunt and uncle taking him there and seeing it."

This must be what David felt when he found a pattern – a Shape. Ariel had thought that before, but this was different. This had a clarity she had never known. She heard her own voice, rolling along on autopilot. The Shape was a tulip, its petals unfolding. "He isn't remembering it, Elizabeth. He is *creating* it."

"That's crazy." The girl kicked against the desk's side. "And Dad's crazy, isn't he? Really crazy. Psycho, schizo, vacationing from reality."

"No, he isn't."

The flower unfolded a new petal, and in this Ariel saw the suicide girl. Lake Waldridge, who looked cold and emotionless, impassive, unreachable, sliding into herself – now bellowing in rage, wailing her fear.

David, you manipulative son of a bitch, Ariel thought, and joy swelled her throat until she couldn't breathe. I know what you did to me back then. Now you're doing it to that child.

Struggling to cope with what was happening to him, David's mind must have gone back to its roots. Not to the twisted psychopath his aunt and uncle spawned, but to the man he had become. Ariel remembered the sharpness in his eyes, that scalpel-edge focus when he spoke of Lake.

She is keeping you sane, isn't she, David? You never were one to leave your work at the office.

"Elizabeth. I mean it this time. Your father will come home. But I need your help."

Memory is a story, Ariel thought. Bennie Shimmerman wrote that.

What if you change the tale?

~

"Who is that?" Uncle Stu asks the boy.

"Suki." The slender girl slows as she nears her bus, waves at him, turns to the steps. She is the only one at school he talks to, even with lies. He has a fantasy world for her, about how Mom and Dad died in a car accident; that's why he is living with Auntie and Uncle.

Uncle glances from him to Suki. The boy sees a familiar hunger in Uncle Stu's eyes.

"Maybe you should bring your friend over sometime. Introduce us."

The boy's fist clenches and slams down on the console. Uncle's eyes grow wide. The boy glares.

Uncle's voice breaks at the edges. "Hey, it's no big deal."

The boy must force himself to look mad. When the boy flares his eyes, pinches his mouth, that is when Uncle's fingers quiver.

Uncle works the shift down into drive. His hands tremble on the wheel. The boy looks away, fixing his gaze on Suki's bus. Hoping his smile doesn't show.

~

Spring 2032

"I haven't cried in nine years."

39

Mom and Dad stride through the airport's metal detector and out of sight. "I hope they never come back," Ari mutters. Gran turns to her and –

"Honey." The old woman looks shrunken. Her cheeks twitch, shedding tears that begin a slow march down along her nose. She slumps to the couch and puts her hand on Ari's leg. Ari is sure her eyes are shinier than normal. "Your parents aren't coming home."

The first thought to slam through Ari's mind is: They don't want me.

"There's been an accident. They were flying out of Athens, on their way to Heathrow." Gran's voice catches. "The plane went down."

"Down."

"They're gone, honey. I'm so sorry."

Ari looks at Gran, uncomprehending, trying to suck the words in and piece them together in some way that fits the image in her mind of Mom and Dad coming through the airport, smiling at her, hugging her, telling her the spectre of divorce has gone.

Ari's voice is soft. Almost a whisper. "They're dead." The word hovers in the space between them. She remembers Gran beside her, weeks ago, watching Mom and Dad at the metal detector. *"I hope they never come back."*

"It's your fault."

The thought slips out. Ari hears the sound of Gran's stifled gasp. "No, Ari. It's nobody's fault. It was an accident."

The thought wasn't meant for anyone else. Ari knows it's her own fault Mom and Dad are gone. She wished it.

But when she looks at Gran she sees pain in the old woman's eyes, and it somehow helps. "It's your fault," she says again. "You should have told them not to go."

"Ari – "

She is on her feet, racing down the hallway to the room that has been hers for five weeks and –

Gran stands in the doorway to her bedroom, voice jagged. *"Ari. How dare you?"* And –

Corey in the coffee shop in Chapters. His girlfriend's name is Wing. He rises, eyes glistening. "Good-bye, Ariel. Don't call me." And –

David is beneath her, hands on her breasts, cock jutting into her, and she squirms on him desperate to see anguish in his eyes and –

*****

A pillow, cold and damp, pressed against Ariel's face. A haze of something not quite sleep lifted. She found her body curled into a ball. The blankets were gone. She wiped sweat from her face with her arm, then she crawled to the foot of the bed and peered down at the heap of sheet and green comforter. Her bladder made itself known. She shifted her feet to the floor and stood. Pain shot through her belly. Her arms and neck felt as though the muscles had been stretched too far. She reached for her robe, slung over the back of the nearby chair, and put it on, wincing at the agony in her arms. The hardwood of the corridor chilled her feet. She padded to the bathroom, sat on the toilet without turning on the light, peed. The bathroom shrank around her, walls leaning in. On her way back to Gran's room she heard the house draw a breath.

Ariel placed her hand on the wall, guiding herself to the door to the basement. The wall felt like cool skin.

Carefully down the steps she went, across the basement, to the door into the garage. Ariel shivered. Feeling with her toes, she found her nest and flung her body into it, burrowing, covering herself with a rough blanket reeking of mildew.

She slept, dreamless, until the house extruded a figure in silhouette in the doorway to the house. Ariel wailed.

"Be quiet." David knelt and tugged the blanket off her. "Come with me."

Unable to think or breathe, she let him lift her to her feet and lead her into the glare of the basement lights. At the steps upstairs, he gestured for her to walk ahead. The house growled, unhappy to find her between its walls again. Ariel shut her eyes, and caught her foot on one of the steps. She tumbled forward, her knee thumping against wood.

David helped her to her feet. At the top of the stairs, he slipped his arm around her waist.

He half-carried her to Gran's room, slipped her robe off her shoulders, lifted the sheet and the comforter over her as she lay down. He tucked her in. "Stay here." His tone made his words an order. He stepped from the room, the door latch clicking into place behind him.

The previous night played itself back in Ariel's thoughts. Stupid baby, she told herself, hugging her belly, aware of the sound issuing from her throat – a sound of something dying in agony, watching its own blood pour from flayed skin.

The room brightened around her. When she heard the first footfall, the clock radio said 8:21. David murmured something, muffled by walls. She heard the bathroom door close, opening a few minutes later. The sound of feet on hardwood shifted to the softer sound of feet on the living room rug. Then the thump of a boot. A rustling sound – David's jacket. The front door squeaked open. It seemed for a moment he hesitated in the doorway. Then came the resolute tone of the door thudding into its frame.

Ariel lay still for half an hour, staring at the ceiling. Finally, relieved, she crawled out of bed and reached for her robe. It reeked of dust and mold. She threw it to the floor and found a green T-shirt, which she tugged over her head. To this she added a blue thong – her only underwear left unworn. The combination looked ghastly. She shrugged, uncaring, and wandered to the kitchen to make coffee.

The empty can sat on the counter where she had left it. "Damn!" She knocked it away. It collided with the wall before rolling across the floor, coming to a stop at her feet. An ugly gash remained in the wall. Ariel sensed the house wince in pain.

In the living room she sat on the couch and picked up the television remote.

"What were you expecting?" she said aloud. "If he was an utter shit to you, would you stick around?"

He would call; she was sure of that. She wouldn't have the guts to answer, would stare at his number on the call display at first. Then later, if he kept trying, she would pick up the phone. Stilted and faltering conversations. Then he would be gone.

Thank God.

Her photo album lay open on the coffee table. Mom and Dad looked up at her.

Ariel was ready when tears tried to come again. She gritted her teeth, then drew four breaths that began ragged and broken but smoothed out at the end.

I wonder if he'll be able to wash the stain of your snotty, runny nose out of his shirt, she told herself.

CNN showed a story about the rebellion in Peru. She flipped past it and kept jumping channels until she reached NewMusic. India Kasman had released a new song, proving the art of writing intelligent lyrics wasn't dead. Ariel closed her eyes and tried to listen. It sounded like ocean breaking on a beach.

The front door swung open. Ariel heard herself yelp. Her gaze, blurred at first, sharpened on an image of David in the doorway, three green shopping bags swinging from his grip.

"Good morning."

Ariel's mouth tried to say something and failed.

David lifted the bags. "Out of coffee. Ever had chai? I bought some. And only one egg in the fridge. Got more. I'm making French toast."

Ariel watched him slide his boots off and reach for a black hanger in the closet for his jacket, each action efficient and elegant, no wasted movement. He picked the bags up and headed into the kitchen.

Oh crap, she thought. The director gave him the wrong script.

Water hissed in the sink. Ariel recognized the sound of the pot being tugged free of the coffee maker.

An hour ago he had walked out of her life for good, and now he was making her breakfast. That peed on her plans for spending the day wallowing in self-pity. What the hell would she do now?

The thought provoked a startled giggle.

David poked his head out of the kitchen. "Laughing? Or crying again?"

"Both."

David stared, then nodded. "Good."

Why is that good? Ariel wondered. Oh, who cares? She sat up and placed her bare feet on the rug. Sounds of cupboards opening and closing, the clang of the frying pan being lifted from its hook on the wall.

David came to her minutes later with a mug and placed it on the table next to the remote. Ariel watched the steam do its snake-charmer act, then noticed the song had ended, replaced by a loud steady beat that hinted at the coming of a crashing headache. She thumbed the remote and killed the video channel. More thumping and banging in the kitchen. Her hand closed on the mug's handle and lifted it to her mouth. Warmth filled her. The drink hit her tongue with spicy fullness, thicker and richer than coffee.

What can you say to him? she asked herself.

David came to the coffee table with two plates in his hands and a bottle of maple syrup tucked under his left arm. He held a plate out to her and, when she took it, let the syrup drop and caught it with his free hand. Then he sat next to her, flipped open the top of the syrup bottle with his thumb, and upended it onto his own plate.

Ariel looked at the bottle, reading the label to keep her attention away from him. Real maple syrup, not the artificial stuff.

"When did you wake up this morning?" David asked.

Ariel swallowed, stared at her plate. The older the bread, the better the French toast. Gran used to say that.

She felt David's weight on the couch shift. He faced her now, probably staring at her stupidly.

He's the stupid one, huh? Keep saying that and you might start believing it again sometime next century.

Her voice had cracks in it. "Eight thirty."

"Heard me leave."

"Yeah."

"Thought I wasn't coming back."

Ariel's fork clattered across the coffee table. "Stop doing that!" A tremor started in the knot in her belly and pulsed up through her ribs into her neck. She flung herself sideways onto the couch, her back to him, shaking. "Just stop it!"

"What?"

"Stop reading my mind!"

40

SILENCE. HER CHEEKS FELT AS though bugs crawled beneath her skin.

David sniffed. "Telepathy. I've read about that. Can't do that. Doubt it's even possible."

Ariel could hear the fractures in her voice. "I never told you I ran into Corey at the bookstore."

David's fork tapped and scraped his plate. She could hear him take a mouthful of sausage or French toast. He ate. Then: "At Katie's apartment. She said Corey had a job at Chapters downtown. You were in the bathroom. I went to the bookstore a few times, worked out his schedule."

"You figured you'd play matchmaker?" Asshole.

"Shay said he was seeing a woman named Wing. Expected me to tell you. You needed to talk to him. But you didn't do it right. Watched you with him in the coffee shop. Sad."

Tears carved lines down her cheeks. One dripped onto her lips. Salty. "You knew about Gran, and Mom and Dad. I never said anything about them." You know what I did.

David's eyes narrowed. "Guilt. You carry it in your face." His fingers touched her cheek, right thumb gliding under her eye. She flinched and drew back, but he reached again and settled his fingers on her skin. "You talk about Corey, the skin here becomes tense. And here, flesh next to your nose bunches up. Same when you talk about your grandmother and parents. Made sense you were feeling the same way." His fingers ran down her neck. "Here, artery is close to the surface. I can count heartbeats when you're upset. But I don't know why you feel that way, or why you want to hurt yourself." His eyes locked onto hers and his voice came out hard. "Tell me about your parents."

The command hit her like a slap. Words rolled out before she could think. The airport. The day Mom and Dad flew out. And later, Gran telling her about the crash.

"I told her I hope they never come back. Got my wish. And then when Gran said they were gone, I blamed her. Right there, seconds after the guy from the airline or the government or whoever the hell he was gave her the news." Ariel's stomach wrapped itself into knots. "I didn't realize till I was fourteen that Gran had lost her own son. It took three years for that to sink in. And I thought *you* were slow."

David was looking at her photo album, ignoring her as she babbled. He turned the page to the photo Gran had taken that summer when she had taken Ariel camping in Washington. The shot showed the tent behind, yellow and blue. Gran had put the camera on the roof of the car, so it was tilted. Ariel and Gran stood smiling at the lens.

Ariel reached for the book's open cover. "Goddamn, you wanted to hear this shit – "

"Why do you do that?"

"What?"

"Only get mad when I turn to a picture of you smiling."

Ariel's jaw fell. She stared at the book, then at David.

He tapped the page. "This. Tell me." Again his voice carried the steel of command.

Memory unfolded in her mind: Gran driving them into Olympic National Park in Washington. Gran had got it into her head to take Ariel camping.

"Ollie and I used to come down here every summer," Gran said.

They had loaded the Duster with a large tent – a bizarre affair which, to Ariel, violated some fundamental essence of *tentness* by virtue of having three rooms in it – a propane-fueled barbecue, two coolers which had been empty until they reached Port Angeles and had stocked up, and a sack of metal struts and black canvas which Gran refused to say anything about.

Ariel was sixteen. She liked Gran's concept of camping. Gran had insisted on picking up a fuel cell to power Ariel's Hyperstream receiver for two weeks, and then keyed up an assortment of movies about campers in the backwoods facing psychopaths, bloodthirsty animals, and supernatural monsters.

Woods sheltered the campsite, just in past the gate to the park. Somewhere beyond it, Ariel could hear a running brook.

"Yoo-hoo," Gran said when Ariel turned to sweep her gaze around the campsite. She opened the hatchback and pointed to a long black sack. "Why don't you set up Couch Thingie over by the fire pit. I'll heave the tent onto that flat bit."

"Couch Thingie?"

Gran smiled. She had lines around her eyes and a thickness to her middle. But that didn't mesh with the view of her clad in jeans and sneakers and a white T-shirt. Her smile stole away her age.

Ariel picked up the sack and took it to a spot near the blackened circle of stones. When she turned the sack over, a mass of articulated struts and black canvas tumbled out. She scowled at it, uncomprehending, then tugged on what looked like one end.

With each tug the thing expanded, until it began to look sofa-like.

Gran came tromping down from the car. "Here. This too." Dropping a sack which looked like Couch Thingie's offspring. "The height of decadence."

Ariel pulled it free, confused. It stretched into a frame that kept a strip of canvas taut, like a firm hammock.

"What is it?"

Gran laughed. "Footrest Thingie." As though it were the most obvious thing in the world.

Ariel came out of the memory shaking, aware that she had been mumbling about "Couch Thingie" and the hours in the evening watching the screen as the fire crackled in the pit.

"Must have been fun," David said.

"We hiked up into the mountains. Snow lay on the ground – in August. And you could see all the way to Vancouver

Island." Ariel's body quaked. She glared at him. "Why are you doing this to me?"

"Do you feel better?"

"Are you getting a kick out of this? Did you enjoy humiliating me in front of your friends? Petty revenge, was that it? You had to cut me down in front of them; it isn't enough to do it like this when we're alone, to pick me apart."

"You: changing the subject." David shrugged. "Fine. You mean Switch and Virgil and Carmen? They had to be there. You hit with words when someone says something you don't like. Then you stop thinking about what they said. But strangers silence you, make you listen. If I left you alone after that, you'd have thought about something else, like visiting Katie and Shay. But you saw me on the bus and the train. Couldn't shoot words at me, so you had to think about what I said."

Ariel's heart wound up. Her palm went to her neck, pressing against the pulsing spot. "You bastard. You did this deliberately. Look at me. I haven't cried in nine years. *Nine years!*"

David watched her, lips pursed. "Why do you think that's good?"

"Because. . ." Because once I start I'll never stop.

David picked her empty cup off the table. "More?"

Ariel sat trembling, hands tucked between her knees. Her breasts jutted against her T-shirt, her nipples pronounced and visible. Her body sickened her.

David returned, placing her cup before her, then put her knife and fork back on her plate. "Eat."

She nibbled, slipping a square of sliced French toast into her mouth. Warmth had fled her breakfast.

"I'm sorry," she said to the silence.

David made no response.

"I'm so sorry. About . . ." About everything. About what I wished on Mom and Dad. About what I said to Gran, who forgave me even though I didn't know it and sure as hell didn't deserve it. And about what I did to Corey.

Her lungs burned. "How many times do I have to say it before I feel like it matters?"

David was quiet. When she looked at him, he stared across the room, gaze fixed on the blank television screen. "Up to you."

Ariel laughed. The sound dissolved into pain in her belly. "I won't live that long."

~

It's strange to find himself hard, the way Uncle gets when he is with Auntie. The boy likes the sensation. Auntie invites him into the shower and gazes at him, then arches her back and waits.

Uncle is afraid. Uncle doesn't touch him anymore. The boy is getting bigger, at thirteen. Or maybe Uncle has shrunk. The boy likes the differences. Auntie is a little afraid too. The boy doesn't care. It's Uncle who needs to be afraid.

And he is. The boy sees it in the tautness of the old man's shoulders and the way he hunches when the boy is near.

~

Autumn 2051

"Change me."

41

DAVID'S SENSES HAD SHARPENED, AS though the chaos of his returning memories forced his mind to counterbalance with a heightened awareness: of Lake Waldridge, of the toxic dynamic between Zeke Crane and the other members of the hospital staff, of the tension in Zeke's body that drove rods up through his back and deepened his voice.

"Thrombophilia," Zeke said.

The word split itself into pieces in David's thoughts. "A blood disorder," he said. "Opposite of hemophilia – causes clotting, not the inability to clot."

The psychiatric nurse nodded, looking impressed. "So you've heard of it."

"A thrombosis is a blood clot; it's obvious. Lake has it?"

For an instant a triumphant smile darted across the other man's face. The father, David thought.

"No," Zeke said. "Her father does."

"Hits in adolescence?"

Again that triumphant look, slipping in around a flare of fear that tugged at the corners of the man's eyelids. "No. Factor V Leiden – that's the inherited type – can strike at any time. Or a victim can go a lifetime without an event."

"Her father: it hit him when he was her age. True?"

"He was sixteen when he had his first stroke. A minor one. He has had seven in his life. But Leiden is easy to test for, and Lake doesn't have it."

David leaned back against the padded wall and eyed the dome in the ceiling. "Still has her father's influence. Hearing him talk about living day by day. It's overriding reason. What prompted you to look for it?"

"A doctor happened to be on the psych floor. She overheard Lake making certain remarks about blood to your wife."

The starfish Shape David associated with Lake hovered in his mind's eye. "Ariel said something, set her off?"

Zeke nodded.

"Good."

The psychiatric nurse wiped his hands on his pants. "I don't see why that was good. The girl had . . . an emotional episode." He licked his lips and cast a glance at the intern standing near the door.

"Good," David said. "Too wrapped up in herself, too much inward looking."

Zeke stood ramrod straight. His eyelids moved with a subtlety that made the movement almost invisible. He, too, had an air of having turned inward in recent days. David shifted his voice into gentleness. "Ever lose a patient?"

Zeke glowered at him, his lips pressed together.

"Or someone close to you?"

The change was immediate: Zeke's body hardened in place.

David slipped a smile into his cheeks. "Tough thing to live with. Suicide?"

Randy stared at the back of Zeke's head, his expression of contempt lurching into surprise – and sympathy. The psychiatric nurse, unaware, lowered his voice. "David, I'd like to ask you some questions."

"Nothing else has come back to me. Nothing has started to make sense. Pure chaos in here." Tapping his temples.

Zeke moistened his lips with his tongue. "Not about you." The man's mouth opened, as though he were struggling to push something out.

The starfish had grown additional limbs, clutching at air and space around it. "Her father. Living a day at a time. She's absorbed that sense, picked it up from him." David squeezed his eyes shut against the distracting dynamic between psychiatric nurse and intern, and studied the Shape. "Bind her to the future."

Zeke was quiet. David opened his eyes. The psych nurse eyed him skeptically. "You think if I tell her she doesn't have this condition and she will live a long, healthy life, that will solve the problem?"

"No. Needs a therapist, someone to talk it out with. But a therapist won't get anywhere, not if she expects to drop dead at any time." The Shape retreated. Chaos enveloped him. "Give her something real. Bind her to it. Otherwise she's dead."

*****

Through the night, Jackie's skin burned, driving her out of sleep. David Glass leered at her, eyes full of hatred and triumph. Unseen mice skittered across her body. In the emerging dawn she saw a bright blue aura hovering over the flesh of her arm where fine hairs rose. The world blinked away.

The sun cast a strip of light across the bed. She lurched up. Her joints ached. The window had a blue corona around it – one of the signs of Vaxodin withdrawal. She saw in her mind the pills tumbling into the toilet in the hospital. That had been stupid, in retrospect. She should have kept them and just held the addiction under control.

Jackie blinked the pattern to wake her contact lenses, and tapped her phone's surface. The keyboard floated before her. She brought up the list she had recorded: psychiatrists and therapists across the west coast of the United States and Canada who had at least some experience in treating what could be considered memory disorders.

Thinking about David left her with no appetite, so twenty minutes later she called a cab. Fortunately, throughout the ride the driver kept busy speaking in quiet tones into a headset. He seemed to be handling a technical support call for the local phone company. A pad lay across his lap with the telecom's website on it.

The car found Kingsway Avenue and rolled east. Jackie stared at the rain on the window. She thought of David in his cell. She liked that word better than "isolation room."

The hospital elevator deposited her on the seventh floor. She found Ariel Morrissey in Ezekiel Crane's office.

Zeke nodded to Jackie. "Good morning."

Ariel cast her a grim smile.

"How are you?" Jackie said, letting her gaze take in both of them.

Zeke pushed his chair back. The wheels squeaked at a pitch that made her teeth buzz. "We were discussing Mr. Glass. He is going to need a good therapist." Zeke turned a gaze toward Ariel that managed to look sympathetic and patronizing at the same time. "I've made some phone calls."

Jackie dropped herself into the seat next to Ariel. "So have I."

"Can I see my husband for a while?"

"David had a rough night – " Zeke began.

"What happened? Is he all right?"

"He's fine."

"Then what's the problem? I've managed to bring him out of it whenever he has slipped away on you."

Jackie expected Zeke to refuse, so his response surprised her.

"I'll give you half an hour," he babbled. "I . . . he seems obsessed with his fellow patient, Lake. Perhaps you can question him about her, to see if he has anything more to offer. It's important that we understand the root of his obsession. For his own sake."

"Thank you."

Jackie watched the woman rise unsteadily from her chair. Ariel's handbag sat on the floor beside her chair, forgotten as they all walked out.

Zeke turned to Ariel when they reached the elevator. "Would you like me to arrange for someone you can talk to? I understand this isn't easy. David isn't the only one who will need a therapist. Your kids . . . ."

A look of raw contempt clouded Ariel's face. The door slid open. Jackie was sure she heard Zeke's jaw clack shut. He thumbed the reader. It flared green, accepting his print. The elevator lurched up one floor and groaned to a stop, opening on a gray corridor and a smell of too much antiseptic. Ariel clamped her right hand over her own neck, giving Jackie the impression she wanted to do that to Zeke. The psychiatric nurse went on ahead and leaned over the counter. His colleague, Jean, sat at the desk with its curving screen. Zeke spoke in hushed tones, then straightened up and smiled. "I'll have David brought to the lounge."

Randy, the day-shift intern, strode out of a corridor to the right. He nodded to Zeke, then to Jackie.

Zeke straightened. "Please take Ms. Morrissey to the lounge to see her husband."

Randy smiled and gestured at the door. Ariel followed. Zeke waited for her to vanish into the lounge before turning back to Jackie. "So. You found a therapist?"

"Nothing concrete. I think we've taken the wrong approach. Forget about finding a therapist with experience in dealing with ERIN cases. David's getting his past life back. He is becoming a 'normal.' All he needs is a therapist who has dealt with violent patients, or patients who have survived violence."

Zeke cast her a wan smile. "What would you recommend, Doctor? What would you do with David?"

Jackie stifled a laugh. "I'm not qualified to offer you advice." But if it were up to me, she thought, I would see him locked up in a psychiatric institute with a gallon of Thorazine in his blood. Do they even use Thorazine anymore? How about electroshock? That would be entertaining to watch.

Her skin began to itch. She raked her nails across her arms.

Zeke shrugged. "I'll start putting feelers out, then. We'll need someone for David, and someone for his wife and children. This family . . . ." He stroked the side of his nose thoughtfully. "That has to happen soon. We can't keep him in this hospital beyond another week or two."

"Where do you put criminally insane cases in this province?"

The psychiatric nurse laughed dryly. "I don't see it coming to that. David has years of therapy ahead of – "

"He burned his relatives to death after a lifetime of rape. How do you think that's going to affect him, when he understands his memories?"

"That's for his therapist to determine." Zeke stopped pacing and eyed Jackie. "Have you told David's wife about your . . . encounter with him?"

My encounter, Jackie repeated in her mind. The bastard tried to rape me.

Zeke read her answer on her face and shrugged. "His therapist will need to know about it."

"Zeke?" the nurse behind the desk called.

"In a minute," the psychiatric nurse said, waving in her direction. He turned his attention back to Jackie. "Anyway, we – "

The nurse's voice grew sharp. "Zeke, you have to hear this."

Zeke turned, shifting mental gears. He leaned over the desk. "What is it?"

"David's wife." Jean tapped her earbud.

"Speakerphone," Zeke said.

Jackie stepped next to him and saw Jean stab the blue button for the overhead speakers. On the screen, upside down from her perspective, Jackie could see Ariel leaning close to David from the camera's eye in the lounge.

Sound exploded around them:

"SO WHERE DID YOU KEEP *YOUR* PORN COLLECTION, DAVID?"

Jean's face flushed scarlet. "Sorry." She turned the volume dial down, sliding her finger along the bar next to the button.

Zeke chuckled. Then his mouth pursed.

Ariel spoke. Her voice had a husky timber.

Zeke's jaw fell. His face paled as he reached for the microphone. "Randy, get David out of that room and away from that – " His throat caught and he threw the mic down; it bounced on the counter and fell to the floor, dangling by its cord. Zeke turned toward the door to the lounge.

"What," he said, "does that stupid woman think she's doing?"

42

DAVID COULDN'T SEE THE FLIES in his room. They came out of the walls and buzzed around his head, until he brushed them away and silence fell like a stone. A hallucination – he knew this. But that knowledge changed nothing.

The door latch thumped, then slid back. The door swung inward. Randy stood in the doorway, another man behind him. "Get up, Mr. Glass. Your wife is here."

David absorbed the scene of the intern in the doorway: green slacks and tunic, name tag clipped to the left pocket. Randy had had some kind of injury to his right shoulder years ago, perhaps as a child. He wasn't aware that he favoured it.

Ariel is here, David thought. Focus on that.

The cloth on his arms and legs rustled. The material felt like tough paper. He wanted to go to the bathroom.

The door clanged shut. David turned back, confused. Randy tapped his shoulder and pointed down the corridor. The two interns followed him two paces behind. David heard their boots on the hard floor, a ticking sound like the clock in the living room before it stopped working and Ariel had it taken down and the man who fixed it replaced a spring and a wheel –

Bedlam in his mind. His thoughts refused to latch on to anything. Find the key, the Shape. On a chessboard, the Shape lay in elegance and simplicity, like music, one note flowing into the next. Pawn here, knight in this square, bishops intersecting so the opposing king couldn't move into either of those two squares beside it.

Rook to king's pawn four. Checkmate.

"Mr. Glass?"

Randy's baritone tore his mind back to his body. Gray passageway, a smell of sweat and rubbing alcohol. David took another step, and another. When they reached the door to the lounge, he stepped aside. Randy tugged the door open.

Ariel sat at the table, her magenta coat open, hands between her knees. A smile flickered across her face. She looked like she had grown older since . . . when had she last visited him? Yesterday? Or before then? David's mind leaped back to the day in the cemetery, to before he even knew her name. When he had seen the young woman with black hair striding toward him, everything about her screamed *pain*: the way she hunched her shoulders, the lines in her forehead, the stiffness of her hips. Broken, he had thought, watching her approach him past manicured graves. Now in this tiny white room he saw something similar to that. And he saw something else, a hardness underneath. Ariel rose and came to him, arms open. He held her, his cheek against the top of her head. Then she took his hand. They sat, turning the chairs to face each other.

David heard that familiar grit in her voice when she spoke. "How are you, love?"

"Been better."

Randy took up his place next to the door through which David had come, the other intern moving to the opposite side.

A smile danced across David's mouth. "You said something nasty to Lake."

"Who? Oh, the girl."

"She came unglued."

"Yes."

"Good. She can get better now."

"She tried suicide twice; she should be up here in one of those rubberized rooms, like yours."

"Told Zeke to let her out."

"You did? Why? No, don't answer that. Let's talk about you. Has anything else come back?"

"More of the same. It's so random, Ari. Can't hold on to any of it." He stared at her knees. "Losing my mind."

Ariel placed her hands on his thighs and squeezed. "Tell me what you remember."

"Told you already. Remember school. On the south side. When I was thirteen: field trip to Victoria. I remember the ferry. Called the *Spirit of Vancouver.* We toured the government building. There were men in dark suits, and I remember some tall kid saying they looked like robots." He fell silent, picturing a broad hallway. An ornate, domed ceiling above.

"What else?" Ariel pushed gently. "You said last time there were two streams of memory." Her forehead glistened. She had more lines around her eyes than he remembered.

I love you more than you will ever know, he thought.

Oh yes: the old game. *I love you. I love you more. Do not. Do too* – and a kiss, silencing the childish retort, dissolving into –

Pressure on his cheek, and he found himself here in this hard plastic seat, Ariel's fingertips touching skin over the bone beneath his left eye. "You say that a lot, how none of it makes sense. I've been thinking about that. I have a question . . ."

*****

What if you're wrong? Ariel thought. David rambled, seemingly unaware of half of what he said. "We toured the government building. And *you'll like the farm, Davey.*" A thin smile. "And some of the kids said – "

It wouldn't be the first time she'd screwed up. David knew her better than anyone – uncomfortably so. He had probed for all her soft spots, her buttons, and worked out how to push them. He could still do it. He understood her in ways she couldn't fathom.

She thought back to yesterday's conversation with Elizabeth. It was Sunday morning and she hadn't been ready to confront David. So she asked her daughter to join her in a drive. Warren hadn't demanded to come along, thank God. Ariel suspected he was struggling with the image of his father in a padded room.

She needed to have that conversation with him soon. But right now, David was the priority – he had to be, or the conversation with Warren would be a lot tougher.

Elizabeth sat in sullen silence in the car as rain lashed the windshield and Ariel outlined her plan. The plot to bring David back.

"Forget it," Elizabeth said. "You can't lie to Dad."

"I have no choice. I know it's usually the wrong thing – "

"That's not what I mean. I mean you can't lie to him. You're a fucking deuce at it."

"Elizabeth, damn it, I need you to help me here."

"I am. You stink at lying to Dad – he reads you like a website, all pictures and sound and shit."

"God damn it, don't speak to me like that. Where did you learn language like – oh."

Her daughter scowled, barking a derisive laugh. "I mean it, Mom. Dad reads you. You put your hand on your neck when you're upset. If you do that when you try bullshitting him, he'll know it. He has you figured out. He was there with you through your breakdown. He has a Shape marked 'Ariel' in his head."

Ariel was sure even the rain stopped for a second. "My breakdown? He told you about that?"

Elizabeth stared, stricken, a flash of guilt coursing across her face. "Yeah. Years ago."

Ariel felt herself shrink in her daughter's eyes. She drew a rough breath, her voice breaking as she spoke. "Does your brother know?"

"Don't be a deuce, Mom – if I told Warren about it, I may as well wide-cast it on the Web. Now listen. Dad has a blind spot. How do you think I get away with all the sh – stuff that I do?"

Ariel stared at the rain-soaked glass and the wipers that swung back and forth, revealing in sweeps the lights of Kingsway traffic. "What do you mean, a blind spot?"

"I know Dad. We talk about how he sees things. Never said this to him, but he isn't perfect." Elizabeth turned a wicked grin on her. "Don't tell him anything. *Ask* him. Make everything you say a question. Do that, and he won't process *you*, he'll process the questions."

She thought about Elizabeth as David's rambling ran down. When he looked at her blankly she prodded him again. "What else?"

David's voice dropped by an octave into a childish parody of an adult's voice. *"It'll be great, Mel. Think about it."* He seemed unaware that this child's voice leaped out among the words of the adult.

I'm not wrong, Ariel thought. I can't be wrong, not this time. She swallowed. What the hell. Go for the Oscar.

*****

"I have a question."

David eyed the tension in Ariel's left cheek, the bunching of muscle beneath the skin. Fear, uncertainty, then resolution.

"What?" he said.

"Who were you interested in at school? The girls, I mean."

The shift in conversation jarred. "Girls? There weren't any."

"Your school had no girls?"

"Of course it did. Don't remember them."

Ariel's tongue darted out and dampened her lips. "Warren has his collection of pornography, and he is only twelve."

Again a shift in direction. David chewed air. He pictured his aunt, kneeling over him on the bed, breasts swaying –

David gasped, pressing his palm to his cheek.

"What?" Ariel demanded.

"It's Auntie. She's not wearing anything." The room gyrated.

Pain. David opened his eyes to find Ariel squeezing his forearm, pressing her thumb into the spot between the bones, using throbbing agony to drag his thoughts out of himself.

"Listen. Where did you keep yours?"

"My porn collection? Didn't have one."

Ariel's cheeks grew hard. "You stupid little fool."

"Ari – "

"You got Bennie's flu when you were a teenager, awash in hormones. Are you telling me you weren't interested in sex at the time? Never looked at the girls in school and wondered what it would be like to do them? Never went on the Net and found yourself some girlie pictures?"

"I . . . no." The answer collided with chaos in his mind. It was ridiculous. Of course he must have at least been curious. "Don't remember."

Ariel laughed, a sound drenched in contempt. "You were fifteen. What the hell else would you have thought about? Warren is thinking about it already."

David's temples began to ache.

"I have a good idea what he does in bed now. Can you imagine what he thinks about, late at night when he and his stiff little friend are alone?"

Something licked out from the corners of David's eyes, as though dancing just beyond his view. Ariel's voice grew louder, filling his mind. "And who do you imagine he thinks about? The girls at school? Maybe his math teacher? Maybe even me, his own *mother?*"

A Shape swelled into being in his thoughts. Incomplete, incoherent, but trembling about like a spider web in a breeze, seeking clarity.

"Warren will never admit it," Ariel said. "He will bury that deep inside himself and trot out those perverse little fantasies only when he is alone. And if he kept a diary like you did, he sure as hell wouldn't write about it.

"So where did you keep *your* porn collection, David? Who did you fantasize about? Your aunt? Maybe you weren't sure which way you swung at that age; did you include your uncle in the fun? And then at fifteen along comes Bennie's flu and wipes you out, right when your brain is drowning in testosterone and God knows what else. That's the state you were in then. So what would stick in your mind when the memories start coming back?"

"My God, Ari – "

A boot thumped linoleum behind him, and Randy spoke. "Ms. Morrissey."

"Just a moment, I'm talking to my husband."

"No, Ms. Morrissey. It's time to go." The big man marched around the table and settled his hand on David's shoulder.

The door behind Ariel swung open. Zeke and a familiar older woman stepped in. Zeke looked wound up like a spring. "Ms. Morrissey, I need to speak with you. Now."

Ariel shook her head. "Five more minutes."

"No."

David felt Randy's grip tighten. The intern tugged him toward the door. The other intern hung back, looking confused. Zeke trembled with rage. That's new, David thought through a translucent haze of newborn Shape.

Ariel shrugged and smiled at him, brittle curves in cheeks and lips. "I'll see you soon. Think about it."

A thousand thoughts competed for space in David's skull. Randy steered him into the narrow gray passageway and palmed the large red button next to his door. David heard the latches grind back. The intern gave him a shove. "In."

The door shut. David stood, unseeing. His thoughts jumped from one stream of memory to the other, seeing his aunt in the kitchen sitting at the table, smiling at him as he tramped into the room fresh from the school bus at the corner. Then that bizarre mental twist, as though his brain were being wrung out, and suddenly Aunt Mel lay on top of him in a scene almost as real as the memories of her and Uncle in the car, speeding along the highway east of Vancouver, cutting through farming country, and David in the backseat listening to them and glancing up from the book of cartoons Auntie had bought him.

Then the twist again, and he heard himself gasp as Uncle touched him and –

You were a warped little bastard, weren't you?

David sank onto the bed and tucked his knees against his chest. His belly convulsed.

The Shape grew solid, its edges and patterns more defined. As though he were looking at stained glass, a portrait of his life in scarlet and green and violet.

He shook, emotion rippling out from the centre of his body. Laughter, silent at first, then swelling into a crescendo of howls and wails. David tumbled onto his back and roared.

An image of Ariel thundered through his mind. She slumped to the carpet against the doorway to the den, body quaking with laughter.

The scene washed away, replaced with a mental film of walking with Aunt Mel along Marine Drive when he was four; then that skipping sensation as the film raced forward into the raw, awkward teenage fantasy of Auntie on her back on the bed. *"That feels so good, Davey."*

David shrieked. His stomach spasmed. He struggled to sit up, shifting his butt until his back leaned against the padded wall.

Warmth in his groin drew his attention. He stared in fascination at the spreading yellow stain.

"Thought that was only a cliche," he murmured, then buried his knuckles in his mouth the way Ariel did to bring himself under control.

At last he could draw a breath and said, in a loud, clear voice, "I've just wet myself. Could somebody come in here and change me?"

43

Ariel crossed her arms and followed Ezekiel and Dr. Olver to the elevators. Zeke reminded her of Warren, stomping around the living room because Elizabeth refused to let him have his choice on the wall screen.

If she was wrong, David was finished. He would ask himself a simple question: what if my journals are bullshit? And then he'd put things together in his mind and come out hating his aunt and uncle. And himself.

You reached into David's head and waggled the wires. Too late to go back.

In those last moments before the intern dragged him away, David had fixed her with his unbreaking stare. He had found a Shape.

Zeke's voice dragged her thoughts back to the present. "What were you trying to do back there?"

"Save it," Ariel said. The psych nurse recoiled. "Let's talk in your office."

The man thumbed the reader on the counter and led her to the elevator. Ariel was sure she looked ready to collapse. Not enough sleep, not enough time to think.

The elevator door slid open. Ariel stepped in and turned. She looked up at Zeke's eyes. He had the kind of face that could ruin an actor: rage made him look comical. Dr. Olver stepped in on her right, and the door whined shut. Ariel sensed them looking at each other over her, the distraught spouse of the crazy patient. Olver hadn't spoken since they had burst into the room and Ezekiel demanded she leave.

Zeke sucked a breath through his nose.

Ariel's throat felt like sandpaper. "Ever been to Aznar Park?"

"What?"

"The busted bust is still there." She laughed, expecting a quiet chuckle, but the sound came out as a girlish giggle.

The door opened on the seventh floor, and Zeke led the way to his office. Ariel listened to the sound of her boots on the tile floor. The psychiatric nurse pushed the door open. Ariel saw her purse sitting next to the chair where she had sat twenty minutes or a decade ago. The man marched around his desk, swaggering like a gunfighter. The door shut behind her.

Ezekiel let loose. "You suggested to David his memories are just fantasy. Now we'll have to start over with him. And there isn't anyone in this city who knows how to handle ERIN survivors."

Ariel lowered herself into a chair. "You have no idea what's good for him, what he needs. You're fumbling around in the dark. You and everybody else."

"The only way David can get through this is if we let the memories return at their own speed."

"Who told you that? Until David came here, you had never even *seen* an ERIN case."

Zeke's fists clenched and unclenched. Her gaze flickered to his neck, looking for the telltale throbbing artery. David could read her, even when she pulled her anger inside and rolled it into a stony ball in her belly. Invariably, at that moment when she felt like she might crack apart like a wet rock in a fire, he would do or say . . . something. She never knew what it would be. But that little stone would crumble into sand inside her.

Her daughter understood him better than she did. The thought unsettled her.

"Ms. Morrissey. Ariel. I understand you're concerned for your husband, but this is not – "

"David doesn't want to remember what really happened back then. Hell, he wrote eight notebooks full of lies and BS. If his journals were true and he still had a family alive, they'd be crowding around him right now. Suppose his aunt were here the way he remembers her. And suppose he told her what he recalls about going to the park and seeing the busted bust. His aunt might say 'Yes, David, and you played with a little girl in a green T-shirt and jeans.' Maybe he has no memory of that little girl. Maybe his aunt is confused, and David never saw the little girl she remembers; maybe she saw some other boy playing with that kid. But now David has a piece of a memory that is complete bullshit, and to him it feels right."

Zeke's eyes rolled. "David's memories of the park came back to him on their own, without help from anyone else – including you."

Olver spoke. Her voice sounded tight, as though she were strangling herself while speaking. "David has to come to terms with what happened to him – with what he did."

Ariel reached for her purse, caught its strap, tugged up on it hard. It seemed to leap into her lap. Zeke looked as if he expected her to pull out a gun when she unzipped the main pocket and reached in. She brought out the pages she had printed this morning and thrust them to him.

Confused, Zeke turned them around and looked at the side-by-side pictures of the busted bust. He dropped the pages onto the desk. "Yes, David remembers this, of course. But you're missing the point here – "

"Read the caption under the photos."

Zeke leaned forward. "I – "

"The date. August 2030. That's when vandals destroyed the bust."

A gasp behind her. Olver's voice was a whisper. "That's not possible."

Ezekiel's eyebrows shot up. "I don't understand."

Ariel grimaced. "David went to the North Vancouver clinic in 2028. His aunt and uncle were already dead. There is no way they took him to this park when he was a kid."

The psychiatric nurse looked past her at the doctor, then back at the pages. "Well. Um. This must be wrong, then. David clearly remembers the park."

"My daughter told me David took her there four years ago. That's when he saw old Aznar's broken head. And that's the problem." Days without sleep settled on her shoulders. She slumped. "Bennie Shimmerman wrote that memory is a story.

We have images and sensations and emotions, but it's the story that puts them in context. David has eight books, all telling the same story. But the memories coming back to him don't fit the context. Without context, they're driving him crazy. But I've given him that now. Good memories are from the past he wrote about in his notebooks.

"All the shit his aunt and uncle did to him is just the product of a hormone-addled teenage mind; that's all he needs to believe." She leaned forward and placed her elbows on the desk. "And let me make something absolutely clear. You will not interfere."

The psych nurse glowered back. "When you brought David here, he became my patient. I'm in charge now." His eyes darted from her to Dr. Olver and back. Afraid of losing control. Not control of *himself*; Ariel was sure of that. No, he thought he might lose control of the situation.

"You have no experience with an ERIN victim," Ariel said. "I've lived with one. Bennie Shimmerman is credited with launching a revolution in neurology and psychology, and *you don't even know her work!* If you say or do anything at all to David, I will end your career."

Zeke paled. "You can't do that."

"David has a condition you don't understand, and you haven't called in an expert – you haven't even brought in a staff psychiatrist. Then David told you to let a violently self-destructive and suicidal patient out of her cell upstairs and put her back down here, and you did it. You've got one patient treating another."

"That's not true!"

"Park it, I'm not finished. On top of this, two children wandered into the psychiatric ward with no adult supervision, and you let them blithely sit down for a chat with your suicidal patient." Ariel pushed herself back and rose. "Say nothing to David. Not a word. Or I will see that your face shows up on *NetNews* in a malpractice suit like this city has never seen."

~

Auntie is on the phone, voice hushed. "Don't argue. This is important. We'll be away for a month."

"But I have school."

Auntie hangs up. The boy shrugs and goes to pack his gray knapsack.

Half the kids at school and a third of the teachers wear breathing masks these days. Auntie's call means a month out of school.

They drive to Uncle Ray's cottage, now Auntie Mel and Uncle Stu's second house. The boy spends the first couple of weeks sneezing, coughing, and spitting phlegm into the toilet at night. But by the middle of their stay at the farm, he is better and so are Auntie and Uncle. Uncle seems to mellow. He sits facing the living room windows and watching the rain. "Always loved a good storm. The way the lightning chops at the sky. And you can feel it in the air, making your hair stand on end." Uncle grins at him. "Makes you feel alive, doesn't it? Like you want to . . . ."

Uncle looks up at Auntie. Her hands settle on the boy's shoulders. She leads him to the worn-out sofa in the living room. Uncle peels off his own clothes and sits watching them. The boy studies his eyes. The old man likes this.

Uncle has started touching him again. When Auntie isn't around, sometimes Uncle takes him. But the boy knows he doesn't swing that way. The boy likes lying with Auntie. Sometimes he wishes for a sister or a niece; he can't imagine doing it with outsiders.

Uncle is no longer afraid. This worries him.

~

Summer 2032

"Two minutes twenty-one seconds."

44

BLUE SKY, CRISP AND PURE, beyond Ariel's bedroom window. The clock radio said 9:48. With a yawn she rose and looked for something nearby to wear. The room looked like a neat-bomb had blown up in it. No clothing lay on the carpet, with the exception of her Chinese slippers. Gran's dresser was tidy, the laundry hamper next to it was shut rather than overflowing with grimy outfits.

The room had looked this way yesterday, and the day before. Ariel was sure of it – and equally sure she hadn't noticed until now.

Nonplussed, she slipped bare feet to the floor, feeling for her slippers with her toes. The closet door opened on her winter jacket, Mom's old trench coat, a row of dresses she hadn't worn in ages, and her gray robe. She reached for the robe and flung it on.

"David?"

No answer. Ariel made her way to the living room. David's knapsack sat next to the couch, pants and two T-shirts folded on the carpet beside it.

The bathroom beckoned. She pushed the door shut behind her, then reached for the toilet lid. Her hand stopped above a sheet of yellow paper taped to it. Ariel peered at David's looping scrawl:

Ariel:
Going downtown. Playing chess. Meet me at
Ayutthaya for lunch?
~ David
PS: Staying at Simon's house tonight. Have to
collect some books. Haven't seen the others in
weeks.

Ariel smiled and crumpled the note in her fist. "The least you could have done is put the coffee on before you left."

Minutes later, her bladder no longer complaining, she wandered into the kitchen. The coffee pot was empty, but a blue sticky note on the coffee maker's base declared:

Not good for you. Chai on stove. Turn on
medium heat, wait till it steams.

A crude arrow pointed in the direction of the stove. Ariel laughed and did as told, tugging the note off. Then something nibbled at the back of her mind. Her palm opened on the balled-up paper she had found in the bathroom. She smoothed it out and read it again. "'Haven't seen the others in weeks.' God, David, histrionics are my specialty; it hasn't been that long. It . . . ."

Just how long had David been here? With that came another thought: the house around her wasn't breathing, wasn't filling the air with its fury.

Ariel reached for the counter and held herself steady. What the hell did that mean, the house wasn't breathing?

The question tumbled down a slope in her mind and shattered at the bottom. The shards coalesced into . . . someone else's memory.

She sits with her back to the couch, quivering. The house whispers in her mind: *You sicken me, you little bitch. David may let it all slide away, but as long as you're here, you will answer to me.*

She bolts to her feet, ignoring the sounds of David in the kitchen. Her belly rumbles. Food. But no, she can't stay here; the house envelops her, its walls moving toward her, squeezing against her. She flees to the basement steps, scrambles downstairs and across the cold floor to the door opening on the steps up to the garage.

The garage isn't as it should be. The black Plymouth Duster is parked where her nest was, the mass of ancient blankets and grimy clothing is gone, and the boxes that used to be scattered about are stacked against the back wall.

"Cleaned it up." The voice makes her shriek and spin around. David stands with his hands at his side, palms on his thighs, his vacuous eyes fixed on her.

"You bastard. I can't. . . "

He waits. "Can't what?"

She struggles to catch the words, but they pour from her throat like vomit. "The house hates me, I can't be inside it."

David's hands grip her shoulders. "House doesn't hate you. You do." He pulls her to him, then pushes her ahead. "Upstairs. Dinner."

The house sneers at her with every step. She leans against him, belly convulsing until she feels as though her middle is on fire.

That didn't happen, Ariel thought. David hasn't had time to clean up the garage; he has only been here for a few days. And I'm not like that, wailing like a crazy person.

In the living room she clicked the television on. CNN appeared. She surfed until she found the weather channel with its perpetual display of the date.

Wednesday, June 30.

Ariel sank onto the couch. "You met Corey at Chapters in early May. And that night . . . ." That night David lay beneath her. "Jesus. He's been sleeping on this couch for seven weeks."

Her thumb settled on the Mute button, and a cheerful yet silent weather woman strode back and forth in front of a map, pointing at colourful patches with numbers on them.

What happened in the last seven weeks of your life?

David leans over Gran's album as Ariel bellows wave after wave of rage. He cowers, eyes locked on the photos, afraid to meet her gaze. Then he speaks, and she realizes all her insults and taunts have washed over him leaving him untouched. "Tell me about this." Lean fingers tap a photo of her school gymnasium, taken when she was seven. Mom and Dad stand next to her. She is a holly tree in the Christmas show, thorny branches jutting from her black dress.

Then: "You look happy there." Motioning at a shot of Mom and Dad at some beach along the coast, Ariel herself three years old, parents holding her up by her tiny arms so she looks like she is standing on ocean.

Rage cracks, and Ariel curls up on the couch, head against his thigh, her body quaking, knuckles pressing against her eyes.

That had to be the first week or two. Days ago, out of sheer boredom, she tidied up the papers in the corner; they were now organized in the den. The house began to look and feel like home again.

She remembered having these same thoughts then, and days earlier as well. But each time, something tore apart in her mind.

Not this time, Ariel decided. Get out of here.

She found her phone in one of its haunts – on the carpet next to the black leather chair. She tapped its screen.

David answered on the first ring. "Hi, Ariel."

"Who's winning?"

"I am."

"So. You want to meet for lunch?"

"Yes. When?"

"Hell, I don't know. I dragged my butt out of bed about ten minutes ago. I haven't even poured chai yet."

"Twelve thirty?" he said.

"I'll be there."

At a quarter to twelve she put on capris and a blue tank top, then opened the closet near the front door to look for her summer jacket, the blue one with stripes down the shoulders.

A white coat with a belt around its middle hung on a wooden hanger. Ariel winced, remembering Corey's hands in that coat's pockets. Was this how it would be for the rest of her life? Everything she saw pushing some large, painful button in her?

Then she recalled the electric razor sitting on a shelf in the bathroom. And Corey, leaning over the basin, working those triple blades over his cheeks. He might want his things back. More likely he'd given up on them – not interested in seeing her after their last spat in Chapters.

Ariel found her keys and purse on the dining table, and tucked her phone in her pocket. She opened the front door. Then she realized she hadn't grabbed her own jacket. But June was hot; sun beat down on her. Warmer now than it was last week, when –

Memory stormed into awareness.

"I can't," Ariel says, but David tugs her hand. She steps down to the sidewalk, leaning against him. Early morning sun glares. They walk along Watling to Royal Oak, and David leads her north. Past the church, past houses with flower beds and lawns. At the Skytrain station, David takes her hand and guides her across the street, and they walk back. The air smells of mowed grass.

That must have been three weeks ago. Last week he had forced her to walk with him to Pedro's down on Rumble Street for breakfast. David had wandered into the computer shop and talked to the old man behind the counter, and when they left he carried a small box holding a fan that would make her computer work properly. It likely did now, though she hadn't turned it on. Hadn't spoken to anyone, not even Katie.

No, wait – Shay phoned, she thought. I told her to fuck off.

Ariel set out toward the Skytrain station. Her hair, for the first time in ages, didn't feel like a bird's nest. She ran her fingers through straight black strands, enjoying the feel of it brushing her shoulders and back. A tall black man who lived in the neighbourhood walked by. She smiled a greeting at him. Moments later she climbed the concrete steps to Royal Oak Station. Then, remembering that her city transit pass had expired weeks ago, she trudged back down and tapped her phone on the ticket machine.

Burnaby flowed past the windows. Stations came and went. The train crossed the suburban border into Vancouver proper. The Science World dome gleamed in the sun.

The train hit the patch of track past Main Street Station that always made it shudder. Ariel clung to the bar across the top of the seat in front of her. At Stadium Station, the train's brakes whined; then the train accelerated away with a new collection of passengers. Darkness fell when the train shot down into the underground. In Granville Street Station, Ariel joined the throng of passengers exiting through white-tiled tunnels to the escalators and staircases and out onto the street.

A red brick pinned Ayutthaya's front door open. David was nowhere in sight. She picked the corner table near the windows and chose the seat that put her back to the wall.

The small Thai man who ran the place waddled up to the table. "Long time. David okay?"

Ariel stared, flustered. "Uh, yeah. He's fine."

The man's shoulders relaxed. "Good."

"He'll be here in a few minutes."

"Very good. Menus?"

"I think David memorized it."

The man grinned. "One for you, then."

He brought her green tea. She watched a tide of humanity flow past the windows, breaking at times on the benches along the street to await southbound buses.

Her stomach knotted at the thought of David striding in. It seemed a kind of visceral reaction to the memory of what she had come to call That Night. David never mentioned it, not since his remarks at the halfway house on the day of her breakdown.

David walked past the windows and in through the open door. He placed his phone on the table, then pulled his chair out and sat. "Good afternoon."

"How is your day going?"

"Seven games. Ordered yet?"

"Surprise me."

The owner materialized, his face warped by a wide grin. David smiled back and fired a string of syllables, which prompted a nod and sent the man retreating into the kitchen.

"You're staying at the house up north tonight?" Ariel asked to make conversation.

"Simon thinks you kidnapped me."

Ariel laughed, hating the undercurrent of desperation in her own voice.

David cocked his head as though expecting her to say something.

To fill the void, she blurted out: "I found Corey's jacket in my closet. And some other things. I'll have to return them to him soon."

David became still. "Want me to come with you today?"

The thought hadn't occurred to her. "Um. No. I'll be fine." And suddenly she realized it would be today that she bundled Corey's things together. The thought sent jagged shards through her belly.

David nodded, eyes fixed on hers. "Have to start looking for an apartment."

"Oh. Good. I guess. What's Friday evening like for you? We could order take-out, and watch a flick. That gambling movie with Reeve sounds good."

"Aces," David said.

"Huh?"

"Film's called *Aces High*. Lots of gambling language in it. You hear people say things like that now. 'Aces,' for 'good.' 'Deuces' for 'bad.'"

Ariel swallowed. "You've seen it. Then we could get something else."

"Haven't seen it. Just listen to people, that's all."

"Oh." Ariel wished she could think of something more to say. "Your knapsack is still in my living room."

"Yes."

Silence crawled. The Thai man arrived with two plates and set them on the table. He smiled and bowed, carefully laying down two sets of black chopsticks. Ariel nodded a hasty thank-you, then looked at David. He gazed back.

"Yes?" he said.

"I . . . ." I'm sorry about everything and I wish there was something I could say and damn damn damn. "Never mind."

David talked about apartment hunting for the rest of lunch, and his plans for taking college courses in computer repair. His choices of conversation didn't jive with the emptiness in his eyes, as though something were missing from him, some fundamental part that might have made him normal.

Ariel made her way home an hour later, feeling hollow.

45

She spent the afternoon hunting the house for Corey's leftovers. In the end, the list was shorter than expected.

One hardcover novel, a techno-thriller called *The Queen of Kashmir*; the cover picture showed a jewelled crown with a rocket launching through it. Two socks, both white, mismatched. His electric razor, no longer charged, and the accompanying power cord. A toothbrush which looked as though it had polished a shoe; she threw that in the trash. And finally, his jacket.

Ariel found a cardboard box in the basement and piled his items into it. In late afternoon, she lugged it to the car. She had switched to shorts and a fresh T-shirt. The Duster purred to life, and she wheeled it out of the garage.

Oh God, Ariel thought. What if he's home? What if *she* is there?

Corey had, at least until a few months ago, four roommates all throwing money into the rental pot for a duplex in South Vancouver. One of them must be home. Ariel retrieved the box from the car's trunk and carried it to the front door. She set it on the step and touched the doorbell. Its double chime came to her muffled by the door.

Footsteps within.

An Asian woman opened the door. Dark hair, taller than she, with a sharp jaw and a quick smile.

Maybe Corey had moved. "Uh, I'm looking for Corey Hewitt."

The woman turned. "Sweetie, it's for you."

Wing. Best case scenario: she could have been a clone of Ariel herself. Worst case: mind of an astrophysicist and body of a porn star. This woman was somewhere in the middle, at least physically.

Corey appeared, eyes bright. The light went out of them when he saw her. "Ariel."

The demeanour of the woman changed from relaxed to on edge, like a cat catching sight of another.

Ariel's throat felt like pumice. She knelt, picked up the box, and held it out to Corey – trying not to shake. "You left some things at my house. I brought everything I could find."

Wing crossed her arms.

"Thanks." Corey took it and backed into the apartment. The woman watched her, jaw clenched. He returned a moment later. "Thanks for bringing it. I didn't expect that." Wing slipped her arm around his waist.

Ariel's heart turned over.

"It was the least I could do. God, isn't that the truth." She forced herself to look at him. "I was awful to you. You tried to help after Gran died and I was a mess. I'm not making excuses, but . . . God, I'm not very good at apologizing."

"Actually, you stink at it," Wing said.

Ariel blanched. A brutal voice in the back of her mind barked: Stupid cow, I had him first.

She laughed, a sharp giggle. Wing's brow pinched in surprise.

"I haven't had much practice." Ariel turned her gaze on Corey. "One other thing. You didn't deserve that scene at Chapters. I'm sorry. I mean it."

It was Corey's turn to look stupefied.

What the heck, Ariel thought. Go for the hat trick. "You two look good together."

Both of them stared. Wing laughed out loud, then clamped her hand over her mouth. "I'm sorry. I just never . . . ."

"Never expected a blessing from me?"

"I would have put the chances of that at about the same as the moon falling into English Bay."

Ariel smiled. "Me too, a few weeks ago. But I mean it." She stabbed her finger at the woman. "Don't screw it up." Then she shifted her gaze to Corey. "And you. Don't take any crap from her."

An uncertain smile hopped around his mouth. "Yes, ma'am."

Wing's eyes narrowed. "Corey has told me about your addiction."

"My what?"

"Coffee. Like to come in? We have a pot on. It's probably awful now. I can make a fresh one."

Corey's mouth hung open.

Ariel laughed again, enjoying the sensation. "Better not. I'm trying to kick that habit. And he looks ready to explode."

She reached the car before the first sob broke in her throat. She climbed in and rested her head against the wheel. After a minute she wiped her cheeks. "At least you don't sound like a dying cat when you do this now."

*****

On Friday, Ariel keyed up *Aces High* on the player, and David sprawled out on the carpet next to the couch. Jackson Reeve was overrated, but Ariel decided by the end of the film that his "my lobotomy was an outstanding success" style of acting suited his poker-faced character. She took the empty popcorn bowls to the kitchen while the credits rolled. She returned to find David peering at his phone.

"What are you doing?"

"Apartments."

"Why don't you use the computer? It's easier to look at than that little thing."

"Thanks." David rose.

"Dr. Markson told me you didn't think you were ready. What changed your mind?"

David stared with that blank look she used to think meant he was stupid. Now it left her with the discomfiting sensation that he could see into her layer by layer like some weird-ass medical scanner.

"You aren't broken now," he said. His mouth pursed. "Like to come with me tomorrow?"

Patronizing son-of-a-bitch. She clamped down on the thought. "Well, if I'm not too broken to be seen with you in public, fine."

David's brow shot up.

"Sorry. Yes. I'd love to come along." Ariel forced her face to remain neutral. "Go ahead. Use the computer. I need to fill the dishwasher."

Ariel wandered to the kitchen. Faint footsteps reached her from the den.

David's choice of words annoyed her. *You aren't broken now.* She chuckled at herself. Weeks ago she would have laid into him for saying that. If nothing else, she wasn't such a witch to him now.

She tidied the kitchen, then eyed the dent in the wall where she had flung the coffee can weeks ago.

You did that, she thought. Pissed off at the lack of coffee. How moronic.

A brisk percussive rhythm indicated that her computer had started. Gran's old broken beast lived again.

The room spun, and a memory fell into place: the cafe near the tombstone shop. When David told her he had taught himself to repair computers, she thought he was a savant.

"Started by reading everything I could find. Made a shape in my head, how all the parts work together." She pictured him sitting across from her, wringing his hands, struggling for words. *"Had to make sure I really got it. The house had a broken one in a closet. Thought: if I can make it work right, I'll know I understand it."*

She remembered David in the cemetery, the day before they visited the tombstone shop. She had been vicious to him, joking about his aunt and uncle, going for the emotional jugular. He didn't care. But he stared at her, locked that lingering gaze onto her. Dr. Markson had called it finding a shape, a sense of meaning. When most people lost themselves in thought they looked around the room, or paced. David simply stared.

Simon Markson had said, "The hardest thing for a Shimmerman's survivor to do is learn how to relate to people again."

How does it feel to realize you were his graduation project? Ariel thought. *And why aren't you roaring mad right now?*

The answer came from that terrible voice in the depths of her mind. *Because you don't get to ride the white horse here. If David has played you for two months, his motives beat yours all to hell.*

Ariel shook her head. Ridiculous. Nobody could be that . . .

.

That smart?

Yes.

There's an easy way to find out. Ask him.

Ariel sucked in a breath to steady herself. Then she strode to the den. David sat at her computer, leaning one elbow on the desk.

"I have to ask you something."

His gaze remained on the screen. "What?"

David, she thought, *did you decide to try a little home-brewed psychotherapy on me when we met? I figured you'd played me just for a week or so, but did you actually start pulling my strings from the moment we met in the cemetery? Did you drive me into a mental breakdown for my own damn good?*

The question refused to come.

Afraid he'll laugh at you, moron?

No, Ariel thought. I'm afraid he won't.

Her gaze found the monitor screen. The blazing red "Vancouver RENTS!" logo burned across its top. Below that hovered a photograph of an apartment building. Silence stretched.

"Yes?" David prompted.

Say something. Anything.

"David," she heard herself say, "why don't you move in here?"

Aw, crap. Where did that come from?

His eyes turned to her. "Here."

"I've been thinking about this for – since – well, all day." *Liar.* "I mean, this place is more than I need, but I don't want to sell it anymore. I'm not thinking long-term here. You won't have to sign a lease, and you can leave whenever you like. God knows there's no way you could stand me for more than a year, tops. I'll charge you rent, but it won't be as exorbitant as you'll find anywhere else."

"I won't have to sell my testicles on eBay to cover the rent?"

Ariel guffawed. "No, you won't. And if they're just hanging around doing nothing, I won't complain if you feel like putting them to work once in a while."

David's eyebrows shot up.

Whoops; too far! "You're not obliged to. The Landlord and Tenants Association will bitch if I try pencilling that into the rental agreement. You can have my old room; it needs cleaning and fresh sheets, but . . . . "

All expression had slipped off his face. An image burst into her thoughts. David, under her, inside her, as she twisted her hips, savouring a savage need to see him in agony.

Tears cut hot tracks down her cheeks. "Maybe you're better off finding an apartment." She choked and wiped her face with her sleeve. "You have no idea how sorry I am. Some things just aren't forgivable, are they?"

"That's not the problem."

"What?"

David's eyes narrowed to slits. "Your motives that night aren't the problem. The problem is the execution."

"I – "

"Shut up and listen."

In surprise her mouth shut with a painful clash of teeth.

"Ariel. I'm nineteen. And male. With appropriate stimulation I can go from flaccid to orgasm in as little as two minutes twenty-one seconds. But that night you had me for more than half an hour and you still couldn't manage it."

Ariel's jaw dropped.

"I have some books up at the house. One of them has pictures. They should help you with the basics. Once you've read them, I can show you some websites that will introduce you to more advanced techniques like the Shanghai Spine Crusher."

Ariel stared in shock. A smile, wonderfully wicked, began to play at the corners of David's mouth.

"You *bastard*," she managed, before a fit of giggles punched her in the stomach and doubled her over. She sank to the carpet, cursing and laughing. David watched her, and each time she looked at him, she howled harder until slivers of agony pierced her body. She leaned against the doorframe, coughing and wheezing. David pushed himself out of his chair and lowered himself to the carpet, sitting opposite her in the doorway. He sat watching her in silence as she contorted.

When she came out of it, Ariel rubbed her eyes. "I really am sorry." She looked away, struggling to breathe. Then she forced herself to glare at him. "But stringing me along that way was cruel. Just for that you can make up your own damn room."

"Then I'll crawl in with you and steal all the blankets."

Ariel could hear her heart, firm and heavy, weighed down with grief and abrupt hope. Then a thought struck her. "Uh, the 'Shanghai Spine Crusher'?"

"I made it up for dramatic effect. Sorry if that ruins your evening."

Ariel snorted. Then she peered at him. "You sound different."

"I'm talking like you. Creepy, isn't it?"

"Yeah. Cut it out." Ariel didn't notice her hand had begun to move until her fingertips touched his cheek. He tilted his head, pressing his jaw into her palm. Ariel let her gaze absorb his face. Pale brown hair, angular face. Empty eyes.

No, not empty. Full of something she couldn't understand.

And you probably never will. Live with it, honey.

"David, promise me something."

His brow rose in expectation.

Ariel let out a long breath. "Promise me that no matter what happens, you will never, ever tell me how you figured out you can pop your cork in two minutes and twenty-one seconds."

~

Back home from the cottage.

Sprawled in his bed, the boy hears Auntie and Uncle through the air vents.

"He'll be new again, Mel. Virginal."

"I don't know."

"It's too late anyway. We're committed."

Committed to what? the boy wonders. This is important. He shuts his eyes, filing away the conversation. Tomorrow he will find out.

~

Autumn 2051

"Hell's Gate."

46

"ARE YOU ALL RIGHT, MR. GLASS?"

The washroom door muffled Randy's rumbling voice. Usually the intern stood with his back against the wall outside the shower stall, where David could see him silhouetted through the thick marbled plastic. Today he remained outside the room, leaving David alone.

Even the showers on the category-two floor took account of the condition of the tenants: gray foam covered the walls and a round grill served as the shower head. In this particular stall were grooves in the foam that reminded him of teeth marks.

A touch to the square blue panel below the shower head turned the water off. David watched steam rise from his bony arms. A face swam across his vision.

David is six. He leans against Auntie, feeling her warmth, feeling betrayed at the same time. She runs her fingers through his hair, beaming down at him. "Don't worry. You'll make lots of new friends here."

The school buses have begun to pull in: long yellow and black monsters. They squeal to a stop at the curb, and kids begin to flow from them. Little kids and big kids. David hugs Auntie harder.

She urges him forward. A tall woman with dark hair stands on the front steps of the school. She has on black pants and a big pink sweater, with a black stripe across her chest. Kids gather around her looking bewildered and frightened.

"Good morning, I'm Ms. Jacobson." She smiles at David. "What's your name?"

Swallowing: "David."

"David. Welcome." Her gaze shifts to another kid, and another, saying a few words to each. "Now let's show you all to your classroom."

Ms. Jacobson leads David and the rest down a wide corridor amid older boys and girls who talk and laugh loudly. She holds a door open and waves them in. The boys and girls spread out and shuffle their way to desks. David's gaze flits right and left. Chalkboards form a strip of green along one wall. Above them are colourful pictures of letters and numbers drawn with crayon. He picks out the letter A, an apple balancing on its pointed top. He can recognize B if he stares long enough; the loops form soccer balls.

"Take a seat, David."

Ms. Jacobson's voice makes him jump. A plump boy snickers. David marches to the middle of the room and sinks into a chair.

Time crawls.

At recess he sits apart from the others in the playground, choosing a spot on the steps where he can watch the kids on the swings.

A shadow falls over him, and he looks up. A girl sits on the steps near the railing on the opposite side. In Ms. Jacobson's room she sat in front of him. She has huge brown eyes and skin the colour of licorice. Her red T-shirt and pink skirt look too big for her.

"Hi," the girl says.

"Hi."

The girl watches him with those big eyes. "I'm Suki."

"I'm David."

Suki moves over next to him and laces her fingers together. "I wish I had a swing."

"Me too."

A silence stretches like a dark pit, and David feels himself slipping into it. He turns to Suki, screwing a smile onto his face. "Want to play in the sandbox?"

"Not really."

"Me neither."

"Where you from?"

David points. "I live over there."

"Oh. You walk to school?"

"My auntie drove me."

"You live with your auntie?"

"Yes."

"Why not your mom and dad?"

"They're dead."

Suki blinks. "Oh. I came by bus."

"Oh."

"The bus stinks like my brother's socks. It stops up on Fifth Street. That's a couple of blocks away from my house. My brother came with me. He is starting grade nine. He skipped a grade. He's really good at hockey; Mom says he is going to be great." Suki picks at a thread in the seam of her skirt. "You got any brothers?"

"Nope."

"Good. Mine's a dickhead."

Randy's voice clutched at his thoughts. "Mr. Glass?"

"Doing fine." David shut his eyes, but the memory had retreated into some recess of his mind.

A subtle loss of brightness on the floor told him Randy had entered the bathroom. David stepped naked from the shower stall. The intern stood with his thick arms crossed, his toe propping the door open. "I'll expect you within two minutes."

"Roger wilco, Captain."

Randy's cheeks twitched into a smile. He backed out of the door and let it sigh shut.

Fresh clothes hung on a rail next to the shower stalls. Clothes was a misnomer: the gossamer thin garments came apart astonishingly easily. If they got wet, they dissolved. David figured a patient could eat the cloth with no ill effects. Someone bent on suicide couldn't even strangle himself with a rolled-up sleeve. When he tugged the pants on he felt the seams loosen. He put on the tunic, then carefully tied the thin strings that served as buttons. The only footwear they gave him were white socks that covered his Achilles tendons but went no farther up his legs.

David pulled on the door. Randy stood near the opposite wall. He motioned down the corridor in stoic silence.

"Hobbies?" David asked. "What do you do when you aren't guarding psychotics?"

The intern said nothing. David stopped and turned.

"I read a lot." Randy motioned for him to continue.

"Like what?"

"Politics."

When they reached David's room, the intern pushed the button. The door slid open, grinding on steel rails. David imagined himself scratching lines into the padding on the walls of his room to mark the days – though what he would do it with was beyond him. He sat on the bed and studied the horizontal stitch-work. Now that he could think clearly, he let his thoughts wind back over the past days. Ariel's last visit had been three days ago – no, four. That put his total stay at . . . twelve days? Thirteen? Or fewer? Breakfast came at eight o'clock; he had seen the time on the phone on the intern's belt when the man brought in a breakfast tray. His shower took place at nine. Every second day, Randy and one of the other interns stood in the bathroom watching him shave with an electric razor which they confiscated immediately after. The lunch tray came at ten past noon, always. Perhaps in the psychiatric wing it helped patients to have their day regimented.

David turned his thoughts inward again. His memories had lost their chaos. He could rummage through them now, turn a thought or question into a scene.

Blessed clarity. The speed of the change in his thinking surprised him. But perhaps it shouldn't. Ariel was right: he had needed to see the Shape of it, to understand the distinction between his boyhood fantasies and the reality of his life, the reality detailed in his journals.

So what turned Auntie into an object of those fantasies? Perhaps –

A thought burst like a firework.

David is on the top stair coming up from his room in the basement when Auntie steps from the bathroom, a towel around her waist. She has left her chest uncovered, and her large breasts sway like pendulums. David steps back down the stairs, feet against the walls to avoid making the steps creak. He hears her turn and stride along the corridor, then the opening and closing of the bedroom door. His heart makes a heavy sound, resounding through his body. Then he becomes aware of pressure in his groin. He runs his hand down his front and feels his cock against the cloth of his sweatpants.

David laughed aloud. What would Auntie have thought if she knew she had fuelled countless teenage masturbations?

The camera eye peered at him from the corner. He waved at it and blew a kiss. Then he leaned back and shut his eyes. There must be something more interesting than teenage fantasies. Like, say, summer, when he was fourteen – months before his aunt and uncle died in the fire. There: focus on that, find something you can grasp.

A new slice of mental video rolled.

Uncle Stu's car smells of oil; Uncle complains about the holes in the front panels, which leak engine fumes into the cab. They are driving the Fraser Canyon. In the backseat David feels the car lurch. The engine needs work. So do the brakes. Uncle hasn't bothered yet, and Auntie has started nagging him about it, which means Uncle will deal with it by the weekend. David knows the pattern. The Shape.

For a moment he feels himself drifting into a padded room two decades from now: *Shape* is not a word he uses here. Force of will drives him back into the automobile as it rolls through the Fraser Canyon on a blazing summer afternoon. He sees a wall of rock, and when the engine dies he hears rushing water.

"Hell's Gate," Uncle says ominously, grinning over his shoulder. "Come on, boy."

They step to the edge and lean on the railing. David sees white rapids below, where tons of water carve away at stone. Auntie stands next to him, fingertips massaging his neck.

David glances at the cars. A mass of people of all colours, shapes, and sizes, wearing T-shirts and shorts. A pretty woman nearby wears a white dress and white sandals. The sun is bright, and David can feel it against his left arm.

The important thing is, he doesn't know these people. None of them come from school. So it's okay to let Aunt Mel run her fingers over the back of his neck. He loves it when she does that. He wipes sweat from his hands on his shorts and gazes at the water crashing into white foam on the rocks below.

Zeke came in to check on him before lunch. "Good morning, David."

David nodded in greeting.

Zeke crossed his arms. "Lake. She appears to be withdrawing again."

"Turning off? Getting quiet? Not answering questions?"

"Her therapist comes in for two hours each day. She doesn't say much anymore. She acts the way she did after her . . . first attempt." Zeke glanced at the camera.

"Told you. Bind her to the future."

"I don't know what you mean."

David injected a note of petulance into his voice. "Why don't you ask anything about *me* anymore?"

The psychiatric nurse put on a condescending smile. "David, you've improved dramatically." His smile looked forced. "It's remarkable, really. I've never seen a transition as rapid as yours."

"Getting better?"

"Absolutely."

"Then, no reason to keep me in this room. Better move me downstairs."

Zeke's mouth opened, then snapped shut as though he were feeling the walls of the trap David had sprung pressing in on him.

"David – "

"Why won't you let my wife see me?"

"What makes you think I've stopped her from – "

"On Ariel's last visit you were upset – dragged her out in the middle of our conversation. Hasn't been here since. So unless something has happened to her or the kids . . . is that it?"

"Your wife and children are fine."

"So: all that's keeping her away is you."

"I didn't say that!"

"Then why hasn't she been here? Wouldn't choose not to see me."

The psych nurse's eyes darted about, discomfited.

David smiled. "You think she shouldn't have said anything to me on her last visit. She pointed out the obvious – I've been mistaking fantasy for reality. You think I should have figured all this out myself."

"It isn't that simple."

"Think I'm dangerous? Obviously not – you cut your entourage."

"My what?"

"Three days ago you brought a second intern or nurse with you. Now you're comfortable with just having Randy here watch me. When he takes me for a shower, he comes without backup. And I had blackouts until a few days ago, didn't I?"

"Well, yes. But – "

"Haven't lately. Thoughts are clear now. I can tell you the time at this moment is between 11:00 a.m. and 12:00 p.m. Fourth day since Ariel's last visit."

Zeke looked like a cartoon tightrope walker who had only just noticed his rope had vanished. "Why don't you tell me what you remember?"

"When someone says, 'Tell me about yourself,' can you ever think of anything sensible to say?"

"I don't understand."

"Ask questions. Be specific."

"Okay. What were your hobbies?"

"Wasn't much of a reader, though my uncle loved books – real, paper books. Thrillers. He read Michael Slade religiously. Me: stereotypical teenager – too much television.

Had a few dozen games. My favourite was called Grey Wolf. You played a werewolf, and you had to battle monsters; trick was, you were human most of the time, so you spent most of the game running for your life. Only became a wolf for short periods, and that was when you managed to score points. Usually you annoyed the monsters enough that you had a tougher time when you turned human again because now they *really* wanted to kill you. Warren would have loved it. Next question."

Zeke rubbed the bridge of his nose. "Do you remember when you collapsed, and your wife called for us? The day we brought you up here?"

The question caught David off guard. Pain flared in his temples.

The cake has five layers of chocolate.

"Make a wish, Davey."

David closes his eyes and wishes with all his might. He blows as hard as he can, squinting beneath his eyelids, knowing his wish will come true only if he doesn't look up too fast.

Auntie claps. Uncle stands behind her, his smile wide and full of teeth.

"Happy birthday, David. You're four years old." He isn't sure which of them spoke. His gaze hunts the room.

"Mama."

Auntie kneels beside him, hand on his arm. "What is it, David?"

"I wished for Mommy. And Daddy."

Auntie's round face fills with lines and curves that meet in the corners of her eyes and the edges of her mouth. "Your mama and daddy are gone. I'm so sorry."

David turns to her and glares. "You said they would be back." It isn't true; he knows it; years ago Auntie told him they couldn't come home yet. He stopped asking. But now this is his birthday, and wishes are supposed to come true. Mom and Dad are supposed to be standing with Auntie and Uncle, Dad's arm around Mom's waist.

"Mama!" he screams. "Mama! Mama!"

Then Auntie's arms enfold him, and he wails against her shoulder.

"Jesus." David's belly muscles bound themselves into knots. "I remember."

Zeke stepped back. Randy moved forward.

David glared up at the psych nurse, knees trembling. "I was four. It was my birthday." Tears welled. "Son of a bitch."

Zeke's voice penetrated his thoughts, soft and distant. "What do you remember?"

"My birthday. Wished Mom and Dad would come home." David guffawed bitterly. "Auntie told me they wouldn't, ever."

Zeke stood in silence, his tongue riding his upper lip. "Well. We should leave you alone. I have other patients to attend – "

David wiped his cheeks on his sleeve. The cloth grew translucent where moisture touched. "When can I get out of here?"

Zeke stopped in mid-turn. "What?"

"Padded box is for people who may hurt themselves or the rest of the patients. I'm not dangerous, so when can I get out of here?"

"David, we have to be sure about you."

"Sure how? Can't see me interact with people. Even a well-balanced person gets peculiar in isolation."

"Very well. I'll consider moving you downstairs. I can't make any promises, of course. We'll see how things go."

The door slid shut behind them. David lay back on his bed and tried to sleep. When that didn't work, he got up and patted his stomach. He settled to the floor and started doing sit-ups. At twenty-five, panting, he stopped and turned over onto his chest to do push-ups. He found himself gasping at seventeen. He moved back to the bed. Over the past week he had managed to count the stitches in two lines across the wall next to the bed. That had lost its entertainment value the first day he tried it, but at least it gave him something to do.

The door whined open. Randy appeared, but his hands were empty. Then Jean stepped in holding a tray.

David raised his brows. "Haven't seen you in a while."

The nurse smiled. David noticed her fingers trembling on the edges of the gray tray as she set it on the bed beside him. "Enjoy, Mr. Glass." The woman straightened and backed toward the door.

David had a vision of a white blouse with white buttons. Then the buttons flew like pearls as he ran his fingers down the front and tore them free. He imagined himself on top of the nurse, her mouth forming an *O* as he pressed himself down on her, erection aching against his undershorts. His left hand gripped her breast while his right worked at her crotch, struggling with the zipper. Jean's face washed away. For an instant she was Auntie Mel, leering at him.

Jean stopped moving, her head twisting slightly in that motion that meant someone had started speaking to her through the bud in her left ear. Something between fear and anger moved through her cheeks and eyes. "Is there anything more I can get you, David?" Her voice broke at the end.

"No. Doing fine." David kept his face impassive. His thoughts sharpened. A Shape moved around Jean, drawing back until he saw it like a latticework. At one intersection stood Jean, at another Zeke, at another Randy and a crew of assorted interns he had seen throughout his stay. The Shape hardened, its intersecting lines growing in clarity and definition. Jean had not been in this room for days. Nor, he realized, had any of the other female staff.

47

BLUE FIRE FRAMED THE EDGES of Jackie's vision, matching the burning sensation in her throat. She had no way to snag a supply of Vaxodin here – the seventh floor of Crawford didn't keep stocks of drugs in a handy unlocked closet. The storage locker had a thumb reader next to its door.

Withdrawal made her bones and teeth ache, and caused indigo coronas to shimmer around anything moving in her vision.

Fortunately Zeke left her alone in his office. She tried to avoid thinking about Ariel Morrissey, keeping her attention on the screen. David muttered to himself in the window showing the view from his cell's camera.

"Farm," he mumbled. "We'll take him to the farm."

She tapped a square on the screen next to the viewing window. The image flickered and jumped. Now David lay against the padded wall. His fingers brushed against the side of his head with a familiar nervous tic. Jackie had watched him mutter to himself, curl up as though a cloud of bees enveloped him, and masturbate violently – not necessarily in that particular order.

The door swung open behind her. "Did you see?" Zeke asked.

"See what?"

"Jean took lunch for David."

Jackie rounded on him. *"What?"*

"He is doing much better."

"Shouldn't you have a trained psychiatrist make that assessment?"

The nurse flinched at the implied rebuke. "I'm qualified to recognize when a patient is a danger – to himself or anyone else."

Ariel Morrissey had scared him. Jackie felt like pointing that out. Zeke spoke up again, his voice brittle. "David has been lucid since the last time his wife saw him. I can't see a reason to keep him up there."

"Fine," Jackie said, more curtly than she expected. "You're right, it is your decision, and your responsibility. I'm just a volunteer."

Zeke leaned on the desk and peered at the screen. "That must be from days ago. He's an entirely different man now."

"So you've made up your mind about moving him out?"

"I'll watch him for the rest of the day. If he seems okay, I'll have him moved down here tonight."

"Tell the night crew to watch him."

"Of course."

No one changes, Jackie told herself. Not like that. You can fake it for a while, paint a smiling mask over it. But eventually the mask falls.

The computer's clock said 12:06. She was late for lunch.

In a Chinese restaurant across the street she found Ariel, cracking open a fortune cookie and laying the slip of paper on the tabletop.

Jackie sat. "Zeke says he is improving."

Ariel's face brightened. Tension seemed to ooze from her neck, softening her cheeks. "What do you think?"

Jackie shrugged, peering at Ariel through a blue haze. If a black market for prescription drugs existed in Vancouver, she hadn't found it in the Hyatt Hotel bar.

Zeke had left himself open to Ariel's threats. Ariel had a strip of iron running through her. She cared about her psychotic husband. That protectiveness would see careers ruined. She could probably even reach down into Baltimore and toss a wrench into Jackie's life. What would Mo think if it came out that Jackie had allowed a patient to forge his own life? That could get uncomfortable.

Ariel hadn't squeezed her, not the way she had Zeke. But she had insisted on these lunch meetings. Jackie loathed herself for this feeling that Ariel held her leash.

"I think there's nothing more I can do here," Jackie said. "You obviously have control of the situation. David appears to be getting better. And I am running out of excuses for being away from my job."

"I want to see him."

"That is up to the staff at Crawford."

"You mean Zeke."

"David wants to be taken out of his cell and put back in the category three ward."

"He's thinking clearly, then?"

"He seems more in control of himself now."

Ariel let out a breath all in a rush. "God. He's actually coming through this."

A somber Chinese couple came into the cafe. The door swung on its worn-out hinges, and a blast of November air prompted Jackie to hitch her coat higher on her shoulders.

"Thank you," Ariel said. "I appreciate everything you've done for him."

Jackie's gaze shifted to her hands in her lap. "You're welcome."

No one changes, she thought, remembering a monster in a tiny room.

~

The boy has questions, and burrowing through papers in Uncle's office he finds his answers folded into a torn envelope.

A blood test. January 20. Uncle Stu. A box says, "Possible exposure: SHV." In red beside it: GPT POSITIVE.

Below it lies an identical sheet, this one dated January 21, for Auntie Mel.

Possible exposure: SHV. GPT POSITIVE.

The twentieth was the day Uncle and Auntie didn't come home. They had returned the next morning, late, and told him they had the flu. Then they told him to pack. With suitcases piled in the back of the car they set off for the cottage and away from the world for a month.

~

Spring 2028

"I am God."

48

STARS EXPLODED IN JACKIE'S BRAIN as the kid slammed her to the wall and drove her to her knees. Jackie twisted and gazed into eyes full of madness and tears. He screamed something incoherent. Jackie put her arms up, and he swept them aside. She felt his touch on her breast, then agony as he clenched his hand into a fist in her flesh. His free hand hooked into the neck of her shirt and pulled down. Buttons flew. Then a snap of her bra, torn open at the strip of cloth between the cups. A hand tugged at the button at the top of her fly.

Then George had his arms around the boy and dragged him away from her. David's elbow slammed back. George's nose made a sickening crunch. Blood sprayed the wall.

Jackie's vision glazed. Then huge hands grabbed David. The boy flew across the room, tumbling against the bunks. He was up again an instant later, and Switch's paw-like hand slammed against his belly, driving the wind out of him.

Jackie struggled to her knees, then slumped back. The room gyrated. Her hand found George's leg. He clutched his nose, his white shirt soaked in blood. When he reached to grasp her hand, she didn't care about the scarlet running from his fingers.

The boy lay on the lower bunk, back against the wall, legs apart. Switch glanced at her, then leaned over him. The man's arm windmilled like a softball pitch, fist going for the boy's groin. David yelped once and slumped into a foetus shape.

Switch knelt beside Jackie and plucked at her open shirt, drawing the sides closed over her chest. "Can't speak for you, Doc, but I feel a hell of a lot better now."

Jackie lay staring at the ceiling of Lions Gate Hospital's emergency ward, trying to assemble the past hour in her mind. George lay in a bed nearby; she heard his breathing, a whistling sound. A doctor came to her bedside and told her she didn't have a concussion, that the worst of her injuries were bruises. She heard the doctor tell George he had a broken nose.

Simon appeared, settling his lanky body into a metal-frame chair.

Jackie glowered at him. "Why are they keeping me here? I just have bruises."

"I asked them to. You can go home tomorrow. Right now I don't think you should be alone."

"Simon, it's not even nine o'clock. You expect me to stay here all day and into tomorrow?"

Simon squeezed her arm. "Our staff psychiatrist will stop in later. Just in case you'd like someone to talk to."

Jackie shook her head in irritation. "This isn't the first time one of my patients has gotten rough with me. Jimmy Francesca relived falling off his parents' boat in the Georgia Strait and blackened my eye when I tried pulling him out of the bathtub. Have you arranged a shrink for George? His injuries are worse than mine. If I need counselling, he needs it more."

"It isn't the same, Jacklyn."

"For all we know, he would have come out of it before he got that far."

"That's not what George and Switch have said."

"Fine then, he wasn't going to stop. But they stopped him. I don't need a therapist to get me through what the kid *might* have done." Jackie sat up and slung her legs over the edge of the bed.

"No, my friend." Simon rose and moved to her. "I must insist. You aren't going anywhere."

"Not even the bathroom?"

The man smiled. "Okay, I think I can permit that."

The smock the nurses had given her chafed her armpits. Jackie wished they hadn't taken her clothing away.

In the little room across the emergency ward, she sat on the toilet and peed. When she rose, her arm brushed her left breast, shooting agony through her torso. She looked at the mirror. Blond hair, loose – David had torn away the band she wore to hold it in a ponytail. Her chest began to throb. Carefully she lifted the smock.

A dark purple bruise lay across her breast in the shape of a hawk's talons.

Jackie lowered herself to the toilet again and trembled, fingers digging into her knees.

Lorne Rainford, the Recovery floor's resident psychiatrist, came later in the day and sat with her. He was tall and plump, a combination that gave him a gangly waddle.

"If you would prefer to talk to a woman, I understand," he said, stroking his trimmed salt-and-pepper beard.

"I don't need a therapist: male, female, or in between."

"I understand, you've gone through a frightening and painful experience."

"Don't you think being constantly told I've been through something awful might actually make it worse?"

Rainford leaned back and crossed his legs in that distinctly male way, resting his ankle on his knee. He looked like he planned to stay a while. Jackie mentally cursed and tried a different tack.

"I need time, Mr. Rainford."

"Please, call me Lorne."

"Lorne. When I'm ready, I'll call Simon. Or you. Maybe you can refer me to someone."

As she hoped, Rainford nodded in satisfaction. He stood and reached for her hand. Jackie let him squeeze it. He stepped back. "Whenever you're ready."

Jackie heard his voice again a moment later, speaking quietly with George Ross.

Someone in the hospital notified the police about a case of attempted rape. Members of the RCMP appeared and insisted on talking to her. Jackie referred the kind but abrupt female officers to Simon.

Simon drove her home the next morning. Jackie left the hospital with a new appreciation of what patients endured. The sheer monotony of being stuck in Emergency for a day with nothing to do but brood had left her feeling oddly drained.

Two years, Jackie thought, surveying her apartment. And this is all you can do with this place?

Spartan furniture adorned her living room. The walls were eggshell white with nothing to break their monotony. The rooms didn't even have a smell to them.

Chicago was home. North Vancouver was just a stop along the way to somewhere else. Beyond the balcony and across the inlet sprawled Vancouver: a mountain range of towers – glass, steel, and concrete.

She was sick of it. Not the city. Just the people she had to cope with, the whining victims of the illness who insisted God meted out special punishment for them. She was done with them all.

Done with fifteen-year-old aspiring rapists.

Jackie channel-surfed, then Net-surfed on her laptop at the little round table in what might have been a dining area if anyone ever dined here. The assorted microwave meals in her freezer testified to her culinary skills. Later in the day she ordered Italian takeout from a restaurant up on West Fourth Avenue, and walked up to it to collect her food.

Late at night she showered. Looking down her body, she saw the imprint of David on her breast, the bruise an ongoing violation. She shut her eyes and felt around on the back of the bathroom door for the Bears T-shirt hanging there. This she tugged over her head and down, then made her way to the bedroom. She pulled the covers to her chin. Time drifted past.

An image burst into her thoughts: Switch, the big man's fist windmilling into David's groin, the boy's face twisting in agony. She slept at last.

Jackie woke at six, her usual time, and dressed in fresh clothing: black pants and a gray turtleneck. She scanned her closet and found her heavy wool coat looking alone and forlorn. Her light jacket must be hanging in her office. She glanced once more at the coat and shook her head. A chilly walk to the clinic would clear her head.

Outside her apartment building she headed up toward West Fourth. At the nondescript green tenement that was the clinic, a figure moved beyond the little hexagonal window in her office.

Her card worked on the lock, which surprised her; she had half expected Simon to cancel her card, to keep her away for a while. She walked the hall, past the locked door to security, on to her office.

Lorne Rainford sat behind her desk.

"You're in my chair," Jackie said.

Surprise flickered across the man's face. "Simon told me we wouldn't be seeing you for a while."

"Simon was wrong."

"Yes. I see."

"We don't need a therapist for these patients. They will be upstairs in no time."

"Simon asked me to take over. Until you're ready to come back, of course."

"I'm going to make my rounds. Please lock my office when you go."

Jackie walked the corridors, stopping in at some of the rooms and saying hello to the patients who hadn't yet made it to breakfast. Then she turned her attention to the common room where she found Switch behind the counter, filling the air with the smell of frying bacon. The Priest leaned on the counter, talking to the big man. Switch caught her eye, and she strode over to him, forcing a smile.

"Back already?" he rumbled.

"I'm fine."

Switch glanced at the Priest. "How is George? He got bloodied up bad."

Jackie smiled at the man with relief, thankful he hadn't asked about her in front of another patient. "A broken nose. He'll be away for a few weeks." She made a mental note to call him and find out how he was.

"What about the kid? Last I heard, he was back in lockup."

Jackie swallowed.

Before she could think of a reply, Switch's thick brow rose and his gaze moved to the doorway behind her. She turned to see Simon Markson rubbing his hands on his khaki shorts. Stifling a sigh, Jackie stepped over to him.

"You should be home, resting," Simon murmured.

"I'll go out of my mind."

"This place isn't healthy for you." Simon led her away from the common room. "You don't have to do this. You don't have to prove something here."

"I'm not trying to prove anything. I'd rather be here doing my job than at home wallowing and thinking."

The security office stood open. Simon strode toward it. "Have you met George's replacement?"

"No."

The short, beefy guard slumped at the desk with his hands on his paunch.

"Dr. Olver, meet Nathan Rosenberg."

The man didn't rise, choosing instead to reach over his left arm to shake her hand with his right. Jackie kept her face impassive. George knew something about psychology – he had been studying it at Simon Fraser University, which helped him land his job here. This man looked as though his response to a crisis would be to knock people over.

Sitting on the security man's desk were two black hardbound notebooks. Jackie picked one up and opened it. David's distinctive looping handwriting filled the pages.

"Picked them up in the room where the kid . . . ." The guard trailed off and shrugged.

"I'd like to see him," Jackie said.

Simon raised his brow. "That isn't a good idea."

"I meant on the screens."

An almost imperceptible nod to the guard. Rosenberg hit a button on the keyboard. The screens shifted, now showing the view from the overhead camera in David's cell.

Simon eyed Jackie. "Lorne tried talking to him. The young man was abusive."

The kid paced back and forth. The cot's blankets had been dragged off and flung onto the floor. David abruptly glared at her out of the screen. His mouth contorted in a silent bellow.

The guard grunted. "He's been doing that a lot. Yelling for his books. You can hear him in the isolation hallway, clear through the walls."

"Then give him his diaries back. It'll calm him down."

Simon picked them up. "Did you have a chance to read them?"

"No."

"They're fiction."

"I thought so."

"For the time being, the lad is to be kept in isolation."

"We can't leave him in that state. He could hurt himself."

"If he gets violent, Nathan has orders to call upstairs for help. We will restrain the lad and sedate him."

A vicious spark of triumph shot up Jackie's spine, quickly subdued. "I want to go in there."

"That isn't going to happen."

"Simon, I need to see him." To look him in the eye, Jackie thought.

Simon stared her down – or tried to. His gaze flickered away after a minute. "Okay. Just once, and you'll have Nathan and myself with you. After that, the lad is to be left alone, with minimal contact by outsiders. We'll keep him alive and fed. That's all." Simon picked up the notebooks.

Jackie led the way, listening to their footsteps and the guard's annoying tendency to sniff loudly. She slowed when she reached the narrow corridor of the isolation wing. At the door to David's room she hesitated, biting her lip. Then she swiped her card over the lock and defiantly shoved the door open.

The kid stood in the middle of the room. He came at her fast, and Jackie flinched back.

"Where are my books?" David stopped, eyes widening in surprise. A grin spread across his face like oil on cold stone. "I didn't expect to see you."

"Do you remember what happened?" Jackie asked, her heart making a heavy sound in her chest.

David shrugged. "They tell me I jumped on you." He snorted. "I didn't know one of the symptoms of this stupid disease is your taste turns to shit." His gaze found the books in Simon's hand. A hunger filled his eyes. Simon tossed them onto the cot.

David's gaze moved to him. "I need more. I'm almost finished with the last one. Did you read them?"

Jackie glanced at Simon, her fists clenching. It seemed the kid thought of her as a piece of furniture to be disregarded and ignored. She remembered Switch driving his fist into the kid's crotch and felt better.

Simon shrugged. "I won't lie to you, David. Yes, I have read them."

To Jackie's amazement the kid's eyes softened. He barked a single sharp laugh. "You know, I was sure you'd try to bullshit me about that."

"That doesn't bother you?" said Simon.

"Why would it? Do you think you're learning my deep, dark secrets?"

"You're falsifying your whole life. You're writing fiction."

"And that bugs you, right? You think I should be honest about it all."

"I don't think it matters, really," said Simon. "Maybe writing a story about someone else's life will keep you from losing yourself in your own. You may have an easier time with phase two than most patients."

"Wow. That sounds almost deep."

"And I can understand you not wanting to write about years of rape."

"I wasn't raped, dumbass."

"You expect me to believe a child could consent to what they did to you?"

"I'm not a child. You have no idea what I am."

Simon folded his arms and looked down at David, putting on his most patronizing air. "Then what are you, David? Enlighten us."

The kid's mouth formed a thin, hard line. "I'm God. Mom and her pussy of a husband are dead, brains all over the ceiling fan. Uncle Ray is in a box. Auntie Mel and Uncle Stu are ashes. My grandfolks out east are all gone too. So I'm God, writing the Bible. Writing those fuckers out of existence."

Jackie grabbed the handle and pushed the door open with her back. The corridor gyrated. She fled along it, hand skimming the wall, until she reached the restroom in the main corridor near her office. She scrambled into a stall, shoving the door shut and sliding the bolt into place. Then she sat on the lid of the toilet, quivering, as fire bit into her chest.

Three months, she thought. In three months, they will wheel him on a gurney into the elevator, his pupils wide, his skin pallid. Sticking a sharp needle into his foot or his arm won't get so much as a twitch out of him. A shell called David Glass will leave here, but the sick thing in that room will be dead.

End of story.

~

The boy spends his school lunch hour at a computer in the library, Googling the terminology.

SHV (Shimmerman's virus): The unidentified virus believed to cause Shimmerman's Disease, a disorder of the brain and nervous system.

GPT (Gentry Prion Test): A simple protein test indicating the presence of a recessive gene which inhibits the development of Shimmerman's Disease.

At a website for the American Medical Association, the boy finds a chart showing how the GPT gene works. Auntie and Uncle are immune to the disease. Mama Izzy probably was too. But Harrison Glass was an outsider. For the gene to work, the boy had to get it from both parents.

He stares at the screen, thoughts whirling into chaos. They twist inside him, too fast to follow, then slow and coalesce into a single realization:

They've killed me.

~

Autumn 2051

"You have no clue how I feel."

49

"ARIEL LEAVE MY JOURNALS HERE?" David asked.

Zeke stood in the doorway, hands clasped in front of him. "She took them, along with your clothes."

"So, stuck with this until morning." David smoothed his paperlike tunic and pants. The bed was as he remembered it: narrow, with a single white pillow and a yellow blanket. Dusk had come. He moved to the tall, narrow window and peered out. "Never thought I'd miss a parking lot." Kingsway Avenue stretched northwest, lined with high-rises and shops.

"I can have the nurse at the desk call your wife, if you like."

"Better to ring her in the morning. I call now, she'll spend the night bouncing off the walls."

A pregnant silence stretched between them, until the psych nurse broke it. "Lake is still here."

"No surprise."

"Her parents are back."

David turned and studied the man. Zeke's shoulders were tight. A muscle along the side of his nose twitched. Lake was, David knew, the reason the nurse had returned him to the seventh floor.

"Better say hello," he muttered.

David wandered into the corridor. Two nurses, both female, sat at the desk near the elevators, and a third leaned on the counter speaking with them in a hushed voice. David looked away when they glanced at him. With a jolt he realized they looked like cardboard cutouts of real people. The woman standing tapped her fingers on her thigh. David sensed something significant in that, but the gesture refused to build a Shape in his thoughts.

Unnerved, he walked on to Lake's room, Zeke's footfalls echoing behind him. He found her lying in the bed on her back, her spiritless eyes staring at nothing. The bandage on her throat was smaller now, and pure white. A new bandage encircled her wrist. David wondered what kind of mark her teeth had left there. Not the smooth slice of a blade – more like gnawed hamburger.

The Shape woke in David's thoughts and stretched its starfish limbs to her. Then the Shape curled into itself, withdrawing. David stepped back – into Zeke, who hovered behind him. He pushed past the nurse and strode back toward his own room.

"That's all?" Zeke said. "You aren't going to talk to her?"

"Nothing I can say. Needs a shrink. I'm not that." David marched into his room, wishing it had a door he could fling shut.

Zeke caught his arm. "You know her better than any of us. She needs you."

David shook the man's hand away.

Zeke stood breathing heavily. "If you can't do anything, if you can't . . . read her, or whatever it is you do, then that could be a sign that your grip on reality is slipping again. We may have to move you back upstairs. Think about it."

David glanced at the man. Zeke's attempt to look threatening would have been ridiculous had naked desperation not crawled into his features.

"Who was it?" David said gently. "Friend? Parent?"

Zeke's glare broke. "My brother." His hands moved in the air before him, as though pulling on a rope. He drew a long breath. "Please, talk to her. We've got a therapist for her, but ever since she spoke with her parents, she has been even more withdrawn."

David shrugged. "They tell her to take it one day at a time. Cliche."

"That sounds reasonable."

"It will get their daughter killed by her own hand."

"You said bind her to the future. What did you mean?"

David found his thoughts tripping over each other. Something fundamental had slipped out of his grasp. Some essential part of him. Yet his memories were so clear. Auntie, standing over the stove. David closed his eyes and savoured the smell of French toast. The image in his thoughts dissolved before he could bring it into focus. Ariel's form swam across his mindscape. His thoughts spiralled back to her last visit. In the room upstairs, holding his hand. *"Where did you keep your porn collection?"*

So much made sense: the distinctions between the two tracks in his mind, the sensations that seemed utterly at odds with one another. But there was a wrongness about it all, as though the Shape couldn't glom onto the underlying structure.

A face drifted across his mental vision, long blond hair, and lines around the eyes.

"Not sure," David breathed.

"Please. You must have had something in mind."

"Probably. Maybe it'll come to me."

"Fine, then. Yes." Zeke set his palms on his hips.

Relief? David wondered. Or anticipation of relief?

"I guess we can pick this up tomorrow," the nurse said. "If there is anything I can do for you . . . ." The words hung in the air, incomplete.

"There is," David said, remembering buttons like pearls, flying up from a white blouse clenched in his hands. The Shape coalesced. He visualized Ariel rising from her seat, the door behind her bursting open and Zeke charging in. And behind the psych nurse, another figure, face framed with blond hair.

"What?" Zeke asked.

David spoke softly to mask the tremor in his voice: "It can wait till morning."

*****

Jackie came to in a warm blue haze of rain. She blinked, and the squares of tile in the hotel shower shimmered into focus. With clarity came pain: her elbows, knees, and breasts felt as though they were full of smouldering coals. She sank into the tub, closing her eyes to the shower spray, imagining the corridors of Johns Hopkins. Back there she could take Vaxodin from the narcotics locker with an indecipherable signature and the name of a non-existent patient.

Beyond the wall of sleep, a beast prowled. "I am God," it muttered.

The bartender had booted her out at one thirty last night. Now, too many beers had left fur on her tongue and a throb in her temples, as if the symptoms of Vaxodin withdrawal weren't enough.

A muffled buzzing reached her. She twisted the shower knob to Off and reached for a towel. Then she noticed she still wore her white nightdress with hearts on it. She stripped it off and flung it, soaked, into the tub. Then she rubbed her hair with the towel and wiped her face and body.

The phone stopped buzzing. Jackie wandered out of the bathroom to the desk where her luggage lay strewn. She picked up a bra and put it on.

Tapping the phone's screen revealed: "Crawford Memorial Hospital, extension 1312." She touched the Return Call icon, then Video Off.

"Hello." Zeke Crane materialized in the little screen. He peered expectantly out of the screen.

Jackie yawned. "I just got out of the shower. What can I do for you, Nurse Crane?"

"I moved David back to category three last night."

Jackie's breathing stopped, then resumed with a heavy tremor that wove up and down her body. "So you don't need me here anymore."

"He has asked to see you."

In the silence of the room, her heart began a jackhammer rhythm. *"Why did you tell him I'm here?"*

"I didn't. He saw you. Remember when I ordered his wife out of the lounge?"

"I'm twenty years older now, and he couldn't have seen me for more than a second or two."

Zeke said nothing.

Jackie squeezed her arms against her chest.

The nurse licked his lips. "If you're not up to this, I can tell him you've had to fly home. An emergency."

"What makes you so goddamn special?" David glares up at her, pinning her in place with his gaze.

Jackie sank onto the bed.

She sees him through a cloud of dancing lights. The kid's hand grips her breast. Pain arcs through her brain and body.

"Dr. Olver?" Zeke's voice penetrated her thoughts. "I understand how you feel. But I don't see any way . . . ."

"I am God." The boy stands straight, proud of himself, uncaring of the agony he caused.

"I'll be there in half an hour." And you have no clue how I feel, Jackie thought.

~

A power drill to grind a delicate hole in an ancient incandescent light bulb. A quantity of gasoline from the jug Uncle keeps in the garage. A drop of fast-drying glue to fill the hole, and the boy now has an explosive. Auntie and Uncle are out when he drags the three propane canisters from behind the house and sets them in the basement next to the furnace.

Auntie is afraid of thieves. Gray steel bars cover the windows, bolted to the house. A lamp in the living room is wired to a security timer which turns it on and off several times a night. The boy resets it to wake at 3:00 a.m.

He replaces its LED bulb with the incandescent he had found covered in dust in the garage.

When they return, Auntie looks into his bedroom in the basement. He feigns sleep. They leave him be.

He hears them retreat to their bedroom, Uncle's voice slurring drunkenly.

Soon their voices grow silent. Then Uncle's snore reaches down through the air vent.

~

Autumn 2028

"Suspensory ligaments."

50

"FOR WHATEVER IT'S WORTH, I'M SORRY." Simon set the pages of the MRI report on the table.

Jackie looked at her fingernails, running them over the palm of her hand. "It isn't your fault."

"That doesn't change anything. This happened in my facility."

"You can't anticipate what patients here are going to do. I sent everyone else out of the room when David started rewinding. You weren't there." The words came easily. She had recited them to herself for weeks as the pain in her breast refused to subside. David Glass had been rolled on a gurney into the elevator to the Recovery floor, the pupils beneath his lids narrowed to pinpoints as Shimmerman's Disease unwound his life.

Simon's gaze lingered on the pages with their full-colour graphics of her upper body, giving Jackie the discomfiting feeling that he was staring at her chest, although MRI images could hardly be called arousing.

He turned his eyes to her, his stubbly face squinting as though in pain. Perhaps he did hurt, an effort born of trying to understand her feelings. It wouldn't be a physical pain for him, but a pain of realization. He pushed the papers toward her, turning them as he did so. Even leaning back, a distance from the coffee table, she could make out the one sentence highlighted in bold midway down the page.

Damage to left pectoral fascia and suspensory
ligaments.

In other words, Jackie thought, a fifteen-year-old creature from hell twisted your tit and left it permanently torn.

"Perhaps a plastic surgeon could . . . ." Simon let the sentence trail away into silence. Her breast ached. The pain had become her life's background noise in recent months.

"I'll think about that. Right now I have to do this." Jackie took an envelope from her coat pocket, smoothed it on her leg, and laid it on the table between them.

Simon reached for it and drew his hand back. "You don't have to."

"My contract expires in two months."

"We can renew it, roll you into a higher salary. Perhaps move you up here." Simon stiffened, his eyes widening at the realization of what he had suggested. "Um. Better still, I'm looking at opening a halfway house for recovering patients like Peter and Lily. Perhaps you could head up that." He paused. "I can ensure David won't be there."

"I'm not a psychologist. Or a bureaucrat. That's what you need."

"You have the chops for it. You have seen these patients and what they've gone through."

Simon watched her, waiting for a response.

"I'm taking time off," Jackie said. "For a few months. Then I'll decide on my options. But they won't include coming back here."

"Are you running away from this?"

"I've looked David in the eye. I've seen all I need to see there."

"Then meet him now. See what he is. Spend time with him. He isn't the young man you remember."

Jackie felt sure the colour drained from her face. "I don't need to spend a moment with David. I'm moving on."

"I have to say, Jackie, you don't sound like it. You sound like you're carrying this around in you." He waved away her retort. "You need to see a therapist when you get home."

Her shoulders grew painfully hard. "I will," she lied.

~

The boy slips from his bed and makes his way to the furnace. He crouches down beside the propane tanks and twists the faucets open. A sharp acrid odour. He backs from the room and climbs the steps. In the upstairs bathroom he collects a white towel, rolls it into a cylinder, and places it against the bottom of Auntie and Uncle's bedroom door – enough, he hopes, to conceal the smell.

He returns to the basement and crawls back into his bed. The smell is all around him. The end will be quick. The grip of fire. Pain. Air sucked and seared from his lungs.

He smiles.

~

Autumn 2051

"Feel better now?"

51

ARIEL AWOKE AT SIX AND made breakfast. Warren spent his first waking hour in the living room with his GameDome. Ariel watched him at the couch while Elizabeth took over the computer in the den.

"Warren," Ariel said finally. "Do you think I could try your game?"

Warren's gaze swivelled to her. His brow rose in a remarkable mimicry of her own expression. "Aces. But I'm busy."

"Oh. Later then?"

"Sure. Or you can go to their website. Google *Panthea*. They've got a three-month trial, free. You don't need a Dome to play, it's just more fun with one."

"Maybe I'll do that."

At seven thirty the pair stomped out of the house to the bus stop.

Ariel found the game's website. A creature with fangs glared at her from the screen. Panthea's logo was a network of intersecting curves and arches that made up a dozen faces, most of them inhuman. She clicked the green blinking "Free Trial" logo. A box materialized.

Select your character race: human, elf, orc, gnome. At random she chose gnome. A short plump figure appeared with questions about gender and clothing. Soon her gnome wore what looked like an evening dress made of leather.

She hopped through a list of questions, then watched her character materialize: a short buxom tracker named Ariela.

She stopped then, the mouse pointer hovering over the *Tutorial* option. You're avoiding the more pressing issue, she thought. Finally she shook her head and reached for the phone to key up Jackie.

The doctor's avatar appeared. Ariel clicked off and, her stomach feeling heavy, keyed the hospital. To Crawford's avatar she said, "Please connect me with the psychiatric ward."

"Yes, Ms. Morrissey." The computer smiled a too-perfect smile amid a corona of dark hair.

Jean appeared. "Good morning, Ms. Morrissey."

"I'm trying to find Dr. Olver. Is she there?"

"I haven't seen her. But I do have good news. Nurse Crane has moved your husband back to the seventh floor."

"Ezekiel let him out?"

"Nurse Crane would like to hold him for another week, just to be sure. But you can visit him whenever you like."

"Like *now?*"

"Visiting hours aren't until ten."

"But, if I just showed up . . . ?"

"You would find the elevator doesn't work without a staff thumbprint until visiting hours begin."

Ariel let her breath out in a long sigh. "Thank you."

The screen dissolved into the Disconnect logo. Ariel watched the neon blue loop twisting around the words. Then with a whoop she bolted to her feet.

Two and a half hours to kill. Damn. She ran a bath, soaked, tried to read a mystery novel from the Burnaby Public Library. That wiped out almost an hour. She spent the next hour sorting clothing on the bed. She soon had half her closet laid out. What did she want? Sex appeal? Or something understated, since she would be surrounded by staff people and neurotics at the hospital?

By the end of the second hour she had opted for an emerald pullover, given to her two Christmases ago by David, and white slacks. Not really the season for that colour, but it suited her mood. Dressed, she sized herself up in the tall mirror. No makeup. Hair showing gray roots. "Screw it."

David's suitcase lay in the bottom of the closet. She dug it out and tossed his shorts and T-shirt into it, along with jeans, sweats, and a blue button-up shirt. That should be enough for the time being. Oh, yes: toothbrush and deodorant.

"What else?" she muttered, drumming her fingertips against her chin.

Four of David's journals leaned against the dresser's mirror, where she had left them a week and a lifetime ago. Ariel scooped them up and dropped them into the bag. As she turned toward the door, her gaze found the nightstand with its picture of David and her. The woods of Stanley Park filled the backdrop behind the two figures in the shot, a dozen shades of green seen through a Y-shaped tree. A decade past. David stood behind her, arms around her middle. Last year he had suggested replacing the photo with a new one showing Warren and Elizabeth with them. Ariel had shot down that idea, saying, "I'm not having the kids staring out of a picture at us while we roll around like monkeys."

A detail the camera hadn't captured was David grasping her breasts and then dropping his hands to her middle an instant before the timer fired the shutter. She tucked the picture down under David's clothes, away from the hardbound books.

At the front door she slipped her sock-clad feet into light-grey loafers, thumbed the lock, and fled out the door.

A sky of broken clouds. She shivered as she pulled the car's driver-side door open and tossed the suitcase onto the passenger seat.

"The hospital," she told the car.

The drive to Crawford Hospital involved the longest fifteen minutes of her life. The car found a vacant place in Visitor Parking. Moments later she strode across the asphalt, David's suitcase swinging against her hip. At a minute after ten, she reached the glass double doors. She smiled at the receptionist and carried on to the elevators.

David, light of my life, lover o' mine. This past week has to be the worst we'll ever see in our lives.

The leftmost elevator ground open, and Ariel stepped in. Numbers above ticked upward. The doors slid apart on the seventh floor. No one occupied the front desk. A muffled sound of voices reached her from the direction of David's room.

Then she heard him. *"Get the hell out of here!"* And her throat cramped like a garden hose bent in two.

She reached the door to find Ezekiel, Jean, and another female nurse standing in the middle of the room. Beyond them, in the corner near the window, David crouched against the wall. His body shook. His face turned, and she saw the gleam of tear-soaked eyes. His gaze caught hers. "Ari." A whisper. He turned his face to the wall. His voice cracked and broke. "I'm sorry." He said it again and again, his voice dissolving into silence.

Ezekiel had turned, following David's gaze. "Ms. Morrissey."

"What's happening?"

David laid his arms across his knees and buried his face against them. Ariel pushed past Ezekiel and knelt. "David."

He spoke, his voice muffled.

"What?"

"I raped her." His voice came louder now. His gaze flickered past her shoulder.

Ariel turned. Dr. Olver stood against the wall, pressing her back to it. The woman's face twisted around an *O* shape of lips and teeth. Her right arm was tucked beneath her breasts.

Ariel's heart ground into a painful rhythm. She glared at Ezekiel. The psych nurse's mouth chewed on air.

When she touched David's arm, he flinched away from her. "Don't."

Ariel dropped the suitcase and pushed it to the wall. For an instant she felt like turning and walking out of the room, getting in the car, driving until she couldn't see anything familiar in the rear-view.

She reached with both hands and lifted his face, forcing him to look at her. "What did she say to you?"

*****

"Well," Zeke said half an hour later in the office down the corridor from David's room. "That could have gone better."

He swallowed and directed his gaze at Jackie. "We can have your . . . issues dealt with here."

Issues, Ariel thought. Such a weak word for it all. Pain. A lifetime of terror.

Feeling stretched like an overworked string, she looked at the woman beside her. Jacklyn Olver's fingertips twitched, jarring with the serene expression on the woman's face. "I'm all right," Olver said.

"There is an addiction blocker for Vaxodin. We can break its hold on you."

Jackie smiled. "I appreciate that."

Ariel felt like screaming until her lungs bled. Her voice came out hoarse, broken. "Feel better now?"

Jackie smiled again, her gaze meeting Ariel's evenly. "As a matter of fact, I do."

Ariel leaned forward in her chair, her elbows on her knees, and rested her face in her hands. I will not cry, she thought. I will not.

~

Two thirty.

He cannot think through the stench of gas. But something in him cries. His temples ache.

He slips from his bed. One foot touches the edge of the popcorn bowl he had brought to his room. He drags his suede jacket from the top of his closet, wraps it around himself and carries the bowl upstairs. He leaves the basement door open to let the gas spread, and looks for his shoes near the closet.

Mom's spirit hovers over him as he makes his way outside and across Marine Avenue, watching for gaps in the traffic. The stench leaves his nostrils. He sets the bowl of popcorn down, then huddles on the bus stop bench with his jacket snug about him.

Two forty-two.

~

Autumn 2051

"Did I hurt you?"

52

A TAXI GOT JACKIE TO the hospital at fifteen minutes to ten. Waving her VISA card past the sensor on her door got her the driver's perfunctory "Thank you." She strode into the hospital on stiff legs, a muscle in her right thigh throbbing. Her fingernails kept digging into her palms. When she told the duty nurse that the Psychiatric Department expected her, the nurse peered at a screen and tapped something. "I've called the elevator. Go right up."

This, Jackie thought, must be the stupidest thing you've ever done. No, the second stupidest – on the gold-medal podium stands your decision to send George Ross and that big patient with the tattoo out of the room so you could talk to David alone.

The elevator opened before she reached it, the walls a dark brown. The blurred vision brought on by Vaxodin withdrawal made it look like an open mouth.

The door closed, and Jackie sagged against the back wall. The seventh-floor button blinked green, indicating the elevator wouldn't stop anywhere else. An indigo corona looped around the button. The addiction sent rippling blues across her vision like northern lights.

The door slid open. Jean, the only other member of staff she had spoken with, sat behind the half-circle desk with its high counter top.

"Where can I find Mr. Crane?" Jackie said, her voice tight like a spring.

Jean had no chance to respond.

"Dr. Olver. Good morning. How are you?"

David Glass stood in the doorway of one of the rooms. He wore a white tunic and trousers made of that paperlike material. A thin line like a cartoon drawing of a distant bird in flight marked where his lips touched: unsmiling, expectant. An itch travelled back and forth between her elbow and wrist. She ran her nails over the cloth of her sleeves and saw the man's eyes track the movement. David blinked once. Then as the moment drew itself out, he stared at her, his gaze moving up from her arms to her face and back. She pictured the boy she remembered, imagined him overlaying the man she saw now. The two refused to mesh. In her mind the boy leered at her chest, and her left breast pulsed with pain. But this man, standing with his hands at his sides, looked as though nothing mattered but how she would answer his question.

"Fine. I'm fine."

David's gaze narrowed. "Ari says that. Doesn't mean she's fine. Means she isn't."

"Well, I am fine."

David's head cocked to one side, jerking, birdlike. "Join me?" he said, making it a request as he stepped out of the doorway, pointing at the room beyond.

Blue flame formed a silhouette around his body. Jackie approached, fingernails raking her arms. At the doorway she stopped, thunder in her heart.

David's voice was gentle, unsettlingly so. "Common room at the bend in the corridor. Maybe you'd prefer there. Probably other people. More comfortable."

Jackie glared at him, aware that he wasn't as tall as she expected.

She had stepped through the doorway and into the room. Her thoughts pulled back, trying to work out why she had done so. The only light came from a window filled with a sky that threatened storms. The man passed her, and for a moment she smelled sweat. He motioned at a chair against the wall, a metal-framed seat with a blue cushioned bottom and back. Jackie reached for it and jerked it to the middle of the room. She sat, glad the doorway lay behind her.

David took a second chair, his gaze absorbing her. His eyes grew narrow.

"Up from the States?" he said.

"Yes. Baltimore."

"Johns Hopkins."

"Yes."

"Long way."

"There is – was – a convention. To do with neurological – "

"The Seventeenth Annual Convention on Neurological Disorders. ERIN: not considered a disorder."

"It's my field!" Jackie blurted out, more forcefully than she expected.

David fixed his eyes on her, unblinking. His gaze carried no malice, no gloating sense of power – hunger to flay and damage. There was, however, a sense of probing, of looking into her. It made her stomach feel squeezed between two stones.

"The Shimmerman's Clinic," he said.

"Yes."

"Remember it. Remember a room. By myself. A green cot. Old computer terminal – big, heavy." He shook his head slowly. "Some of it: out of sync. Remember my birthday. No sense, that."

"Um."

"Tell me about it."

"The clinic? I had about fifteen patients at a time. Roughly. From Western Canada and the States."

"Tell me about me."

Jackie's knees and ankles ached. Another sign of withdrawal. Part of her followed the checklist: blue halos, check; hypersensitive skin, check; muscle ache, joint ache, nausea, check, check, check. "You kept to yourself." Because we never let you out, not after what you tried to do to me.

"You isolated me."

"You know about that?"

"Remember it. Remember that room. I think. I can picture the corridor. Walls. Nothing else."

"Do you remember how you came to us?"

"Social Services. Bald man brought me. At some kind of centre before then. Remember thinking: traded prison for Death Row." A quiver moved through the muscles in David's neck. "You look scared. Scared of me."

The statement, so unexpected, stabbed through her chest.

"It's true," David said, and Jackie felt a pulse of triumph when pain lurched across his face. "I remember . . . think I remember, buttons. White. Flying." His gaze switched to her chest. "From your shirt. White too." His voice began to pick up speed. "I can see them now. Tore your shirt open. You were on the floor. I was on top of you. You writhed – " His voice cracked. "I raped you."

Her skin became fire under her nails. Colour leached from David's face in the silence.

"You fought. I hit you. Remember blood. Broke your nose."

In the face of her would-be rapist, Jackie laughed, an abrupt bark which caught in her throat. You tried to rape me, she thought. But George got in the way; you broke his nose, not mine.

David's eyes took on a faraway look. As a second or two passed the look grew hard, fierce. He shoved his chair back and stumbled to the wall. His fist swung like a hammer against the window. The temperglass thumped. His foot struck his chair, sending it smashing against the bed in a clang of metal on metal.

Jackie stood abruptly, sending her own chair tumbling.

David's breath came out like the rattle of train wheels on a track. "Shit. I remember it. Tearing your shirt open. You were in my room with the cot and the computer."

For a moment Jackie saw it. Then her mind flipped. No, she thought. It was in the room he shared with Switch. She had sent George out, leaving her alone with a monster.

"You were on the floor. You had gray pants and a black leather belt."

Jackie felt the wall press against her back. Her skin burned with addiction withdrawal. I've never worn a belt, she thought dimly. Not with clinic clothes. And David never got far enough to try peeling my pants off.

It was ridiculous.

David's gaze darted away. Jackie wrenched her head sideways, following it, and saw Zeke Crane and another nurse, a black woman.

"What's happened?" Zeke demanded.

David slumped into the corner near the window. "Get out." His voice broke, and tears burst out on his cheeks and rolled down past his nose.

Zeke looked at Jackie, his face knotted with confusion. "Doctor, what is happening?"

"Get out." David's voice rose. "Get the hell out of here."

Images bubbled through David's mind: buttons exploding from Jackie Olver's blouse; his hand pressing between her legs, forcing them apart. The visions twisted his stomach and filled his throat with acid. Dr. Olver had her back to the wall, arms crossed, hands clenching her forearms. Fright was a palpable barrier around her.

I did this to her, he thought. I made her this quaking shadow.

"Get out," he stammered. "Get the hell out." His fist pounded the wall beside him, the pain a welcome distraction. *"Get the hell out of here!"*

Thank God Auntie and Uncle were dead. What would they have thought, knowing what he had done? He saw Auntie in his mind, her face contorted, teeth white against flared lips, a bellow erupting –

Then Ariel pushed between Zeke and the other nurse, to stand before him, his aged suitcase swinging in her grip.

"David," she began, and stalled before the words came.

Not you, Ari; not here, not like this.

"I raped her." His voice came out weak, flaccid. He said it again, his throat stronger now, making the words more real.

Colour drained from Ariel's face as she turned and saw Dr. Olver. Her breath escaped in a whoosh.

David turned toward the wall, unable to meet her gaze. Then her hands were on his cheeks forcing his vision back. "What did she say to you?"

"She lied. But I can read her."

"David," Ariel said. "You're wrong." But Ari's body betrayed her; the tension in her shoulders, the throbbing artery in her neck, the way the fingers of her left hand splayed themselves, all told him she didn't believe her own words.

"My God, Ari. I'm so sorry. Auntie would be sick if she knew."

Dr. Olver made a sound deep in her throat. Ariel glared at her, a look of raw hate carved into her face.

"Ari. Don't. Had to know."

Dr. Olver spoke, her voice hard and smooth. "Nurse. Vaxodin. Two hundred milligrams."

As she spoke, Jackie felt like laughing at the surreality of the situation. David huddled, crying over something he had never done, in anguish over what an aunt more monstrous than himself might think of him. His wife knelt next to him, desperation giving her voice a strident edge.

Ariel heard the doctor call for the drug. She glared at the woman, then turned her attention back to David.

"You're wrong, David. Whatever you think you did, you're wrong. You must be."

The words did nothing to the anguished resolve cutting across his face, turning the lines around his eyes into grooves. I've lost him, she thought.

The psychiatric nurse slapped a syringe into Jackie's palm. "Two hundred mills. But that's not – "

"It's enough." Jackie pushed herself free of the wall and moved to David. Ariel Morrissey glanced up at her, a look that said she would be happy to cut Jackie's throat. Then Ariel's gaze found the injector. David followed it too, even as his body shook. Sweat beaded across his forehead.

Expectation filled his face. He loosened his arms from around his middle and turned the left one up.

Fool, Jackie thought as she pressed the penny-size head of the syringe against the crook of her own arm. Time slowed around her. She knew the injection took a fraction of a second, but she was certain she felt the cold of the antiseptic against her skin, then the rolling sensation of the probe hunting the vein, and finally the mosquito bite of the needle piercing her skin.

"If you're so good at reading people, David – " she began. Ecstasy flooded her brain in waves of blue. She drew a shuddering breath, squeezing her eyes shut as her heart began to steady. " – then why haven't you realized I'm hooked on this stuff? What makes you think this is about you?"

Then she opened her eyes and looked into the shocked faces of David Glass and Ariel Morrissey.

The injector slipped from her fingers. "I've been addicted for months. A week ago I quit – cold turkey. I haven't slept in days."

A gasp from one of the nursing staff. She ignored them. Her voice came out strong and even now. "I suppose I should be flattered. Some women actually like rape fantasies. However, I am not one of them." She smiled, savouring the sensation in her cheeks. "I never knew you felt that way about me. I shouldn't be surprised, I suppose. You were fifteen at the clinic, and I'm the only woman you saw for a long time.

"Listen to me carefully, David. There were patients who hurt me, usually when they were rewinding and losing themselves in painful or intense or even incredibly happy memories. You were not one of them. Now tell me: Am I lying?"

Ariel blinked at the sight of Dr. Olver pressing the syringe to her arm. The woman's neck arched, a motion both orgasmic and despairing. After Olver spoke, a second of hope burned, because doubt flickered in David's eyes. Then his gaze narrowed, fixed itself on the woman.

He didn't see it coming. Ariel's palm pounded across his face, snapping his head sideways.

"Goddamn, David!" she bellowed. "How dare you? You almost convinced *me!*"

That brought his attention spiralling back to her. "Ari. I'm sorry."

"Jesus H. Get off my wagon and get your own. Doesn't this crap you've been spewing sound a little old? Look at me. Remember when we met? Remember my breakdown?"

"Oh God, I'm so sorry, Ari. I never should have – "

"Think, idiot! You listened to me whine about my childhood for weeks. About what a bastard I was to Gran, and Mom and Dad, and Corey, and everyone else in my life.

"And now you're telling me what a bastard *you* were? You spent a week in a rubber room, convincing yourself you used to screw your aunt, but somehow you're still an expert on human nature? Simon said you learned that skill to adapt after what you lost. Now you're getting it all back – all the twisted, clouded memories the rest of us have lived with for a lifetime. But you think you're special? You think it isn't going to affect you?"

There it was again, the instant of doubt. It had to be enough.

"Tell me, David," Ariel said. "Who do you trust the most?"

"You, of course. But – "

Ariel's hands darted out and gripped the lapels of his tunic. The paper gave way comically, prompting a muttered curse. She grabbed his head and tugged him close.

"Wrong, dumbass. The answer is *you*."

~

Sweat chills the boy's forehead. Two fifty-eight. The numbers refuse to penetrate his mind. Then he comes awake and straightens. He checks his watch again and starts to count down the seconds.

Three o'clock. The flies begin to gather about him. He waves them away and waits. And waits.

Three oh-one. The boy tucks his legs beneath himself. The flies crowd around him, buzzing against his ears. Mama materializes in his thoughts. "Should have let me kill you," she says, her voice bleak, her eyes like black balls.

"The house was full of bugs when they found you, boy," Uncle said. "Clouds of them buzzing around. And the stink. Pheweee."

Three oh-two. The lamp must have failed. Or his watch is fast. His body shakes. Tears land on the jacket, drawing dark lines.

The world roars.

Glass showers from the living room windows onto the front lawn. A hot wind sweeps across the street. The flies around him scatter until the only sounds are the hissing and crackling of the house. Lights flare in the neighbouring homes. Soon people begin to pour into the street. A man in dark blue pajamas and a ski jacket. Two teenage girls in parkas.

Sirens wail to the north. Just like on TV.

~

Autumn 2051

"Get on with it."

53

I will not cry, Ariel told herself. Exhaustion dragged at her chest and sat on her lungs.

Ariel looked up at the doctor beside her. Olver's face was a cocktail of serenity and ecstasy.

"My husband raped you." There, Ariel thought. I've said it. We lied to David, but there it is.

"No." Olver drew the word out like a song. "He tried. A guard and another patient stopped him. He broke the guard's nose."

Ariel massaged her eyes with her knuckles. "I'm sorry."

Olver smiled, angel-like.

"You lied to him. You told him he had never hurt you."

"He didn't. I've never met your David before. The David Glass I knew was a psychopath." Jackie's smile vanished, as though a switch had been flipped. "I wish I'd met your David sooner."

I won't cry, Ariel thought. Then she did.

54

EMBARRASSMENT WAS A KNOT IN David's belly, humiliation a rope across his shoulders. Had Ariel felt this way when she came apart, wracked by guilt and fear and pain? Her pain at least was real, not a forgery.

David sat on his bed with his knees beneath him. Ariel had brought him shorts and a T-shirt; cotton felt pleasant against his skin. His hospital trousers and torn tunic lay on the floor where he had discarded them. Randy had begun to look bored. He sat near the wall to the right of the doorway.

David's face burned where Ariel had slapped him. Four of his journals lay open on the yellow blanket. He liked the feel of the heavy paper.

> Uncle was skinny. Auntie was roundish. Auntie used to make French toast on Sunday mornings, with real maple syrup which Uncle said was hideously expensive though it didn't keep him from emptying half the bottle on his plate. (Ha ha.) Auntie would chase me out of the house and tell me to go for a walk, and when I got back this smell of eggs and sausages would be so thick you could almost chew the air.

The reality of it, a simple scene of breakfast in the old house, made him smile. Ariel was right when she asked him who he trusted the most. "The answer is you." Her hands had tugged the zipper of his suitcase open, flipped it over. Clothing and books poured onto the floor. "You wrote these. Find the part where you say you raped Dr. Olver. Show me where there is even a change in tone, anything to hint at it."

David stared at the books, a heap of them, one opened on its spine, pages fluttering.

"Ariel."

She picked herself up. "Read. This is you. You know it. All this confusion in your head? That's a bunch of wet dreams that you take way too seriously. You want to get back in touch with yourself? Read, damn it. You're in these books. Or do you think you made all this up?"

He stared at her back as she strode toward the doorway. Zeke and the other nurse stood together, looking uncertain. Jackie Olver glanced at Ariel, then back at David. She smiled at him. Her body had become preternaturally calm thanks to the drug.

The room emptied, save for Randy who took Jackie's toppled chair and moved it back near the doorway. He sat with his arms crossed, watching.

All that remained of his collapse was this vague sense of embarrassment. He should have seen Dr. Olver's addiction – it had scrawled itself into every gesture, every fingernail against her sleeve, every twitch of her cheek, every motion of her arms folded beneath her breasts. He had missed it regardless.

"Get on with it," David muttered, then chuckled to himself. His aunt might have said that. Normals learned to live with this perpetual uncertainty, this constant roiling of conflicting feelings and memories. He could, too.

At least he had his journals. David turned the page, then shrugged and reached for another book. When he opened it something whispered out. It fell to the blanket: a small clear card. The moment he picked it up, the gold and silver logo for Bitwise Perceptual Technologies materialized within, the letters winding in and out of each other. Months seemed to have passed since he had last seen the offices, though in truth it must have been only two weeks.

Randy straightened in his chair when David stood.

David grinned, hoping it looked genuine. "Not going to crack up again."

"We'll see." The man's voice was like flowing oil.

"Like to use a phone."

The intern motioned at the doorway and followed as David stepped into the corridor. Lake Waldridge wandered past. David stopped and stared at her back. A starfish hovered around the girl, almost invisible now. Lesions marked its limbs. David felt a tug of pain in his neck and arm. The girl slowed at the doorway to her room and vanished within.

David stepped that way, then looked at the card in his hand. He chose left instead and made his way to the bank of phones near the elevators. "Bitwise Perceptual Technologies," he told the phone. "In Burnaby."

Vanida answered on the third buzz, smiling from the screen. "Good morning, Bitwise Tech."

"Thought I fired you."

"Oh, you did! Like Mexican cuisine, I keep coming back." A momentary silence. "You're calling from the hospital. Haven't they let you out yet?"

"Soon. I hope. How is work?"

"Educational. I ran one of your tutorial presentations a few days ago." A shiver ran through her shoulders. "I could feel it digging into my brain. I actually understand the visual processes now. It's bizarre."

A starfish flailed in David's thoughts. Vanida said something else, and he had to ask her to repeat it.

"Are you okay? Dad misses you."

Image of Granville Street, Arutthaya's door held open by a brick. Thak had got a new sign, had replaced the old tables years ago.

"I'm getting better. Ari and I, we'll be there soon. Haven't had a belly full of fire in some time."

The starfish flexed its limbs.

"Van. Gotta go. Just thought I'd check in. No emergencies?"

"You mean like the building flooding, the staff ripping off the bank account, and the city closing us down, thanks to safety hazards? Nope, nothing like that at all."

"Good. Go away."

"I love you too, boss."

"Get back to work."

"Pffft."

David tapped Disconnect. Randy stood near the elevators, looking infinitely bored.

Yes, David thought. Get on with it. "Where's Ari?"

"Talking to Dr. Olver and Nurse Crane. I can get her."

"Don't." David looked at the card still clutched in his hand. Then he tapped it, the distinctive dut-dah-dah rhythm that unlocked its recorder.

"Exchange this card . . ." he began, and the words materialized across it, embossed in onyx.

Randy gave him a look, brow raised.

David smiled and finished the recording.

Lake sat on her bed, her back to the wall. David waited for her to notice him. Her fingers touched the bandage on her wrist. No emotion tinged her voice, as though feeling had bled from her wounds. "What?"

David moved to the bed and lowed himself next to her. "Got something for you."

"What?" she said again, peering vacantly at him. David had a sense of how small and thin she was, hardly a shadow. He held the card to her. Lake took it and gazed at the Bitwise logo hovering within.

"Pinch it."

She did. The card flared like a sunrise. Across it, black letters unrolled left and right.

> Exchange this card for one summer job
> beginning July 8, 2052.

The girl looked at David in silent confusion.

"You're going back to school when you get out of here. You and your parents will see someone to help with what you've been through. But this will all be behind you in a few months. You'll need a job in the summer. You're old enough to start thinking about college or university."

Lake's gaze lingered on the card. "You don't understand." Her voice was free of emotion, but the card began to tremble.

"Actually I do. You're not going to die. Father has a condition. You don't. So, time to start thinking about a future."

"Deuce. You don't get it." A shudder ran through her shoulders. "What if . . . ." Her fingertips touched the bandage on her wrist.

David waited. "You won't," he said when the rest of the question refused to come. "I'll expect you in my office at eight thirty. Don't be late. Train you on the front desk; the phone system. You're bright; shouldn't take long."

Lake quivered. A sob cracked free of her lips. Then the crying began. It was a soft sound, like rain and wind in trees. David slipped his hand into hers and squeezed. She leaned against him, quietly weeping. Receding footsteps told him Randy had fled. A moment later two pairs of footfalls echoed. David looked up to see Ezekiel Crane standing in the doorway. And Ari, hands on her hips. Grinning, she mouthed, *You bastard.*

David put his finger to his lips, then settled his arm around Lake's shoulder. The girl's crying grew louder and more forceful, as though a gate had opened to pour out anguish and fear. The starfish wrapped limbs around them both, and a moment later Lake hugged him, bursts of grief and terror catching in her throat and erupting into tears.

It was the last time he ever saw a Shape.

2052

"Take me home."

55

ARIEL WOKE IN AN APRIL night, aware of a chill in the bed. Her arm snaked out. No David beside her. She lay still, expecting to hear his footsteps down the corridor any moment. When nothing came, she struggled to sit up and set her feet on the floor. Her toes hunted for her slippers. By instinct her hand reached for the light on the little table beside her. Before the glare could steal her night vision, she stopped, drew her hand back, and rose. With the arrival of spring she had gone back to sleeping with nothing on. She reached for her robe, visualizing Warren padding out of his bedroom at an inopportune moment.

She made her way along the hallway to the living room and saw David's silhouette in the chair near the curtains. The drapes were partway open, and David sat with his back to her, his left elbow on the arm of the chair, fist propping up his chin. Clad in undershorts, he sat motionless but for an occasional tightening of the muscles in his neck.

David spoke first. "Bad dreams."

Eyes in the back of his head, damn it. "About what?"

"The fire."

Ariel took a tentative step toward him, then another. Now David turned, and in the blue-grey of the street, she saw the sparkle in his eyes.

"You were wrong," he said. "Back in the hospital. About me co-opting your guilt. Got my own. I remember the smell of gas in the house."

"And?"

"Couldn't think. Got outside. The street was cold. Got to the bench across the street. House turned into a fireball."

"David, you were a kid. You were disoriented from the gas or the smoke. You couldn't have – "

"I know. If I had been alert, I would have done something. But: late at night. Three in the morning – I remember the time. Couldn't think clearly, but I remember that." His palms rubbed tears from his cheeks. "Doesn't stop this, this loathing. Told myself I was a coward. Then: found out I was going to lose it all to ERIN. Made me happy, that."

When Ariel neared him, he reached for her, slipping his arms into her robe, pulling her to him. He pressed his forehead against her breast and held her, his breath on her belly. Ariel let silence fill the space around them. She imagined gears in his mind grinding at his past, wearing away his memories.

"Odd thing about the fire," David murmured.

"What?"

"The smell. Like overcooked popcorn."

56

DAVID HAD COME TO SUSPECT there were darker aspects to his past, pieces that hadn't made it into his journals. Perhaps he had been too young to understand them – or had wilfully chosen not to include them. Maybe his youth hadn't been quite so idyllic. Perhaps Uncle Stu had bequeathed to him a subtle, unconscious brand of sexism. Or perhaps Auntie Mel could at times be recalcitrant and hurtful, and David remembered without knowing it.

Whatever it was, it must have given him a mistrust of females. He had over the course of the past months sensed that Ariel was lying to him, each time she uttered a breath. It was there in her body, in the way she looked at him, in her smile. He found it too in those phone calls to Baltimore months ago, when he spoke to Dr. Olver. He had questions about the clinic. She answered, and he sensed in her voice and in the view of her on the phone's screen that she was lying.

It was all utterly silly. He knew this because the sensation extended even to Elizabeth.

The realization, when it came to him in the summer, unsettled him. Ariel was right: normals had to dig into themselves, to make a leap of faith because they had no skill at reading each other. Memory was a perpetual din, a rolling chaos, easily confused.

So he fought the feeling, battled it in secret, until he pushed it into a corner of himself where it couldn't cause harm. And there he left it to be forgotten.

57

ARIEL COULD TRACE BACK TO the very day when David's confidence began to return. Early July. The day Lake Waldridge walked into his office and dropped his card in front of him. Beside it, she dropped her own.

David had brought the card home to show Ariel. With a squeeze it shimmered green, then opened like drapes to reveal the girl's face. Her eyes flashed white. Beneath her face were the words, "Perceptual-Applications Developer – Apprentice." She had, in the intervening months, taken a series of online courses using a Dome like Warren's.

"She's good," David had said. His throat moved. Nerves and excitement. "Scarily good."

Ariel laughed. "She'll have your job in no time."

David didn't smile. He considered her remark seriously and nodded. "Likely."

58

THE WORST PART ABOUT GETTING his past back, David decided, was that he couldn't win a chess game against Elizabeth to save his life now. She stood over him, tapping her knee against the side of the table, while he stared at the board. Her queen and most of her men stood on the tabletop around the board itself. All except for that damn rook and both her knights – enough to box him into a corner.

"Dad. Give it up. Checkmate."

"Where's your mother?"

"Playing that dumb game in the living room."

"Your brother and your friend?"

"In the car."

"So why aren't you out there with them?"

"Because I'm kicking your ass all over this chessboard."

"Don't speak that way to your father. Show a little respect for your elders."

"Yes, sir. Sir, I'm respectfully kicking your ass around this chessboard."

"Better." He looked at her oversized faded blue shirt and clinging orange pants: "Going to the cemetery in that?"

Elizabeth looked down at herself. "What's wrong with what I'm wearing? I'm just going to sit in the car. And now you're stalling. Dad, I can fix this."

David's six pieces, including his queen, were scattered across the board. He had the uncomfortable sense that Elizabeth had somehow tricked him into moving them away from his king. She had left her own queen and both bishops open in what looked like an amateurish effort to checkmate him from across the board. Her queen was too tempting a prize, and he had fallen for it. How many players at the library had he beaten with the same set of moves?

Six pieces: enough to win the game through attrition, if he could get his king out of the cross hairs of those two black knights. "There's a way out?"

At one time, a glance at the board would have shown him the Shape of the game, all the permutations three, five, eight moves ahead. A circuit would snap into place, and he would *see* it, see how the game could follow no other path.

But here, with his king in the corner, the Shape eluded him.

"It's simple." Elizabeth tapped his king with her fingertip. It tumbled over, clattering across the board. "That's called the hara kiri gambit."

David grunted and rose. "Smartass. Go join your brother."

Elizabeth rolled her eyes and set off upstairs. David followed. The girl picked up her shoes at the doorway, making a show of a colossal eye roll for his benefit at the sight of Ariel at the coffee table. She had bought a smaller GameDome, not the large deluxe model Warren had insisted on three years ago. It had its controller attached, not separate, and she worked her thumbs and fingers across its keys and joysticks. Within, a gnome in a swirling dress battled a trio of ogres. David watched them fall to the slashes of the gnome's sword.

"Coming, love?"

Ariel glanced at him, scowled, and returned her gaze to the Dome.

Ariel worshipped her son, something David had commented was deeply wrong. Ariel had grinned sheepishly at that.

More accurately, her character, Ariela, worshipped Warren's newly minted deity, Thundarre. Warren had begun work on a world of his own, insisting she become one of his followers. Apparently if she prayed to him in the game, voicing a plea into the mic beneath the Dome, he could rain terrible wrath down upon her enemies.

"Levelling up," Ariel muttered. "I'm almost at fifty-seven."

"Gran's waiting."

"She isn't going anywhere."

David crossed his arms and clicked his tongue against the roof of his mouth. Ariel grimaced, setting the Dome down. Then she rose and made a theatrical stretch. David did a double-take. She had put on a snug white shirt, black vest, and gray hip-hugging pants. It all looked sprayed on.

"Let's not keep the relatives waiting," she said brightly. She came to him and kissed his mouth, then stepped back and watched him through narrowed eyes. "How do you feel?"

He shrugged, then tapped the side of his head with his knuckles. "Anything I can take for the chaos in here?"

"Get used to it; the rest of us do." Ariel smiled a pink crescent.

At the door she pried her black boots out of the corner near the closet with her toe and slipped them on. They donned their magenta coats. He followed her into the cool November afternoon.

The car purred. The kids whined.

"Mom, Elizabeth won't sit still."

"My butt hurts."

David's voice oozed innocence. "What's the matter? Should we take you to a doctor?"

Ariel poked his thigh and glared a warning at him, stifling a wicked grin. Two days ago she had taken their daughter to Santiago's office, where the doctor had sutured a contraceptive ring into Elizabeth's buttock. David glanced back. Elizabeth turned crimson and sank into her seat, twisting herself to keep her weight off her left side. Between her and Warren, Lake rolled her eyes in classic teenager style.

The trees along the avenue had shed their leaves, leaving them barren and with all the appearance of death. Gran had chosen the right time of year to die.

David squeezed his eyes shut. Sometimes it quieted the noise in his mind. Was this really what normals had to endure, this perpetual racket? For the first two months after Crawford Memorial Hospital's psychiatric staff had set him free, he hadn't been able to work, thanks to the turmoil of images and sensations in his mind. When he finally returned to the shop, he couldn't focus. He could no longer latch his attention on to an idea and watch it peel open like a flower. The loss, it seemed, was the price of remembrance.

Fair trade. Now he could picture Auntie sitting on the back porch of the house, watching him from the swinging chair as he lay in the hammock. He could smell Uncle's famous (according to him) barbecued chicken wafting through the house. And now he could visualize Uncle's broad shoulders and his fringe of cotton-like hair, and smell his musky scent when he came into the kitchen for coffee before heading for the bathroom and a shower.

With a jolt he felt Ariel's hand squeeze his. She watched him from the corner of her eye. "Enjoying the movie?"

"Uncle used to make chicken on the barbecue."

"Hey, can we have chicken tomorrow night?" Warren piped up from the back seat.

The car found a parking spot along the loop of road next to the cemetery. David pushed his door open. Behind him, Warren climbed out of the car also. Elizabeth and Lake remained behind, two silver visors attuned to Elizabeth's netpad. Their heads moved back and forth in the kind of rhythm which made David certain he would cringe if he could hear the music. Ariel rose from the car and rolled her eyes in a parody of Lake. David grinned at her across the car roof.

A rare November sun blazed. The grass had been cut recently; David could smell it. Short shadows cast by cedars cut across the path. Ariel squeezed him when they reached Auntie's and Uncle's plots. Then she continued with lazy strides toward Gran's grave. Warren followed her. David watched her, the boy trailing a few paces behind. Was it possible to love someone by proxy? he wondered. The thought struck him as strangely profound. He loved Gran. He felt sure of it. Ariel had told him about her, had over the course of twenty years slipped so many details of the old woman's life into their conversations that David could picture her in his thoughts, the way he had for years imagined Auntie and Uncle.

Decades ago the stones before him had gleamed white in the glare of the sun. He preferred this, the gray hue of age. The stones looked more real, more solid. Like his memories.

Ariel had long ago given up on bringing flowers to Gran's grave. She knew the old woman would have guffawed at the gesture. She glanced back at David. He stood with his hands behind his back, thumbs crossed over each other. That was new, she couldn't remember him standing that way before.

Warren: "Can we go now?"

"Why don't you tell your great-grandmother what you want for Christmas?"

Warren rolled his eyes. The whole family had picked up that gesture. Even David did it now.

In the past year Warren had grown until he matched Elizabeth's height. Soon – before the Christmas holidays – he would need a ring in his butt. Let David explain that to him.

She turned back to the black stone, imagining Gran's voice: *You're getting old and gray from raising teenagers – just like me, Ari.* Laced with laughter.

David heard Ari's footsteps, followed by Warren's. She wore her hair loose today, letting it hang down her back in a thick mane. She strode toward him with purpose. He knew what to expect now; they had come to the cemetery at Easter last spring. She had knelt and touched Auntie's stone.

Sure enough, she went down on her right knee and touched the stones, first Auntie's, then Uncle's.

Warren gave a loud, theatrical sigh.

David waved in the direction of the car. "Go; we'll be there in a few minutes." The boy shrugged and trudged off.

Yes, it was possible to love someone by proxy. Ariel looked beautiful when she laid her fingers on the granite, as though she were speaking to Auntie and Uncle, the way she sometimes spoke to Gran, silently in her mind.

Ariel felt the weight of David's gaze on her. She drew a smile across her face like an archer drawing a bow. *If there's a hell, you assholes are in it. And I hope whatever demon got the job of turning you on a spit and squirting you with a turkey baster takes time out to let you have a good look at David. You don't get to leave a mark on him, you bastards — not one scar on his mind.*

Ariel rose. "Where did Warren go?"

"Sent him to the car. Feel better now?"

"Much. have a brilliant idea: why don't we drop the kids off with their friends, then you take me home and boink me till I can't walk?"

David slipped his arm around her shoulder. "Sounds lovely."

"What'll it be this time, Doctor And Patient or Auntie And Nephew?"

"That's disgusting. Hold that thought till we get home."

"Mmm." Ariel leaned against him and kissed his throat. "Love you."

"Love you more."

"Do not."

"Do — "

Note to Readers

Independent authors survive on word-of-mouth and reviews. Please take a moment to post a review at the site where you purchased *Oblivion's Wake*. Your words make a huge difference and are very much appreciated.

I am working on three new novels at the moment. *Judgement Daze* is a contemporary fantasy action-comedy, the first in the *Armageddon Boys* series. *The Frog of War* is the second of that series. I am also wrapping up a hard science fiction novel called *The Gimp*. If you would like an email when these or other books are released, use the link below to join my notification list. Your address will not be shared and you will only hear from me when a new book is being released.

http://www.jslyster.com/sign-up/

If you would like to discuss this book or indie publishing in general, feel free to contact me at jonathan@jslyster.com.

You can find out more about my writing (and read some free stories) at my website: www.jslyster.com.

Did you spot a grammar, spelling, or continuity error in *Oblivion's Wake*? If you're the first to email me about it, you will receive my next novel as a free ebook the moment it is released.

Acknowledgements

This is the crew who helped bring Oblivion's Wake to you.

Alpha readers:

Karilee Orchard – long-time friend, science fiction fan(atic), and marketing wizard (http://outcomemarketing.com) – vetted the earliest versions and was the first to suggest the indie-publishing route.

Myst de Vana first edited this story soon after we started seeing each other. She caught the truly embarrassing errors, cracked the whip when the deadlines loomed, invented perceptual engineering, and married me.

Krista Wallace – fantasy author, afficionada of fine single malts, and fellow writing conference alum – worked with me through endless Skype chats to polish the story and rid it of unintentionally hilarious continuity errors.

Rowan Jespersen is the insightful stepdaughter responsible for my addiction to texting. She caught numerous snags regarding the technology of the story.

The Malaspina Writers' Association read the story in bits and pieces as it came together. I know it was a frustrating process, having only a chapter or a part to review at a time and wondering where the hell this story was going. (I didn't know, either; it appeared to be approaching five possible endings before doing a Schrodinger's Cat trick and collapsing into the conclusion you just read.)

Editors:

Andrea Howe of Blue Falcon Editing (http://www.bluefalconediting.com/) waded through the manuscript, found all kinds of issues that I hadn't noticed, and supplied a wealth of suggestions – including that I should get a copy editor, which leads me to . . .

Linda Devendorf, who did a remarkable job of vetting the manuscript and cross-referencing with the Merriam-Webster dictionary and the Chicago Manual of Style. (If you're looking for a copy editor, contact her. Right now. No, put the coffee mug down, you can drink it later. Email her here: goldfishlinda@yahoo.com.)

Beta readers:

Heartfelt thanks to Katherine Aiken and Cheyenne D. Barnett for your suggestions and corrections. You did an amazing job on short notice, for a strange guy who was also a stranger to you.

About the Author

Jonathan Sean Lyster writes stories, designs software, and messes with new technologies.

He lives on Vancouver Island with his wife Myst, two cats, and an insanely long-lived newt.

Check out his blog at:
www.jslyster.com.